VICES *of* MY BLOOD

THE MURDOCH MYSTERIES

MAUREEN JENNINGS

Vices
of My Blood

A Murdoch Mystery

McCLELLAND & STEWART

LIBRARY AND ARCHIVES CANADA CATALOGUING IN PUBLICATION

Jennings, Maureen
Vices of my blood / Maureen Jennings.

(A Detective Murdoch mystery)
ISBN 978-0-7710-4332-1

I. Title. II. Series: Jennings, Maureen. Detective Murdoch mystery.

PS8569.E562V52 2010   C813'.54   C2009-906983-0

We acknowledge the financial support of the Government of Canada through the Book Publishing Industry Development Program and that of the Government of Ontario through the Ontario Media Development Corporation's Ontario Book Initiative. We further acknowledge the support of the Canada Council for the Arts and the Ontario Arts Council for our publishing program.

Published simultaneously in the United States by
McClelland & Stewart Ltd., P.O. Box 1030, Plattsburgh, New York 12901
LIBRARY OF CONGRESS CONTROL NUMBER: 2009942501

Typeset in Caslon Book by M&S, Toronto
Printed and bound in Canada

This book is printed on paper that is 100% recycled, ancient-forest friendly (40% post-consumer waste).

McClelland & Stewart Ltd.
75 Sherbourne Street
Toronto, Ontario
M5A 2P9
www.mcclelland.com

1 2 3 4 5   14 13 12 11 10

To Iden, as always

And to Al and Barbara Lyons,
who have been there from the very beginning

. . . as truly as to heaven
I do confess the vices of my blood,
So justly to your grave ears I'll present
How I did thrive in this fair lady's love
And she in mine

— William Shakespeare, *Othello*, Act I, sc. iii

Prologue

ESTHER GOT OUT OF BED, wrapped a shawl around her thin shoulders, and shuffled over to the window. The winter morning light was dull, the sky heavy with unshed snow, and the window itself was crusted with a rime of frost on the inside. She peered down into the street below, where a few men were making their way to work, all huddled into their coats against the cold. She must have slept longer than usual. She glanced over at the bed where her son Wilf was now awake. He started to make a tortured, guttural sound, which she knew meant that he needed to use the commode.

Her daughter was still asleep, the threadbare quilt pulled over her nose for warmth. Strands of her dark hair were spread on the pillow, and Esther felt an unaccustomed rush of tenderness at the sight. They'd had a bad row last night when she'd tried to tell Josie she had to be up early for the Visitor. Josie had cursed, upsetting Esther with the vileness of her language and told her daughter so. Josie had laughed at that. "I should think that's the least of your worries, Ma. I doubt God is going to punish me for a few cuss words and overlook everything else. But you never know, maybe he's just like you."

It was as if she had stabbed her mother in her heart, the sensation so physical Esther had been forced to sit down. Later, trying to explain to Josie what she had done that afternoon, Esther said it was because of that one remark. She felt as if she had been living in a fog and an icy wind came and blew it away. She could see clearly the squalor of the room where all three of them lived. She knew she'd grovelled before the authorities to get their charity. She stared into a pit of despair and saw her own destroyed soul reflected back at her.

"So you might say, 'The worm turned.' Yes, that's the best way to put it, 'The worm turned.'" Esther laughed as if she'd said something witty, but a soft, plump-bodied worm wasn't anything like the hard, sharp anger that suddenly bit at her guts, like a cancer she'd been carrying for a long time without knowing it.

Chapter One

WILLIAM MURDOCH HAD RECENTLY been promoted from acting to full detective and given a raise in wages of three dollars a month. But his new status was not reflected by a better office, and from his desk he was contemplating the same old furnishings of a battered metal filing cabinet and a visitor's chair that the rag-and-bones man would have rejected. The walls, he noticed, would benefit greatly from a fresh coat of paint, as he was wont to use the one wall as a blackboard and the chalk marks never quite rubbed off. He needed a new lamp, or at least some better oil, as the one on his desk was smoking badly.

Having made this gloomy assessment, he took a gulp of the hot strong tea that he'd brought in from the duty room and got back to his task. He dipped his pen into the inkwell. He had a fine working fountain pen in his pocket, but he couldn't bring himself to write a letter to his absent mistress with a pen his beloved deceased fiancée had given him.

Dear Enid. I haven't yet received a letter from you, but I hope that is only because of the bad weather and not because you don't want to write to me. How is your father faring?

He paused. That last line seemed ridiculously stiff. But he'd have to leave it. This was the third draft he'd started. Oh just cross out *faring,* for Christ's sake.

How is your father? I do hope his health is improving.

Of course, the reason she had not written could be because her father had died. If that was the case he wondered if she would return to Canada. And then he wondered how he would feel about that if she did. It had been almost two months since she had been summoned back to Wales to take care of her ailing parent. This had been the primary and acknowledged reason for her departure, but they both knew that sitting just behind it was Murdoch's inability to make up his mind to marry her.

Another dip in the ink and he made a large blot on the page. *Damn.* These pens were police issue and leaked badly. His fingers were stained already.

Tell Alwyn I am thinking of him. I have still got his sled and . . .

He'd been going to write *and I look forward to the time when he returns,* but that was implying a promise he didn't know if he could keep.

He looked at the letter. It was a mess with two

4

crossing-outs and three blots. He crumpled it up and threw it into the basket with the others. He'd write later at home, not here at the police station where there were distractions. He'd heard the clack of the telegram machine in the front hall and decided to get up and see if anything interesting had come over the wire. It had been a quiet day so far.

He swallowed the rest of his tea and went out into the main hall.

There were no miscreants or supplicants gracing the wooden bench that ran around the room and it wasn't time for the shifts to change so the only two officers present were the stenographer, Callahan, and the duty sergeant, Gardiner, who was sitting at his high stool behind the desk. He grinned when he saw Murdoch and waved a piece of paper.

"We've got a telegram from Hamilton. Callahan just typed it up. You might want to have a look at it." He handed Murdoch the wire.

BE ADVISED STOP WATCH FOR QUEER PLUNGERS STOP
WE SUSPECT A SUPPOSED FAMILY OF THREE STOP
WOMAN MID AGE STOP YOUNGER MAN STOP ONE BOY
ABOUT EIGHT TO TEN YEARS OLD STOP COULD BE
RELATED TO EITHER STOP PROBABLY IN TORONTO
AND WORKING THE KING STREET AREA STOP ALIASES
GIVEN AS MRS WRIGHT AND SON BOBBIE STOP NO
NAME FOR MAN STOP VERY CONVINCING STOP

Murdoch saw that Callahan was watching him curiously, but he averted his eyes immediately when Murdoch glanced his way. The constable was almost obsequious in his dealings with the detective, whom he feared. With good reason. Murdoch couldn't stand the fellow.

He walked over to him. "You're no doubt wondering, young Liam, what a queer plunger is."

Callahan nodded, apparently unsure how he was supposed to reply. Murdoch perched on the edge of the desk. "Never be afraid to admit you don't know something, young Liam. You don't want to be a constable third class forever, do you?"

Callahan flushed. "No, sir."

"Thought not. Our lad is ambitious, sergeant. Don't let that fresh-faced, just-off-the-boat look fool you. Right, Liam?"

Murdoch was goading him to the point of eruption, but the stenographer swallowed hard. He smiled a snake smile, but his eyes were dark with anger, and Murdoch could see that thoughts of revenge were churning in his mind. He didn't care. He knew very well that Callahan was as two-faced as the month of January.

He gestured at Gardiner, who looked puzzled by Murdoch's uncharacteristic incivility. "Explain to the lad, sergeant."

Gardiner pursed his lips, going along with it.

"Queer plungers is a cant term for folks who commit fraudulent acts upon the public. Typically, they work in groups of three or more. For instance, a favourite trick is for one of the group to pretend to be despondent, and in full view of a crowd, he will plunge into some water, the lake or a river like the Don. The second member of the gang will then effect a rescue. The half-drowned one will be taken to the closest house. They always make sure it's a tavern or failing that a church just emptying of the congregation. Then there is some cock-and-bull story about why the poor man wanted to commit self-murder in the first place. Debts of honour, most like. A go-around is suggested so he can redeem himself. Another go-around for the rescuer. Get the picture?"

"I do, sir, thank you. I suppose they can only really pull that one in summer."

"Mostly. They do other things, of course. If there's a woman involved, the boy acts as her son and he might take a dive under a carriage and then pretend to be injured. Or he might be a pickpocket and take off with her savings that she was just about to deposit at the bank. The possibilities are endless, the common denominator is the go-around, where they rely on public sympathy. As long as they move from place to place, they can get away with a lot, and believe me, if they get a good crowd, the takings can be more in one day than Murdoch and me make in a week. Last Christmas Eve, we nabbed two young tads who'd got fifteen dollars in their pockets."

7

Callahan looked impressed.

"Mind you," interjected Murdoch, "the one titch had a broken collarbone from being stomped on by the horses, so the price can be high."

"Yes, sir. I wasn't considering taking up queer plunging, if that's what you are implying." Callahan tried a tentative smile.

"Of course not, constable, I know you're too canny for that. But it's one way to earn your daily bread."

The constable spat out, "It almost sounds like you condone what they do, sir. But they are breaking the law after all."

Murdoch shrugged. "They're harmless enough."

"Judge Rose doesn't share your opinion, sir. I heard he sent down a pickpocket for two years' hard labour. And Judge Pedlow ordered ten stripes of the lash for a man who robbed a farmhouse in Markham."

"So they should," chipped in Gardiner. "You've got to put the fear of God into people like that or there's no knowing what they'll do."

Murdoch went back to the duty desk. The disparities between certain crimes and the punishments they were accorded had bothered him for a long time, but this wasn't the place to debate it. The sergeant was an affable sort to those he considered peers but punctilious to a fault when it came to lawbreakers.

"Anything else I should know about?"

Gardiner gave him a rather sheepish look and

8

lowered his voice. "Not in the work line, but I wanted to let you know that Mary and me are going to have a young 'un."

Murdoch thrust out his hand. "Congratulations, Henry. What's that now, your sixth?"

Gardiner shook hands. "Seven, actually. Mary dearly wants a little girl this time. And by the way, she wanted me to ask if you've heard from Mrs. Kitchen as to how Arthur is getting on?"

"He's doing well. Mrs. K sounds quite optimistic."

"That would be a miracle if he recovered. Mary don't think he'll see spring."

They were interrupted by the shrill ring of the telephone. Callahan picked up the receiver and put it to his ear.

"Number four station."

There was a pause while he listened to the message being relayed, some alarm on his face. He scribbled something down on the message pad in front of him, as the other two watched. He replaced the receiver on the hook, and swivelled around to address Murdoch. He was excited.

"The alarm has been sounded at Jarvis Street and Carlton, sir. Headquarters says to get over to Chalmers Church right away. Apparently, the pastor there has been found murdered."

"Good heavens, that's my own church," exclaimed Gardiner. "Surely it's not Mr. Howard."

9

Callahan checked the notepad. "Yes, sir. That is the name I was given. Reverend Charles Howard."

"Do you have any details?"

"Only that it has just been discovered. One of the parishioners found him. He had been stabbed and beaten."

Gardiner flinched. "Any culprit apprehended?"

"Not so far, sir. Constable Fyfer raised the alarm. He is at the church now."

Murdoch was already over at the coat rack retrieving his coat and forage hat.

"This is absolutely dreadful," said the sergeant. "I can't believe it. Reverend Howard is a fine fellow. As good as they come."

"We'd better order out the ambulance," said Murdoch.

"Shall I telephone for a physician, sir?" Callahan asked.

Murdoch nodded. "I'll meet him at the church." He hustled into his coat. "I'll ride my wheel, it'll be faster."

Gardiner leaned his head on his hand, and Murdoch went over to him and touched his shoulder in sympathy.

"I'm sorry, Henry."

"I just saw the man on Sunday. As hale and hearty as you and me. And he has a young family. How his wife will take it, I don't know. She is devoted to him. What the deuce could have happened?"

Murdoch headed for the door. "Send Crabtree over as soon as he comes back from his tea, will you?"

Once outside, he grabbed his bicycle from where it

was leaning against the station wall, lit the oil lamp, and pedalled off along Wilton Street. The year was still more on the side of winter than spring and there was a vicious bite in the air. Darkness was taking over and the streets were full of people hurrying to get home to a warm fire and their tea. As he turned right onto Church Street, a streetcar clanged by, jammed to capacity with passengers. Murdoch kept to the side of the road. It was all too easy to catch a wheel in the tracks. He'd crashed twice before in that way and still had a lump on his elbow to show for it.

Some people on the streetcar were watching him and, not for the first time, Murdoch was struck with the separateness of human life. A man was lying murdered, a good man, said Gardiner. His wife was now widowed and children orphaned. Their lives were changed irrevocably and yet the lives of everybody else continued. Once again some poor woman would be struggling to understand how God could have mercy and yet so cruelly take away.

Murdoch had investigated murders before, of course, and he was experiencing his usual feelings of both apprehension and excitement as he approached the place of the crime. "What happened?" Gardiner had moaned, and for Murdoch the reason for being a detective was the need to find the answer to that question.

11

Chapter Two

CHALMERS PRESBYTERIAN CHURCH was a large grey stone building that sat at the northwest corner of the Allan Horticultural Gardens. Murdoch was there within six minutes. Constable Fyfer had positioned himself at the top of the steps and in front of the double doors. A dozen or more people had already gathered to one side and were standing together watching expectantly.

Murdoch dismounted, caught hold of one of the spectators, a clerk by the look of him, and told him to take care of the bicycle. Then he joined Fyfer, who gave him an almost-military salute.

"What's happened, constable?"

"It looks like the pastor of the church has been murdered, sir. His body's in his office at the rear of the church. He's been stabbed."

They were interrupted by the bike-minding clerk,

who called out, "Give us the truth, officer. What's going on?"

"Never you mind," Murdoch shouted back. He couldn't stand the morbid curiosity that came out when there was a police affair.

"I assume you haven't seen anybody leaving the church," he said to Fyfer.

"No, sir. Not a soul. From the feel of the body, he hasn't been dead that long, but as there was just me, I didn't try to search the church proper. It seemed the most sensible thing to do was to keep watch until help arrived. I came out and blew my whistle to summon the closest constable. Fortunately, Constable Dewhurst was at the end of the Carlton Street beat and he came running. I sent him to guard the rear while I dealt with the lady."

"Surely not the pastor's wife?"

"No, sir, the lady that found the body. She is one of the parishioners who was coming for a meeting. Not surprisingly, she was quite hysterical, and I didn't know what the heck was happening because she had blood on her face and hands and down her cape. I thought maybe she'd hurt herself. Finally, I got out of her that she'd found a body in the church. Somebody named Charles. Lucky for me, a man who lives on Carlton heard the commotion and came to see. I put him in charge of her while I went into the church."

"Where is she now?"

13

"He's taken her to her own home. I've got names and addresses."

"Good work, constable."

Fyfer was a new transfer to number four station and Murdoch hadn't worked with him before. He was impressed with the young officer's brisk, efficient demeanour.

Just then they heard the sound of the ambulance bell and the clatter of hooves as the horses galloped up Jarvis Street. Constable George Crabtree was seated beside the driver, and as soon as they pulled over, he jumped off and, pushing through the onlookers, bounded up the steps. He was a giant of a man, made taller by his helmet and winter cape, and the crowd parted in front of him except for one woman who yelled angrily, "Oi, who'd you think you're shoving?" as her wide, over-trimmed hat was tilted to one side, almost bending one of the tall purple feathers.

Murdoch nodded at him. "George, take over from Constable Fyfer while we go inside. Keep the vultures at bay. Don't let anybody in or out, and for God's sake, don't get drawn into talking to them. We don't want the man's wife to hear anything until we have a definite confirmation it is the minister."

"Right, sir. And the physician should be here in a tick."

Murdoch beckoned to Fyfer. "Show me where he is."

"This way." Fyfer headed down the steps to the brick walkway that ran between the church and Carlton

14

Street. He opened the side door and let Murdoch through into a hall. "In there. It's a mess, sir. Worse'n a butcher's shop."

Murdoch went to the threshold. A butcher shop, indeed. A man was sprawled, twisted half on his back in the middle of the room, with what looked like a narrow dagger protruding from the right side of his neck. The weapon must have severed the artery, for blood had spurted everywhere. The front of the man's clothes were soaked and the pale blue carpet was drenched around the upper torso of the body. The side of the man's face was smashed in, the right eye socket completely destroyed. His other eye was open and staring.

Murdoch looked over at the constable. He knew it was important to present a good example to the new young officer, but his own heart was beating faster. The murderer had left behind his own violence, it hung in the air and it was impossible not to be affected by it.

"Are you all right, Fyfer?"

"Quite all right, thank you, sir."

"Is this your first murder case?"

"Yes, sir. A few assaults and drunk and disorderlies is all I've dealt with to date."

"The vile smell is because his bowels have evacuated. That usually happens with sudden death."

"Yes, I know, sir. My father was a butcher. I'm used to death."

15

Murdoch thought surely there was a difference between slaughtered cattle and a human being who had been brutally murdered, but he wasn't about to argue the point now. Better an officer who had his wits about him than one who didn't.

He glanced around the room. The curtains had been drawn and, on a desk to the right, a lamp was burning.

"What would help is to have more light in here. There's another lamp over there on the mantelpiece. Bring it over, will you?"

Fyfer went to do his bidding and Murdoch moved in closer to the body. The dead man was middle-aged, with thick dark hair liberally streaked with grey. Except for full side whiskers, he was clean-shaven. A handsome face, Murdoch thought. He was wearing the typical clothes of his profession: a black suit and a black waistcoat. His once-white shirt and cravat were crimson with blood.

The constable brought the second lamp over.

"Put it on that table and turn both wicks up as high as they will go. Don't tread in the blood."

Murdoch squatted on his heels, trying to get a sense of what had happened. He could see now that the weapon was a letter opener, and it had been plunged with such force into the pastor's neck that only three inches of blade were visible. He touched the man's forehead. The skin was cool but not yet icy cold. Fyfer was right, he had died quite recently. Gently he lifted both hands. They were covered with blood and he took

16

out his handkerchief to wipe it away. There was ink on the forefinger and thumb of the right hand.

"I don't see any defensive wounds, so the blood is probably because he was clutching at his neck to pull out the knife," he said to Fyfer.

"What about the other injuries, sir? It looks like somebody gave him the boots."

"The post-mortem examination should tell us more exactly, but I'm sure you're right. Speaking of boots, his have gone. And hurriedly, by the look of it." The socks were half off the man's feet. He leaned in. "Look at this, Fyfer, the buttonhole's torn on his waistcoat. Unless he's habitually an untidy man, I'd say his watch and chain were also snatched."

"Seems to indicate a burglar, doesn't it, sir?"

"Possibly. It was certainly a violent attack." Murdoch got to his feet. "But where was he when he was hit? From the spray of blood across the top of the desk and the wall, I'd say he was sitting down when he was attacked. He was hit from behind and slightly to the side. He stood up, clutched the letter opener, turned to face his attacker, then fell backwards to the floor."

Fyfer nodded. "The odd thing is he couldn't have been taken by surprise, could he?"

"Why do you say that?"

"Look where the desk is in relation to the door. The attacker had to come right into the room in order to be behind him."

He was right. "Let's not jump to conclusions. Maybe he was asleep. He could have been having an afternoon nap."

Fyfer's eager look vanished. "Yes, sir, of course. I was getting carried away."

"No, no, lad, what you say is quite plausible. Anyway, we'll do a more thorough examination later. Right now we'd better see if we have a predator to flush out or not. My hunch is we don't, that our murderer fled immediately, but we've got to have a look."

Fyfer removed his revolver from the holster. "Do you want my gun, sir?"

"No thanks. It's been a while since I was on the beat, I might be more of a liability than an asset. Give me your truncheon. And when I said *flush out* that's what I meant. If the murderer is hiding somewhere in this church, you can bet he's desperate. Let's not have any unnecessary heroics."

Fyfer's flicked at his wide moustache. "I'd say between us we'd be his match. I've been in training all winter for the police games, same as you."

"Bicyclist are you?"

"Yes, sir. And I know this isn't the time to go into it, but I would dearly like to talk about your training schedule one of these days. You got nipped at the wire last summer by Varley, but I'd wager you can beat him this year."

Murdoch stared at the constable for a moment. He

18

was a good-looking fellow with clear blue eyes and the fresh complexion of an athlete. His uniform sat well on him.

"All right then, let's check the rooms in this area."

"The halls have all got a hemp floor covering, and I don't think they would hold any trace of footprints. I took a quick look before."

He was right again, but Murdoch said, "We'll do a thorough examination in daylight with more officers."

They walked across the hall to the room opposite. Murdoch leaned his ear against the door, then signalled to Fyfer to stand on one side of the threshold. He took the other. He couldn't hear any sound from the room so he turned the knob and flung the door open. Another pause, then he peered around the door frame. Nothing stirred and he motioned to the constable to follow him. The room was large and looked as if it served as the parish hall. Several rows of chairs faced a long table covered with a white cloth upon which were stacks of cups and saucers. A bank of windows at the far end gave sufficient light even at this time of day that he could see the place was empty and there was no other exit and no hiding places.

"I came here for a Boxing Day festivity," said Fyfer. "Chalmers Church has a long tradition of Christian charity. They invite all of the poor parishioners to come in for a meal at Christmastime."

Murdoch was startled. "Is this your church?"

19

"Oh no. I attend Sherbourne Methodist, but our churches have a cordial relationship and I had no family commitments that day so I thought I would help out."

"You knew Reverend Howard, then?"

"No. He only received his call to this ministry in January. The position was vacant for six months after the death of Reverend Cameron."

"You are an unexpected font of information, constable."

He indicated to Fyfer that they should go back across the hall and try the room that adjoined the pastor's. According to a brass plate on the door, this office belonged to Reverend Swanzey. Murdoch went through the same procedure as before and thrust open the door. His heart gave a painful thump as his eye caught a dark shape standing in the corner. He actually raised the truncheon before he realized he was looking at a coat tree with a fedora hanging on it.

Fyfer grinned at him. "I almost put a bullet through it myself, sir."

Murdoch looked around. This office was smaller than Reverend Howard's, with minimum furnishings: a rolltop desk and two plain chairs; a single bookcase against the wall. There was no wardrobe or cupboard. The fire was set in the grate but not lit and the curtains weren't drawn. Through the window, he could see the gardens, patched with snow and bedraggled and dreary in the encroaching night. There was a single lamp on the desk and Murdoch walked over to it and touched the globe. It was cold.

"Let's check the other hall," he said to Fyfer.

This ran perpendicular to the one that led to Reverend Howard's office. To the left were two doors, one marked Water Closet, the other Storage. Murdoch proceeded with the same care and opened the first door to the water closet, which was surprisingly spacious with a small sink and one of the newer types of flushing toilets. There was a delicate flower motif in the bowl and a matching decoration in the sink.

Fyfer whistled softly. "I think the station would benefit from a toilet like this, don't you, sir?"

Murdoch agreed. The earth closet in the lower room of the station was noisome most of the time.

They moved on to the storage room. This proved to be crammed with the usual debris from a building used by the public. A couple of broken chairs, a pile of has-socks in need of repair, a bin of assorted umbrellas, an open drawer filled with gloves, a coat stand loaded down with forgotten scarves, but empty of anyone hiding.

At the end of the hall was a door, the twin of the one by which he had originally entered. He pushed it open and a wave of damp, cold air blew in. A flight of steps led to the path that seemed to circumnavigate the building, but this side was lined by a high hedge, at the moment all bare branches except for a few with-ered leaves and bits of paper that had blown there over

21

the winter. Beyond the hedge was the Horticultural Gardens, and he saw the lamplighter was starting to light the lamps along the pathways criss-crossing the park. Snow was drifting through the pools of light, but it wasn't yet sticking on the ground.

Murdoch turned back to Fyfer.

"Where is the church proper?"

"Through those doors, sir."

At either end of the hall were two closed doors.

"You take the first one, I'll take the second. Wait for me to give the signal."

A moment of attention, then they each flung a door open and entered the nave.

It was much bigger than he'd expected and in spite of the circumstances, Murdoch felt a twist of curiosity. Ever since he could remember, the priests had drilled into him the peril to his immortal soul of associating with any Church other than the true Faith and to his mind that carried over to the buildings themselves. Murdoch remembered his mother, on their way to mass, hurrying him, Bertie, and Susanna past the Protestant church in the village as if it would reach out a tentacle like a giant octopus and suck them in.

The tall windows here were plain glass, no glorious depictions of Christ and the saints, and in the dim light, he could just make out the high ceiling where the large gasolier hung. There was a balcony and in the nave, rows of plain, straightbacked pews were arranged not

22

as he was used to, perpendicular to a central aisle, but in semi-circles fanning out from the pulpit and divided by two aisles. There was not a wink of gold, no painted statues nor richly embroidered cloths to be seen. Instead of the sanctuary and the altar of his church, here was only a platform on which stood a pulpit reached by two curving sets of stairs on either side. So this was what a Protestant church looked like. Here the congregation presumably believed just as fervently in Jesus Christ and no doubt were as certain as any papist that they knew the truth, that they had the ear of God Almighty Himself.

He noticed that Fyfer was watching him from the other side of the church, waiting for further instructions, and he shifted his thoughts back to the investigation. The high backs of the pews would make this a great hiding place.

He called out. "I am a police officer. If there is anybody in here, show yourself in the name of the law or accept the consequences."

His voice echoed faintly in the empty church.

"Light your lantern, Fyfer. You can walk up on that side, I'll keep watch at the other end of the pews."

The constable obeyed and began to flash the light along the rows. As they walked, Murdoch realized that what was absent was the familiar smell he associated with God, the sharp, acrid whiff of incense. There was just the odour of wax polish, gaslights, and a faint dank

23

smell, but he assumed that was from the winter clothes of the congregation.

Nobody flew out at them and by now, Murdoch was sure they weren't going to find anyone. Nevertheless, they went up to the balcony, searched up there, then returned to the main floor.

"The problem is there are several possible points of entry, wouldn't you say, sir? Two side doors, one quite hidden from view, a rear door that comes in from the park, and the two Jarvis Street main entrances into the church."

"Thank you, Fyfer, I had worked that out myself."

"Yes, sir."

Murdoch immediately felt a pang of guilt at his own curtness. Who was he to suppress eagerness and initiative in a young officer?

"I see they have a gasolier in here. We'll have to get somebody to light it and we'll give everything a thorough going-over."

"I know how to light it, sir. The ladder is kept behind the pulpit."

Murdoch shook his head. "Leave it for now. We can't do anything further until the doctor has made a formal pronouncement of death. We'll have to swear in a jury and Crabtree will need you. I'll go and talk to the woman who found the body. What was her name again?"

"Miss Sarah Dignam. She was dreadful upset. She's a spinster lady."

Murdoch thought any woman would have been shocked by her discovery, but he assumed Fyfer was informing him Miss Dignam was no longer young or marriageable. Whatever she was, he wasn't looking forward to the prospect of interviewing her.

Chapter Three

AT THAT MOMENT, THEY HEARD the north side door open and a woman entered. Murdoch frowned, about to usher her out again, expecting to have to deal with the hysterics of an unwary parishioner when she smiled politely.

"Good afternoon, I'm Dr. Julia Ogden. I am here to act as coroner."

Murdoch recovered quickly. "Yes, ma'am."

"Where is the body I'm to examine?"

"In here, ma'am . . . Fyfer, go and report to Constable Crabtree."

The doctor looked at the young man in surprise. "Hello, Frank. I didn't expect to see you here."

"Good afternoon, Dr. Ogden. The church is on my beat. Er, this is Detective Murdoch."

She offered her hand. "Why is your name familiar?"

"We met last summer, I believe. That is, not met exactly,

we spoke on the telephone because you performed a post-mortem examination for us."

"Ah, yes, I remember."

Murdoch wasn't sure she really did. He recalled speculating at the time about what the good doctor looked like, as her voice was youthful, English in intonation. She was older than he'd expected, almost of middle age, tall and thin with greying hair. She was wearing a black mackintosh cloak and she reminded him of a nun who'd taught him when he was in standard two. Sister Regina had the same air of unshakeable composure and competence. He'd found her most intimidating.

"I'll report to Constable Crabtree," said Fyfer and he left.

"I know his family," Dr. Ogden said to Murdoch. "He's a very fine young man. The police force is lucky to have him."

"So I am learning, ma'am. This way, please."

He indicated the pastor's office and opened the door. She stood in the doorway and regarded the dead man. Her expression changed and her hand flew to her mouth. Her composure was not so unshakeable after all.

"Oh dear me, it's Charles Howard. I wasn't told anything except that somebody had died. I never dreamed it would be him. I thought . . . Oh my goodness . . . excuse me, detective, I . . ."

She stopped, struggling for control.

"You knew him, ma'am?"

"His wife is one of my patients. This is quite, quite dreadful. What happened? Who did this?"

"I'm afraid we don't know as yet. One of the parishioners found his body hardly more than half an hour ago and I've just been called in."

Murdoch waited a moment to see what she was going to do. She breathed deeply and braced herself. Control was back.

"Do you want to examine the body now, ma'am?"

"Yes, of course."

She had her medical bag with her and she placed it on the floor. She unfastened her cloak, removed it, and put it carefully on top of the bag. Then she pulled off her gloves and, with a steady hand, reached forward to touch the minister's forehead. Murdoch knew that sort of discipline. Sister Regina would have stared down the devil himself if she thought it was her duty.

"He is barely cold. Death has occurred within the last two hours." Without looking at Murdoch, she said, "I have to remove the dagger."

She leaned over the body, put her left hand on Howard's shoulder, and with her right grasped the handle. With strength worthy of a teamster, she gave a jerk, and with a soft, gulping sound the weapon came out, the blood seeping over her fingers.

"That was in quite deep." She held out the thing to Murdoch. It was about nine inches long, of brass or gold, the handle carved in the shape of a serpent, with leaves and tendrils curling about the blade. "It looks like a letter opener."

He took it from her and wrapped it in his own handkerchief. He would examine it later to see if it had any more to tell them. She looked at the pastor's hands. "There are no cuts on his fingers."

"I believe the blood on his hands is from him trying to pull out the letter opener, ma'am."

"Ah yes, good thinking. He would try to do that, of course."

"Would he have died instantly?"

"Quickly, but not necessarily instantly. But those wounds to his head look very severe. They probably finished the job."

"I think he was kicked while he was on the floor."

She nodded. "It appears that way. Two or three times, I'd say, but I can confirm that when I do the post-mortem examination." She sat back on her heels. "Who would do such a thing? Charles Howard was such a kind, friendly man. I cannot believe he would have an enemy in the world."

"It's likely it was a thief. His boots have been pulled off and his watch and chain appear to be missing, but we'll have to confirm that with his wife."

Again there was a crack in the doctor's composure. "Poor, poor Louisa. Does she know?"

"I don't believe so, ma'am."

"She won't take it well. She is of a most highly strung disposition."

Rather stiffly, she got to her feet. "You'd better start to summon a jury, detective. In the meantime, I will deliver the news to Mrs. Howard."

"I would prefer to be present when you tell her, ma'am."

Not that he relished witnessing the inevitable shock and grief the woman was going to experience, but this was a murder case and at the moment, nobody was excluded as a suspect.

Dr. Ogden regarded him frostily. "It would be far better if I were alone. She will probably need a sedative as it is. And you are a stranger to her, are you not?"

"We have never met and I have no desire to add to her distress, but I am investigating a murder."

"Good Lord, detective, surely you aren't implying Louisa Howard had anything to do with her husband's death?"

"I'm not implying anything, ma'am, but at this time, all possibilities are on the table."

They eyed each other, trying to assess the extent of the other's stubbornness. It was Murdoch who backed down. Calm and controlled on the surface, Dr. Ogden had a core as stiff and unyielding as a whalebone corset – which she probably didn't need to wear, he thought uncharitably.

"Perhaps you could on ahead, ma'am, and I will follow in about a half an hour. As you say, my presence may be too hard on her."

"Very well. After she is settled, I will return and instruct the jurors." She picked up her medical bag. "You had better have a constable stand guard here and perhaps you should go to talk to the woman who discovered the body."

"I was intending to do that."

His voice must have been sharper than he realized because, unexpectedly, she turned rather pink. "I beg your pardon. Telling people what to do is an occupational hazard with doctors."

He liked her better for her discomfiture and smiled. She went to the door.

"I should go at once. Louisa mustn't hear the news from anyone else, least of all prurient neighbours. You will follow me then?"

Murdoch almost answered, "Yes, Sister," but caught himself in time.

After she left, he stood for a minute in the doorway of the office. He wanted to get a sense of the man who'd used it.

It was a spacious room, the furnishings simple but pleasant and comfortable looking, not as austere as he had imagined a Presbyterian minister's office would be.

Opposite the door, a marble fireplace dominated the wall and the fire was lit and well drawn. Two floor-to-ceiling, glass-fronted bookcases, the books sober and neat as a library's, flanked the fireplace. Close to the brass fender was a brown leather armchair and across from it a straightbacked wooden chair. Lined up along the wall to the left of the door were half a dozen identical chairs. Above these hung some oil paintings, all of them still-lifes of fruit and flowers. The floor covering was a pale blue wool rug, well worn.

He went over to the armchair. Beside it was a small table on which was an open book placed spine up. It turned out to be a book of sermons by a Reverend J.T. Lanceley, volume one. Tucked into one of the pages was an envelope and inside it was a catalogue from a supplier of church goods. It looked as if Howard had sat in his chair, opened the envelope with his letter opener, then put the pamphlet in the book. If he had put the letter opener on the table, as was most likely, it would corroborate that in order to get hold of the weapon, his assailant had come right into the room. The single wooden chair was out of place from the others. Was this its normal position or did it indicate Howard had company?

Murdoch turned to the curtained window. If the pastor had been killed two hours ago, it was early to close the curtains, but perhaps it was because the day had been so dull and dreary. He drew one aside. Reverend Howard hadn't had a good view. His window overlooked the side path and the tall hedge that ran around the property.

Murdoch returned to the blood-spattered desk. Constable Fyfer was astute in his observation. Whoever

32

Howard had allowed in was somebody he knew or, at least, somebody he saw no reason to fear because at some point he had turned his back as he sat at his desk. Unless of course he was asleep, but somehow Murdoch doubted that.

There were no signs of a struggle. The attack had been swift and unexpected. He'd noticed that Reverend Howard's index finger was ink-stained, just as Murdoch's was. He'd been writing something and he had been using the pen recently. Yes, there it was beside the blotter, but there was no paper or letter to be seen. A sheaf of unused notepaper and envelopes was neatly stacked in a tray. Murdoch checked the wastebasket beside the desk, but it was empty. On the floor was a briefcase made of gutta percha, labelled PERSONAL PORTFOLIO. It was untied and inside were cardboard pockets sorted alphabetically and stuffed with papers. He closed the case. He'd take it back to the station with him later.

Howard had been a tidy man and the top of his desk was clear except for the brass lamp, the tray of note-paper, and a photograph in a silver frame. It was a studio portrait of him as a youthful-looking pastor with a pretty young woman on his arm. They were both dressed in formal attire. She was wearing a wide-brimmed hat with ostrich feathers and holding a bouquet of cascading flowers. Murdoch assumed this was their wedding picture. They were solemn and unsmiling as one had to be for photographs ten years ago, but even so, they seemed happy to be together.

He looked down at the dead body. Even with the dreadful disfiguring injuries, it was obvious he had been an attractive man.

He made the sign of the cross.

"May the Lord have mercy on his soul."

He wasn't sure how a Presbyterian minister would take to being blessed by a papist, but he hoped doctrinal differences weren't important when you were dead.

Chapter Four

MURDOCH WAS ADMITTED into the house by a young, frightened-looking maid.

"I'm Detective Murdoch. Is the doctor with your mistress?"

"Yes, sir. They're in the drawing room."

Even in the hall, he could hear the sound of anguished weeping. "Would you announce me. Just speak quietly to the doctor."

"Yes, sir."

She disappeared through the chenille *portière* of the drawing room, and Murdoch began to pace up and down slowly. He tried to concentrate on one of the paintings on the wall, a fierce biblical scene of Abraham about to sacrifice Isaac. It was a story that Murdoch had never liked, as blind obedience was not his idea of virtue regardless of whether you believed the order was from God. The crying stopped abruptly and the maid

35

emerged followed by Dr. Ogden, whose face was stiff with strain.

"You can speak to her now, Mr. Murdoch, but not for long. Please ask only the most pertinent of questions."

She stood aside to let him enter, then followed him into a small dark room, its furnishings heavy and sombre. Mrs. Howard was seated on the sofa, a hoop of needlework beside her. What jolted him was that the informal silk tea gown she was wearing revealed she was *enceinte*, perhaps six months.

"Louisa, this is Detective Murdoch. He needs to ask you some questions. Can you do your best?"

The other woman managed to nod. She had fine reddish-brown hair and was probably normally fair-skinned, but now her face was blotched with red, her eyes already shadowed.

Without being asked, Murdoch sat down on the nearest chair across from her. He felt he was less intimidating that way. Dr. Ogden took the chair to his right.

"Mrs. Howard, please accept my deepest condolences. I would not trouble you at a time like this, but I want to find the man who is responsible for this crime and I need to act promptly."

36

He had taken out his pen and notebook when he was in the hall and he kept them discreetly at his side.

"First of all, will you tell me when you last saw your husband?"

She could barely manage a whisper and he had to lean forward to hear her.

"We had our luncheon together as we usually do. He left just before one o'clock. Tuesday is his day to be in his office." She licked her lips. "Could I have some water?"

Dr. Ogden immediately stood up and tugged the bell pull beside the fireplace.

Murdoch resumed. "Was it common knowledge that your husband would be in his office at that time?"

"I assume it was. He was there on Tuesdays, Wednesdays, and Fridays. The other afternoons, he made calls in the parish." She broke off. "My husband was one of Christ's most diligent servants, Mr. Murdoch. Who would do such a thing to him?" There was a rising note of hysteria in her voice. The doctor came over to her and laid a hand on her head.

"Louisa, calm yourself."

There was a tap at the door and Dr. Ogden went to answer it.

After a short, whispered conversation, she closed the door and returned to Mrs. Howard.

"Doris says that Mr. Drummond is here. He would like to speak to you. Do you want to receive him?"

Louisa had been slumped against the back of the sofa, but she suddenly sat upright.

"No, I will not. How dare he come here!"

"I'm sure he wishes to express his condolences, my dear," said the doctor soothingly.

37

"He does not. He wishes to gloat." Louisa was virtually shouting.

Dr. Ogden pursed her lips. She turned to Murdoch.

"As you can see, Mrs. Howard is in no condition to be interviewed. I must administer a sedative and perhaps you should return to the church."

"Of course." He picked up his notebook. "One more question, if you please. Mrs. Howard, was your husband in the habit of wearing a pocket watch?"

"Yes, he had a lovely silver engraved one that had belonged to his father. Why do you ask? Has it gone?"

"It appears to have been snatched from his waistcoat."

Louisa abruptly got to her feet. "I want to see him. I want to see Charles," she said to the doctor.

"Absolutely not. I cannot allow it."

To Murdoch's distress, the widow turned to him. "You are the detective in charge. Surely it is up to you. It is my right to see my own husband."

"That is true, Mrs. Howard, but I do not recommend it. Better to remember him as he was."

But he regretted the words even as they left his mouth. Her imagination was going to paint the picture now. She was going to fill in what he hadn't said.

"I'm sorry," he said. But he knew whatever she might imagine had happened could not possibly be as shocking as the actual thing.

"Louisa, you really must . . ." At that moment they heard voices outside in the hall.

"I have sent for some of the women to be with you. I have to return to the church."

Mrs. Howard caught the doctor by the hand. "How shall I tell the children?"

"You won't tell them anything for now. When I have finished my duties I will come back and deal with it for you."

"Who is here?"

"The Misses Frobishers and Mrs. Watson."

"Not Miss Dignam. I will not see her. Nor Miss Flowers."

"No, not them. Just the ones I mentioned."

Just then, they heard the sound of the door knocker, followed almost immediately by a man's voice, raised and excited. The door opened and a man burst in, Doris following helplessly behind him.

"Mrs. Howard, my dear lady –" He halted when he saw Murdoch and Dr. Ogden. "I beg your pardon. I was just at the church and heard the news. I had to come and see you."

"This is Reverend Swanzey," said Louisa. "Dr. Ogden and Detective Murdoch."

Swanzey hovered awkwardly by the door. "Have you arrested the culprit yet?"

"Not yet, sir."

"Do we know what happened?"

"Mr. Murdoch says that Charles's watch has been stolen."

"Ah, a burglar then, I thought it must be that."

"Why so, sir?" Murdoch asked. He'd kept his voice neutral, but Swanzey flinched.

"Charles Howard didn't have an enemy in the world. He was truly a vicar of Christ on earth."

His words made the new widow weep once more, exhausted, almost tearless crying that was painful to see. Dr. Ogden went and sat beside her.

"I have asked some of the women from the parish to stay with Mrs. Howard," she said, her tone making it clear this was no place for men. Swanzey promptly edged toward the door. He was a tall, gangly man of middle age with a lantern jaw and bristling side whiskers. The wind had reddened his cheeks and nose in an unattractive way. His awkwardness was not soothing.

"Of course. I don't wish to intrude, but I couldn't, er. I couldn't not come." He turned to Mrs. Howard and gave her a quick bow. "I will call tomorrow. If there is anything at all I can do, please send for me."

She gave him a wan smile. "Thank you, that is very kind." She began to stroke her distended stomach in an unconscious search of comfort. Murdoch noticed the embroidery she had been working on was a nursery sampler.

40 Swanzey bowed again to Murdoch. "Good day, sir. I will make myself available at any time if you need to speak to me."

He backed out of the room, and Dr. Ogden exchanged

a look with Murdoch. It was time for him to leave as well.

"Mrs. Howard, I will have to come back at a later time. Again please accept my sincerest sympathy."

She nodded and turned her head away. He was now the enemy.

Out in the hall, Murdoch tipped his hat to the three women who were standing there. Older, respectable women whose faces reflected the shock and sorrow of what they had heard, they were here to offer support to the new widow. He wondered how many times through the centuries women had come in such a way to comfort their bereaved sisters.

Chapter Five

MURDOCH RETURNED TO THE CHURCH. In spite of the increasingly heavy snow, a large crowd had gathered; people quietly talking among themselves, waiting to see the body removed. The police ambulance was drawn up in front of the steps, the horses jingling their harnesses and snorting from time to time. Fyfer and Crabtree had done a good job and quickly assembled the "good men and true," who would be jurors at the inquest. They were all standing at the top of the steps by the doors. Because the church was located in a well-to-do area of the city, they were better dressed than most jurors Murdoch had seen in the past and they didn't seem to be grumbling about being subpoenaed and losing a day or two of work. The constable was informing them of their duties in his loud, unmistakable voice. It was the juror's duty to view the body and the scene where the crime had taken place. When the inquest was conducted, they were expected to offer an informed opinion about what had taken place and, if appropriate, point an accusing finger at the one they considered the guilty party.

Murdoch leaned his wheel against a tree and went up to talk to him. "How are things going, George?"

"I just need one more to make the twelve, sir . . . Ah, you over there." He called out to a man in a tweed ulster who had just joined the crowd. "Come over here."

The man shook his head, "Not me."

Some of the onlookers, mostly women by now, giggled at his defiance, but Crabtree was on him in a minute. "I need one more juror, mister, and you'd better give me a very good reason why I shouldn't subpoena you."

"I'm a businessman, I can no afford to lose time away from my shop."

He was an older man with a pinched, craggy face and a full, grey-streaked beard. He spoke with a strong Scottish accent.

"That's not good enough. It's your civic duty same as the other men up there. I'm going to subpoena you."

"I've already helped the police once today to do their job, I dinna think I should do more."

"What do you mean, helped the police?"

"He was the gentleman who took care of the lady for me while I went into the church," interjected Fyfer. "Mr. Drummond, isn't it?"

"Ay."

43

Fortunately for Drummond, another man, a young, smartly dressed fellow who heard this, put up his hand as if he was in school.

"Excuse me, officer. I'll be glad to serve."

"Can you read and write?"

"Yes, sir. I got to the sixth standard."

"I don't need your school record, just your name. All right, come up here. But, Mr. Drummond, we can always do with extra jurors. I'm going to subpoena you anyway. You can get somebody to mind the store for you."

"I've already been closed down for the past two hours. I'll be pauperized."

But Crabtree was a stickler for civic duty and he hated dodgers. He began to write out the subpoena and, reluctantly, Drummond climbed the steps and took it.

"Good," said Crabtree, "that'll do us. Now listen, you men. First off you need to elect a foreman, then we view the body, I will administer an oath. Are there any Jews among you?"

There was a general shaking of heads. "I need to know because that's a different oath, but it makes my job easier if you're all Christian. Now then. Who's going to be foreman?" Nobody stirred. "Chamberlin, you've been on a jury before, why don't you do it?" Crabtree spoke to an elderly man who was sporting an impressively long white beard. "Any objections? No, then that's resolved. Mr. Chamberlin is your foreman and he will take the oath on behalf of all of you when we get inside."

44

The men shuffled their feet and a couple of them shook hands with Chamberlin. Murdoch tapped Drummond on the shoulder.

"I'm Detective Murdoch. I was just about to go and talk to Miss Dignam. How is she?"

The Scotsman eyed him mistrustfully, but Murdoch was beginning to think this was his habitual expression.

"She's got the look of wet clay about her, but she'll live I'm sure."

Just then Dr. Ogden arrived and, without wasting time, ordered the men to follow her. She went down the path, the jurors trailing after her like courtiers. Crabtree and Murdoch went with them.

They crowded into the hall and Crabtree directed them into the study until they were standing around the body. The sight of the corpse sobered even the enthusiastic young volunteer, but the constable didn't give them a chance to become maudlin.

"Listen up and hearken to your foreman's oath." He faced Mr. Chamberlin. "You shall diligently inquire and true presentment make of all such matters and things as shall be here given you in charge, on behalf of our Sovereign Lady, the Queen, touching the death of Charles Howard now lying dead, of whose body you shall have the view; you shall present no man for hatred, malice or ill-will, nor spare any through fear, favour, or affection; but a true verdict give according to the

45

evidence and the best of your skill and knowledge. So help you God. Do you so swear?"

"I do."

Crabtree addressed the remaining men. "The same oath that James Chamberlin, your foreman, hath now taken before you on his part, you and each of you are several well and truly to observe and keep on your parts. So help you God."

A spatter of *amens* from the less worldly of the men, then Dr. Ogden took over and began to describe what had happened to Howard. Her terminology was clinical, but no language could bleach the horror from the description. Midway through, Murdoch was afraid he might lose some of the jurors. He sent the young man of sixth-standard accomplishment out to get some fresh air. Fortunately, the process didn't take long and there were no questions.

"The inquest will be two days from now, March 5 at eleven in the morning at the Humphrey Funeral Home," said Dr. Ogden. "The constable will inform you where it is and what you should do when you get there." She nodded at Murdoch. "You can have the body taken away now. I will perform the post-mortem examination tomorrow."

46 The jurors talked among themselves briefly before leaving. At least half of them seemed to have known Howard, and Murdoch was struck with the genuine dismay they expressed.

Dr. Ogden said she was going back to the manse and Murdoch returned to the front of the church.

"George, start the rounds. See if anybody heard anything, saw anything, the usual procedure."

"Can I assist, sir?" asked Fyfer.

Murdoch hesitated. "Somebody has to stand here." But he knew from experience how dull it was to be assigned that task and Fyfer was looking at him like an eager pup. Two other constables had been sent up from the station and were waiting for orders. "All right. Start with questioning those who're hanging around. Just get names and addresses for now. If they have anything to say unsolicited, make a note of it, but tell them we'll be coming to interview them as soon as we can."

"Ugly business, isn't it, sir?" said Crabtree. "A man ripped from his family like that. And a decent man by all accounts. The inspector is going to be on our backs about this one, sir. If I may take the liberty of putting it that way."

"Indeed you may, George. The exact thought had crossed my mind. The deceased was a pastor of the Presbyterian Church. Inspector Brackenreid is always consistent in these matters. If you were important in life, you will be as important in death. Privilege doesn't vanish at the Great Divide."

47

Murdoch mounted his bicycle. He had discarded his muffler and gloves a few days earlier, hoping this would encourage spring to come. It hadn't. He turned up his collar and pulled his sleeves down as far as they would go over his hands.

"Anyway, I'm off to talk to Miss Dignam now."

"I gave you the address, didn't I, sir?" said Fyfer.

"Yes. Thank you, constable."

"Good luck, sir. I consider you have the worst job of all."

Murdoch was inclined to agree with him.

Fyfer had given Miss Dignam's address as 420, just north of the church on the west side of Jarvis Street. The house was impossible to miss as it was blazing with lights. As Murdoch approached, he saw a man and a woman turning away from the front door. Another couple was waiting for them on the sidewalk and he heard, "won't see us . . ." Some of the people who had gathered at the church seemed to be here, and there were three or four clumps of people standing on the street. They watched intently as Murdoch opened the wrought-iron gate and walked up to the front door. He didn't even have time to knock before it was opened. A wizened little man, in the formal clothes of a servant, frowned at him.

"Miss Dignam is not receiving callers, sir."

He handed the butler his card. "Detective William Murdoch. I must speak to her."

The little man's attitude changed. "Thank goodness. She has been waiting for you. We've already been swamped with neighbours and such who want to see her. Not that they were stomping down the weeds

48

before, I'll have you know. But now, suddenly she's the belle of the ball, the toast of the town. Poor dear thing."

For a moment, Murdoch wondered if indeed he was speaking to a servant.

"And you are?"

"Walters. I'm the general dogsbody here and have been since Miss Sarah was in short skirts. My actual job is valet to Mr. Elias Dignam, but there's just me here now so we don't stand on ceremony."

He stepped back into the hall. "Come on in before you get gawked to death. Miss Sarah is in the parlour. Her friend Miss Flowers is with her, but Mr. Dignam is in his study. Will you be wanting to talk to him?"

"I'm not sure just yet, Walters. Let me start with Miss Dignam."

The valet-cum-butler led the way down the hall, which gave the impression of having seen better days. The red flocked wall covering was dingy and the one rug on the floor should have been long ago relegated to the attic by the look of it. Walters seemed to pick up his thoughts.

"We aren't grand here, Mr. Murdoch. Mind you, we used to be when Mr. Dignam Senior was alive. Five servants then, and company all the time. But he lost all his money in a foolish investment in America and the two children were left with almost nothing."

Murdoch thought that the old servant was probably as loyal as he was indiscreet.

49

"Here we are. I'll bring in some tea."

There were no *portières*, so Walters tapped lightly on the door and, without waiting for permission, he went in.

"I've got a Detective Murdoch here to see you, Miss Sarah."

The parlour Murdoch stepped into was almost completely dark. Most of the light was coming from the blazing fire in the grate. Only one lamp was lit, and it was turned down low. He could just make out a smallish room crammed with furniture. Close to the fire were two shadowy figures. One of them stood up and came toward him.

"Good evening, I'm Miss Flowers, a dear friend of Miss Dignam," she said in a breathy voice. "As you of course realize she has had a most dreadful shock, but she has expressed a desire to speak to the police, which is why we have permitted you to come in."

Miss Flowers seemed to be trying to live up to her name. Past mid-age, she was short and stout but not deterred by her own physique. She was wearing an afternoon dress whose full skirt of heavy green satin was lavishly appliquéd with white daisies and roses. She was rather like a walking meadow. Her hair, although abundant and loosely pinned, was more grey than brown. She wore a pair of gold pince-nez.

The other woman had not stirred from her seat by the fire. Miss Flowers grasped Murdoch's arm and stepped forward. They were only three paces from the fireplace, but she said in a loud voice, "Sarah, my dearest, I have a Mr. Murdoch here from the police. He wishes to speak to you."

Finally, the other woman turned around and Murdoch saw that all the overdone solicitude on the part of her friend was justified. Even in the dim light, he saw the grief in the woman's face. Miss Sarah Dignam was suffering more than shock and horror at what she had found. She was also experiencing profound loss.

Chapter Six

IN CONTRAST TO HER FRIEND, Miss Dignam was wearing an unadorned dress of navy wool, extremely plain with old-fashioned tight sleeves. The only jewellery was a silver pendant watch. Murdoch thought he was in the presence of yet another nunlike woman, although Miss Dignam was too distraught to command much authority and he doubted that even in her normal days she would do so. She was small in stature, slight and bony, her skin suggesting that she had been drying up for a long time. However, as she offered her hand in greeting and managed a ghost of a smile, he saw that she had fine blue eyes that in her youth must have brought her many compliments.

"I am sorry to have to speak to you at this time, Miss Dignam, but I am sure you can appreciate the necessity for the police to pursue the matter of Mr. Howard's death as soon as possible."

"Of course. I expected you." Her voice was soft but not without crispness. She looked at her friend. "May, I believe it would be better for me to speak to the detective alone."

For a moment, Miss Flowers looked as if she would flat-out refuse to leave, more from prurient curiosity, Murdoch thought, than genuine concern for her friend. But rather surprisingly, Miss Dignam stood up, went over to the door, and opened it.

"Perhaps you would be so good as to look in on Elias. He's quite upset at the news and does so need cheering up. And would you tell Walters to wait on serving us tea until I ring. Thank you, May, I am much obliged."

"As you wish, my dear." With something of a pout, Miss Flowers swept off with a rustle of taffeta. Miss Dignam returned to her seat by the fire.

"Please sit down, Mr. Murdoch."

Her manners were those of a woman of polite society, but Murdoch had the impression she was barely keeping other, more passionate feelings in check. He took the chair opposite, put his hat on the floor, and removed his notebook from his pocket.

"Miss Dignam, I will have to write some notes. Do you mind if I turn up the lamp?"

"Not at all. I cannot sit in darkness for the rest of my life, can I?"

An odd remark, he thought, but he turned up the wick of the lamp and took out his fountain pen.

"Will you tell me what happened, Miss Dignam? Please don't hurry. Any details that you remember no matter how trivial may be of great importance so I do ask you to include them."

She stared at him blankly as if the word *trivial* had no place in her universe any more. There was no longer anything associated with the death of Reverend Howard that could be described in that way.

"Will you tell me exactly what happened this afternoon?" he repeated gently.

She shifted away from him so that she was staring into the fire. "In a way, there isn't much to tell. Tuesday is the afternoon when the study group meets. We discuss a biblical text that Reverend Howard assigns us – I should say, assigned us."

"And what was the text for this week, ma'am?"

Murdoch doubted if he really needed to know this, but he found working around the edges of the significant issue sometimes made his witnesses reveal unguarded things.

She glanced over at him nervously. "We have been studying the Song of Songs."

"Ah yes, a magnificent piece."

"Yes, indeed it is." She seemed to vanish again into some interior world of her own.

54

"What time did you arrive at the church, ma'am?"

Another nervous glance. "I, er, I went a little earlier, it was my turn to provide refreshment and I had a seed cake, caraway seed." She paused. "Reverend Howard was quite partial to my caraway seed cake."

She turned her head away and wiped at her eyes. Her shoulders shuddered and Murdoch was afraid she wouldn't be able to continue. He waited. Finally, she regained control and turned back to face him.

"I do apologize, Mr. Murdoch, but my eyes are burning dreadfully. Would you mind if I put the lamp in a different place?"

"Of course. Allow me."

Murdoch shifted the lamp to the table behind him and lowered the wick. Miss Dignam's face was more shadowed now. She folded her hands in her lap.

"I beg your pardon, I was distracted. As I said, I went to the church early. Our group meets at four o'clock and I must have been there at half past three."

Another pause. She was coming to the centre of the horror now. "I went in through the front door and walked down to the pastor's office, which is at the rear of the church."

"Did you notice anything amiss in the church itself, Miss Dignam?"

"Nothing. It has been a gloomy day and it was rather dark in there, but no, I saw nothing out of place."

"Do you usually enter by the front doors, ma'am?"

"Yes. Is that important?"

"I merely wondered if you had tried to go in by the side door and found it locked."

"No, I, er . . . I like to go in to the church so I can offer a short prayer before our meeting."

"And is that what you did today?"

Another sharp glance. "Is that relevant, detective?"

"It may be. I'm trying to get an accurate time sequence."

"Of course, I'm sorry. No, I did not stop to pray. I had taken a little longer than usual and I didn't want to be late so I went directly to the office."

Murdoch braced himself for the breakdown he anticipated would occur when she had to put into words what she had seen, but Miss Dignam simply clasped her hands even more tightly together and said in a voice that had gone as bloodless and light as an autumn leaf, "The door was open and I could see Charles lying on his back on the floor. There was blood everywhere . . ."

"Did you go into the room?"

"Of course. I had to make sure he was indeed dead and that there was nothing I could do."

"That was very brave of you, ma'am."

"Was it? I don't see it as an act of courage. If there were the slightest possibility he was still alive, I would have –" She stopped, but once again Murdoch had an eerie sense he was talking to one of the nuns he had known. Miss Dignam would have walked through fire if need be. "I could see that the injuries he had sustained were very severe. I had to leave him and I ran to fetch help. By good fortune, I encountered a constable on his beat right outside the church and directed him to the office . . . do I need to continue, Mr. Murdoch?"

"Just one or two more questions, Miss Dignam. Did you touch the body at all when you went into the room?"

"No."

"The constable said that your face and hands were quite bloodied and that you had blood on your cloak."

"Then I must have . . . it's all so dreamlike, frankly. But, yes, perhaps I did touch him, to see if there was any possibility that he was alive."

"Did you touch anything else, either on his person or in the room itself?"

Her reply was quick. "No, of course not. I had no occasion to."

"Did you hear anything at all when you went into the church? Footsteps, for instance? A door closing? That sort of thing."

"No, I did not. I have had some time to think about the matter. I realize Charles, er, Reverend Howard must have been killed very shortly before I arrived, but I had no awareness of anyone either in the church or the hallway."

"You said the church was dark. The pews are all tall. It would be easy for somebody to hide there, would it not?"

"Yes, I suppose so."

Murdoch made a note. "Did the minister have any enemies that you are aware of, Miss Dignam?"

57

Even in the shadowy light, he could see how much that question upset her.

"Absolutely not. Charles Howard was a truly good man. His eyes were as the eyes of doves, by the rivers of waters, his lips fitly set and terrible as an army with banners."

Murdoch barely had time to register that she was quoting from the Song of Songs when she suddenly gulped in air and began to gasp, fighting for breath. She was shaken by uncontrollable sobs that were virtually soundless and the more pitiful for it. He got to his feet, not sure how to help her, and gently touched her shoulder.

"You've had a terrible shock, ma'am. Shall I fetch Miss Flowers?"

With a tremendous effort of will she made herself stop crying. "No, I would prefer to be alone." She managed to suppress another shudder. "Would you be so kind as to hand me my bible, which is on the sideboard. I will take the word of our Lord as my comfort."

He did so but she didn't open the book immediately, waiting for him to leave.

"If you think of anything else at all, please send for me, Miss Dignam. I am at number four station on Parliament at Wilton Street."

"Yes, I will do that. Can you let yourself out?"

He left her, wondering if he should send in the friend regardless. He didn't need to worry. As soon as he

58

closed the door behind him, the kitchen door opened and Miss Flowers popped her head out.

"Have you finished?"

"For now."

"I'll go into her."

"She said she wanted to be by herself for a little while."

"Nonsense. Right now, she doesn't know what she wants." And she swept down the hall and into the drawing room.

Murdoch let himself out of the front door. As he cycled away from the house, he was struck by a memory that had haunted him for years. "Monk" Brodie and his dog. What was the mongrel's name? Ah yes, Paddy. A mangy stray that Brodie had adopted. Murdoch doubted if he would ever forget what had happened that cold winter night when the little dog had gone missing.

He leaned his wheel against the station wall. Why was he remembering that now?

Chapter Seven

THE DAY HAD BEEN more like November than March, as almost every customer had remarked to the cabbie, who had pulled his muffler up around his face for protection. His latest fare, a man in a hurry to get to Union Station, had asked him to whip up the horse, twenty-five cents extra if he made his train on time. Later, trying to tell his wife what had happened, the cabbie, Mick O'Leary, admitted that he hadn't seen the child's hoop as it came rolling across the road in front of him until it was too late.

"Where's there a hoop, Lal, there will a boy surely follow, but that lad dashed like a devil out of the other place, right into me path. I pulled up Jeb as smart as I could, but we was already out on the canter. He reared in the shafts so I afeared he might break the leads and bolt. Then this woman let out the most God-awful scream I ever did hear. *Timmy!* Or maybe it was *Tommy!*

I don't know. Then the man I'd picked up, who in my mind is the one responsible, so help me God, this fellow leaned his head out of the window and yells, 'Stop. You've run over a child. Stop at once.' Which he didn't need to shout because that's what I'd already done. We was right outside the Golden Lion and of course all the customers were just coming in or out. There was two or three other coachmen outside waiting for their missus, but do you think they'd so much as step down to give a fellow a hand? Not them. All of them, three it was now I think, all of them sat like they was Lot's wife. 'Course, I jumped down right smart to see the worst. The woman, who it turned out was the boy's ma, was on her knees trying to see underneath the carriage. My fare had got out too and he was down there looking.

"I can tell you, Lal, those were some of the worst moments in my life. I could see this lad lying still as a dead cat. There was blood coming out of his mouth and I swear I didn't know as he was quick or dead. I said a Hail Mary I can tell you. 'Move your carriage forward, but don't deviate an inch to either side,' said the fare, who was a bossy sort of cove. So I got Jeb's bridle and walked him on. He was a trembling poor beast, what with the pulling up that had torn his mouth and this woman carrying on to wake the dead, which we all thought she might need to do. But there was quite a crowd gathering now, and I heard somebody say, 'Look, his eyes are fluttering. He's alive.' The woman tried to

61

pick him up, but Mr. Bossy stopped her and lifted the
lad himself. 'We need to lie him down somewhere,' he
says. And wouldn't you know, one of the la-di-das said,
'Bring him into the shop. There's a couch.' That was
noble of her, seeing as how the lad was bleeding and
covered with mud and some horse plop. I could tell as
soon as I saw the look on that clerk's face that he wasn't
too pleased with the idea. But no, she had to be a good
Samaritan. Wasn't going to cost her anything if he
ruined the furniture. She had a walking stick with a
silver head and she waved it in front of her, like Moses
at the Red Sea, no I'm not blaspheming, that's how she
did it." He demonstrated to make his wife laugh. "Well,
everybody moved aside and the man carried the lad
into the store. I tied up Jeb and followed quick as I
could. 'Give him air,' says Mrs. La-di-Da. So Mr. Bossy
– they deserved each other, in my opinion – laid the
boy on the velvet couch. And it *was* velvet, blue velvet.
I wager it hadn't seen so much filth in all its born days.
And all this time, you understand, the mother is sobbing
and carrying on that she can't lose him too. Not so
soon. Then I paid attention to the fact that she was in
mourning. Mr. Bossy tries to calm her down.

"'He's not dead, madam. Look, Tommy, or Timmy,'
whatever it was, 'open your eyes.' And the lad did,
which made his mother scream more than if he'd died
on the spot.

"'What happened?' asks one old geezer and I knew

62

I was going to get it in the neck. I just knew it the way Mr. Bossy glared up at me. 'It was your fault,' he says. 'You were driving recklessly.' As if it weren't him that'd told me to whip up my horse. 'It was an accident,' says I, but I knew I weren't going to get much sympathy from this lot. They see us cabbies as some species of low life like you might find under a rock if you was ever to turn it over, which in their case they wouldn't do without a gardener.

"'He should get to a physician,' says the old geezer. The number of people who suddenly promote themselves to captains never ceases to amaze me. So the lad tries to sit up, scared I suppose. I don't blame him. I wouldn't want to see a sawbones either. You come out worse than when you went in, if you ask me. But sitting up made him yelp out with pain, like a little dog, and that set his mother off again. The lad whispered something and Mr. Bossy leaned down with his ear next to the boy. 'Say that again.' Well, I knew what the boy was trying to say without he needed an interpreter. I could tell by looking at them that they didn't have a penny to rub together. Clean, mind you. She'd dressed them both as decent as she could, that was obvious.

"So Mr. Bossy addressed the first good Samaritan, like they was of like mind. 'He says they can't afford to go to a physician and he's quite all right, thank you.' But he didn't look all right to me. He had a goose egg over his eye the size of the knob on the woman's cane and who knows as he hadn't broken some bones that we couldn't see. 'Nonsense,' says Mrs. Good Samaritan. I could tell by the Moses act earlier that she was a woman who got her own way. Probably has a dozen servants and fart-catchers." O'Leary saw the expression on his wife's face. "Sorry, my dear, but you know how I feel about women like that. Anyways, she reaches into her reticule and pulls out a five-dollar note. Yes, five dollars. 'Here,' she says to the widow who'd stopped wailing a bit by now. 'Here. Take this and pay for the doctor.' 'Oh no, ma'am, I couldn't possibly. He'll be right as rain in a minute.' At which point the lad started to heave like he was going to do a big toss-up. And did that turn Mr. Clerk's face green, I can tell you. But the lad kept it down and Mr. Bossy says to the widow, very stern like he was a magistrate, 'My good woman. I understand you are a decent woman and you have pride. But you must put that aside for the sake of your son. Look,' he says. 'Where'd you live? We'll get the lad to your house.' 'Oh,' says she, snivelling again. 'I don't live in Toronto. I've just arrived from Chatham and I haven't got a place yet.' 'Just as I suspected,' says Mr. Bossy. Then he snatches off his own fedora. 'Tell you what, why don't we do a go-around right now. Get you enough money for a night's lodgings at least and the fee for a physician. What do you think, ma'am?' he asked Mrs. Silver Cane.

"Well, she was a bit uppity because she had been the

first one to come up with the five dollars and she wanted all the glory. But before you know it all the ladies were dipping into their purses and dropping money into the hat. I tried to get a good look at how much was in there when it came to me. Yes, I had to put in something, they'd have had my hide otherwise. I reckon there was close to a hundred dollars. I made sure Mr. Bossy gave it all to her and some didn't fall into his own pocket on the way. Somebody piped up and said that I could take them to the closest doctor, which I thought was a right cheek. They didn't offer to pay my docket, I noticed. But by now, Timmy seemed somewhat improved. So Mr. Bossy helped the lad to stand up and he showed he could walk all right. 'You're lucky,' says this man to me, wagging his finger. As if it were my fault. The boy were the lucky one, if you ask me. He could have been killed. As he hobbled by, he looked up at me with his big brown eyes. 'Sorry for all the trouble, sir,' he says. 'But can I have my hoop?' Fortunately, somebody had already got it and straightened it out.

"Ah, you're forever saying I'm down on the human race, Lal, well all this kindness would have warmed your heart. Mr. Bossy says as how he'll escort the lad and his ma. 'What about your train?' I asks. 'You'll have missed it by now.' He gives me a look. 'There are more important things in life than catching a train,' says he, and I know he also means than getting a fare. So off they went. I hung around a bit, in spite of the nasty

65

looks I was getting from the clerk. I hoped I'd pick up some business, but most of that lot have their own carriages and I got not a nibble. Besides, they all wanted to sit around and talk about what just happened, which was probably the most excitement they'd had since the undermaid fell down in a fit in the scullery." O'Leary took a deep pull on his pipe and eyed his wife, who was sitting quietly in the inglenook with her mending.

"So what do you think of all that, my dear?"

Mrs. O'Leary bit off the end of the thread. "I'd say it was a queer from beginning to end."

O'Leary laughed and puffed out smoke at the same time, which made him cough. "I thought as how you wouldn't be fooled," he said, his eyes watering.

"Are you going to report them?"

"Nah. It's not my tit that they milked, was it?"

Chapter Eight

IT WAS ALMOST TEN O'CLOCK by the time Murdoch
returned to his lodgings. He was dead tired, famished,
and in decidedly low spirits. The house was in darkness, but when he let himself in, he saw there was a
light in the kitchen. A smell of sausages lingered in the
air and he hoped there were some left. Since Mrs.
Kitchen had packed her and her husband off to
Muskoka to see if they could cure Arthur's consumption, one of the new lodgers, Katie Tibbett, had taken
over the cooking. And truth be told, however fond he
was of Mrs. Kitchen, the one thing Murdoch didn't
miss was her cooking. Katie was a good cook and now
he looked forward to coming home to tasty meals.
Murdoch, his old friend Charlie Seymour, and Amy
Slade, a schoolteacher, were the others who now
boarded in the house and they paid Katie a small wage
in exchange for housekeeping duties. She was the

young mother of twin baby boys and would be destitute if it weren't for this arrangement.

Good food wasn't the only reason Murdoch liked being at home these days. Charlie, a sergeant at number four station, was a bachelor whose taciturn speech belied an intense and passionate nature. They had great animated discussions about life, death, and God, not to mention bicycles. Murdoch knew it was Charlie's night to be on duty at the station, but he wished he was available to talk to.

And then there was Miss Amy Slade. They had met in January, when she had asked for his help with a police matter that involved one of her pupils. Murdoch found himself in a constant turmoil of feeling, which had started almost as soon as he met her. If he were to be honest with himself, which he didn't particularly want to be, he had to admit that it was partly because of Amy Slade that he hadn't proposed marriage to Mrs. Enid Jones.

The kitchen door opened and the woman in question emerged. She was in a quilted red house gown and her hair, usually so neatly confined, was loose about her shoulders. Murdoch almost missed the peg on the coat tree as he went to hang up his coat.

"Good evening, Will. You are very late tonight. You must have been working on a case."

She wasn't at all uncomfortable about the casualness of her dress, which paradoxically made him more so.

"I was indeed."

"Come into the kitchen. Katie has left some delicious toad-in-the-hole in the warming oven. Your case must be a difficult one, by the look of you."

He followed her, marvelling yet again how she was able to pick up his mood so easily. He also marvelled at the beauty of her fair hair, which was thick and curly and reached almost to her waist. All this marvelling made him irritated with himself. He was as fickle as water, pining for one woman after another.

As if on cue, Amy turned to him and gave him a rather enigmatic smile. "I picked up a letter from the post for you today. I believe it's from Mrs. Kitchen."

"Oh, good." Murdoch rubbed his hands together with excessive zeal. He didn't want Amy to think he was waiting on a letter from Enid.

The envelope was on the table, propped up against the salt cellar.

"Why don't you sit down, and I'll get your supper."

This was not usual for Amy. She'd made it clear from the beginning that in her view, men and women were equally capable of making a meal, getting it out of the oven, and cleaning up after themselves. This was all new to Murdoch and he was still getting used to it. Frankly, he'd rather liked the way Mrs. Kitchen and then Enid had looked after him.

69

He headed for the stove. "That's all right, I can do it . . . Ow." He'd underestimated the heat of the warming oven and the plate was hot.

"Use the teapot holder," said Amy. She didn't jump up to help him. He did as she said, gripped the plate, and came back to the table. The toad-in-the-hole looked delicious, the plump sausages sticking out through the pastry, the gravy thick.

Amy sat across from him and leaned her elbows on the table. With her hair unpinned in that way, she looked like a young girl. The house gown was fastened to the neck, but the sleeves were loose and she was revealing her bare forearms, well shaped, pale-skinned with a smattering of freckles.

He speared one of the sausages. "How were the twins today?"

"They were a bit mardy. Katie says they are teething. You'd better be prepared, they might wake you up tonight."

"I'd better put cotton wool in my ears then."

"You already look exhausted, Will. What has happened?"

"Let me feed the beast within first, then I'll tell you." He picked up the letter, immediately getting gravy on it. "Damn."

"Shall I read it to you while you eat?"

"That'd be swell."

70 Too late he realized Mrs. Kitchen might have made a reference to Mrs. Enid Jones, her former lodger. Or worse, some shrewd comment about the new boarder, Miss Slade. But Amy was already slitting open the

envelope and it would seem churlish, if not suspicious, to snatch the letter away from her. He gave a little mental prayer and concentrated on stuffing pastry into his mouth.

Amy began to read. "'My dear Will. Life here continues to be quiet. Now that I have a routine, my work is not arduous. I am not used to giving orders to other people, but that is what I am supposed to do so I do it. The girls are for the most part industrious and honest, thank the Lord. I am happy to report that Arthur continues to gain strength. He frets at the idleness as he puts it, but it is obvious the air and rest are doing him good. I would never have known what fresh air really is if we hadn't come here. Toronto is dirty indeed. The patients are weighed every week and he has actually put on two pounds. We celebrated by a little party with the others on his floor. We were all wrapped up against the cold because, as much as possible, everybody stays on the veranda for the air. Arthur complained that if the consumption doesn't get him, the cold will, but there are hints that spring is coming and that will be more comfortable. He says to tell you he misses the smell of your tobacco and especially the evening talks you used to have. There is a young boy two beds down who is only seventeen, and he is the most ill of all of them. The nurses shake their heads at us behind his back, meaning he is a hopeless case. Arthur has taken him under his wing and is telling him the stories of your cases and how

71

you solved them. The boy's name is John and he begged me to tell you that when he is better, he would like to come down to Toronto and meet you. He'd like to be a police officer. I say my prayers that this might be. How is everything in the house?'" Amy paused and Murdoch braced himself. Here it comes. Amy continued. "'How is Mr. Seymour? And that poor young girl with the babies? Is Miss Slade behaving herself?'" Amy stopped reading. "Why would she say that? What sort of impression did I give her?"

Mrs. Kitchen had met Amy once just before they were leaving for Muskoka. The schoolteacher had been wearing her pantaloons and jerkin and even though her manners were impeccable and she was very well spoken, Beatrice had been shocked.

"It was your, er, your Rational Dress. Mrs. K is quite conservative."

Amy sighed. She had experienced such reactions many times. "She signs off by saying, 'I say my rosary constantly. Remember us in your prayers, Will. Yours sincerely, Beatrice Kitchen.'"

They were both quiet for a few moments, Murdoch thinking about Arthur and the precariousness of his life. Then he picked up his plate and stood up. "I'll make a pot of tea."

He lifted one of the lids from the stovetop and dropped in a piece of coal to build up the fire. While they waited for the water to boil, he started to tell her something of what had happened that day. He had too much respect for her to treat her as if she were a potential hysteric, so he told her about the murder, glossing over the more horrendous injuries but sparing nothing else.

She straightened in her chair. "What a dreadful thing. I do pity his wife. Do you have a notion as to the culprit?"

"It looks very much like a thief. Howard wore a silver pocket watch, but it is gone. His boots were also taken. I don't know if anything else is missing yet."

"Who found him?"

"One of the parishioners. A woman by the name of Sarah Dignam. She was coming for a prayer meeting."

"Poor woman."

"Indeed. She is dreadfully upset."

He hesitated, wondering whether he should share his thoughts about Miss Dignam, but they seemed rather unfair and he had tangled with Amy before about denoting strong emotions in women as hysteria.

"It's funny, after I left her I was reminded of this chopper I knew at the camp. His nickname was 'Monk' not because of any pious habits, far from it, but because we all thought he resembled a monkey. He had abnormally long arms and short bandy legs and masses of hair all over him."

Amy smiled. "Surely it wasn't a physical resemblance to Miss Dignam that made you think of him?"

"Hardly. Brodie was something of an outcast, but he found this stray dog about the camp and he became a

73

changed man. He loved that mongrel and became friends with any other chopper that paid attention to the little creature. There was a lot of snickering behind his back, as you can imagine with that bunch of hard hearts, but they wouldn't have dared say anything to his face because Monk was far too tough." Murdoch started to fold the tea towel. "Anyway, what came back to mind so vividly was the night he discovered his dog, Paddy was its name, was missing. He was beside himself. We weren't supposed to leave the camp after dark because it was too dangerous, but I couldn't stand to see him so I agreed to go with him in search of Paddy." Murdoch hesitated, not sure how much he should tell Amy, but she was obviously listening intently and he could feel how much he wanted to unburden himself. He'd never told anybody the story before. "We didn't have to go far because we soon picked up a trail of blood leading off one of the runs. Paddy had managed to drag himself to the shelter of the trees. He must have been attacked by a coyote because his ear was half off and he had several deep bites on his head and legs. The worst was the one at his throat."

"Oh how dreadful."

"It was. At first I thought he was dead, but Monk dropped to his knees beside him and Paddy moved his head and tried to lick his face. Brodie just recoiled in horror and he yelled at me. 'I can't bear it. We must do something.' I tried to tell him that the dog would die soon enough, but Paddy whimpered and tried to crawl toward him. Brodie screamed and before I could stop him, he reached for a nearby stone . . . with two blows, he dispatched the creature on the spot."

Amy was gazing at him, her hand to her cheek in horror.

"After that he cried, clutching the dog to his chest, rocking back and forth . . . I didn't know what to do or say. Finally he stopped and I persuaded him to bury the little mongrel, which we did."

"Oh Will, that is such a sad story."

"There was an expression in Miss Dignam's eyes and the way she cried for those few moments that reminded me of Monk when we first found the dog and he knew he'd lost him. It was as if a door had opened up into the sorrow of all their lives." He averted his eyes. "My God, that sounds fanciful."

Amy reached out and touched his hand. "No, it doesn't at all. I had a pupil once whose mother died suddenly, influenza I think it was, the girl was about twelve years old. When she came back to school, we happened to be studying *Romeo and Juliet*. The girl wasn't a particularly good student or had never before shown much response to Shakespeare, but this afternoon when we got to the passage where Juliet dies, she burst out crying. I couldn't soothe her. She was only a child, but she had known much loss in her young life."

Murdoch smiled at her gratefully. "Monk left the camp at the end of the season and I never saw him

75

again. We never talked about poor Paddy . . . I was also troubled by the way he killed the dog."

"I suppose it could be considered as an act of mercy. The dog must have been suffering."

"He was, but Brodie went into a kind of panic as if the sight was more than he could bear. Whether that was for the dog's sake is debatable. I hope I'm never faced with a situation like that." Murdoch shuddered. "I still have nightmares about it."

At that moment, the kettle began to whistle.

"Good timing. A cup of tea will hit the spot," said Murdoch and he got up and went over to the stove. While the tea was poured and sipped, he resumed his narrative of the day's events.

"I spent the evening going through Howard's personal portfolio. He was very organized and everything was filed under subject matter, including sermons, church business. There was quite a bit of correspondence and minutes of meetings about the installation of a new water closet. Apparently, the proposal was controversial. There were those who thought it was a ridiculous expense and the earth closet was quite adequate and those who thought it would enhance the public standing of the parish to have such a fine piece, not to mention being more suitable for the older members of the church."

Amy smiled. "Surely the poor man would not have been killed over the matter of a water closet?"

"Let's hope not. I saw the new facility and it is indeed very handsome and probably cost a lot of money. As far as I can tell Reverend Howard was generally keen to improve the church furnishings. But except for minor quibbles from a few of the elders, I couldn't find any evidence that somebody was sufficiently enraged to murder him over it." Murdoch poured them each more tea. "The letter opener told me nothing new other than that the thrust was a single one, made hard and deep. There was no sign of footprints inside or out. So that's it for the silent witnesses. As for human witnesses, that was equally as unproductive. Crabtree and Fyfer questioned as many people in the area as they could, but so far nothing at all has emerged. It was such a dismal day, there was hardly anybody out to see anything. The murderer came and went without a trace. He might as well have been a spirit."

Amy blew on her tea to cool it. "You've been saying *he* all the time when referring to the culprit. Do the injuries preclude a female attacker?"

He reflected for a moment. "The letter opener had been thrust into his neck very deeply and then I'd say he was kicked hard when he was on the ground, but he would have been defenceless by then. So, no, alas, we cannot at this point eliminate the possibility it was a woman who killed him. The coroner, who is a woman by the way, said she will do a post-mortem examination in the morning. I'll attend that. Sometimes there are surprises."

77

"Such as?"

"Oh, I don't know, maybe the pastor was an opium eater or a drinker or had syphilis."

Amy looked at him in amazement. "Is that likely?"

"Believe me, anything is likely."

She gave him a slightly teasing smile. "Are you becoming cynical, Will?"

"Perhaps. I'd like to believe Mr. Howard was as good a man as everybody says he was, but if that's true how can we explain such a tragedy?"

"Ah, we're back to the inscrutable nature of God's intention, are we?"

"That sounds awfully much as if I'm becoming boringly predictable."

"Not at all. Not predictable, just forever questioning." Her eyes held his for a moment. "You've been in the presence of too much human misery, Will. You can't take the sorrows of the world on your shoulders."

Murdoch grabbed at his own neck. "Heck, I thought all that stiffness was from too much riding on my wheel."

Amy pushed back her chair and stood up. "I should go to bed. I am tireder than I realized."

And that was that. Without more ado, she picked up her candleholder.

"I wish you good night."

To delay her, he said, "How were your pupils today?"

"Let me say, I felt as if I were trying to hold down

twenty balloons all at the same time. It's a wonder we didn't float away."

She left and Murdoch groaned to himself. Why had he made light of her remark when she was trying to be kind? What a boor she must think him. He reached for his pipe and tobacco pouch, although he didn't usually smoke in the kitchen. He tamped down the tobacco in the bowl of his Powhatan and struck a match.

He supposed it was true what she'd said about him. He still went to mass but less and less frequently, and he was often restless when the priest delivered his homily, which was usually about some doctrinal issue that Murdoch couldn't completely accept. Amy made no secret of her atheism, although she was obliged to attend church if she wanted to keep her job. She had opted to go to the Presbyterian church on King Street. "If I have to spend two hours of my precious Sunday going to an institution I don't believe in, I might as well get a good sermon out of it and the Presbyterians are the best as far as I'm concerned."

Murdoch had considered inviting her to come to mass with him, just so she could see what it was like, but he knew all too well what she'd think of Father Fair and all the crossing and genuflecting that went on.

He sat for a long time thinking about things – or, more specifically, love and the human heart.

79

Chapter Nine

Inspector Brackenreid was in the irascible frame of mind that was so typical of him these days, it would have been something to remark on if he had been otherwise. Murdoch was standing in front of his desk waiting for permission to sit down. Sometimes, the inspector was petty enough to make his officers stand for an unnecessarily long period.

"I'll give you Dewhurst and Birney. You've got Crabtree and Fyfer already. As long as nobody's shirking their duty, that'll be enough, don't you think, Murdoch?"

"Nobody will shirk, sir. They're good officers. But I'd be glad of any constables we can spare from other duties. As you no doubt noticed in this morning's papers, the city is quite caught up with the crime. I'm sure the chief constable would like us to make the case our top priority."

Brackenreid looked as if he wanted to argue the

point, but he didn't have the energy. He rubbed his temples.

"Ach. I feel as if there's some malevolent little devil in my head, playing a tune on an anvil."

Murdoch knew exactly what that devil was. He could smell it from where he stood.

"Perhaps a strong cup of tea will help, sir."

"You're right, Murdoch. I'll have one sent up." He flapped his hand. "Sit down, for goodness' sake. I can't keep looking up at you, it makes things worse."

Murdoch took the chair in front of the inspector's desk. He almost felt sorry for the man, he looked so bilious. The whites of his eyes had a yellowish tinge.

"I want every single person interviewed who lives in the vicinity of the church. Somebody must have seen somebody. I don't care if it was the mayor himself taking a stroll with his paramour, I want to know about it."

"Does Mr. Kennedy have a paramour, sir? I hadn't heard."

Brackenreid groaned in irritation. "No, of course not. It was a figure of speech. You know perfectly well what I mean."

"You mean that as the Reverend Howard was a man of prominence in the community, we must leave no stone unturned to find his murderer, even if that proves to be another person of prominence."

"What? No, for heaven's sake, Murdoch I didn't mean that. We all know he was killed by some passing tramp.

81

Find him and soon. I want a daily report from you. Don't forget, Murdoch, I promoted you and I can unpromote you just as fast."

"Yes, sir. It's not something I would forget."

Brackenreid's flash of anger seemed to have aggravated his headache and he sat for a moment with his head in his hands.

"Is that all, sir? Shall I have Gardiner send up that tea?"

"Yes, good idea. What is your plan now?"

"I'm going back to see Mrs. Howard. I hope she is able to talk to me."

"Mrs. Brackenreid and I met her just after the pastor's appointment to Chalmers. Some charity concert, I think it was." He struggled to remember. "Or was it at Mrs. Maclean's soiree? Oh blast, I don't know. It doesn't matter, does it?"

"Probably not, sir. Unless you think that somebody at the concert is a likely suspect."

"What? Dammit, Murdoch, you go too far."

"I beg your pardon, sir."

"As I was saying. I met the Howards not so long ago. She is a handsome woman and I preferred her to him. Decent-enough fellow, don't get me wrong, but a bit airy-fairy for my taste. I like to see a fellow with some fire to him. Nothing like a tip-top sermon to set a man up for the day."

Sermonizing hadn't had much impact on Brackenreid's need for the little devil drink, thought Murdoch. He shifted slightly in his seat. Whenever the conversation approached even obliquely to the topic of religion, he knew that he could expect some kind of riposte. Ah here it came.

"I don't know how you manage in your religion, Murdoch. With all that Latin, you can't get any direction at all, surely?"

"The prayer book does have an English translation on one side of the page, sir. And the sermon, or homily as we call it, is in English."

Brackenreid started to shake his head in ostentatious disbelief but thought better of it.

"All right. Get on with it then. I suppose I don't need to remind you to handle the poor woman with kid gloves, do I?"

"No, sir, you don't."

"Quite. That's something I've noticed about you Catholics, you are good at dealing with women."

This remark was so stunningly peculiar that Murdoch had no reply. He stood up.

"Don't forget the tea," said Brackenreid as Murdoch left.

The maid's face was puffy and blotchy from crying. "Mrs. Howard is in the drawing room with Mr. Swanzey, sir."   83

"I do need to talk to her, Doris."

"Yes, sir." With the merest tap on the door, she showed him in.

Louisa Howard was sitting on the couch by the window, Swanzey beside her. He stood up to greet Murdoch, but Louisa didn't even turn to acknowledge him. She was staring out of the window and he presumed her expression was grief-stricken, but he could see nothing because of the obscuring widow's veil she was wearing. She was already dressed in deepest mourning and Murdoch wondered not for the first time if every married woman of affluence had black clothes in her wardrobe on the ready for such an eventuality as widowhood.

Reverend Swanzey hovered uncertainly between them. He had a long neck and his prominent Adam's apple bobbed visibly.

"I'm sorry to disturb you, Mrs. Howard," said Murdoch, "but as I'm sure you can understand, I am anxious to find your husband's murderer as soon as possible."

There was no other word he could use other than killer but even at the word *murderer* he saw her flinch. She turned to face him. Her voice lacked energy and her breath rippled her crepe veil as she spoke.

"I do understand, Mr. Murdoch. And since last night, all I have been able to think about is your question whether Charles had any enemies."

Swanzey interjected. "Mrs. Howard and I have been discussing this very matter this morning, detective. At first we both as with one voice said no. Charles was a good man, beloved by all he came in contact with." He paused and glanced anxiously at Louisa. She remained steady for

84

the moment. "However, in the course of his work, he had occasion to do things, to make decisions that for the people involved might have seemed harsh. They were not likely to step back and say, 'This good man is merely doing his duty. I have no right to hate him for it.'" Again he paused and looked at Murdoch expectantly.

"I'm afraid I don't know what you are referring to, sir."

Mrs. Howard explained. "My husband was a Visitor for the House of Industry. It was his job to visit the homes of the people who had applied for charitable relief and decide whether they were deserving."

"It is something I do myself," said Swanzey, "and believe me, Mr. Murdoch, not all the cases that come before us deserve help. But these tend to be the kind of people who will rail against the Visitor himself rather than look to their own shortcomings that have brought them to their predicament. And there is only so much the city can do. I myself have agonized over whether I can grant a coal allowance or food to a poor woman who has neither heat nor sustenance but whose husband I know has succumbed to bad habits."

He meant he was a drinker.

"That must be difficult, Reverend. Especially as it is not the woman herself who is to blame."

Swanzey swayed on his tiptoes. "Ah yes, but we encounter many tricksters. The women come to the House to apply because they think we will be more indulgent of them, but they know perfectly well that

85

the husband at home is a drunkard and should be working. And sometimes, I regret to say, they join him in his habit."

"Quite so. But to return to Mr. Howard for a moment, are you saying, ma'am, sir, that through this work, it is possible he made an enemy, angry enough to kill him?"

"Yes," whispered Mrs. Howard.

"Did he ever mention such an encounter to you, ma'am?"

"No. He did not. But he never brought the burdens of his work to me. I wanted it that way. I strove to make our home a haven for him, where all those cares could be put aside."

Murdoch thought of the comfort he himself found from talking over his cases with first the Kitchens, now with Seymour and Amy Slade. He wondered if there had been some place else where Reverend Howard had unburdened himself.

"Where can I get a list of the homes he inspected?"

"The House of Industry would have that," said Swanzey. "And I should add that his territory was in this area. We are all assigned places that are easily accessible –"

Mrs. Howard interrupted him. "The work is voluntary, detective. It is in addition to all the other duties that a minister in a large parish has to execute."

And she didn't approve of her husband doing that unpaid work, thought Murdoch.

"As you say, Mrs. Howard, being a Visitor is voluntary,

but I myself consider it my civic duty," interjected Swanzey. "But more to the point, detective, if Reverend Howard had antagonized somebody, that person most likely lives not too far from here. And it is highly likely that they would know that he had office hours on Tuesdays."

Murdoch got to his feet. "Thank you, reverend. And you, ma'am. There's just one more thing. I wonder if I could ask your maid to accompany me to the church. I assume she would be the one who would dust the office and I'd like to know if anything else has been taken."

"Is it absolutely necessary? There is so much to do here at the moment."

"I wouldn't ask if it weren't, ma'am. I shan't keep her for long." He knew Mrs. Howard was bereft, but he was finding her rather irritating. There was something sour and self-pitying in her manner.

"Very well, but I warn you, Doris is a rather empty-headed girl, Mr. Murdoch. She might not notice if somebody had walked off with his chair."

Murdoch took his leave and Mrs. Howard returned to gazing out of the window. Reverend Swanzey perched himself beside her on the couch. He was clearly not comfortable in his role as chief comforter. He should have been a Catholic. According to Inspector Brackenreid, *we have a certain facility with women*, thought Murdoch.

———

The poor maid was initially afraid to go with him to the office after Murdoch warned her she would have to see the blood stains. But when he explained the importance of knowing if anything was missing, she braced herself and agreed to accompany him. They entered the office, which still had the curtains drawn although the fire had long died out and the room was cold. Doris shuddered once when she saw the blood on the carpet and on the desk, but on Murdoch's instruction she walked slowly around the room, taking note of everything. Far from being empty-headed, she seemed to be a servant who took pride in her work and knew exactly what belonged where.

"He had a very fine letter opener that always sat on his desk. I don't see it."

"You are right, Doris. It is in the possession of the police."

She blinked as she comprehended what that meant, but she didn't say anything.

She picked up a silver snuff box that was on the lamp table next to the armchair. "Usually this is on the mantelpiece. He loved his snuff, but the mistress didn't like him to use it so he only did when he was in here. But he was trying to break himself of the habit and so sometimes he'd put the box where it was less convenient to reach." She replaced the box. "I can't see what harm it did."

"Is the chair usually across from the armchair?"

"No, sir. It lines up with the other ones for when he has his meetings."

They took the next half an hour going over the room carefully, but Doris was adamant everything was in place except for the letter opener.

Murdoch thanked her and commended both her courage and her awareness. He was gratified to see the shy blush of pleasure on her face.

"Reverend Howard's boots were removed and as they are nowhere to be found, I assume his attacker took them. Were you responsible for cleaning them, Doris?"

"Yes, sir. I did the boots every night before I went to bed so as they'd be ready."

"Can you describe them for me?"

She looked a little puzzled. "They was just ordinary boots, sir. Black of course. Not new though. He didn't like waste and rather than buy new when another would, he'd mend and make do. Those boots were mended sole and heel at least two times." Murdoch made a note. It was something distinguishing at least. Suddenly Doris tapped her fingers to her forehead. "I'm sorry, sir, but the shock has fair blown my idea pot in two. I was almost about to forget his laces. In the morning, he broke one of his laces. We didn't have any spare and he said he didn't have time to buy some more so he took one from his other pair of boots." She looked at Murdoch expectantly. "Oh dear, what I mean is that the second pair of boots is brown. So he had one pair of black laces and one brown. Mrs. Howard would have had a conniption if she'd seen, but those sort of things weren't important to him."

"Thank you, Doris. That could be very helpful indeed. I have one more question. Did Mr. Howard post his own letters?"

"No, sir. I did."

"Did he write a letter on Tuesday morning?"

"Not that I know of, sir. He could have written something when he went to his office after his luncheon, but that wasn't usual. Friday was letter-writing day and I would take them to the post office that afternoon." Again there was the sad little smile. "Mr. Howard liked his routine. He didn't change it, ever. He always said that the earth was without form until God created it and it was up to us to follow in God's will by making order throughout our lives." Her voice was wistful and Murdoch felt a pang of pity.

"How long have you worked for Mrs. Howard, Doris?"

"Since I was fourteen, sir. I came up with them from Buffalo."

"Is your family still there?"

"I don't have a family anymore, sir. They all died of the smallpox. Mr. and Mrs. Howard took me in."

90   She was a young girl, surely not yet twenty, and however grateful she might be, her life as the only servant of a man who hated variety must have been dreadfully dull.

Murdoch walked her back to the manse and took her round the rear of the house to the servant's entrance. Here with sweet, natural good manners, she offered him her hand.

"I'll say good morning then, sir. I hope I have been of help."

"Indeed you have, Doris. Thank you."

She blushed again, but there were tears in her eyes.

"The master was good like you, sir. I will miss him terrible."

Chapter Ten

MURDOCH SAW THE HORSE MANURE just in time, but as
he swerved to avoid it his wheel skidded on a patch of
ice and he almost lost control of his bicycle. If it hadn't
been for that moment of distraction, he would probably
have seen the boy sneaking up on the elderly woman
who was hobbling down Yonge Street. As it was, he
heard a cry, saw that a woman had collapsed to the
ground, and a boy was running as fast as he could away
from her. A passerby stopped briefly to see if the old
lady was all right, then he took off after the boy. He
was a husky fellow and his frame couldn't keep pace
with his good intentions. Murdoch hesitated. A woman
was helping the old lady to her feet. There wasn't much
point in his racing after the boy until he knew exactly
what had happened. This section of Yonge Street, where
stores lined each side of the street, was always crowded

at this time of day and several people were already surrounding the woman.

He pulled over to the curb, dismounted, and eased through the group of spectators.

"Excuse me, I'm a policeman, excuse me."

Close up, the woman who was the centre of attention wasn't quite as old as she had first appeared. Her face was thin and toothless, but what he could see of her face was relatively unlined. She was holding a silk handkerchief to her eyes and repeating in a quivery voice, "Dearie me, dearie me. He took all my money."

"Ma'am. I'm a policeman. Can you tell me what happened?"

"She was robbed, that's what happened," said a young woman next to her. "That street arab just came up and snatched her purse."

Murdoch saw that the man had given up his chase and was coming back. He came into the circle of helpers.

"He got away from me. I'm so sorry." He was still panting, his weatherbeaten face flushed from his exertions.

"Did you lose much, ma'am?" Murdoch asked.

She shook her head, the handkerchief still at the ready. "Just my streetcar tickets. I was on my way to see my daughter. Oh dear. That's all I had with me." 93

"Don't you fret yourself, ma'am," said the lad. "I'm sure there's folks here that'll help you out."

"I have an extra ticket," said the young woman. She reached into her glove. "Please accept this. I'm so sorry about your money."

"Here," said the young fellow. "I've only got fifty cents, but I'd be obliged if you would take it." There was a sympathetic shift among the bystanders and the beginning of a shuffle with purses and pockets.

The old woman shook her head vigorously. "Thank you, sir. I couldn't possibly. This gentleman here says he is a policeman and I'm sure he'll be able to retrieve my purse for me."

The young man glanced over at Murdoch. "Good thing you was on the spot. Did you get a gander at the lad? All I saw was his backside, begging your pardon, ladies."

"No, I too saw him only from the rear. Can you describe him, ma'am?"

"Alas no. He came up behind me, snatched my purse, knocked me to the ground, and ran off. I cannot say I noticed anything at all. He could have been a red Indian for all I saw."

The woman next to her burst in.

"I saw. He was wearing a checkered cap, brown knickerbockers, and a plaid jacket."

Murdoch took out his notebook. He'd seen that much himself, but he wrote down what she said out of courtesy. She leaned over his shoulder to see what he was writing.

"I'd say he was about ten years old, dark skin."

Murdoch smiled at her. She was a pretty woman, with lively brown eyes. She was neatly dressed in a plum-coloured walking suit with a matching wide hat on which bobbed two long plumes. On her chest was pinned the white bow of a temperance advocate.

"You're a good witness," he said.

"He seemed older than that to me," interjected the country man. "More like fifteen or sixteen. But the lady's right about the skin, I'd say he was a quadroon."

"Can anybody else add to this description?" Murdoch asked the onlookers, but all he got was a gabble of confusing statements: "Too far away, definitely dark. Yes, dark-skinned like a Negro, older, younger."

He turned back to the victim. "I'll have to make a report, ma'am. Can I have your name and address?"

"Really, officer, I am quite all right. My daughter will be worried, so I must get along. Thanks to this young lady, I can continue my journey. If the poor lad was driven to rob me, he must be one of our unfortunates. I don't want to press charges. There was only a small amount of change in my purse."

"I'm afraid that I will still have to write up a report, ma'am. We will try to apprehend the boy." He could see her alarm was growing at the thought of continuing police involvement. This was by no means an uncommon reaction among the public.

"Don't worry, ma'am, you'll have nothing further to do with us unless necessary."

"Very well. My name is Mrs. Agnes Pierce and I live at 720 Queen Street East. I am a widow."

Murdoch wrote it down. The onlookers were starting to drift away. "Will you describe your purse to me?"

"It was black silk with a gold-coloured clasp and a strap. It contained two blue tickets for the streetcar and perhaps twenty cents in coins."

"Where does your daughter live?" asked the young temperance woman.

"Oh, she resides on Church Street near St. Michael's Cathedral. "

"I'll take you there."

The elderly woman shook her head even more vehemently.

"No. Please. I do appreciate your kindness, but I am quite all right. I'll get along now. My cane please."

Another bystander, a man, had collected her cane for her and he handed it over. With a murmured "Thank you, kindly," she took it and began to shuffle off. The temperance woman looked as if she would follow her, but the boy's pursuer said, "We'd better let her be. She's got pride, that lady, bless her heart."

"I'll take down your names," said Murdoch. "If we catch the thief, I might have to call you as witnesses."

The man gave his name as Joshua Winters. He was from a small town north of Toronto and just visiting the city. The young woman was Helena Martin. She gave her address, describing exactly where it was. For a moment, Murdoch imagined she was going to invite him for tea, but then he was embarrassed at his own conceit. They had only had a few minutes of contact, for goodness' sake.

That done, he tipped his hat and remounted his bicycle. He had the feeling that Miss Martin continued to watch him as he cycled down Yonge Street until he turned right onto Elm Street where the House of Industry was located.

Chapter Eleven

THE HOUSE OF INDUSTRY was a flat-faced, two storey building and everything about it seemed pinched, from the dun-coloured brick to the low roof and narrow windows. A high fence enclosing the entire building kept the curious from observing the supplicant paupers as they lined up daily to get their bowl of free soup. Murdoch opened the gate and walked up to the door, which was tall and wide with a stained-glass fanlight and arched lintel. The elegance was unexpected, like a friendly smile on the bailiff's face. He pulled on the bell and the door was opened promptly by a white-haired old man in a dark formal suit.

"You'll be wanting to see Superintendent Laughlen, I presume," he said in a hoarse voice, as if he had spent his life shouting. Murdoch wasn't sure why the porter made that presumption, perhaps nobody else in the

House received visitors. He handed over his card, which the man glanced at briefly.

"Ah yes," he croaked. "Come this way."

He ushered him into a hall that was so ill-lit, Murdoch could not tell what colour the walls were painted. Something dark and sober, but there were no decorative pictures or furniture as far as he could see. He wasn't surprised. This was a charity house funded by the city taxpayers, no luxury would be allowed. The old man, he almost called him a gaoler, shuffled across to a door to the left, tapped and pressed his ear against the door. In response to a command that Murdoch could not hear, he then beckoned and opened the door.

"Detective Murdoch to see you, sir." He backed out. What had he been? A circus barker? A music-hall master of ceremonies? Murdoch thought perhaps he should burst through the portières with a triumphant hurrah.

"Go in," the old man whispered and he shuffled off.

When he entered the room, Murdoch could understand why he hadn't heard Superintendent Laughlen answer the knock. He was seated behind a massive desk at the far end of the room that was spacious but as dreary as a Trappist refectory. There was no other furniture except for two plain wooden chairs in front of the desk. This was a business office, with one small fireplace, plain Holland blinds on the windows, and

99

walls lined with filing cabinets and shelves of what looked like bound annual reports.

There was one lamp on the desk, the wick turned low, throwing Superintendent Laughlen's face into shadow except where the light reflected from his bald head. As if to balance the dearth of hair in that location, he had a full beard that jutted out from his cheekbones to the top of his waistcoat.

He got to his feet immediately and came around the desk with his hand outstretched. He was a big man without his flesh conveying in any way that he was convivial.

"Good day, Mr. Murdoch. I was expecting somebody from the police to come. It's concerning the tragic death of Reverend Howard, I presume."

"Yes, sir, it is. And may I express my condolences."

"Thank you. We are all quite devastated."

Laughlen pulled over one of the straight chairs for Murdoch and eased himself into a second one so he was facing him without the barrier of desk or privilege. Murdoch liked him. His brown eyes were sincerely doleful.

"How is poor Mrs. Howard?"

"As well as can be expected."

100   "Have you made progress with the case?"

"We have not yet caught the person responsible, superintendent, but we are making progress." Murdoch took out his notebook. "One of the reasons I am here is because Mrs. Howard told me her husband did visiting duties for the House of Industry and I wondered if I could have a copy of his list."

"Of course." Laughlen got up at once and headed for the filing cabinet. "But I heard that Charles had surprised a thief. Is that not the case?" He opened one of the drawers, flicked through the folders, and removed one. For a big man, he moved lightly and quickly. He returned to Murdoch.

"We're by no means ruling out a thief, sir, but I don't think he was taken by surprise. The evidence suggests that Reverend Howard allowed his attacker to enter his study."

Laughlen looked shocked. "Do you think it was somebody he knew?"

"That or somebody he might expect to be there. Tuesday was his regular office day."

"I see." Laughlen took a sheet of paper from the folder. "Here is the most recent list. He made his monthly visit just last week. He had a heavily populated district and he had twelve applicants. You can see he gave tickets to all but four of them."

The superintendent sighed. "Reverend Howard had only been with us since January, but he showed signs of being an excellent Visitor. His inexperience made him a little too generous perhaps, but he was not without perspicacity. He could detect frauds as well as any of our more experienced men." He handed the piece of paper to Murdoch. "You can keep that sheet, detective, I have a copy." Like a lot of bald men, Laughlen had a habit of stroking his head as if unable to accept the loss it revealed. He did so now. "Am I correct in assuming that you suspect the, er" – Laughlen stumbled over the word *murderer* – "the, er, culprit, might be one of our applicants? Somebody the pastor rejected perhaps?"

Howard was not the only one who showed perspicacity.

"I am exploring that as a possibility. Did Reverend Howard ever mention any trouble to you?"

"Not at all. As you see, this month, he refused help to only four families. One of those is well known to us and they were turned down without ceremony. The husband is a lazy good-for-nothing and he always sends his wife to beg for him."

Even lazy-good-for-nothings have to eat, Murdoch thought, but this wasn't the time to discuss the limits of charity so he made no comment. There were three other names on the list with a stamp beside them, *Refused.*

"Do you know anything about these ones, sir?"

Laughlen glanced at the list. "No, they are not known to me. Last year we had well over two thousand families who applied to us for relief so alas, I can hardly know each one personally." He sounded genuinely regretful rather than defensive. "I can look at the slips and see what Reverend Howard wrote on them if you wish."

"Thank you, sir, that would be helpful."

102

The superintendent returned to his desk. "They are all here, as a matter of fact, I haven't yet pasted them into the report book." He riffled through a pile of papers, pulled out four, and brought them over to Murdoch. "He rejected a Mrs. Tugwell, a widow; the Gleeson family; a woman, Mary Hanrahan, not married; and Thomas Coates."

Murdoch looked at the slips. They recorded the name, address, and age of each applicant, the number of people in the family, and a comment in Howard's neat handwriting. All four of these applicants had been refused as "undeserving." Mrs. Tugwell was cited as living with her daughter, who was *a known woman of intemperate and immoral habits*. Gleeson was *malingering and capable of working*, Miss Hanrahan was a *drunkard*, as was Thomas Coates.

"What is the procedure for somebody in need of relief, superintendent?"

Laughlen sat down and leaned back in the chair, as much as he could without imperiling his own safety. "Every weekday afternoon from two o'clock until five, one of our trustees receives applications from those who consider themselves to be destitute."

He must have seen something pass across Murdoch's face because he added quickly. "Please don't misunderstand me, my good sir. I would say that the majority of the cases that come before us are genuinely in need of assistance. Often the husband is ill or injured and

103

unable to work. More often than I care to say, it is a woman, close to her confinement who has been abandoned by her spouse, leaving her with children to feed. Those are our most heart-rending cases and I would say the most deserving."

Murdoch remembered what Amy had said to him. He couldn't rule out the possibility that the murderer was a woman. Laughlen continued.

"But we also have to sort out those who would not work for a living if the Lord Jesus himself asked them to. All applicants are assigned to one of our Visitors, who then goes to their residence to see if that person is deserving of the relief. If he considers them to be so, he will give them tickets so they can receive bread and coal, and they can also come to the House for a daily bowl of soup."

"If a family is refused help, what would they do?"

"Oh, believe me, Mr. Murdoch, they find somewhere. Hunger is a strong motivator. And as I say, these are people who prefer to drink and live off the charity of others rather than work." He tucked his hands under his beard like a man accustomed to giving interviews. "It is my duty as superintendent to be frugal with public money. We can accommodate about a hundred permanent residents in the House itself, mostly elderly, decent folk who have ended up friendless and alone and no longer capable of fending for themselves. However, our primary work is with outdoor relief. Last year, we gave out relief to more than eleven thousand persons, men, women and children, at a total expense of thirteen thousand five hundred dollars. That works out to one dollar eighteen cents per head."

"Economical for sure."

Laughlen missed the irony in Murdoch's voice or chose to ignore it. He was warming to his subject, a man who took pride in his work.

"Our volunteers are mostly men of the cloth, but we do have two or three laymen; one is an eminent lawyer, one a grocer who is a respected elder of his church. We could not afford to do our work without their contribution." Another head patting. "Our biggest headache continues to be the casuals. You're probably more used to calling them vagrants. Men for the most part, although I have seen an unfortunate woman or two." He shook his head sadly at those particular daughters of Eve. "These men have no home, some of them have come into hard times through no fault of their own and those men I am only too glad to help, but too many in my opinion have chosen a life outside that of normal men where they have no responsibility and subsist through the good nature of others. You must know the kind of man I am referring to, Mr. Murdoch. You've had to arrest a few of them, I'll warrant."

Murdoch nodded. The question of vagrancy was a bone of contention at the different police stations. The law said any man thought to be a vagrant had to be charged and brought before the magistrate. In the winter, the cells were frequently clogged with men on their two-week sentence, glad to be out of the cold in spite of the discomfort of the jail. They invariably brought bedbugs and lice with them to the cells. Most officers wanted the House of Industry or the religious House of Providence to house the men instead. Murdoch agreed with that. In his experience, the majority of these vagrants were too beaten down by poverty and drink and their attendant ills of malnourishment and disease to be true criminals. But they were a nuisance, begging for money from respectable citizens when they dared or were desperate enough.

Laughlen patted his head again in a search for hair. "Of course, since we instituted the labour test, we have been able to weed out the corrigible from the incorrigible. We show compassion to the elderly and the infirm but not to the lazy. Any man that refuses to work is, by the same token, refused another night's lodging. If we are looking for criminals, there would be a place to start. Many of them take actual pleasure in defying society's rules."

"Would Reverend Howard have had anything to do with the casuals?"

Laughlen pursed his lips. "He had no need to. Other volunteers manage the casual poor and the Visitors are not required to come to the House. Once a month,

I gather up the applications and send them over to them."

"So he would not necessarily have known any of the casuals or they him?"

"That is correct. They come here by five o'clock in the evening for a bed for the night. During the day, after the work is complete, they are not allowed to stay here. You never know where they are wandering. They go to another institution, most likely. There is the House of Providence that the Sisters of St. Joseph run. Apparently they insist that the receivers of their charity stay for prayers. We are non-denominational so the men usually come here first. You'd be surprised how ungodly many of these people really are, Mr. Murdoch. Some of them avoid prayer as much as they avoid water. But it is not inconceivable that one of them would know of the pastor's habits and go there to dun him. It would fit your picture of somebody he'd let into his study."

"Do you have a list of those men, sir?"

"Yes, we have a register. I'll get the porter to make a copy for you. Not that it will help that much. They are not allowed to stay more than three consecutive nights in the casual ward and when they leave here, we have no way to trace them. Almost three-quarters of our tramps are not from Toronto and none of them have proper addresses. They are like sharks that I believe never rest. Homeless, friendless, they wander the land searching for who knows what. Are they Christ among us, Mr. Murdoch? Come to test us? Sometimes I wonder about it."

A little surprised by such a poetic turn of phrase from this practical man, Murdoch could only nod.

Chapter Twelve

MURDOCH WAS LATE getting to Humphrey's Funeral Home and Dr. Ogden made it clear she was not happy at his tardiness. He muttered his apologies. Cavendish, the police photographer, was standing with his tripod at the ready. He looked uneasy, but then he always did. An older, spry-looking man with a notebook open on his lap was perched on a high stool close to the examining table.

Dr. Ogden waved her hand. "This is my father, Dr. Uzziel Ogden. He has offered to serve as both a second medical witness and our clerk."

The man hopped off his perch and held out his hand to Murdoch. "Good day to you, sir. Nasty business this." His cheery tone belied the words and his blue eyes actually twinkled. He was enjoying himself. His daughter must have inherited her stature from her mother because she was a good seven or eight inches taller than her father, although she did have his keen blue eyes and rather sharp nose.

"I didn't know the poor fellow personally, but Julia did and I thought I could come along and make sure she didn't miss anything in the shock of it all."

Dr. Ogden smiled briefly and Murdoch couldn't tell if she was offended by this remark or not. He had the feeling she wouldn't take kindly to women being considered the weaker sex.

"Well, I'm ready to begin," she said. "Would you like an apron, Mr. Murdoch? Father?"

She was wearing a heavy brown holland pinafore. Murdoch remembered Sister Regina had worn something very similar when she'd conducted her natural science classes. Not that she'd cut up anything more fleshy than mushrooms.

Dr. Ogden pulled back the canvas cover, revealing the grey, stained body. Murdoch had seen corpses before, but they never failed to jolt him. The utter absence of life where there had so recently been one was always troubling. Howard's clothes had been removed, but the body hadn't been washed and the blood had turned black around the side of his face and where it had spilled down his shoulder and chest from the stab wound. Dr. Ogden took a sponge from a dish on the nearby table and wiped away the congealed blood from his neck. Her father handed her a measuring stick with which she checked the wound.

110

"Seven-eighths of an inch across," she said and he wrote it down. "It was not a sharp instrument so the skin and flesh around the area are depressed and bruised. There is a torn fragment of his shirt visible in the cut." She pulled it out with a pair of tweezers and placed the fragment on a dish. Uzziel wrote a label. Murdoch noticed the pastor's body was quite hirsute and rather flabby, which was consistent in a man of his age and sedentary profession. His male member was a good size.

Dr. Ogden sponged away the blood from the side of the face. "The orbital bone is fractured, the eyeball crushed, and the cheekbone is depressed. I'm sure we will find it is fractured in more than one place. The cause of these injuries was a blunt instrument and we have a rather clear imprint here on the cheek." She took the stick and measured the marks carefully, calling out the numbers to her father. "It is roughly in the shape of a crescent, the bruising is uniform, so I would agree with you, Mr. Murdoch, that it is likely caused from a vicious kick. I think we can safely assume that the blows to the eye and the eye socket were also from kicks. You can see the eyeball has been pushed down slightly to the left, which would be consistent with the victim being prone and on his back at this point. Would you agree?"

Murdoch didn't particularly want to examine the bloody mess of an eye, but he peered more closely and agreed with what Dr. Ogden had said.

111

"Now, I can't say with any certainty whether the boot was worn by a man or a woman. The mark is definitely rounded rather than pointed, which would rule out a woman's fashionable boot, but as far as I can tell the mark could indicate either male or female ordinary footwear. What do you think, Mr. Murdoch? Have a look through the magnifying glass. And, father, perhaps you could offer an opinion as well."

Murdoch took the glass and bent forward to see. "It's hard to say. Could be either."

"I'd say that was a man's boot that did that," Uzziel said. "A woman couldn't have used that much force."

Julia made no comment, but she glanced at Murdoch.

"I think a healthy woman in a state of extreme rage would have been able to inflict such an injury," he said.

"Ah, you are probably right, you're the detective after all," Uzziel said.

Dr. Ogden lifted and rotated both of Howard's arms so she could examine them.

"No sign of bruising on either arm, which suggests that he had no chance to defend himself. The nails on each hand are intact. This dark splotch between the index finger of the right hand appears to be ink. Had he written a letter recently?"

112 "It would seem so, ma'am, but I haven't found it yet. I am pursuing the matter."

"Well that's your province, not mine."

Dr. Ogden walked slowly to the end of the table, making a close observation of the body.

"He is clean and well nourished." Suddenly, she leaned forward and pinched at something on the chest hair. "He has, however, acquired lice." She went back to examine the hair on Howard's head, parting the strands carefully. "I don't see signs of bites, so I assume this louse is a recent guest."

"Are we going to mention the louse?" asked Uzziel.

"It doesn't seem significant. He was a minister. He probably had some parishioners of the poorest kind."

She continued with the external examination. "There is a scar on the right thigh reminiscent of a chicken pox scar, otherwise the body is unmarked." She moved aside the flaccid penis. "Testicles intact and normal size. Penis uncircumcised."

She took some long swabs from a jar on the movable table. "I'll check his orifices. Will you label the appropriate bottle, father?"

She went back to the head of the table and inserted the swab into Howard's right ear, removing it and sniffing it. "No infection." She dropped that swab into one of the clean jars that Uzziel had at the ready, then wiped out the other ear and, with a fresh swab, inspected Howard's nose and mouth. "He was fond of snuff I see and he was just getting over a bad cold, but there is no blood in the mucus, which suggests there was no concussion. The

113

kicks to the side of the head, although severe, were not the *coup de grâce*; most likely, he would not have died from them if he had not been stabbed. The cause of death was undoubtedly the massive bleeding from the carotid artery. Will you help me turn him over, Mr. Murdoch? No, it's all right, father. We can do it."

Murdoch took hold of one arm and leg and pulled, as she simultaneously pushed from the other side and they rolled the body onto its stomach.

"Other than lividity staining, there are no marks." She took another swab and inserted it into the anus.

"There was a loosening of the bowels and the bladder, but that is to be expected." She wiped her hands on her apron. "Let's reverse him again, Mr. Murdoch."

They did so.

She nodded over at Cavendish. "Will you take your photographs now, Mr. Cavendish, before I begin the dissection. I'd like three or four pictures of the head wound as close up as you can get it and the insertion point of the letter opener." She pointed to one of the shelves. "The weapon is over there on a linen cloth. You might as well take a picture of that as well."

The photographer began to set up his equipment, and the two doctors retreated to a corner of the room to confer over Uzziel's notes. Murdoch went to the shelf where he could see Howard's clothes had been piled and tagged. Every item of clothing was bloodstained, including the one-piece undergarment. His suit was worsted but not of especially high quality. His white cravat was fine silk, but his shirt collar was starting to fray at the neck and had already been turned once. Murdoch took a closer look at the tear in the waistcoat. The pocket where he'd kept his watch was slightly stretched. A large watch then. The trouser pockets were empty except for a crumpled and stained white handkerchief and a wrapped cough lozenge. He wore leather suspenders for his trousers and New York garters of an atypical cherry red, kept up his socks that were darned at the heels. His wife or the maid had made sure he went out into the world well brushed and mended, but either from moral conviction or financial necessity, Reverend Howard had not been extravagant in his attire.

Cavendish had finished and he backed off to the far corner of the room with his equipment. He might still be needed, but this next part was nothing he liked.

Dr. Ogden walked over to the table and her father hopped onto the stool.

"I'm going to commence the dissection now, Mr. Murdoch. Am I correct in assuming you will not faint on me like a green boy?"

"I have seen other post-mortem examinations, ma'am. You don't have to worry about me."

He hoped that was true. It wasn't as if he watched a scalpel slicing into dead flesh every day. Dr. Ogden wheeled over a small table on which she'd fastened her

115

surgical instruments in loops on a roll of cloth. She
selected a scalpel and tested it on her thumb.

"You need some more chloride of lime," said her
father. "It's starting to pong in here." He went to a
bucket in the corner of the room. While he was doing
that, Dr. Ogden leaned over and made a Y-shaped inci-
sion from Howard's shoulders, down the breast bone
to the top of the pubes. Then she pulled back the skin
and flesh as if she were opening a valise. All of Howard's
inner organs were exposed.

"Clippers please, father."

Uzziel handed her what looked like a pair of pruning
shears, and with the decisive, vigorous snips of an
assured gardener, Julia cut through the cartilage attach-
ing the ribs to the sternum.

"Saw, please."

Except that it was clean and shiny, the saw looked
to Murdoch exactly like the kind of tool used to cut
branches. Dr. Ogden sawed through the ribs, dropping
the cutoff bones into a dish. She acted quickly and
efficiently and Murdoch was glad when she'd finished.
The sound was not pleasant. That done, she picked up
a long scalpel and severed the valves that connected
the heart to the bloodways of the body, then she lifted
out the organ from the chest cavity and placed it in a
dish that her father had ready for her. There it sat, an
inert piece of red meat, once the source of all Howard's
fears, angers, and passions. In spite of what he'd said

116

earlier, Murdoch felt a rush of bile come into his mouth.

"Are you all right, detective?"

"Yes, ma'am."

She looked at him kindly. "My tutor used to think we should hang up a sign in the morgue. *Hic locus est ubi mors gaudet succurrere vitae.* Or to translate, 'This is the place where death rejoices to teach those who live.'"

Ah, but what is the lesson? Murdoch thought.

Chapter Thirteen

"Here you go, Will. This'll wake you up."

Sergeant Charlie Seymour plonked down a mug of steaming tea on the table. Murdoch could see that he'd made the pot of tea so strong, a spoon would stand up in it, but he didn't mind. He needed it. He yawned again and Seymour laughed.

"If you don't stop that, you'll set me going too and I've got a few more hours on my shift to go."

They were sitting in the duty room where the officers were allowed to have their meals. Seymour looked tired. All of the police sergeants worked twenty-four hours at a time. One turn of duty on, one off. If the station was quiet, they could nap during the night but never for more than two hours at a stretch. He sat down across from Murdoch, who was cautiously sipping at the tea.

"Did anything come out of the post-mortem examination?" Seymour asked.

"Not unless you count the smell that's stuck in my nostrils. The doctor said she thought Howard had been kicked at least three times. The wound to the neck killed him, but he would have lasted a few minutes probably before he died."

"Poor soul. Not the way he expected to go out, I'll wager. What about the search of the church? Did that bring us anything?"

"About two dollars in coins, two lady's handkerchiefs, both silk, three men's umbrellas, and four different ear bobs, which had fallen under the pews. Nothing that seems important."

Seymour had a thick slice of meat pie on a plate in front of him and he stuffed a forkful into his mouth. "Delicious," he mumbled.

"Katie's?"

"Hmm." He wiped away some crumbs from his moustache. "Crabtree should be due in soon. He was doing house to house along Gerrard Street with Fyfer. Dewhurst and Birney were both doing Jarvis Street."

"Tell them I'd like to talk to each of them when they report in. I'm going to check on the reverend's relief list. I don't know how long I'll be, but they'll have to wait for me even if their shift is over. I also have a list of the casuals who were taken into the House of Industry last week, but tracking them down is going to be a headache."

"Do you think the inspector is going to assign us more men?" Seymour asked. "It's a bloody large area to cover."

"That's it for now."

"I don't understand him sometimes. The pastor's death is the biggest news the city has seen for months, you'd think he'd throw everybody into the investigation."

Murdoch sighed. "He always wants to appear self-sufficient to the rest of the police nobs, if you ask me. And as you know he hates spending money. He won't pay for extra shift work if he can avoid it."

"Right, but I noticed he had a new filing cabinet delivered the other day. His other one looked fine to me."

"Hey, mine is falling apart, perhaps I can nab it myself. Where is it?"

"Out in the stables."

"Anyway, Charlie, do your best with what we've got. I'll also put an advertisement in the newspapers, see if anybody comes forward. We'll get that in tomorrow's editions."

"Do you want a pipe before you go?" Seymour asked as he took out his own bag of tobacco.

"No thanks, Charlie. I'd better kick off."

In fact, Murdoch had decided to give up his pipe smoking for Lent, but he felt rather uncomfortable telling Seymour. He wasn't sure himself why he was doing it as he was more and more alienated from the practices of his church. Somehow, however, he could accept the notion of a small sacrifice to remember a greater one. Besides, not many women liked the smell of tobacco on a man's clothes and breath.

120

Murdoch shoved a piece of paper across the table. "This is a list of applicants for city relief that Howard visited on Monday. I'm going to start with the four he turned down, but there's nothing to say somebody on the list didn't have a miff at him. Maybe they didn't get everything they asked for. Two soup tickets instead of three. It matters when you're starving. Any names you recognize?"

Seymour studied the list. "Coady, of course. He's a guest of the city on a regular basis, but I can't see him murdering anybody. He's too drunk to stand most of the time . . . there's nobody else that I know." He stood up. "Heck, I wasn't watching the time. I'd better get back to the desk. Best of luck." He crammed the tobacco pouch in his pocket and left.

Murdoch lingered for a few moments, enjoying the warmth of the fire on his back. The station cat was rubbing her head vigorously against his leg.

"All right, Puss, all right. You'll wear a hole in my trousers at that rate." He pushed back his chair and the cat gave a loud meow of triumph and ran ahead to the cupboard beside the fireplace where the milk was kept. Murdoch followed her, took out the bottle of milk, and poured some into her saucer. "There. And when you've finished how about doing some work. I found some little black droppings in my cupboard this morning and you know what that means, don't you?"

The cat ignored him.

———

The first name on the list was the Gleeson family, who lived in a small workman's cottage on Wellesley Street. As Murdoch leaned his wheel against the curb, he could hear the sounds of an angry squabble going on inside, children, from the pitch of the voices. Then the front door was flung open and a boy ran out, a bigger boy close behind him. They both collided with Murdoch. He went to grab hold of the smaller lad, but he squirmed away and took off down the street, running hard. This was no happy game Murdoch had interrupted. The older boy hesitated, torn between his anger and a quick fear about the visitor's presence. Murdoch relieved him of the choice by blocking his path.

"I'm looking for Mr. Gleeson. Is he your pa?"

The boy didn't respond to the question but managed to slip in a shrewd appraisal of Murdoch. He didn't like what he saw and he began to back away, hands held out in supplication.

"I don't know nothing, mister."

"Who was that boy you were so intent on killing? Is he your brother?"

A reluctant nod. "He took my last piece of sausage."

Murdoch fished in his pocket and brought out a twenty-five-cent piece.

"Here. I'd rather you go buy yourself another sausage than be guilty of homicide."

The boy accepted the money and stepped back

immediately in case Murdoch should change his mind. "Thanks, mister."

"Is there anybody else in the house?"

The boy's expression became opaque. "My ma and pa are, but they're both taking a short kip right now."

"Unfortunately, I'll have to wake them up. I have some important business I need to discuss with them."

"Are you a bailiff?"

"No. I'm a detective. I'm not going to report them to anybody, I just need to ask some questions."

"What about?"

"Before I answer that, how about telling me your name."

Reluctantly, the boy answered. "I'm Jethro."

"Jethro Gleeson?"

A brief nod as if even that much commitment was dangerous.

"Did you ever meet Reverend Howard, Jethro? He would have come to see about your pa's request for relief."

That was easy. Jethro shrugged. "I don't know nothing."

Murdoch sighed. "All right then, my lad. Why don't you go and get your meat pie or sausage or whatever you want while I talk to your ma and pa."

Jethro was probably about ten years old, skinny and dirty-faced. His trousers were too short and his shirt had big holes in it. He smelled of neglect. It was far too

123

cold to be out long without a coat, but Murdoch guessed the boy didn't own one. He dipped into his pocket again.

"Here's another two cents. Have some gravy as well. Go on, get off with you."

Jethro didn't wait to be told a second time and he bolted down the street. Murdoch watched him go for a moment then walked up to the house.

The boys had left the door open and Murdoch stepped into the dank, stinking interior. It was gloomy, no candles or lamps, and only a dull fire in the grate. He could just make out two lumpy forms on the bed in the corner. He walked over to them. Mr. and Mrs. Gleeson, lying curled up together in sodden intimacy. The smell was vile. Unwashed linen, stale beer. He grabbed the man's shoulder and shook it hard.

"Mr. Gleeson, wake up. Mr. Gleeson."

The man stirred, mumbled, saw Murdoch leaning over him and went from drunk to sober in a matter of seconds.

"Who're you?"

"My name's Murdoch. I'm a detective. I need to ask you some questions."

"I don't know nothing about it."

Murdoch almost smiled. "I haven't said what it is yet." He moved away from the bed more for his own self-preservation. "I'd like you to wake your wife and to sit up."

Both commands were easier said than done. Gleeson was pinned under the heavy embrace of his wife, who

124

was locked in a deep stupor. Finally, he got out from underneath her arm, sat up, and started to shake her.

"Mags. There's a frog, er, officer here who wants to talk to us. Get up, old girl. Come on." His rather endearing tone was for Murdoch's benefit and it didn't last. When his wife showed no signs of responding, Gleeson, in exasperation, suddenly pinched her nose closed and the consequent spluttering and gasping for breath jolted the woman awake. She hauled herself more upright. It was a ludicrous scene. The two of them still in bed, nightcaps on, dirty quilt pulled up to their chins, Murdoch standing at the bedside like an invalid's solicitous visitor. Or two invalids, in this case. He decided that making them get dressed would be more trouble than it was worth.

"You recently applied for relief, I understand."

"Thas right."

Murdoch could see Gleeson struggle to assess whether this question boded well or ill.

"I'm sorry to inform you that your Visitor, the Reverend Howard, has been killed."

A pause, more from puzzlement than fear or guilt.

"Whatch ya mean, killed. Was he run over or something?"

"No. Somebody stabbed him, then kicked him in the head."

Definitely fear now. Even Mrs. Gleeson seemed to comprehend what Murdoch had said.

125

"We don't know nothing about that. We didn't do anything to him, did we, Mags?"

Still mute, she shook her head then winced.

"Why're you telling us?" Gleeson asked, recovering a certain belligerence that Murdoch suspected was his habitual manner.

"I understand your application was rejected by the minister."

"It was, but that don't mean I up and killed him. I'd have 'alf the city dead if I followed that line."

"Where were you Tuesday afternoon?"

"Here in bed like always."

"What do you mean, like always."

Margaret Gleeson found her tongue at last. Her voice was roughened. "Show him, Tom."

Gleeson pulled back the quilt and for a moment Murdoch almost flinched. The man's feet were swollen to twice their size and a livid purple colour. In a couple of places, the skin had ulcerated.

"He can't hardly get himself to the chamber pot," said his wife.

"What about you, ma'am? Where were you yesterday afternoon?" Murdoch said. He saw the glance of triumph that flashed between them. They'd got him.

126

"I was in bed beside him," she answered. "See," and she too pulled back the quilt. She was in a state of advanced pregnancy. "I've got to rest my legs." She raised her stained nightgown so Murdoch could see the purple swollen veins, snaking up from her ankles. She patted her mound of a belly. "I've lost two before this one, so I've got to be careful."

Murdoch felt like yelling at her that sobriety might help the unborn even more than lying in bed, but he held his tongue.

"What can you tell me about Reverend Howard's visit?"

"Not much. It didn't matter to him that Mags here is expecting and I can't work. He's a nob. They're all nobs and they don't give a piss for people like us. If we starve to death, we're one less name on the books as far as they're concerned. He didn't stay long. Just said that he couldn't give us any tickets. We'd have to find another source of charity."

Gleeson hawked and spat on the floor, just missing Murdoch's boots. He'd seen his own father do that many a time and he'd heard that tone of voice before. Aggrieved, self-righteous, defiant. *He used to be a good man, Will,* his mother had whispered to him once as he lay in bed smarting from the most recent beating. *Try not to think too harshly of him. He just can't abide it when you talk to him that way. He sees his own failure.*

Murdoch had been full of helpless rage and in no mood for forgiveness. He could feel that old anger stirring at the back of his mind, stiffening his neck in a way he had no control over.

"You seem to have found enough money to buy drink," he said. "You could have got food instead."

127

Gleeson didn't answer, but somewhere in his ruin of a face Murdoch saw a glimpse of desperation. They were both beyond redemption, but they also had two sons and a baby imminent. He felt disgusted with them and with himself for having a reaction he had tried so desperately for years to control.

"Listen. I'm not going to give you money, but I'm going down to the pie shop at the corner and I'll have them send down some bread and soup."

Margaret looked as if she were going to thank him, but Gleeson gave him a vile, unrepentant glare. Murdoch dropped a dollar bill on the table.

"Kill yourself then."

Chapter Fourteen

THOMAS COATES WAS ALSO DRUNK, but his wife was sober, as were his four children, all of them huddled around a tiny fire in the dark backroom of a house on Bleeker Street. He had nothing to say about his Visitor except that Reverend Howard didn't understand how hard things had been for him with a bad back and no work. He was a whiner, but the children were obviously in dire straits, Murdoch wondered why Howard hadn't granted them relief. He supposed he was under strict orders to refuse tickets to anybody who was undeserving, that is, a drunkard and a malingerer. Murdoch left a dollar with Mrs. Coates, who immediately hid it in her apron pocket. He felt confident that she and the children at least would have supper that night.

Miss Mary Hanrahan's room was filthy. She didn't seem to understand any of his questions and she reeked of stale beer, but Murdoch wondered if her lack of coherence was caused by something else. She seemed lost and frail and in need of care. He crossed her off his list of possible assailants. Even in a rage of disappointment, she couldn't have overcome a healthy man like Howard; she could hardly walk. He left her a dollar bill on her table.

The fourth name on his list was Mrs. Esther Tugwell, who lived on Sherbourne Street at the boundary of Howard's district. As he approached the dilapidated house in the deepening gloom of the early evening, Murdoch wondered how much *this* visit was going to cost him. He didn't have much money left. Each window had a different covering, from what looked like a table-cloth to a proper blind so he knew there were several tenants living in a house that was small to begin with. He wasn't surprised there was no bell and he banged hard on the door that hadn't seen paint for many years. No answer. The butler's day off, he said wryly to himself. He turned the doorknob and stepped into a dark hallway that was fetid with neglect and the odour of many years of unwholesome meals. He waited for a moment until his eyes grew accustomed to the gloom but realized he was going to need some light. He went back to where he'd left his bicycle, removed the lamp from the handlebars, and went back inside the house.

130

The beam of light revealed a bare wooden floor and grimy walls. His light picked out a well-polished brass plate on the nearest door, shining like a piece of gold on a midden heap. The plate read, THOMAS HICKS, ESQUIRE. He could hear a low murmur coming from inside the room but only one voice as far as he could tell.

Murdoch rapped on the door and the murmuring stopped abruptly.

"Yes?" It was a man's frail voice.

"Mr. Hicks, I'm a policeman. I'm looking for Mrs. Esther Tugwell."

Various creaks then the sound of a bolt being shot back. The door opened a crack and the face of an elderly man peered out at him. Murdoch had expected a sullen response, but the man actually beamed at him, revealing yellow teeth as prominent in his gaunt face as those of an old horse's.

"Come in, come in." He stepped back and beckoned Murdoch into his room. "Have a seat, sir." Hicks suffered from a severe curvature of the spine, which brought his chin close to his chest and movement was obviously difficult for him. He shuffled over to the table in the middle of the room, removed a newspaper from a chair, and pulled it out. "I must apologize for the untidiness of my abode, sir, but I don't receive many visitors, especially illustrious members of the city's police force." Hicks's voice was that of an educated Englishman and at first glance, his abode, as he called it, resembled the private library of an aristocrat. Tall bookcases lined the three windowless walls. There was a comfortable armchair in front of the fire and a faint

131

smell of singed leather suggested Mr. Hicks had been propping his slippered feet on the fender. A brass oil lamp on the table cast a warm glow. However, as his host fussed with the chair, Murdoch had an opportunity to observe a little more closely. There was a simple couch in the corner, which was presumably where Mr. Hicks slept, and next to it a washstand. Two worn druggets were on the planked floor and the window had a decent-enough blind, but it was obvious that if Thomas Hicks, Esquire had ever, in fact, been affluent, he was no longer so.

The chair cleared of newspaper, the man offered his hand.

"Thomas Hicks at your service, sir."

"Murdoch. William Murdoch. I'm a detective at number four station."

"Ah, yes, I know it well," said Hicks ambiguously. He waved in the direction of the hearth where there was a kettle steaming on the hob. "I was just about to prepare some tea when you knocked. May I offer you some?"

Murdoch was about to refuse, but he knew the man's eagerness was a measure of his loneliness.

"Thank you kindly. It's damably cold out there and a hot cup of char would hit the spot. As long as it's no bother."

"Not at all. Not at all. I always have my tea at this time." Hicks flashed his powerful teeth again. "It is probably not such a good thing to be a creature of habit the way I am, but ever since my dear wife passed away, I find it a comfort to continue with our little customs." He tapped on the table. "She would sit here and I in my armchair and we would read to each other, often for hours."

Murdoch glanced at the bookshelf behind him, which was lined with leatherbound books stamped with gilt letters. "I see you read German."

Hicks was busy pouring boiling water from the kettle on the hob into his teapot. "Alas no, sir. To be frank I got all of the books on that shelf as part of a job lot from a gentleman's estate. I find to be surrounded by books, no matter what language, is like being in the middle of a company of loving friends." He brought the teapot to the table, which was covered with a too big but clean red damask cloth. "The two shelves just above your head are also from an estate. They were going to be thrown away. They're written in a language I don't recognize. Portuguese perhaps and I do believe they are medical textbooks." He chuckled. "I think they must have belonged to a specialist in diseases of the skin, the illustrations are quite gruesome."

There was a book turned face down on the table, which was the one Murdoch presumed Mr. Hicks had been reading aloud.

133

"Ah yes. That is a book of sermons, which was kindly lent to me." His lined face looked wistful in the shadowy light. "I do sometimes pine for the robust humour of

Mr. Dickens or the rollicking yarns of Mr. Scott, but as they say beggars can't be choosers." He spoke about the books the way another person might describe missing a tasty roast beef or apple tart. "The public library is farther than I can manage in the wintertime. But soon it will be spring and things will improve considerably."

He took two cups without saucers from the cupboard in the washstand and poured them each some weak tea.

"I'm afraid I cannot offer you milk or sugar, Mr. Murdoch, but I'd be more than happy to share my biscuit with you."

"No, really, sir. I prefer my tea this way."

Mr. Hicks took a sip with the slow appreciation of a man who is forced to apportion out meagre amounts to himself. Murdoch didn't know what had brought the old man to this state of poverty and he wasn't about to ask for his life history, but he found himself running through his own mind some way he could help financially without offending Mr. Hicks's pride. Oh Lord, he hadn't even got past the first tenant. He put down his cup.

"I am actually looking for a Mrs. Esther Tugwell. This is her address, I understand?"

Hicks's eyes flickered. "That's quite correct. She lives directly above me." At that moment, they heard the creak of floorboards from overhead as somebody walked across the floor. "That is no doubt she. She is a hard-working soul, a seamstress by trade, who takes care of her invalid son. She also has a daughter. She . . ." He drank more tea and didn't finish the sentence. Murdoch had the sense he had more to say but chose not to. "My immediate neighbours are the Misses Leask, Emma and Larissa. Next to the Tugwells are Mr. and Mrs. McGillivary, a young couple who are expecting their first child soon. Then on the top floor we have Mr. and Mrs. Einboden, recently arrived from Germany, and Mr. Taylor, who is a bachelor and quite reclusive alas." He grinned. "We are quite crammed to the rafters, you might say. But we do look out for each other when we can."

Murdoch put his cup on the table. At least the tea had been hot. "I wonder if I might ask you one or two questions, Mr. Hicks?"

"My pleasure, sir."

"Did you ever meet the Reverend Howard?"

Hicks smiled at him.

"Oh yes. He is a Visitor from the city relief fund and Miss Leask needed help, as, I believe, did poor Mrs. Tugwell. I was calling on her the first time he came and he kindly furnished me with Dr. Lanceley's book. We had the most entertaining conversation for almost an hour."

Something in Murdoch's expression must have communicated itself and Hicks frowned. "Why are you asking, sir? Is there something wrong?"

135

"I'm afraid so." There was no way Murdoch could soften the reality of what had happened. He said quietly. "Mr. Howard has been murdered."

Hicks gaped at him. "How can that be? He was the kindest of men."

Kindness was not unfortunately always a protection against violence, thought Murdoch. "His body was found in his office yesterday. We believe he may have surprised a burglar."

The old man pulled out a handkerchief from his pocket and blew his nose vigorously so Murdoch wouldn't see his eyes had filled with tears. "I had such expectations we would become friends. He was a most lively conversationalist."

"I intend to find the perpetrator, Mr. Hicks."

"Even if you do, and I have every confidence that you will, it won't bring him back, will it? I cannot say I knew him well, but I do believe that Reverend Howard was one of those rare human beings who is truly good."

He was stroking the cover of the book as he spoke, as if it brought him closer to the man who had loaned it to him.

"I'm very sorry to have brought you such bad news, Mr. Hicks," said Murdoch, "but the reason I am here is because Mr. Howard was, as you say, a relief officer. I want to speak to the people on his list."

Hicks glanced over at Murdoch sharply. "Do you suspect one of them to be his killer?"

"I have no suspects at the moment. But it's regular procedure to follow up on the victim's movements prior to his death. He made his rounds on Monday. Did you speak to him at all?"

Hicks shook his head. "Unfortunately, he must have been too busy to drop by."

He averted his eyes, a man accustomed to people being too busy.

"Did he visit Mrs. Tugwell?"

"I assume he did. I thought I heard him come in and go upstairs, but I haven't spoken to her so I cannot say for certain."

Murdoch hesitated. "Did Mrs. Tugwell or Miss Leask ever say anything to you that would indicate they were angry with Reverend Howard?"

Hicks pulled his lips over his prominent teeth. "Not at all. Absolutely not. I know that he was unable to give Mrs. Tugwell a docket, but she never spoke a word against him. She knew all too well why she was turned down."

"Why was she?"

Hicks cocked his head at Murdoch. "Are you going to speak to her directly?"

"Yes."

"Then you will see for yourself and it's far better that you do than I say a word."

Murdoch got to his feet, picking up his bicycle lamp and his hat. "Thank you so much for the tea, Mr. Hicks."

"You are most welcome, sir. But tell me, has a date been established for Reverend Howard's funeral?"

137

"Not yet. It will have to wait until after the coroner's inquest. But I will make a point of informing you."

This elicited from Hicks another clearing of his nose into the handkerchief. They shook hands again and Murdoch stepped out, back into the dank hallway.

Chapter Fifteen

MURDOCH FOLLOWED THE BEAM of his lamp up the uncarpeted stairs to the landing. Here there were two doors and at the far end a farther flight of even narrower stairs led to the third floor. A sliver of light was showing underneath the first door, but before he could knock, it opened and a woman emerged. She was dressed in a brown coat, plain enough, but enlivened by a wispy purple feather boa and a beribboned red hat. He presumed this young woman was the problematic daughter. She was young, but any prettiness she might have had was obliterated by the anger held in her mouth and eyes. She flashed him a tawdry seductive smile.

"What can I do for you? Lost your way, I'll wager. I'll help you find it if you like."

"I'd like to speak to Mrs. Esther Tugwell."

The false smile vanished immediately. "You a bailiff?"

"No. My name is Murdoch, I'm a detective at number four station."

Now he saw an all too familiar look. Fear, hostility, wariness. He met it all the time.

"What you want with my ma?"

Her tone of voice was so belligerent, Murdoch felt his own flash of temper.

"As I said, I'd like to talk to her. Are you Josephine Tugwell?"

"The same. And as *I* just said, what you want with us?"

"I'm investigating a murder and I'd like to ask her some questions."

"Ha. Who the hell's got the big bird that my mother'd know anything about it? She never leaves the house."

In spite of her question, Murdoch thought she wasn't surprised to see him and she did know why he was here. Then he recognized her. She was the woman in the red hat who'd taken exception to Crabtree as he came through the crowd outside the church. She must know that Charles Howard was dead.

"Didn't I see you at Chalmers Church yesterday afternoon?"

For a split second, she considered her answer. Then she shrugged. "Your peepers do not deceive. I came over to see what the fuss was all about."

"So you do know who got the big bird?"

"Didn't have to be him, did it? There could be a cove

140

doffed every hour for all I know. What's it to do with my ma?"

"Reverend Howard was a Visitor for the House of Industry. Your mother is on his list. I understand he turned down her application for relief."

"He did. Man with a poker up his arse, as far as I could tell. He thought I wasn't deserving so the rest of the family could go starve. But I hope you ain't thinking my own mother did for him cos she was miffed?"

"I have no thoughts at the moment. I'm interviewing everybody who was on Reverend Howard's list."

"That's a clever thing to do. The prospect of some soft-handed toff having the say-so as to whether you eat for the next month could get a person all riled, couldn't it?"

"Do I take that to mean you don't have a high opinion of Reverend Howard?"

"I don't have an opinion, high or low. He looked down his nose same as all of them."

"Your downstairs neighbour, Mr. Hicks, thought he was a good man."

"That's Christian of him."

Josie had doused herself with some kind of strong musky scent that was overpowering in the small space of the landing.

141

"Given what you just said, I'd like to ask you where you were yesterday afternoon, round about three-thirty," Murdoch said.

"That's a laugh. I was here, shivering myself to death. Why? Don't think I went up there and stabbed the bloke so I could get blood out of a stone, do ya?" She laughed at her own joke.

She was getting on Murdoch's nerves. "Show some respect, young woman, or I'll bring you into the station. Besides, how did you know he'd been stabbed?"

She grinned. "You didn't say so, if that's what you're getting at, but that's what everybody was nattering about up at the church. He'd bin stabbed and the boots put to him, from what I heard."

The door behind her opened and a thin-faced woman poked her head out.

"Josie, what's going on? You're disturbing Wilf."

"Sorry, ma. I was talking to the detective here. He's come to take you to jail."

Mrs. Tugwell was an older, worn version of her daughter, the same narrow nose and sharp chin but without the bold, defiant expression. She looked frightened at Josie's words.

"What for?"

Murdoch tipped his hat to her. "Your daughter is teasing you, ma'am. That's not the reason I'm here, ma'am. I am investigating the murder of the Reverend Howard. I would like to ask you some questions."

Esther glanced at Josie nervously and her daughter sighed impatiently.

"I ain't never going to get out of here. You'd better

let him in, Ma. Don't worry, I'll come too and make sure he don't knock you about."

Mrs. Tugwell backed into the room, Josie went in, and Murdoch was left to follow her. The air was unpleasantly close and the front windows were uncurtained and grimy. Underneath them was what seemed to be the only real chair in the place. A couple of packing boxes served as seats. Even those meagre furnishings made the room seem crowded because most of the space was taken up by the stove and the family bed. On the floor was a pallet where he could make out a boy's sleeping form.

Mrs. Tugwell spoke softly. "That there's our Wilf. He's got St. Vitus's dance, so I'll thank you not to raise your voice. Any loud noise sets him going."

Josie plopped on one of the boxes. "I'd offer you some tea, but we drank the last of it this morning. And I hope you ain't hungry because the larder is empty. So you'll just have to forgive our bad manners. We wasn't expecting company."

Murdoch knew quite well she was baiting him, but he felt a pang of pity. Their state was every bit as wretched as the others he'd seen. Esther fluttered around and pulled the chair closer into the room.

"Why don't you sit here, officer."

She sat down on the other box and Murdoch accepted the chair. The two women were lower and close to his knees, which made him feel like a schoolmaster addressing his pupils.

"Reverend Howard came here on Monday afternoon, I understand?" he spoke to Esther Tugwell although he could tell that the real authority in the family was Josie. It was she who answered.

"That's right. He stayed for what, Ma? Ten minutes. Decided we weren't deserving of no meal ticket and shoved off."

"He told you right away, did he?"

"Oh yes. They have to. Gives you a chance to go somewhere else. We went to the Sisters, who at least have some charity."

"How did you feel when the pastor told you he wasn't going to grant your application?"

Both women looked at Murdoch in astonishment, then Josie laughed.

"How'd you think we felt? Use your noggin. Three mouths to feed, no coal even if we did have food. Wilf is sickly, as you can see. What you think? We were happy as larks." She slapped her knee. "Wait a bleeding minute. I thought you even gave a toss. But you mean, did we want to kill the bleeder? Well I know I did. What do you say, Ma?"

Esther shrank. She was wearing a brown velvet wrapper that must have been passed on to her from a charity. It was too big and the shoulders drooped down her arms.

144

"He was only doing his job, Jo. He was a good man, really."

Josie glared at her. Not said but hanging in the air was the knowledge that she was the reason they had been turned down.

"My mother's a real Christian, Mr. Murdoch. She thinks Old Nick himself is only doing his job when he roasts sinners in hell."

Her tone was cruel and Esther flushed. "Josie, that's not true." She turned to Murdoch. "We was disappointed of course we were, but like Jo just said we was able to go to the Sisters."

"And Monday was the last time you saw Reverend Howard?"

Josie jumped in. "Of course it was, Mr. Sly Boots. He wasn't likely to drop in for supper, was he? Yesterday was Tuesday, and Tuesday was when he was went to the Grand Silence."

Murdoch looked at the older woman, who'd folded her hands into the sleeves of her too big dress. "Is that the truth, Mrs. Tugwell?"

She nodded. Murdoch might have pressed her but at that moment, the boy on the pallet groaned. His arm jerked out from the blanket covering him. Esther got to her feet quickly and went to him.

"He's awake, is he? Mama's here, lambie." Her voice was tender when she spoke and Murdoch saw the anger flit across Josie's face. She'd seen that tenderness lavished on her brother all her life, something she wanted and didn't get. She jumped to her feet.

"If you're done now, mister, I'll be off." She gave him an unabashed leer. "I'm meeting a friend and I'm late already."

Murdoch didn't think he was going to get any further and he wanted to get out of the stifling atmosphere of oppressive poverty. Wilf was making strangled noises and his arms were jerking wildly. Esther understood what he was trying to say and she fetched a mug of soup from the stove.

"Here, lambie. I saved it for you."

Murdoch stood up.

"I'll be going now, Mrs. Tugwell, but I may have to come back."

"She'll be here," said Josie. "She never goes out. She's always worried about brother Wilf. "

Esther straightened up and gave Murdoch a wan smile. "I'm sorry I can't be more help, sir. I'm sorry to hear about the pastor. He seemed like a kind man."

Josie snorted derisively. "Kind, my arse. He didn't care if we were starving."

Her mother sighed and turned back to helping Wilf with his soup.

Josie grabbed Murdoch by his sleeve and grinned up into his face. "Now why don't you do me a favour, mister, and light the way down the stairs so I don't trip and break my bleeding neck."

146

Murdoch followed her from the room, leaving Mrs. Tugwell to minister to the skeleton-thin, twitching boy.

Chapter Sixteen

MURDOCH CALLED ON SEVEN other applicants on his list, all of them "approved." Only one of these, a man with a broken leg, whined that Howard had not given him as much help as he needed and he was worried that the pastor's death might slow down his ongoing application for relief. There were few comments from the others, who all had learned to be wary of policemen asking questions. Self-interest was uppermost and they were all concerned about who would take over now that Howard was dead. "He treated me like I were a real person, not a number on a list, the way most of them do," said one woman who was close to her confinement and no husband in sight. By eight o'clock, Murdoch was tired and ravenous. He decided to start fresh in the morning and finish for the day.

As he got to his lodgings, he could see there was a party going on. The curtains were not yet drawn in the front parlour and light was spilling out onto the street. All the movable furniture had been pushed back to the walls. Amy was standing on a chair with her hands cupped in a whistling position and Seymour and Katie were executing an energetic, if constricted two step in the tiny space in the centre of the room. Murdoch could hear Seymour's whoops and Katie's laughter. He stepped up to the window and, leaning in close, rapped hard. Seymour waved, twirled his partner wildly, and they both dropped breathlessly onto the couch. Amy stopped whistling, jumped off the chair, and beckoned to Murdoch to come in. She was wearing the smock and pantaloons that she favoured for home.

Perversely, he felt a pang at the scene as if he were an outsider, the hungry boy at the butcher's shop window. He let himself into the hall, hung up his hat and coat, and opened the door to the parlour. Seymour greeted him with more exuberance than Murdoch had ever seen him express before.

"Will, come in. Katie and I just did a Scottish reel, would you believe? At least I think it was a reel. I know there was a lot of leaping about on the part of my partner and I just tried to imitate her as best I could."

Katie, who usually looked pale and worried, was flushed with the exertion, her hair dishevelled and her eyes shining. Murdoch saw how pretty she could be when she wasn't weighed down with the care of her children.

148

"Miss Slade is as good as an entire military band," she laughed. "And I was not leaping about, as you put it, Charlie. You have to do pirouettes."

"It certainly looked energetic at least," said Murdoch. "The entire street was enjoying the show."

"Oh dear, I'd better draw the curtains," said Katie and she hurried to do so.

"Why don't you have a go, Will," said Seymour. "Katie can manage another dance, I'm sure."

Murdoch backed away. "Not tonight, thanks. I'd be worse than a sack of potatoes."

They all sensed the change of mood he'd brought into the room but mistook the reason for it.

"You look famished," said Katie. "Come into the kitchen and I'll get you your supper. I made a pork hash tonight and I know you like that."

Murdoch glanced around the room. "Where are the boys?"

"In my room," answered Amy. "They're sleeping soundly."

"Not for long, I'm afraid," said Katie. "They're teething and it's making them mardy. I hope we won't disturb you tonight."

"I think I'll sleep like a log, don't worry."

A wailing from the other room corroborated Katie's 149 statement and she laughed. "I'll tend to them and be with you in a minute, Mr. Murdoch."

"I can handle it myself, Katie, don't worry."

"I'll keep you company," said Seymour. "Are you coming too, Amy?"

She shook her head. "I have to prepare my lessons for tomorrow."

Murdoch felt a pang of disappointment, which he quickly suppressed. "What are you going to do with the little arabs?"

"I was going to teach some Canadian literature for a change, but the inspector will be dropping in this week so I had better impress him." Amy had strong views about the school system and had got into hot water a couple of times for criticizing the curriculum. "I'll have to find yet another poem about the lovely birds and woods of England." She clasped her hands together, blew through her laced fingers, and made a few birdlike trills.

Murdoch and Seymour applauded her, then reluctantly Murdoch followed his friend to the kitchen, which was fragrant with the smell of fried onions.

He took the plate from the oven. His dinner was strips of pork from the previous night's roast, cooked with fried onions and served with generous helpings of boiled cabbage and potatoes. He sat down at the place prepared for him. Seymour took the chair across from him.

"Any progress?"

150

"None at all, I regret to say. As far as I can tell he didn't have an enemy in the world. He was a saint walking the earth."

"A surprise attack, then? A burglar?"

"Most likely."

Katie came into the room. "They've quieted down. Oh you got your dinner already."

"I did and it smells wonderful, thank you."

"We have a currant pudding for the sweet, so leave a bit of room for that."

"Katie says it's called half-pay pudding because it's cheap to make but it's delicious," said Seymour. He smiled so fondly that Murdoch blinked. Good Lord, was the bachelor sergeant falling in love with the young widow? Enid Jones had warned him months ago about affection engendered by proximity not being the same as true love, but he could see why it might happen. Welcome a man home after a long shift of duty, feed him hot tasty food, do his laundry for him, which he knew Katie did, be glad to see him, and before you knew it, romance blossomed.

"I'd better get back," said Katie. Murdoch noticed how Seymour followed her with his eyes as she left.

The two men talked more about the case while Murdoch ate, then they lingered for an hour to smoke a pipe. Murdoch had been intending to resist the temptation, but the sight and smell of the tobacco was too much and he joined Seymour. Katie did not return and Amy Slade remained in her room. Finally Seymour stood up.

"I'm on duty tomorrow, so I'd better climb the wooden hill. You should too, by the look of you."

"I will. I'm just digesting my dinner a bit longer."

"Good night then."

They shook hands and Seymour left. He didn't call out a goodnight to Amy, so Murdoch assumed she had extinguished her lamps and gone to bed. He hoped the inspector's visit would go well. He knew she was an excellent teacher, he'd observed her once or twice before, but she was so radical in her methods that more than once she had upset the school trustees. One of them had heard her whistling to the children and told her dourly, "'A whistling woman and a crowing hen, is no good to God or men.'"

Amy had laughed at that, but Murdoch knew she'd had to be more careful with what she did in the class-room. And her clothes. Rational Dress, she called it and she was right it was very sensible and rational for an active woman, but she'd told him that more than once she'd been shouted at by men as she walked home. Murdoch's thoughts jumped to Liza. His fiancée had been radical in many ways too but conservative in others. He suddenly wished he had her photograph in front of him. Her face was becoming less vivid in his mind. It had been more than two years since she had died suddenly from typhoid fever and the feeling of loss came and went in its intensity. Tonight it was acute and he wasn't sure why. Perhaps it was seeing what was happening to Seymour. Did Katie return his affections? She was considerably younger, but Murdoch thought

152

she did have that soft glow about her these days that women get when they are falling in love and are loved in return.

He banged his pipe on the side of the stove to knock out the ashes and went his own way up the wooden hill.

Katie had been right when she warned him about the twins being in the throws of teething. Their intermittent crying had kept him awake most of the night. Finally, at four o'clock he put on his shirt and trousers and went downstairs. As he approached the parlour that was now Katie's room, both boys were in pained and lusty voice. He had to tap on the door twice before it opened a crack and Katie's haggard face peered out.

"Mr. Murdoch, I'm so sorry you've been wakened as well. I can't quiet them no how."

"I thought another pair of hands might help matters."

Katie was holding one of the twins and Murdoch took a quick glance at the baby's clenched fist as he waved it ferociously in the air. James had a small birthmark on his wrist. This was Jacob.

"Why don't I give him a walk around the premises. A change of scene might help."

"Well, I . . . oh thank you." She was too tired to argue. Murdoch put his candlestick on the hall table and accepted the transfer of the tightly wrapped baby.

"I'll tend to James," she said and retreated into her room where the other twin was wailing.

153

Whether from surprise at this new person, or whether he was just too exhausted to carry on, Jacob stopped crying. Gently, Murdoch straightened the baby's bonnet that had slipped down his forehead and wiped away some of the tears and drool with his cuff. Jacob grabbed his hand and immediately tried to stuff the knuckles into his mouth. Murdoch could feel the bumpy edge of the gums as the baby chomped down. Murdoch started to walk down the hall, jiggling the boy as he did so.

"Teeth are good things on the whole, little fellow. You can get to bite into all sorts of things like apples and pears. The best kind are the ones you can pick right off the tree, even better if the farmer is an old coot who doesn't want you to. Those taste real good." He paused and looked into Jacob's wide eyes. "No, forget I said that. I don't want you starting into a life of crime. Let's see, what else? You can eat crusts of bread that are still warm from the oven with fresh butter and a piece of cheese on the top. And sometimes the best thing in the world is a thick pork chop slathered with onions. Hmm, you need teeth to do all that. So this bit of suffering now is going to be worth it."

He didn't think this was the time to warn Jacob that later in life teeth could be a big problem if they decayed, as he knew only too well. The baby sniffled a little and looked as if he was going to howl again. Murdoch balanced him in one arm and loosened up the tight blanket.

"How's that? You seem hot to me."

154

Jacob looked into his face with the into-the-soul stare that infants have, but he didn't cry. By the time they'd made the third trip down the hall, he even seemed to be on the verge of nodding off. With a groan at his aching muscles, Murdoch shifted him to the other arm, just as the door to Amy's room opened and she emerged, in the red quilted house gown he'd seen her in yesterday.

"William, I didn't expect to see you up at this hour."

"Jacob and I are having a little constitutional. I've been telling him about the value of teeth."

She smiled. "It sounds as if you need to give the same talk to his brother." James was still yelling.

She tapped at Katie's door and went in. Murdoch heard murmured voices, then the baby stopped crying and a few minutes later, Katie emerged.

"Miss Slade has ordered me to go to bed. I'm going to get a little nap in her room. Please wake me in half an hour, Mr. Murdoch. And thank you so much."

She didn't even check her child, the lure of a short sleep propelling her away. She went into Amy's room and closed the door. The house was suddenly quiet. Jacob was asleep, making little snuffling noises and Murdoch withdrew his knuckle, wiping it on his shirt. His arms and back were aching and he suddenly felt desperately tired. He didn't dare go back to Katie's room, where it sounded as if Amy had calmed the other twin, in case they both woke up again. He walked to the hall stand and sat down on the chair next to it. He

155

leaned his head against the wall, wedged the baby in the crook of his arm, and closed his eyes.

He didn't know how long he'd been asleep, but he woke with a start. The light in the hall was the grey of dawn and he saw that his candle had burned down. He was no longer holding Jacob. Somebody had removed the boy from his arms. He sat up straight and almost yelped at the stab of pain from the crick in his neck. The hall was chilly, but there was a cover around his legs and bare feet. He yawned and heard the clock in the kitchen chime the hour. It was six o'clock. Katie's door opened and Amy came out. She was dressed and had even pinned up her hair. He couldn't believe how fresh she looked considering she too had had a broken night.

"Good morning, William," she said, speaking in a low voice. "Everybody's asleep, but I thought I might as well light the stove ready for breakfast."

He rubbed his neck. "You took Jacob, I assume."

"Yes, you were both dead to the world. The twins are still sleeping, bless them, and Katie hasn't moved in the last two hours."

"What about you? Did you get back to sleep?"

"Not really. When I'm up, I'm up. Why don't you come down to the kitchen and I'll make us some tea."

Stiffly, Murdoch got to his feet. He couldn't turn his head.

"You look as if you've got a crick in your neck," she said. "Let me get the fire going then I'll give it a rub.

I used to do that for my brothers and I warn you I have fingers of steel."

"I'll accept any pain if you can restore my neck to flesh."

He followed her into the kitchen. In spite of his fatigue and soreness, he was suddenly very happy.

Chapter Seventeen

ALL OF THE DAILY NEWSPAPERS had made headlines of
Reverend Howard's murder, so Murdoch wasn't surprised to find the chapel of the funeral parlour packed,
the crowd spilling to the outer rooms. He recognized
several reporters, notebooks on their laps, who had to
a man wedged themselves into the end seats of the rows
in order to exit quickly when the verdict was announced.
Their young runners were squatting on the floor beside
them, ready as hunting dogs. Mr. Royce, the coroner,
was seated at a table facing the thirteen members of the
jury who were in the first two rows. He was busily filling
out his forms. Even an inquest into such a violent
murder had its tedious formalities. Murdoch hurried to
a bench near the front, which was reserved for witnesses. Constables Dewhurst and Fyfer were already
seated beside Dr. Julia Ogden and her father. When
Murdoch slid into the remaining empty space, she

turned and frowned. He smiled apologetically. Late again. He resisted the impulse to launch into an explanation about being delayed at the station while he had quickly sifted through the reports of the constables who had been on the night shifts. Nobody had reported anything untoward. The east end of the city had been wrapped in virtuous sleep.

The spectators were as quiet as if they were in church and the room was silent except for the odd choked-back cough. Royce was not intimidated by the pressure from the waiting crowd, even though one woman suddenly burst out weeping and at least two others followed suit. Finally, he affixed his seal to the document he'd been filling out, picked up his gavel, and rapped on the table.

"We will begin this inquest conducted by me, Walter Fuller Royce, on behalf of Her Majesty, the Queen. I will ask all of you witnesses to speak clearly and slowly. Remember, I have to write down what you say, as does our clerk."

Constable Crabtree was standing beside the table, ready to take instruction, and Royce nodded at him. "Call the roll of jurors and make sure they are all present. Then get them to sign their names next to their seal."

Crabtree did so. "Doctor William Caven, Angus Drummond, Joseph Lyons . . ." And so on until all thirteen had called out their varying *presents*. The jurymen on the whole were a well-dressed lot, almost all of them in formal frock coats, even Joseph Lyons,

159

who'd given his occupation as reporter. We could be in a gentleman's club, thought Murdoch.

Royce raised his hand. "This is a public inquest and we know already that the evidence we will hear from some of the witnesses will be most horrific. I suggest that any of the ladies leave now if they wish. And I will also have the court cleared of the newsboys, who are far too young to be here in the first place."

There was a sudden rumble of indignation from the reporters. Royce was a retired solicitor and was notoriously hostile to the reporting of criminal cases in the newspapers. He claimed, and rightly, that the reports were invariably both lurid and inaccurate. In retaliation, the reporters were unkind to him in their reports, mocking his bulbous nose and florid features. Murdoch's sympathies were with the coroner, although he doubted that the newsboys had a sensitive bone in their bodies considering the life they led. There were five of them, each paid a pittance by the reporters to run their stories to the respective newspaper offices in time for the evening edition.

"Come on," said Royce. "Get those lads out of here. Constable Crabtree, please escort any ladies who wish to leave."

With a great show of reluctance and much grumbling, the scruffy-looking street arabs reluctantly filed out of the courtroom. Two women in the back row stood up and left.

160

The coroner consulted his list. "Call the first witness, Miss Sarah Dignam, if you please."

Miss Dignam was at the end of the row, Miss Flowers next to her. At the sound of her name, an elderly man with full side whiskers and shaggy beard, who was seated directly behind her, patted her shoulder solicitously. She got up slowly and walked to the chair beside the table. She was dressed all in black and her felt mourning hat was trimmed with ebony flowers, one of which drooped over the brim to touch her pale face.

"State your name in full, your place of abode, and your occupation," said Royce.

"My name is Sarah Emily Maria Dignam and I live at –"

"Speak up, if you please, ma'am. I can hardly hear you, which means the jury most certainly cannot."

Royce was not a man inclined to sympathy. Miss Dignam shrank down into the chair at the reprimand and repeated her name in a slightly louder voice.

"I live at 420 Jarvis Street, which is one of the row of houses just north of the church."

Royce flashed her an impatient look. "Your occupation, ma'am?"

"I take care of the household for my brother and myself."

"Spinster," he said, making a point of writing that down. "Swear her in, constable."

161

Crabtree handed Miss Dignam a bible, which she grasped in both gloved hands.

"Raise your right hand, if you please, ma'am. When I've finished, you must answer, *I do.*"

The constable smiled kindly at her and Murdoch saw her blink away quick tears.

"Do you, Sarah Emily Maria Dignam, hereby swear that the evidence you shall give to this inquest on behalf of our Sovereign Lady, the Queen, touching the death of Charles Edmund Howard, shall be the truth, the whole truth, and nothing but the truth, so help you God?"

"I do," whispered Miss Dignam.

The coroner looked as if he was going to order her to speak up again.

"Miss Dignam, I realize, as I'm sure do all the members of the jury, that you have suffered a dreadful shock and that this inquest can only be an ordeal for you. However . . . it is our duty to determine the cause of death of the Reverend Howard and we must all rise to the challenge no matter what. In the interest of justice we can spare no one. Do I make myself clear?"

"Yes, sir."

"Good. Now, I would like you to relate in your own words, but slowly if you please, and loudly, especially, loudly, what happened when you went to Chalmers Church on Tuesday afternoon. March third."

The room was completely hushed as Miss Dignam

162

related her story. She was unable to raise her voice, but everybody heard what she said and there were gasps when she described her first sight of the pastor.

"I went into the office. The door was open and the pastor was lying on his back in the middle of the floor. I saw immediately that there was a knife protruding from his neck. He was soaked in blood, which seemed to be everywhere as if the entire room had been doused," she paused here and dabbed at her mouth. Murdoch realized he was holding his breath like most of the spectators and he was glad Mrs. Howard was not present. Miss Dignam swallowed and continued. "I could see his right eye socket was destroyed . . . I first ascertained there was nothing that could help him and then I ran out of the church –"

"Wait a moment, ma'am." Royce held up his hand. "In what manner did you determine he was beyond help?"

"I put my ear to his chest and I drew off my glove and put my fingers underneath his nose to see if he was still breathing."

"Did you indeed? That was most collected, if I may say so."

His comment brought a rush of colour to her pale face but her voice was more spirited. "I did not feel in the least collected, I assure you, sir. But as I told the detective who came to question me"– she nodded over at Murdoch – "if there had been any way to resuscitate Mr. Howard, I would have done it."

She hadn't mentioned exactly what she'd done, thought Murdoch, but then he had interviewed her very soon afterwards. Royce held up his hand again to signal she should wait while he wrote down what she had said.

"Continue."

"As I ran toward Jarvis Street, I was fortunate to encounter a police officer immediately. I told him what I had found. He seemed at a loss as to what to do, but at that moment Mr. Drummond arrived." She nodded in the direction of a man in the first jurors' row. "He stayed with me while the constable went into the church. I'm afraid what happened next is hazy in my mind, but eventually the police constable emerged. He sent Mr. Drummond to sound the alarm. Miss Flowers, who had also come for the prayer meeting, arrived and he asked her to escort me to my home, which she did. It is, as I have said, just north of the church."

Royce looked over at her. "When you first left your house, what time was it?"

"I would say about half past three."

"Did you see anybody on the street or in the vicinity of the church itself?"

Miss Dignam lowered her head but her voice was clear enough. "It was a cold dismal afternoon so there really wasn't anyone about. I saw no one."

164

The coroner leaned toward her. The quieter she became, the louder his voice was. "Please remember you are under oath, ma'am. I must ask you . . . do you have any knowledge of who might have murdered Mr. Howard?"

"No, I do not. It is incomprehensible to me. He was a good man. One of Christ's chosen few."

She shuddered and Murdoch thought she might break into tears, but she held on.

"Very well, you may step down, ma'am. Constable, escort the lady to her seat." He consulted the piece of paper on his desk. "Call the next witness, Francis Fyfer, constable second class, number forty-seven."

Fyfer jumped up and strode over to the table where Crabtree administered the oath. The constable's, "I do swear" was loud and Royce beamed his approval. Then Fyfer launched into his tale.

"I was on duty on the afternoon of March third and I was just approaching the end of my beat, which is at Jarvis Street and Carlton, when a woman comes running out from the side path of Chalmers Church. That woman is here in the courtroom, seated in the first row."

Murdoch couldn't help but smile. The young constable must have been a witness before at a formal trial. On the other hand, his demeanour was rather unfortunate, as there was the slightest implication that Miss Dignam was herself on charge. Murdoch knew enough about the collected ignorance of any emotional group of people and he feared what rumours might be getting spawned.

165

"At first I thought she was hurt because she had blood on her face and hands and garments –"

"One moment, constable." Royce turned over his sheet of paper. "Miss Dignam has told us that she attempted to ascertain whether or not Reverend Howard was quick or dead. Would you say that the amount of blood you observed on her person was compatible with her pressing her head to the dead man's heart?"

Fyfer paused and flicked nervously at his moustache. "It is possible, sir. She was certainly covered with it."

Royce made a note and Murdoch saw the covert exchange of glances among the spectators, the ripple and shift of reactions. Miss Dignam had her head lowered as if she were praying.

The constable continued his statement in his loud, confident voice. "When I determined that she was un-injured and when I could make out what she was saying, I told her to stay where she was. Mr. Drummond, one of the parishioners who is also present in the court-room, had arrived at this point and I left the lady in his care while I myself went into the church. I discovered the body of a man lying in one of the rear offices. This man was later identified as Reverend Howard, the pastor of the church. He appeared to have been severely beaten about the head and he was also stabbed in the side of the neck. I could see he was beyond human aid, so I ran back through the church to where I had left the lady in question, now identified as Miss Sarah

Dignam. Other people were now standing outside of the church and I ordered one of them, a Miss Flowers, also here present, to take her home, having first obtained her name and address. Then I sent Mr. Drummond to sound the alarm while I did my best to watch the church in case anybody left. Detective Murdoch arrived shortly after, and we went back into the church to get a better look at things. We saw no one other than the dead man."

"Thank you, constable. Please step down and come and read over your statement. If you are satisfied it is as you said, sign your name to the bottom left of the last page."

Royce glanced over at Miss Dignam. "Dear me. In all the excitement, I forgot to ask you to do the same. Please come forward, ma'am."

Miss Dignam stood up, suddenly covered her mouth with her hand, retched, then as quietly and smoothly as a suit of clothes falling from a coat hanger, she sank to the floor.

Chapter Eighteen

MURDOCH AND BOTH of the doctors Ogden sprang forward at the same time. Miss Dignam was crouched on the floor retching bile, which spilled out over her gloved hands onto the floor. Murdoch grabbed his handkerchief from his pocket and handed it to Julia Ogden, who held it in front of Miss Dignam's mouth. The stench of vomit was sharp and sour in the air.

"Court is adjourned for fifteen minutes," called Royce.

"Jurors, you will please move to the other room, immediately. Constable, remove the lady from the courtroom and have somebody clean up that mess." He banged with his gavel and, presumably confident that Miss Dignam was in good hands, he strode out of the room. The two doctors helped Miss Dignam to her feet and, followed by the stares of the spectators, Murdoch led the way to the outer lobby. Here they placed her on a bench. She vomited once more and this time it was the elder Dr. Ogden who volunteered his handkerchief.

"Thank you, I'm so sorry," Miss Dignam whispered.

"Do you still feel faint?" Dr. Julia asked.

"No. I think I will be all right now. I'm so sorry to have acted like that."

"Nonsense. It wasn't your fault," said Dr. Uzziel. "It's damnably upsetting for a woman to have to testify in court, especially with such an insensitive clod running the show."

Murdoch glanced around at the curious onlookers. He recognized one of the funeral parlour attendants, who had come to watch the inquest.

"You, Thompson. Run and fetch us a glass of water."

"Would this help, sir?" The man reached into his inside pocket and took out a small silver flask. "I always keep this handy."

He handed the flask to Dr. Julia, who unscrewed the top and held it out to Miss Dignam.

"Take a sip. That's good. Now another, not too much."

Miss Dignam shuddered and gagged but didn't vomit the brandy back.

"One more."

A little colour began to return to the woman's face, but she still looked wretched. There were deep shadows under her eyes and the lids were reddened from lack of sleep.

169

"She should go home at once," Julia said to Murdoch. "There is no reason for her to stay, is there?"

"She has to sign a copy of her statement. But I can bring it out here for her."

"Thank you, Mr. Murdoch, I don't think I could bear to . . . to go back in there." Miss Dignam stuffed both soiled handkerchiefs into her reticule. "I do apologize to you, gentlemen. I will have these washed and returned to you as soon as possible."

Murdoch could see Constable Crabtree in the door of the chapel, his helmet visible above the crush of people in the lobby. Nobody inside had moved although they were talking in low voices to each other.

"The court will reconvene in five minutes, Mr. Murdoch."

"George, bring Miss Dignam's statement and a pen and inkwell. She's going to sign it here. And ask Miss Flowers if she'd join us. She's the lady in the grey furs."

Dr. Julia offered Miss Dignam more brandy. Seeing Thompson's anxious expression, Murdoch tapped him on the arm.

"Don't worry. Send your bill to the police station. You will be reimbursed. "

Crabtree soon returned with an inkwell and paper in his hand and Miss Flowers in tow. She approached her friend nervously.

"How are you feeling, Sarah?"

"Much better, thank you, May, but I am being sent home."

"Would you mind accompanying her, ma'am?" Murdoch asked Miss Flowers.

It was obvious that May did mind. "But the inquest isn't over yet. And I can't leave Elias in there by himself. You know how he is."

Suddenly, Miss Dignam reached forward and caught her by the sleeve. "Please, May. I must go to the church."

"To Chalmers? What on earth for?"

"I want to pray."

"Good gracious, Sarah, isn't that being rather morbid? After all . . ."

She didn't finish her sentence but Miss Dignam shook her head.

"I will be closer to Charles's soul in Chalmers. He loved his church. I know I will be able to feel his presence there."

It was clear what Miss Flowers thought about that.

Murdoch's eyes met those of Dr. Uzziel's, who indicated Miss Dignam should be indulged. He also thought it advisable to keep an eye on her.

"I tell you what, ma'am. Miss Flowers seems to want to stay until the inquest is finished. Why don't I assign Constable Fyfer to go with you to the church? Then he can escort you to your house after that."

171

"Splendid idea," said Dr. Uzziel.

Miss Dignam gave Murdoch a feeble smile. "Thank you, sir. That would be most kind."

"Now if you are feeling better, I should return to the courtroom," said Dr. Julia. "I think they have returned and I have to give my testimony."

"Thank you, doctor. I am quite all right now."

Uzziel offered his daughter his arm.

"Make way," he called out. "Doctor coming through."

Miss Flowers waved her fingers at her friend but didn't embrace her. "I must join your brother. I'll tell him you are quite recovered. I'll stay and tell you what transpires."

Let's hope the jury doesn't accuse Miss Dignam of murder, thought Murdoch. It was in their jurisdiction to name a culprit if they felt confident of the evidence. He'd seen it happen before.

"Read this through and sign it here, if you will, ma'am," said Crabtree.

Miss Dignam gave the statement a perfunctory glance. "I'm sure it's quite correct," she said and wrote her signature in a shaky hand. They heard the coroner thumping his gavel to signal the court was reconvened and the attention of the onlookers switched abruptly to what they could see in the chapel.

"I must leave you to Constable Fyfer," said Murdoch. "I will call on you soon."

172 The constable didn't look too happy about leaving the excitement of the inquest, but ever polite, he offered his arm to the lady, who got to her feet and leaning on

him heavily made her way to the door, the crowd parting before them like the Red Sea.

Murdoch followed Crabtree back into the chapel.

In case any jurors had tried to evade their civic duty by slipping away during the adjournment, the roll call was taken again and the court settled.

Dr. Ogden was the next witness and she delivered her report in what Murdoch now knew was her customary self-contained manner. One of the jurors was also a physician and when she had finished he asked several highly technical medical questions relating to the manner of the injuries to the skull, but it was obvious to Murdoch the man simply wanted to show off his own knowledge, evidently superior in his own eyes.

"And what is your opinion as to the cause of death, doctor?"

She'd already given her opinion, but she was unflustered, answered him calmly, and repeated her last sentence.

"The pastor bled to death because the weapon pierced the carotid artery."

"I have to ask this question, doctor, even though it might seem superfluous. Could the wound to the neck have been self-inflicted? I have known the most bizarre cases of self-murder."

173

"No, sir. I do not believe so and the damage to the side of the head was far too severe to have been caused by him falling down. Although the blows to the side of the face were grievous indeed, they would not themselves have caused death. Mr. Howard died from a massive hemorrhage."

Mr. Lyon's hand shot up. "How long before death actually occurred?"

"Given the depth of the wound, I would say it would have happened quite quickly. Perhaps a few minutes at the most."

"Would he have been conscious long enough to confront his murderer?"

"Perhaps."

"Is it possible then that the, um, the one eye was destroyed so that the image of the murderer could not be detected?"

"I cannot speak for the motivation of the murderer, sir, but I assure you we saw no such image in the post-mortem examination."

Lyons had a pencil in his hand and he tapped it on his teeth. "Another question, doctor, if I may? In your expert opinion, was the piercing of the artery accidental or deliberate? What I mean is, did the assailant intend to commit murder? Did he know exactly what he was doing, or was he only striking out blindly in the course of which he managed to hit that particular spot?"

174

"Even if the actual entry point of the knife was accidental, everything seems to indicate that there was a murderous intent. Mr. Howard was obviously kicked repeatedly when he was lying on the ground. I would say his assailant most certainly wanted to kill him."

This comment was too much for the spectators and there was an outburst of chatter and more noisy crying from some of the women.

Crabtree called for silence, Royce rapped his gavel, and finally everybody quieted down.

"Are there any more questions for Dr. Ogden?" the coroner asked.

A tiny, rabbity man who had given his name as Moses Galt and his occupation as a buyer in Mr. Simpson's drapery department raised his hand.

"Given the amount of force necessary to thrust a knife that deeply into a man's neck, can we assume without question that the murderer could not be of the fair sex?"

This question caused another ripple through the crowd, and Dr. Ogden waited for a moment before answering.

"I would say, we can assume no such thing. Both men and women are capable of unusual strength when the blood is up, whether that is in feats of heroism or acts of blind rage. I have known a woman of quite average build lift a carriage from off the legs of her child who had been run over. It was something she could not possibly have done in normal circumstances."

175

More reaction from the crowd and various nodding and exchanges. The juryman doctor called out that he had known such cases himself.

"In your learned opinion, Dr. Ogden, would the assailant have been marked with blood?" asked the journalist, who obviously was hoping for the most lurid story he could concoct.

"Perhaps less than one might think. The blood probably spurted to the side on one gush. If the murderer was directly behind Mr. Howard, he, or she, would have been able to avoid it. When the pastor fell to the ground, the blood flowed out but as he died almost immediately, it would not have pulsed and again would have been easy to avoid."

"So the murderer could have been bloodstained or totally untouched, either one?"

"That is correct. It is impossible to say with surety."

There were no more questions, and Royce asked Dr. Ogden to sign her statement. She did so and returned to her seat. Her father tapped her lightly on the elbow to signify his pride in her performance.

Murdoch was called next and he added to the doctor's report by mentioning the missing watch and boots.

"You'd say a thief then, would you, detective?" asked Royce.

"That or somebody wants us to think so."

Mr. Lyons indicated he had a question. "Dr. Ogden in her excellent testimony has told us that there is every indication that the assailant was in a mad fury. I wonder then, if a person in such a state would have the presence of mind to deliberately mislead the police. I beg your pardon, Mr. Murdoch, I have no wish to cast aspersions on your competence."

In fact Murdoch thought the man's question was a shrewd one and he'd thought of it himself.

"Frankly, sir, I don't know at this point. It would have taken seconds to snatch the watch and only a minute or two at the most to pull off the boots. I could see even a person in a state of blind rage, having both time and sense to do those things with the intention of throwing suspicion elsewhere."

"Or there could have been more than one assailant," piped up the buyer.

"That is not out of the question."

There were a couple more questions about his opinion on the injuries from the doctor who was still trying to discredit Dr. Ogden, but Murdoch deferred to her judgment and the juror was forced to sit back and resume twiddling with his gold watch chain.

Murdoch signed his statement and returned to his seat. The next witness was a Mrs. Emmeline Bright, who was the matron of the girls' home on Gerrard Street. Fyfer had taken her original statement and Murdoch knew he would be disappointed not to hear her testimony, which he considered of vital importance. Murdoch was less sanguine about the reliability of eyewitnesses.

177

Chapter Nineteen

MRS. BRIGHT WAS SURPRISINGLY YOUNG for her position, and belied her name by her sombre, authoritative manner, which a dowager might have envied. Murdoch imagined she would be most intimidating to her young charges.

Crabtree swore her in and she gave her testimony. "I was walking along Gerrard Street going toward Jarvis. The time was exactly a quarter past one o'clock. I was on my way to visit my sister-in-law, who resides on Church Street and who has recently been delivered of her first child. I noticed a man was crossing the Gardens in the direction of Chalmers Church. He was wearing a long dark coat and a dark fedora hat. He was carrying some sort of sack over his back. He looked like a tramp."

The officious doctor raised his hand and, getting the nod from Royce, he asked, "Was this person running or walking?"

"He was hurrying."

Royce frowned. "May I remind the good men of the jury that Tuesday was a miserably cold day and any sensible person would be in a hurry to get indoors. We cannot make more of this witness's testimony than is called for."

Moses Galt indicated he had a question.

"How can you be so certain about the time of day, Mrs. Bright?"

The matron smiled. She'd been hoping somebody would ask this. "I was due to meet my sister-in-law at one-thirty and I was delayed because I had to admit a new girl. I looked at the clock as I was leaving. It was ten past one. The home is only a few minutes walk from Jarvis Street."

Lyons put up his hand. "You seem quite certain the man you saw was a tramp. Other than the fact that he was carrying a sack, what else was there to identify him as such?"

Mrs. Bright fidgeted with her glove, the first sign of uncertainty she had yet shown.

"The park is a favourite spot for tramps, who often go to the churches in the area to beg for money. They are quite a plague, I might add. This man had a thick black beard and he walked the way tramps do. His clothes were not good quality."

"Did you see him enter the church?"

"Yes," she hesitated. "Er, that is I didn't see him open the door, if that's what you mean, but where else would he be going?"

179

Lyons would have made a good lawyer, Murdoch thought, he didn't give the woman a chance to compose herself. "You said he walked the way tramps do. How is that, may I ask, ma'am?"

"Well, they sort of shuffle."

"You said he was hurrying."

"He was, but he still dragged his feet." She frowned at Lyons, obviously not used to being questioned in this way. Murdoch wondered briefly what sort of man she had married. She would have to be a widow to be employed at the home, but she wasn't in mourning dress so the bereavement must have happened a few years ago. She had a full, smooth face with well-shaped brows, but the hardness of her expression was not attractive. He tried to be more charitable. Perhaps she was covering profound loneliness.

There appeared to be no more questions from the jury and Royce took his large gold watch from his waistcoat pocket and consulted it.

"It's almost dinnertime and I should begin my summing up so we can –"

The Reverend Swanzey was sitting in the row behind the jurors and suddenly he jumped to his feet. "I do apologize for the late notice, Mr. Royce, but I would like to be sworn in. I believe I have some evidence to add that could be of the utmost importance."

He had a fleck of saliva at the corner of his mouth and he actually swayed a little so that Murdoch was afraid he might collapse. He could feel Dr. Ogden shift beside him, so she too was at the ready.

"Good gracious, sir. Why didn't you tell the constable earlier so he could put you on my list?"

Swanzey gulped and Murdoch saw his prominent Adam's apple move up and down.

"I beg your pardon. I realize that was remiss of me, but frankly, the frightful events drove it completely from my mind. However, after hearing Mrs. Bright's testimony, I think perhaps it might be significant."

"Very well. Swear him in, constable, if you please."

Swanzey went through the ritual, seeming nervous and on edge. He sat down in the witness chair.

"Give your statement, Mr. Swanzey, and do speak up," Royce said. "The previous witness set an excellent example."

"Yes, sir." Swanzey took a deep breath and when he spoke his voice was loud and resonant. There would be no difficulty hearing him at the back of the room. "It is my habit to take an afternoon constitutional as often as the demands of my work permit. I find it is an opportunity for inner contemplation and even in the most inclement weather I do so. However, on Tuesday, I decided that the raw afternoon was too much even for me and after a short walk around the Gardens I went into the greenhouse. The greenery is so soothing to the eye at this time of year." He paused and looked about the room. Murdoch could feel how intently the

181

spectators were listening to him. Swanzey was demonstrating the skill and pacing of a good preacher.

"It was as I was making a turn of the building when I encountered a tramp. I did not think much of it because it is not unusual for wanderers to go inside the greenhouses where they have some protection from the elements. However, this man, I now see exactly fitted the description of the man seen by our estimable matron hurrying toward the church." There was a murmuring from the spectators. "He was of middle age, tall, and broad-shouldered with long, grizzled hair and beard. His coat, albeit ragged, was dark, and he was wearing a soft-brimmed black hat. He also had a sack of some sort, although when I met up with him, he was not carrying it but rather had set it at his feet." He paused again.

"Did you speak to the man?" Royce asked.

"I merely bid him good afternoon. He was a rather sullen fellow and didn't give me much of an answer. As I said, I would have thought no more about him except that I now realize he had a watch in his hand, which he had been in the process of winding when I came across him."

"Was it a silver watch?" one of the jurors called out.

"I wouldn't swear to that, but I did remark to myself that such a fellow had a watch at all."

"Did you notice if there was blood on him?" Lyons asked.

"No, I did not. It was quite gloomy inside and he wore dark clothes."

182

Royce leaned toward the pastor. "Mr. Swanzey, I want you to consider your answer to my next question very carefully. If you do not know, say so. I don't want any exaggeration or twisting of the facts because you think it will suit us . . . Now then. What time of day was it when you encountered this tramp?"

Swanzey's Adam's apple bobbed vigorously. "I left my lodgings on Gerrard Street shortly after three, as is my wont to do. I walked around the park as I said, then I went into the greenhouse where I walked some more. I met the man on my third perambulation, so he must have entered after I did." He hesitated, biting on his lower lip. "I would estimate the time was approximately a quarter to four o'clock or shortly thereafter. I decided to resume my walk and I bid the fellow good day and left. As far as I know, he remained in the greenhouse. I myself proceeded across the park toward Sherbourne Street. It was later that I returned to the church and saw a crowd of people had gathered. Then, alas, I was told the sad news."

He swallowed hard and Murdoch thought for a moment he was going to burst into tears, but he clamped his teeth and remained in control.

Royce looked over at Murdoch. "Detective, you have heard Mrs. Bright's and Reverend Swanzey's testimony. It is not a leap of credibility to assume the two men are one and the same. The man could easily have escaped to the greenhouse from the church after the attack on

183

the pastor. I assume you will be doing everything in your power to find the wretch."

"Yes, sir, of course."

As far as Murdoch was concerned the evidence was not conclusive, but there was no point in going into that now. Certainly, the tramp needed to be found.

There were no more witnesses or questions and Royce's summation was short. He then withdrew to the rear room and Crabtree directed the jurors to the adjoining room for their deliberations. One of two people in the audience stood up and stretched, but mostly they just sat quietly, the weeping women were comforted but all the voices were low and respectful.

It was hardly more than fifteen minutes later when the jurors returned and filed back to their seats. Royce took his seat and Crabtree took a roll call again.

"Mr. Chamberlin, have you and the jury agreed on your verdict?"

"We have, sir."

"As foreman, will you please address this court and state what conclusion the jury has reached."

The elderly man stood up, adjusted his pince-nez, and, holding his notes in front of him, said, "We the jury here gathered today declare that on the third day of March, 1896, between the hours of three and half past three o'clock, in the offices of Chalmers Presbyterian Church, a person or persons to the jurors aforesaid unknown, did feloniously murder the Reverend Charles Edmund Howard."

This verdict was not a surprise to anybody and there was no reaction from the spectators.

"All of you must come forward and sign beside your seal that you agree with this verdict," said Royce.

When that was done and they all sat down again, Royce addressed them once more.

"Gentlemen, hearken to your verdict as delivered by you. You find that Charles Edmund Howard was murdered by person or persons unknown, so say you all. The body can now be buried."

It was Crabtree's turn. "Oyez! Oyez! Oyez! You good men of Toronto who have been empanelled and sworn of the jury to inquire for our Sovereign Lady, the Queen, touching the death of Charles Edmund Howard and who have returned your verdict, may now depart hence and take your ease. God save the Queen."

Royce gathered his papers together. "Thank you, gentlemen. You are invited to join me in a small repast at the Crown's expense." He banged the gavel. "I hereby declare this court adjourned."

The reporters made as fast an exit as they could. Murdoch stood up, ready to let the crowd leave ahead of him. Two rows back, a skinny arm emerged from a heavy raccoon coat and waved at him. As the wearer of the coat was also wearing a matching fur cap,

Murdoch hadn't recognized him. Then he saw it was Mr. Hicks. Next to him was a woman who was so muffled in a woollen shawl, he hadn't recognized her either. It was Josie Tugwell. He nodded at her, but she didn't acknowledge him.

Chapter Twenty

TELLING CRABTREE TO FOLLOW on as soon as he could, Murdoch went straight back to the police station. He parked his wheel outside and walked into the front hall. Sergeant Gardiner was sitting at his high stool behind the desk.

"Don't bother taking off your coat. Miss Dignam rang through. She wants to talk to you as soon as possible. In person, not on the telephone."

Two young women whose provocative dress proclaimed a dubious occupation were sitting together on the public bench that ran around the room. They made ostentatious giggling noises.

"Cut that out, you two," bellowed the sergeant and they stopped abruptly. They couldn't afford to alienate him.

Murdoch approached Gardiner. "Did she say anything else?"

"No, just that it was urgent. It was about half an hour ago."

"Has Fyfer reported in?"

"Not yet. What was the verdict?"

"What you'd expect, homicide by person or persons unknown."

"Well, I'm warning you. Don't leave me alone with the culprit when you do find him." The sergeant's normally affable face was contorted with anger. "How dare that scum take down a man of the church."

Murdoch started to leave, then he paused. "By the way, what is your opinion of Miss Dignam?"

"She's a very well-bred lady. She's always had a greeting for me and my wife, whereas there are some whose faces would crack if they smiled a good morning to the likes of us."

"Do you think she is prone to hysteria?"

"Not that I know of. But I've only seen her on Sundays, mind you. She's never married and has no chance of a dowry as I've heard tell, so I'd say she's probably lonely, but sensible with it."

"And Angus Drummond? What's your view of him?"

"Salt of the earth." The sergeant gave a wry grin. "A bit too salty for some tastes, but then you can't please everybody, can you?"

"Mrs. Howard refused to admit him when he came to offer his condolences."

188

Gardiner sighed. "I can understand that. Angus hasn't minced words when he's had something to say about the pastor. But that's just his way. He's a good man who's devoted to the church."

"Thanks, sergeant. I'd better get going."

Murdoch headed for the door. The two women watched him go and the older one in the scarlet hat managed to whisper, "'ave a nice time."

In the fading daylight, Murdoch could see that the Dignam house, while large and elegant, was not in a good state of repair, something he hadn't noticed previously. The paint on the door and windows was peeling and the garden was overgrown and neglected.

Unexpectedly, it was Miss Dignam herself who answered his ring.

"Thank you for responding so quickly, Mr. Murdoch. Please come in."

He stepped inside and she waited while he took off his hat and coat. She accepted them from him as if she were a maid and put them on the hall stand.

"This way, if you please."

She led the way, holding aloft a single candle. Her black gown seemed to him to be excessively tight at the waist and the skirt was pulled back into a no longer fashionable bustle. There was a definite whiff of camphor coming from her. She had taken out a dress from a previous mourning period and she even had a weeping

189

veil pinned to her hair. She opened the door to the drawing room and they went in.

"I must thank you again for your kindness at my, er, my indisposition." She gave him a faint smile. "You remind me of Charles. Even though you are a police detective, I observe that you have the same air about you. 'His eyes were the eyes of doves.'"

Murdoch knew by now what she was referring to and he acknowledged the compliment with a slight nod of his head. He had been compared to various things before but never to Solomon.

"I know the verdict of the inquest," she continued. "Miss Flowers and my brother together with our servant are presently in the kitchen discussing every word that was said. However, they might be done momentarily. Elias has a limited tolerance for company, even in these exciting times."

Murdoch could see a tea tray with silver teapot and china cups was set up by the fire, but he took her last words as a cue and forestalled her invitation to take tea.

"I gather it was a matter of some urgency on which you wished to speak to me, Miss Dignam."

She sat down in the fireside chair, which was pulled as close to the hearth as possible, and again he took the one opposite her.

"I was wondering if you found my cake tin?"

If it weren't for her complete composure, he would

have considered she had dropped into some kind of dementia.

"I beg your pardon, ma'am?"

"I had made a special cake for the prayer meeting that I was carrying when I went into the church. I don't have it here so I can only assume I dropped it . . . when I . . . when I tried to ascertain whether Mr. Howard was alive."

"To my knowledge no cake tin has been found, Miss Dignam."

"Then that is not without significance, wouldn't you say?"

Caught up in the world of spinster ladies and tea and cake, Murdoch looked at her blankly for a moment.

She sighed. "I see I am not making myself clear. Forgive me. The tin is a pretty one with some sentimental value, but that is not the point. If you have not found it, then it was stolen." She looked away from him into the dancing flames. "I told you that when I found him, the pastor's body was still warm to the touch. It is possible that his assailant had remained in the church, perhaps hiding. When I ran out I must have left the tin behind. It is likely that the murderer took it."

She had a point, but a cake tin!

"You say the tin had no particular monetary value, ma'am."

"That is correct but the murderer did not necessarily know that, did he? It could have contained something

191

of value. He probably took it with him to find out."

"How big was it?"

"It was large enough to hold a cake that would feed eight people. The colours were gold and pink with a motif of peacocks and roses."

Not an object that could be easily overlooked.

"I'll check with the constables who were searching the premises, ma'am."

She leaned toward him. "There is one more thing, Mr. Murdoch. I didn't mention this to you before because frankly in the upset of the moment, it slipped my mind. I also didn't think to say it at the inquest. There was a most disagreeable odour in the church when I first went in. I have been thinking about this most carefully, how I would describe it to you. Rotten eggs combined with a stale dirty sort of smell as if dish-cloths had been allowed to stand damp for a long period of time." There was a muffled sound of laughter from the next room and she frowned. "Elias told me that one of the witnesses saw a tramp going into the church –"

Murdoch interrupted her. "He was observed crossing the Gardens, ma'am, not actually seen entering the church."

"But he must have gone inside. Tramps do have the odour I mentioned. I have smelled it before. They often come to Chalmers to beg. The fact that my cake tin is missing would confirm that. He would have expected it to contain food."

She was making sense, but Murdoch found himself reluctant to pounce on the "tramp" theory. On the other hand, he couldn't deny that was what it was starting to look like, especially given Reverend Swanzey's testimony. If the man he had encountered and the tramp noticed by Mrs. Bright were one and the same, the likelihood was such a fellow could have entered the church, killed Howard, and escaped to a temporary hideout in the greenhouse. The timing fitted.

"Is that all you wanted to tell me, Miss Dignam?"

"Yes it is. I'm so sorry I didn't say this earlier, but it had left my mind completely until now. It was only when I walked into the church again that I remembered."

Murdoch wondered if she had communicated with the dead man's spirit as she had hoped.

"There is something I meant to ask you, Miss Dignam. I do understand that you were in a state of shock when you came upon Reverend Howard's body, but perhaps more things are coming back to you now."

She stiffened. "I don't know what you mean, Mr. Murdoch."

"Constable Fyfer says you were covered with blood when you came running toward him, particularly your hands . . . why was that, Miss Dignam?"

Her hand flew to her cheek. "You heard what I said at the inquest. I bent down to his chest to check for a heartbeat. There was considerable blood on his coat. It must have . . ." She didn't finish.

193

"Ma'am, essentially you are still under oath to tell the truth."

"Of course. I don't know why you are speaking to me this way, detective. "

Watching her try to puff herself up was like seeing a kitten fluff itself in front of the dog.

"Miss Dignam. Did you attempt to remove the knife from Mr. Howard's neck?"

She turned quite white. "I . . . er . . ."

"I must have the truth, ma'am."

She stared at him for a moment with horrified eyes, then she shrank back into her chair. "I did try, yes, but it was immovable."

"You should have told me that before."

"Forgive me. It was cowardice on my part. I was afraid how it might seem to the world, to my brother, for instance. Elias is already disgruntled with me for my behaviour at the inquest. And it is one thing to chance across such an unsavoury event, to use his words, it is another to be actively implicated. I shudder to think what he would say if he knew to what lengths I went in my desire to resuscitate Charles."

"Is there anything else you have not said, Miss Dignam?"

194

She looked away from him. "Nothing. I have told you everything."

They heard the sound of voices from the hall. Miss Flowers, laughing merrily, and a deeper voice, who Murdoch assumed was Miss Dignam's brother.

"Ah, she has finished."

Miss Dignam got to her feet.

"I would rather they didn't know you are here, Mr. Murdoch. They think talking to you will further upset me. I will draw them both away to the kitchen. Please wait here."

She put her finger to her lips and hurried out, closing the door behind her. He could hear her talking and Miss Flowers answering but could not make out what they were saying. Then she came back into the room. "I've sent her off to make some tea. My brother has returned to his room. We have a few minutes only. I will give you the cake tin."

Murdoch was beginning to suspect that the poor woman really had become unhinged through shock but she went on, keeping her voice low. "I thought it might be helpful for your investigation to see the twin of the one that is missing. My dear mother purchased several at once some years ago. Every Boxing Day, she liked to dispense Christmas cakes, mostly to my father's employees but also to the families she knew who were impoverished."

She listened for a moment to see if her friend was returning but all was quiet. She quickly went over to the tea trolley, pulled up the white damask cloth, and took a colourful cake tin from the rack.

"Here, you can take it with you for comparison. There is cake in it. I had made a second one and there is no sense in it going to waste. Elias doesn't like caraway seed. I hope you do."

"Er, yes, thank you."

"Please eat it then."

She thrust the tin, indeed pink and gold with a pea-cocks-and-roses motif, into his hands. Then she went to the hall stand for his hat and coat.

"I'll keep May in the kitchen and you can slip away and let yourself out. We are on the telephone and you can ring me as soon as you have any more information. Goodbye, Mr. Murdoch."

She went to the door, opened it a crack, and peeked out. She turned to him and nodded. "It's all clear."

Holding his hat and coat, the tin under his arm, Murdoch slipped away.

Chapter Twenty-One

A LIGHT SNOW WAS FALLING as Murdoch left the Dignam house, which made bicycling unpleasant. He turned left from Jarvis on to Carlton Street and rode up to Drummond's grocery store. At first he thought the grocer had not yet returned from the inquest, but there was a dim light burning and, drawing close, he could see the grocer standing behind the counter, reading a newspaper. There were no customers. Murdoch propped his bicycle against the curb and went into the store.

Drummond looked up, his expression was sour. "Is this official business, detective, or are you in search of fresh vegetables? I'll tell you right now, the potatoes aren't very good and the carrots are woody. The cabbage is all right though, as long as you're not sick of cabbage by now."

Murdoch thought that if this was the way Drummond welcomed all his customers, it was no wonder his store was empty. Honesty might be a sign of virtue, but it could put a damper on business.

"I'm here officially, but I will take a pound of oatmeal while I'm at it. We're running low."

Drummond came from behind the counter to serve him from one of the bins. He didn't seem to have much stock and the potatoes and carrots did indeed look wizened and the few Brussels sprouts were yellowing. Murdoch glanced over his shoulder. There was a big tree a few paces to the west of the store, but it was bare of foliage. He could see the side door of Chalmers Church quite clearly.

"Here you are. Two cents." The grocer thrust a crumpled brown paper bag at him.

Murdoch handed him the money and Drummond held it in the palm of his hand and squinted through his glasses.

"That won't bury me, will it? Are you sure there's nothing else I can get you?"

"No thank you." Murdoch accepted the brown paper bag, then he pulled the cake tin from the front of his coat where he'd wedged it.

"Have you seen this before?"

Drummond looked surprised. "Of course I have. It belongs to Miss Dignam. She uses it all the time at church bake sales. Why have you got it?"

"Actually she tells me this is one of several that she possesses. She says that she took some cake to the

198

church on Tuesday and in her shock she left the tin there. It has not been found. She has lent me this so if I do come across a cake tin I can compare the two of them."

"That's proof then, isn't it?"

"Of what, Mr. Drummond?"

"Come on, detective. You know what I mean, don't play the dummy with me. That verdict of person unknown we brought in was a pile of horse manure. A waste of time, mine and the taxpayer's. We all know who the culprit is. And this business with the tin proves it. The tramp must have picked it up. He's the one you should be after." He glared at Murdoch in exasperation. "You kenna have forgot already what the matron said?"

"You mean that she noticed a man crossing the Gardens who in her opinion was a tramp?"

"'In her opinion'? My that's a wee too lawyerish for me. That lassie is as sharp as a thumbtack. She saw a tramp all right and you don't have to be a clever detective to work it out. He went into the church. Had some sort of quarrel with Charles Howard, for God knows what reason, killed him, then hoofed it over to that greenhouse where Mr. Swanzey ran into him. With a silver watch I might add, that just by coincidence was missing from the pastor's waistcoat."

He was right, but there was something smugly know-it-all about Drummond that Murdoch found intensely irritating.

"You saw him, did you, Mr. Drummond?"

199

"What do you mean, 'saw him'?"

The grocer's cheeks, what was visible of them, were already rosy in colour, so Murdoch couldn't tell if the man had blushed. Nevertheless, the question seemed to disconcert him.

"You have a good view of the church and the park from your shop. I noticed you seem to spend a lot of time gazing out of the window. I was asking a simple question. Did you see this tramp either enter or leave the church?"

"No, I did not. I would have said so if I had." He dragged up a semblance of a smile. "Don't mind me, Mr. Murdoch. I can be a rough old fox, but I'm harmless. You appear to be taking offence at my tone and I didna mean anything by it. The whole affair has got us all riled up and short-tempered. Miss Sarah Dignam is a good-hearted soul and she doesna deserve to be drawn into the whole bloody godforsaken mess. I blew off a slate when you showed me that cake tin and what it implied. No hard feelings, I hope." He stuck out his hand and Murdoch was forced to shake it. He wasn't sure why the grocer was doing such an aboutface and trying to placate him. Drummond went over to one of the bins and picked up an apple.

200 "Here, peace offering. I know it's as wrinkled as an old man's behind but it's still sweet."

"Thank you." Murdoch put the wizened apple in his pocket. "You said a few minutes ago, 'for God knows

what reason,' when you referred to the possibility that
a tramp may have murdered Reverend Howard."

"Ay. I canna imagine Charles Howard refusing to help
any tramp if they came a asking. He was as soft as
butter." His tone was neither contemptuous nor admir-
ing. "Strictly speaking, it wasna his own money he was
giving out, it was the kirk's. I believe if you're trusted
with that responsibility you have to be doubly careful.
You can waste your own muck, but not the public's."

Something struck Murdoch and he said, "Mr. Howard
was a Visitor for the House of Industry, is that work
you've done yourself?"

"Ay. I volunteer when I can. They need somebody
like me." Murdoch pitied the applicants who would be
on Drummond's list.

"By the way, Mr. Drummond, I understand there was
some enmity between you and Mr. Howard."

"Who the devil told you that?" He stepped away and
folded his arms across his chest. His eyes were partially
obscured by the spectacles, but Murdoch could sense
that he had once again hit on a nerve.

"Never mind who told me, is it true?"

"No. Not the least. We didna see eye to eye about
some matters of doctrine, but it wasn't personal and I'd
no call it enmity."

201

"You're an elder at the church, are you not? I
understand Reverend Howard had to be elected to
his office by the church council. Did you vote for him?"

"That's a private matter within the church."

Murdoch leaned forward. "I'm investigating the brutal murder of a man in the prime of his life, Mr. Drummond. At the moment, there are no such things as private matters. Please answer my question."

"I dinna like the way the wind is blowing. I had nothing to do with Howard's death, as you seem to be insinuating."

Murdoch threw his hands out in mock indignation. "Good heavens, sir. All I asked was if the pastor was your choice."

"No, he was not. And there you have it. The blunt unvarnished truth. He was too –" Drummond waved his hands. "Too florid. Chalmers is an old and dignified church. We came here and broke off from the previous congregation just so we could maintain our traditions, not melt and merge into Baptists or Methodists. Ach, Howard was well educated enough and I dare say the ladies found him charming, but I have no desire to belong to a mongrel church, thank you very much." He touched his finger to the side of his nose. "Between you and me, I wouldn't be surprised if he didn't have a sly fondness for popish practices."

"God forbid," said Murdoch.

202 "It's true. He wanted us to start a subscription for stained-glass windows. He was devilishly keen on music, and some of his interpretations of the scriptures were bordering on blasphemous in my opinion."

Murdoch was curious to know what those interpretations were, but he didn't want to get off track.

"Who was your choice, if I may ask?"

"Matthew Swanzey. He might look like a dry stick, but he's got God's fire in his belly. You should hear the man preach."

"He was in the running then?"

"That's right. And he should have got it. He's been with Chalmers for the past six years as an associate pastor. We all expected he would be called when Pastor Cameron died. I didna understand it. The Kirk session was beguiled by a smooth tongue, if you ask me. And Howard won the vote. Why bring in a newcomer at all, I'd like to know? Besides which the man was originally a Yankee."

"Mr. Howard knew of your views, I presume?"

Drummond patted his skinny stomach, as if he'd had a good meal. "I'm not one to hide my opinions in namby-pamby language. Ask anybody as knows me and they'll tell you Angus Drummond is a man who calls a spade a spade even if others want to name it a golden shovel."

Murdoch was saved from the impulse to be rude by the tinkle of the bell as a customer entered the store. Drummond turned to greet her.

"Ah Mrs. Reid, come for your dinner, have you? Well you'd better take one of the tins of salmon I got in. Unless you've got some butter, which you probably don't, the potatoes aren't worth the water."

203

Murdoch headed for the door and called out, "If you do come across the cake tin, please let me know right away."

Drummond barely deigned a nod and Murdoch left him to browbeat his intimidated customer.

Chapter Twenty-Two

THE LAST TIME Murdoch had been in the horticultural gardens pavilion was with Liza. They had gone to hear the Grenadiers band and he remembered it as being unbearably hot inside the pavilion, because even with all the windows opened wide to get a cross breeze, the sun had beaten down all day on the glass. Ladies fanned themselves desperately but sweated nonetheless. In spite of the heat, a small area had been cleared for dancing and several couples were jumping around with more vigour than grace, to the military two step. Murdoch didn't know how to dance then and no amount of cajoling on Liza's part could get him onto the dance floor. He wasn't about to make such a fool of himself. Since she died, he'd taken dance lessons and had to admit he had enjoyed himself. *If onlys* were useless, but they slipped into his thoughts more often than he liked.

A long greenhouse abutted the pavilion porch and its entrance was from the porch. Murdoch pushed open the double doors and felt as if he had stepped into summer. The air was warm and moist and heavy with the smell of vegetation. He was in the main pergola and even though outside was grey and sunless, here the lush green plants and banks of multicoloured flowers made the day seem much brighter. The horticultural gardens and the greenhouses were the pride of the city and were as well tended as any private garden.

Just inside the entrance a young couple was sitting close together on a bench. They quickly moved apart as he came in and the woman straightened her hat. She was fair-skinned and her blush was obvious. Her sweetheart also looked discomfited. Murdoch realized he must have frowned at them, but it was not from disapproval, it was envy. He made himself smile, touched his hat, and walked around to the other side of central island where the trees and shrubs hid him from view. A squirrel had got trapped inside the pergola and it was chittering in fear and indignation, otherwise the greenhouse was quiet, any noise of drays or carriages shut out by the glass.

Murdoch looked around him. There were more benches on this side and behind them was a wide flowerbed. Each variety of shrub and flower was labelled. Many of them were unfamiliar to him, but he didn't have time or inclination for horticultural lessons. In the middle of the island was a fanciful structure set up as part of a living room. A fireplace was made of ivy that had been trained to grow around a wooden frame. Above it were blue and yellow patches of some other climbing plant masquerading as the kind of marble you might find in a nobby house. There were real pieces of coal in the grate and red and orange flowers growing among them to simulate fire. A birdcage of twigs swung from a branch of a nearby tree. There was a fake bird in the cage made also of intertwined twigs, but the bars were wide enough to allow real birds to enter and a sparrow was hopping in and out of the cage. Murdoch was about to walk on when the bird fluttered down and lighted on the arm of the bench close to him. It took a couple of quick pecks at something between the slats, then hopped to the path and pecked some more. Murdoch dropped into a crouch, scaring the bird into flight. It was a big assumption, of course – who knows how many people had come through this pergola? – but he wanted to see what the bird was eating. There was a light scattering of crumbs on the bench and the path and he could see they were cake, not bread or biscuit. He took a blank envelope from his pocket and scooped up as many of the crumbs as he could. Later, using a magnifying glass he might be able to determine what kind of cake it was.

At that moment, he heard the ring of hobnailed boots and Constable George Crabtree appeared.

"Good afternoon, sir."

"How'd you track me down, George?"

"Sergeant said as how you'd been called up to Miss Dignam's and I was heading up there when I seen you going into the greenhouse. I thought I might be some help."

"Good man. Among other things, I'm trying to see if I can find a cake tin here somewhere."

He quickly filled in the constable on his interview with Miss Dignam and her story of the missing tin and the bad odour in the church.

"It looks like we're after a tramp then, doesn't it, sir? When she ran off, he went back to his prey, took the boots and watch, saw the cake tin and picked that up as well. He'd hightail it over here till the coast was clear, I'll wager."

"It's looking that way. But what we need is some hard evidence. So let's start where Reverend Swanzey says he met up with the wayfarer. He was in the adjoining greenhouse."

Murdoch led the way through the connecting doors. This building was warmer and even more lush than the pergola.

"The wife and kiddies love coming here in the winter," said Crabtree. "She says it shortens the season. She even talked me into coming to a concert in the pavilion last summer. Very good it was. Some cove was a whistler, you know, he sort of cupped his hands

208

and blew through them. Sounded exactly like a flute."

"Ah yes. I've heard that. I know somebody who does it."

"Did you ever go yourself?"

"Not to that one . . . anyway, George, I know the constables searched this entire place, but we've got to go over it with a toothcomb. "

"Do you really think a tramp would throw away a cake tin, sir? The ones I've known wouldn't. They always prize something where they can keep their baccy or any extra food."

"You're probably right, George. I'm thinking we're more likely looking for old boots," said Murdoch. "If he stole good boots from the pastor, he'd want to wear them right away. In which case he would have to get rid of his own. Why don't you start on the other side and we'll meet at the far end."

Like the pergola, the greenhouse had a central island of tall shrubs and flowering plants that the path encircled. Crabtree turned to the right and Murdoch began to walk slowly down the path to the left. He was using his eyes, but he was also trying to put himself into the skin of the unknown tramp. In spite of what Dr. Ogden had said, Murdoch thought it was likely the murderer would have some traces of blood on his trousers and shoes. In which case he would want to get rid of them. A few feet down from the entrance was a rock garden, and water cascaded from a discreetly hidden pipe near

209

the ceiling, over a manufactured rocky incline, and into a pool below. He could see fat goldfish swimming lazily among the lily pads.

There was a low railing around the pool, presumably for the safety of the public and no doubt the goldfish. There were masses of small cresses growing around the rocks, and he thought some of them near the lip looked crushed. If you wanted to clean off your boots and trousers, this was the easiest place to reach the water. He wished he'd brought his magnifying glass. He examined the spot as closely as he could but couldn't really see an imprint of a boot or shoe. A slate slab overhang was chipped at the end, but that could have happened a long time ago. Not yet what could be considered hard evidence. He straightened up and continued to move slowly along the path.

He had only gone a little way when he was struck by a sweet scent drifting on the air. He halted. Surely not! But there they were, a mass of purple hyacinths in the flowerbed. He always thought of them as Liza's flowers now. "Oh my dear," he said softly.

"Mr. Murdoch, sir. Over here."

Crabtree was calling to him, his voice excited. Murdoch ran around to the other side, where he saw his constable kneeling by the edge of the path. Here there was another small pond and on its far bank were a shed and a small water wheel that was revolving slowly. Crabtree, his sleeve rolled up, had his arm thrust deep into the water.

"I think I've got something, sir."

He bent even closer to the water and with a tug, like little Tom Horner, he pulled out the plum. One black boot, soles split, dirty. He repeated the action and fished out a second boot.

He beamed at Murdoch. "That wheel was making a funny noise. It was hitting something as it went around. I thought it was a good idea to see what was the trouble."

"Well done, George. Well done. Is there anything else in there?"

Crabtree fished around. "I don't think so."

Murdoch knotted the shoelaces together so he could carry the boots. "Let's continue the search, but I think we've got as much as we're going to get."

They stayed in the greenhouse for another half an hour but found nothing more that could be remotely seen as significant. There was no sign of a cake tin, with or without peacocks.

Chapter Twenty-Three

Louisa Howard and Reverend Swanzey had been sitting in silence for several minutes. Louisa was sewing her initials in black thread on new black-bordered hand-kerchiefs. She was glad of the lack of conversation, happy not to have to respond to the endless comments, mostly from the ladies, who had been calling on her. *Such a good man, so kind and generous.* They all said varia-tions of the same theme. It wasn't that she didn't believe Charles to have been a good man, she did, but first of all, each remark made her weep afresh and second an insidious snake of resentment was stirring underneath her grief and shock. It was she who was left to raise their children, she who had to deliver his fatherless baby. She would have to move from this house now, and she had enjoyed her brief reign as pastor's wife with the prestige it accorded her. Oh there'd be pity and apologies from the committee of elders, but another pastor had to be found. Where would she go now? She had sent a telegram to her parents who lived in Buffalo and she knew they were coming to visit her. But in the meantime, there was so much to see to. Both children were coming down with colds, which didn't help matters. Charles had been an affectionate father, spending time with his children as often as he could and she could see how much they missed him. Louisa shifted her position as best she could. Her pregnancy wasn't yet that advanced, but she was uncomfortable in the mourning dress Miss Smith had sat up through the night making for her. The crepe at the throat was stiff and scratchy and even with her corset, which she wasn't ready to abandon, the waist was too tight.

"Is there anything I can get for you, Mrs. Howard?" Swanzey asked. She shook her head and he returned to his ruminations. He was probably thinking about when he'll be offered the position of pastor, she thought with a puff of spite. There was little doubt he would get it. When Reverend Cameron had died, Swanzey and Charles had both been candidates for the position. The decision process had taken many months and even though there were countless prayers for God's guidance, when the final vote was taken and Charles Howard, an American, was called from Buffalo, a few of the ladies of the congregation had let slip to Louisa that the final appointment had caused much acrimony. Well they'll be happy now, she thought. Swanzey would take over.

213

The elders were unlikely to go to the bother of finding somebody else. Swanzey wasn't married, so perhaps he wouldn't want to live in this house. It would be large for a bachelor. But then if he was offered the position, he would soon be looking around for a wife, she was sure of that. She glanced at him covertly. He was sitting across from her, staring into the fire. He was more handsome in profile, she thought, with his strong nose and lean jaw. Face to face, his eyes were unattractive and his lips ill defined. He suffered from a chronic eye irritation and his lids were reddened, the eyelashes often crusty. The lips he attempted to hide with a full moustache. His conversation was virtually non-existent as far as she was concerned, and she never felt comfortable in his presence, suspecting he found her wanting in seriousness. Nevertheless, if he became the pastor of Chalmers, which was supported by a large and wealthy congregation, she was sure he would find some young woman willing to marry him.

The clock on the mantelpiece chimed the quarter hour. He'd been here at least twenty minutes.

"I'm sure you have a lot of matters to attend to, Mr. Swanzey. I shall be quite all right by myself for a little while."

He started and turned toward her. "Nothing is as pressing as your well-being, Mrs. Howard. I wonder . . . would you like me to say a prayer?"

"Thank you, that would be a great comfort." Louisa

214

put aside her sewing. One of Reverend Swanzey's greatest attributes was a facility with extemporaneous prayers.

He perched on the edge of the couch and covered her hands with his.

"Let us pray."

Louisa closed her eyes, but she was conscious of the dryness of his hands and the heat they generated.

"The Lord said to Cain, 'What has thou done? The voice of thy brother's blood crieth unto me from the ground. And now art thou cursed from the earth, which hath opened her mouth to receive thy brother's blood from thy hand . . .'"

Louisa felt a fine spray of spittle on her cheek, but she couldn't remove her hand from his to wipe it off. He was gripping her tightly. His voice had become louder and more resonant.

"And no less shall the Lord mete out his punishment to the wrongdoer yeah even more mightily when the innocent is struck down just as Abel was slain by his own brother as he walked in the field. Lord, we pray to you this . . ."

At that moment, there was a knock on the door and Doris entered. Swanzey stopped in mid-sentence. The maid curtseyed quickly.

"I'm sorry, ma'am, but I have the afternoon post. Would you like to see it now?".

Swanzey released Louisa's hands, but his mouth was pinched with disapproval at the interruption.

"I beg your pardon, but I am anxious for word from my parents," she said placatingly.

"Of course. That is quite understandable. I'm sure the Lord will wait for us."

He seemed to grimace, but Louisa realized this was his way of signalling he had made a joke. She nodded at the maid.

"You can put it here."

Doris deposited the silver letter tray on the lamp table beside her mistress, curtseyed again and left.

"Will you excuse me, while I see if they have replied, Reverend Swanzey?"

"Most certainly." But he made no attempt to leave.

Louisa picked up the letters, leafing through them first. None bore her mother's familiar handwriting, but one still caught her eye. The envelope was small and rather grubby and the writing ill formed.

"Who is this from, I wonder?" She glanced over at Swanzey, who had returned to the chair by the fire. "Would you be so kind as to hand me the letter opener? I believe it is on the mantelpiece."

He handed it to her. She slit open the envelope and took out a piece of lined paper, also grubby, and began to read. Her hand flew to her mouth and she drew in her breath sharply.

216

"Mrs. Howard, what is the matter?" asked Swanzey.

She closed her eyes as if she could efface what she had just seen.

"Mrs. Howard?" he said again, but she didn't answer and for a moment she swayed as if she would faint. Swanzey came over to her. The letter was in her lap and he picked it up.

"Read it, oh my dear God, please read it."

March 6.

Dear Madam. You must know that yore husband, Charles Howard is not what he seemed. He was a wicked man and I can prove it. It was because of him that my daughter lost her innocence. We are willing to keep silent on this matter because of yore conditioin which as a mother I can understand. But we will want rekcompence. You can send the sum of 200 dollars or we will go to the newspapers. You can send it to the following address, who is a friend.

Mrs. Esther Tugwell

343 Sherbourne Street.

Yours faithfully,

One who has been wronged.

P.S. you must act immediately. Don't forget I can prove what I say.

"What does it mean, Matthew?" Louisa could barely speak.

Swanzey's hand was shaking. "Alas, it means that there are evil people in the world who will take advantage of another's tragedy in the most despicable manner."

"But why would she say Charles was not what he seemed and she can prove it?"

"Do you know this person, Esther Tugwell?"

"Not at all. Who can she be?"

Swanzey folded the letter and replaced it in the envelope. He took her hand again.

"Your husband's death has been reported by every newspaper in the city. I've heard before of vultures who scour the death columns and concoct such letters to see if they can take advantage of the bereaved family."

Louisa started to weep. "Oh what is going to become of me?"

Swanzey patted her awkwardly on the shoulder. "Try not to upset yourself, madam."

"But she says that Charles violated her daughter. That couldn't possibly be true, could it?"

He patted some more. "Come now, Mrs. Howard. Do you yourself believe it?"

She dabbed at her eyes with one of the handkerchiefs. "Frankly, sir, I feel as if I am standing on quicksand. If you were to tell me the moon is truly made of green cheese, I would be inclined to believe you."

She could see her response shocked him. "My dear Mrs. Howard, take a good look at the letter. It has obviously come from the lowest class of person. This woman has seized on an opportunity to extort money from you. Nothing more."

"Perhaps I should notify the detective who was here."

218

Swanzey pursed his lips. "Frankly, I would not recommend that. I don't believe our police force is entirely
comprised of the better elements of society and it would
not be advisable for this news to be bruited abroad."

"So you do believe it to be true?"

"No. Absolutely not. But vile gossip sticks no matter
how pure the object."

His words frightened her. "But what shall I do then?"

"What you must do is to put the matter completely
out of your mind." He tucked the letter into his pocket.
"I shall deal with it myself. We have a name and an
address. I shall call on this Mrs. Tugwell. 'A friend'
indeed! Well I will put the fear of God into this friend,
I promise you."

Swanzey stood up. "I shall see myself out. Please get
some rest."

Louisa leaned back against the sofa cushions. She felt
exhausted, as if she had been fighting a fierce tide for
a long time.

Chapter Twenty-Four

THIS STRETCH OF ONTARIO STREET, below Wilton, was inhabited mostly by working-class people. The houses were well tended, but they were small and close together; no grand gardens here. Mrs. O'Brien was sitting at her front window, nursing the latest arrival, a girl, Beattie, whom she'd named after her former neighbour, Mrs. Kitchen. Her three other little ones were kipping in the backroom so she was enjoying a rare moment of peace and quiet. The afternoon was drawing in and she'd have to stir soon and light the lamps before the rest of the brood came home from school. Mrs. O'Brien was normally a cheerful-enough soul. She had to be, with eight children to take care of and a husband more often away than not. He said it was hard bloody work being a fisherman and having to deal with all the different kinds of weather that God sent. Why don't you stay home and take care of the other things that God sends, all eight of them, and I'll be a fisherman, she'd said to him once, jokingly of course.

She sighed. Perhaps it was the dreary grey afternoon that was making her blue, sitting here watching the wind stir the bare branches of the trees and blow thin plumes of snow from the rooftops. A bit of green would be a balm for her eyes. Mostly, though, she missed Mrs. Kitchen. They had managed to get in a good chin at least once a day, even though Beatrice had a lot on her hands taking care of Arthur. But she had always managed to slip Mary a bit of the roast that they didn't finish or some tarts she'd made. O'Brien made good wages, but the money didn't always reach her regularly and eight growing children would eat you out of house and home given half a chance. They'd all of them been upset when Beatrice said she and Arthur were moving to Muskoka so he could get fresh air. She couldn't blame her, of course, it might be his only chance to get better but she did miss her. The new tenants were friendly enough, but the young one with the twin boys hardly stuck her nose out of the door and the schoolteacher never came round. Mr. Murdoch dropped in last week to see how she was, but a man just wasn't the same. She couldn't have a good gab with him, could she?

The baby had fallen asleep and she was about to lay her down when she saw a man coming up the street. He looked well off in his black fedora and long fur coat, but she didn't recognize him and she had the impression

221

he was looking for an address. Sure enough, at the Kitchens' house, he paused, checked a piece of paper in his hand, and walked up the short path to the door. He made no attempt to knock but bent down and slipped something underneath the door. Then, quickly, he turned around and walked away briskly the way he had come.

And who are you when you're at home? she wondered. I hope that's not bad news you're delivering. He was far too well dressed to be a mere messenger, so who the devil was he? She'd stood up to get a better look and disturbed Beattie, who scrunched her face preparatory to a good wail. At the same time, one of the boys called out to her from the backroom. Hoisting the infant over her shoulder, Mrs. O'Brien shuffled off to tend to him.

Murdoch put the wet boots on a piece of newspaper on top of his desk and began to make notes. The boots were black, badly scuffed, and the soles on both toes were parting company with the uppers. The heels were worn down and the lace in the right boot was broken and reknotted in three places, the left was laced with string. Typical footwear for tramps. He looked at the string under his magnifying glass, but there was nothing unusual about it. The boots measured twelve and one-quarter inches in length and four and a quarter inches wide, which meant the original owner was about Murdoch's height of six feet. That didn't mean that the last wearer was that tall, of course, he could have used them regardless of the fit. Murdoch thrust his hand into the right boot and sure enough his fingers touched something soggy. Carefully, he pulled out the newspaper that was stuffed into the toe and placed it on the desk. The paper was too sodden to make anything of it, he'd have to let it dry.

He upended the boots and examined the soles with his glass. There were several small seeds and bits of straw wedged into the grooves around the nails and he pried them out with his knife onto a piece of fresh paper. Under the glass, the seeds looked like wheat. The boots hadn't been in the water long enough to eliminate the stink from unwashed sweaty feet, but he thought he could detect a whiff of manure mingling in there like a tenor note in a requiem. Toronto streets were perpetually dotted with horse plop of course and as he knew to his cost, it was all too easy to walk in it. However, this smell had survived at least two days of immersion in water so he thought the manure was more ingrained. He stared at the bits of straw, wishing he had a way of determining if they'd come from a stable or a cow barn. He'd make a tentative guess then that the boots had belonged to a man who'd been on a farm fairly recently.

223

He turned the boots over and studied them again, but there wasn't anything else he could deduce. If blood had been splattered on them, it had washed off in the pond water. He pushed them to the edge of his desk and took a piece of notepaper from his desk.

Callahan: send this to all the newspapers right away:

Detective Murdoch of number four station is interested in speaking to anyone who noticed or was in contact with a man who meets the following description. Between five feet eight and six feet tall. Of middle age with full black beard, wearing a long black coat and black fedora and carrying a sack across his back. It is possible this man is a tramp and/or a farm labourer.

Murdoch hesitated, wondering whether to add that the man might be dangerous. He had often complained that the police were all too ready to jump on somebody from the lower classes when a crime was committed, "guilty until proved innocent," but a solid case seemed to be building up that Reverend Howard's murderer was a wayfarer and Murdoch's stubborn refusal to put all his eggs in that basket might be prejudice in reverse.

He added to the note:

This man is wanted for questioning in the murder of the Reverend Charles Howard. He should be considered dangerous.

224

The response from newspaper advertisements was limited. Not everybody could read and especially in the wayfaring class. He wrote another note to Callahan to be telegraphed to the city's other police stations, in which he added a description of Howard's stolen boots and the silver watch. Not that there was any guarantee the man was still be around. He could easily have caught a train and be miles away by now. It wasn't going to be easy to find him. He'd better send Dewhurst to the station and see if anybody fitting the tramp's description had boarded a train in the last two days. He wrote a third note for Callahan to send to police stations in the small towns and villages in the surrounding area. Responses from them would be much slower, as few of them had a telegram line.

He picked up his notes and was about to go down to the front desk when he heard hurried footsteps coming down the hall. Crabtree's large frame appeared in the doorway.

"Come in, George, what's the matter?"

The constable was rather breathless.

"Don't tell me you found our tramp?"

"No, I'm afraid not, sir, but I may have made a pretty big catch."

Murdoch indicated the worn chair that was opposite him. "Sit down and tell me first. I've already got a crick in my neck, I don't want to make it worse."

Crabtree balanced himself in the chair. "After I left you at the Gardens, sir, I was making my way down Jarvis Street. There were one or two people I'd missed when we was going around and I thought they might

225

be home now. I'd just got as far as Wilton when the next thing I know there was screams and shouts going on, 'Thief, Thief,' and this fellow comes running around the corner. Well you don't run like a hare with people shouting *thief* if you haven't been up to something. I sees a couple of gentlemen running after him, but he's fast and is easily outdistancing them. Then he sees me on the opposite side of the road and that gives him the fright of his life so he turns south on Jarvis, like the devil has lit his trousers. I sets off after him, but I wouldn't have stood a chance of catching him when darned if he doesn't put his foot in a pothole and goes a crash. He tries to get up but he can't run a yard and I'm on him like a flash. I can see guilt written all over him. By that time the two gentlemen catch up to us and say as how he'd just stolen a purse from a poor widow woman who was walking on the street. The cove can't even deny it because when I shake him down a little red silk purse falls out of his pocket."

Crabtree patted his jacket. "I've got it here."

"Well done, George," said Murdoch. "I don't mean to spoil your triumph, but at the moment I can't see why this cove is such a prize nab."

The constable grinned. "I'm getting to that, sir. So I grabbed the fellow by the scruff and made him hop with me to where there were a group of people standing around a poor blind woman and a young tad who turned out to be her grandson. It was her purse all right. The boy identified it and said the man I'd nabbed had just come on them all of a sudden and snatched it from her belt. I had the devil of a time persuading the old lady to come to the station and press charges, but I told her as how it was her duty and so forth and we would if she didn't so she agreed."

Murdoch looked at the constable, who was relishing his moment of drama. "Go on."

"She seems like a good old soul and she's concerned that my poor klep has hurt himself. 'Maybe we should have a look at his ankle,' says she. At which point I notice his boots . . . They're *his* boots, sir, Mr. Howard's."

"What! How do you know?"

"Remember the maid said Mr. Howard's had been recently soled and heeled but he had broken his lace and he replaced it with a brown one in his right boot? Well these black boots the nab had on his feet have an exact same brown lace and they've been recently soled and heeled."

Murdoch whistled through his teeth. "Did you ask your nab where he got them?"

"I did and he said he didn't remember and that he'd had them for years."

"Do you believe him?"

227

"Not a jot. I thought he was lying in his teeth. Anyway, I brought him into the station and had him take his boots off so we could take a look at his ankle and as I suspected, he was a lying bugger . . . he has bad blisters on the heels of both feet."

Murdoch slapped the desk. "So they're not likely to be boots he's had for years." He jumped up. "Let's go and have a little chin with our widow robber. Where is he?"

"In the hall, sir. The lady has been weeping non-stop and says she don't want no trouble. You'd think we were arresting her. The lad is crying too and the nab is moaning so it's quite noisy out there."

"Did you get any names?"

"Yes. She's Mrs. Annabel Shorter and her grandson's Bill. They're from Markham and just here for the day. The thief says he's Peter Somerset, but I doubt it's a name his own mother would ever know him by."

"Let's go and talk to them, shall we, George? A recently repaired black boot with a brown lace is a bit too much of a coincidence to swallow."

Chapter Twenty-Five

CRABTREE'S NAB WAS SITTING on the bench a few feet from an elderly lady and a young boy. He was indeed moaning, the woman was weeping rather noisily, and the boy was trying to comfort her, also loudly. She was in full widow's weeds with a long black crepe veil that covered her face and fell as far as her waist. The boy was also in black with knickerbockers and jacket. A velvet cap was pulled down low and the lower part of his face was wrapped in a black scarf so that only his eyes were visible.

"Grandma, hush. Here's the detective come to talk to you."

She turned in the direction of the door, although Murdoch was coming from the hall behind the counter. He walked over to her. Her grandson was speaking so loudly, Murdoch assumed the old lady was deaf and he too raised his voice.

229

"Mrs. Shorter, I'm Detective Murdoch. I wonder if you could tell me what happened."

He glanced over at the man, who had sunk back on the bench and buried his face in his muffler.

"My grandma is too upset to talk much," said the boy. "She don't want to press charges. We have to get back to the train station before three o'clock."

Murdoch sat on the bench beside the old woman who was staring straight ahead. He couldn't make out her face through the dark veil, but he could see she was trembling. He tried to speak gently, which was difficult at full volume.

"Mrs. Shorter, your purse was stolen and we have caught the thief. You won't have to stay long if we write up a charge. You'll just have to sign it. Why should he get away with frightening elderly citizens?"

"I'm blind, I didn't see him," she said, her voice was shrill.

"I realize that. But we have other witnesses. And your grandson must have seen him."

The boy shook his head, still focused on his grandmother. "No I didn't. I was looking after grandma when she fell down. Then I saw a man running away and men yelling and chasing after him. I just thought he hadn't been looking where he was going and knocked her over."

230

"Then you saw that your grandmother's purse had gone."

"I noticed it then, but she could have lost it earlier."

The woman stretched out her hand in search of her grandson's and he clasped it tightly.

"I'm a Christian woman, Mr. Murdoch," she said, "and I believe that we should forgive those that trespass against us. If indeed this young man did rob me, I have my purse returned, I am not harmed, and that is all that matters. There was nothing in it but some streetcar tickets and a little change. We really do have to catch our train, my daughter is expecting us."

Murdoch peered at her, but her face was obscured by the thick crepe veil. Then he glanced over his shoulder at the thief. In spite of his attempt to burrow into his collar, Murdoch could see a broad forehead and ragged sandy-brown hair.

Mrs. Shorter went to stand up, but Murdoch blocked her with his arm.

"Why do I have the impression we have met before?"

She recoiled, bowed her head briefly, then with one swift movement, she jerked upward, threw off his arm, shoved him away from her, and kicked him hard in the shins. With a yell to the boy, she ran for the door. Startled by the pain, he couldn't move fast enough. Somerset tried to follow her, but even though he hopped with astonishing speed, he was no match for Crabtree, who got him from behind. The woman would have got away, but her long veil, flowing out behind her, caught on the edge of the stove in the centre of the room. The bonnet came off, but it was tied underneath her chin

231

and she was stopped in her tracks, giving Murdoch a chance to seize her arm and twist it behind her back.

She cried out in pain, but as it was now obvious she was no old woman, he held on. In the meantime, Gardiner and Callahan had run from behind the counter to help. The sergeant grabbed the boy, who fought desperately, until Callahan managed to hold his legs and Gardiner pinned his arms. In minutes the struggle was over.

"Mrs. Shorter, or should I say, Mrs. Pierce?" shouted Murdoch. "Whoever the hell you are, you're under arrest," He was panting from the struggle and the rush of anger beyond his control at the painful kicks that had been inflicted on him. "I'm going to let go of you so I don't break your arm, but if you move a muscle, you will be cuffed. Do you understand?" He gave her a little shake that made her yelp again. "Do you understand?"

"Leave her alone," yelled the boy and he somehow jerked out of the grasp of both constables who were holding him and ran to help the woman. His cap had fallen off and Gardiner grabbed him by the hair, shoved him to the floor, then dropped, putting his knee on the boy's back. He administered a couple of hard slaps to his head while Callahan once more held on to the boy's ankles. Murdoch let go of the woman's arm and shoved her onto the bench.

232

"Let him go," she screamed at the other two officers.

She probably would have got up again, but Murdoch yelled at the top of his voice.

"Stay there." He looked over his shoulder. "Sergeant, let him get up."

Gardiner looked as if he was going to defy him, but then he reluctantly got off the boy and stepped back, clearly ready to pounce again if necessary. Callahan released the lad's ankles and also stood back.

"You, boy, come over here and sit beside your mother," said Murdoch.

Now that she had lost her black bonnet and veil, the woman's dark hair was revealed. She was not in the least elderly, probably in her thirties, maybe even younger but she had no teeth, which aged her face considerably. The boy's face had gone quite white and a bruise was vivid above his eye. He looked unsteady, but he rushed over to her and she pulled him close to her side. Both of them sat staring at Murdoch with a mix of defiance and fear. The third member of the little trio wasn't saying anything. He wasn't that tall a man and Crabtree, who had pulled his arms back and put the cuffs on him, towered over him.

"Now then. The excitement's over," said Murdoch. "Madam, do I have your word, you won't try to make a bolt for it?"

"I'd sooner trust a rabid fox," said Gardiner. "Put the cuffs on her. And the whelp."

233

The woman had stepped across the line from respectable victim to criminal scum in his eyes. He started over to them but Murdoch warned him off.

"It's all right, I'll deal with it." He addressed the woman. "Shall I call you Mrs. Shorter or Mrs. Pierce?"

"Whatever you like. It don't matter to me."

"So neither one is your real name?"

She shrugged.

"Look, ma'am, you're going to have to talk to me sooner or later. You delivered some pretty vicious kicks to my shin and I could lay charges against you that would have you in the Mercer for a couple of years. Your lad would go to the industrial school and I doubt he'd like that." Murdoch nodded at the other man. "Is he your husband?"

"Not him. I've never seen him before. And you can't charge me with nothing. You grabbed ahold of me and I was just defending my honour."

"You were pretending to be blind and you claimed this man had robbed you."

"I didn't say he'd robbed me. And there's no harm in pretending to be blind. It ain't a crime. It was just a game I was playing with Tim."

"I see. This isn't the first time you've been in a police station, I take it?"

"'Course it is. And it will be last, the treatment you coves dish out. I'll speak to the chief himself, I will."

The preposterousness of the statement made Murdoch grin. He couldn't help it.

"I tell you what, ma'am. This has been very strenuous. I, for one, need a cup of tea. Give me a name that I can call you by for politeness' sake and I'll have our constable here make us a pot. What do you say?"

"Are you going to charge me?"

"I haven't heard your story yet, nor your friend's."

Gardiner was still hovering behind Murdoch, his face dark with anger. "'Course he's going to charge you. You and your bastard assaulted police officers."

The lad had an angry red mark on his cheek where Gardiner had hit him.

"I'll handle it, sergeant." Murdoch turned back to the woman. "Given that this is a public hall and we need some privacy, I suggest we have our tea in one of our jail cells."

"All three of us?"

"Yes." She was about to protest but he held up his hand. "I know, I know. This man is a complete stranger. But as this is the second time I've seen you in the same company, I don't believe you. You're queer plungers and your names are on a bill that I was just looking at on Monday."

The woman's eyes scanned the men gathered around her. Gardiner, red-faced and angry, Callahan eager for another fray, Crabtree just very large.

235

"All right, me name's Bagley, Mrs. Olivia Bagley. This is my nipper, Tim, and that's Ed Parker, a friend."

The redhead gave Murdoch a knuckle salute like a sailor.

Still keeping a wary eye on the woman, Murdoch said, "George, remove the cuffs from Mr. Parker and then escort him to the rear cell. Get him a cold bandage and some opium lotion if you can find it for his ankle. Mrs. Bagley, you and Tim follow behind Constable Crabtree and I will walk behind you. One move in any other direction and I will put the cuffs on. You can't get away, there are four of us here."

"Can I have me bonnet? It cost a dollar."

"Constable Callahan, will you hand the lady her bonnet. It's over by the stove."

The clerk did as he was asked and gingerly held out the hat to the woman. Then, led by Crabtree and the silent Mr. Parker, limping painfully, they moved slowly down the hall.

Chapter Twenty-Six

GIVEN THAT MRS. BAGLEY'S ATTITUDE had been as tough as any man's, Murdoch wasn't sure if he was going to get anything from her, but after two cups of tea and a thick slice of cake that Crabtree donated from his own dinner, she capitulated. They were seated on the hard bunk beds of the jail cell and even though he'd left the door open, the iron bars were enough to scare anybody into co-operation.

He showed her the poster about the queer plungers and she admitted with a touch of pride that they were the trio it referred to.

"We've got several turns. You didn't see the best, which is Tim here rolling under a carriage."

"I taught him how to do it," said Parker. "I used to be an acrobat with a circus." He gazed at the boy fondly. "He's good at it. He can hold his breath for two minutes."

He didn't say so, but Murdoch assumed that was so the boy could play dead.

"How often do you do the little thief act, the one I witnessed?" Murdoch asked.

"As often as we can, don't we, Ed? We have to move around so as nobody recognizes us. Sometimes Tim is a coloured boy, sometimes he's not. People aren't that observant really." She had previously soaked her cake in the tea and more or less sucked on it. "I lost all my teeth when I was only twenty-two. I thought it was the worst thing that had ever happened to me, but it turned out to be useful." She fished in her pocket and took out a kerchief. It was wrapped around a set of gleaming white false teeth. She popped them in her mouth and smiled at Murdoch.

"They're not so good for eating, they're really just for show, but they take years off my age, don't they?" Her words were a bit slurred but with the dentures filling out her hollow cheeks, Olivia looked quite pretty.

"Indeed they do."

Olivia removed the teeth and wrapped them up again. She bent over, tilted her head slightly, and sucked in her cheeks. "I can go all rheumatic and frail in a tick. Usually I powder my face white and put some red rouge under my eyelids, but I had on the blasted veil today so I didn't need it. Phew. How women breathe under those things is beyond me. If ever I married which I won't and if ever I was really a widow, I wouldn't wear one of them veils, I can tell you that."

She slurped the last of her tea and put down the cup, looking over at Murdoch shrewdly.

"So are you going to charge us or what? We're just actors, you know. We don't take anything that don't belong to us."

"You're frauds and your intention is to deceive people to get money from them. That's a crime."

"Oh come on, mister. The coves who give us money don't miss it. We cost no more than a hot-cross bun to them. You saw them when I was poor Mrs. Pierce. They enjoyed themselves being kind to an old lady. It made them feel like good Christian folk. That's worth a few cents, wouldn't you say? And what did you think about that bloody bossy woman who wanted to take me to the station? She was having a great old time being a good Samaritan." Olivia sniffed disdainfully. "I thought it was put on for your benefit. She fancied you, she did."

Murdoch was rather taken aback by that but before he had a chance to comment, Tim, who had been sitting on the bunk, dangling his legs, fell backwards. His entire body was gripped by dreadful spasms so that his head was banging on the bed. Spittle ran from the side of his mouth. Murdoch jumped to his feet, calling to Olivia.

239

"What's happening? Is he having a seizure?"

Neither she nor Ed Parker moved and she said calmly, "Yes. The poor child has fits all the time."

Tim's eyes had rolled back in his head and the spasmodic jerking of his body was violent.

Murdoch grabbed the straw pillow that was on the bed, thinking to put it under the boy's head. "Mrs. Bagley, please do something or tell me what to do."

She put down her teacup and came closer to the bed. Blood was coming from Tim's mouth. She bent over the stricken child, then snapped her fingers.

"Enough, Tim."

As if she had turned off an electric light switch, the jerking stopped. The boy opened his eyes, looked at Murdoch, and grinned. His teeth were red with blood.

"What the deuce . . . ?"

All three plungers burst out laughing. "Fooled you, didn't we?" exclaimed Olivia. "That's another of his good turns. I taught him that one. I seen this boy in the orphanage where I grew up throwing fits so I knew what they looked like."

Murdoch didn't know whether to laugh as well or be annoyed at the trick.

"Tim, you've cut your lip or your tongue."

The boy smiled again with his bloodstained mouth. Then he stuck his finger inside and fished out a rubber nipple. "No, I ain't. I popped this in my mouth when you weren't looking. See."

Gingerly, Murdoch accepted the slimy teat. "How do you do it?"

"It's filled with cherry extract and tied at the end. I just have to bite down is all."

"We used to use real beef blood, but he didn't like the taste," said Olivia. "This does just as well if you aren't too close. Usually I wipe his mouth off and he spits it into my hand. Or he can stow it at the back of his teeth if he has to." She held out her hand and Murdoch gave over the nipple. "We can't afford to waste it." Olivia gave him a gummy smile. "I told you we was in the entertainment business. We took your mind off your troubles for a minute there, didn't we?"

Murdoch had had enough. "They're not my troubles, Mrs. Bagley, they're yours. I'm investigating a murder and you three seem to be implicated."

That certainly got a reaction and they gaped at him. "What you mean, a murder? We ain't killed anybody."

Murdoch pointed at Parker's boots. "Where did you get those?"

Ed shifted uneasily. "I bought them."

"When?"

"I dunno. Last year sometime. I got them at a Jew's shop on Church Street."

He was sitting next to Olivia on the narrow bunk bed, Murdoch was on a stool in between the beds. He stood up. "They belonged to a man who was

241

brutally killed. I'll ask you again, where did you get them?"

Olivia looked alarmed. "Hold on, mister. Ed ain't killed nobody. What makes you think his boots belonged to the stiff?"

"The dead man's boots were taken off his feet and the right one had a brown lace instead of a black because the poor cove had broken his lace that morning and had to use a temporary replacement. That looks exactly like the boot we removed from your foot, Mr. Parker. And your boots don't fit very well, do they? They've rubbed blisters on your heels. How did that happen with year-old boots?"

Ed shrugged. "I dunno."

"He's got a hole in his sock, that's why," said Olivia. "Let me see."

Ed reluctantly pulled his sock from his pocket. It had been darned at the toe and the heel but there was no hole.

"What I meant to say is that he did have a hole but I darned it and the darn must have been rubbing."

"Mrs. Bagley, I am a detective at this station but I'm only one man. The other officers, such as Sergeant Gardiner, have their duties to do. I don't feel as if we're getting anywhere here so I'm thinking I should turn the three of you over to the sergeant and see if he is better at getting the truth out of you."

He could see Tim involuntarily shrink back against the wall and the worried glance he sent to his mother.

242

"Don't be silly," she said briskly to Murdoch. "We're willing to co-operate, aren't we, Ed? But you're not telling us anything. Who was this cove and how and where was he done for?"

"If I tell you that, you can manufacture a story to protect yourselves. "

Olivia shook her head. "We could do that if we had something to hide, but we don't. You've been decent to us and maybe we could repay your kindness by helping you out if we can."

Murdoch knew exactly what she was getting at. "We'll see about that. You tell me the truth with no little darns in it and I'll *consider* dropping charges of public mischief against the three of you, Tim included. But I said consider, not promise. Agreed?"

Nothing seemed to ruffle Olivia, but Murdoch had seen the fear in her eyes. She had been on the wrong side of the law too many times not to know where the real power lay. She nodded at Ed.

"Tell him where you got them boots, Eddie."

"I picked them up in the workhouse on Tuesday night. We'd had a bad couple of days and we had nowhere to go. Livvy and Tim got into the nuns' house, but the men's side was full so I went down to the city workhouse." He paused and looked at Olivia to get the go-ahead.

243

"Well, I was coming in as a casual see, so I had to take a bath and get deloused. It's a bugger, begging your pardon, because I was quite clean and the sulphur chokes up my lungs. But they won't let you in unless you go through it. Anyway all the tramps have to get undressed and put their clothes and boots and hats on a shelf while they're in the bath. There's an attendant who's supposed to watch, but this one was blind as a bat. I seen a good pair of boots that looked my size and mine had got a big hole in the sole. So I did a swap."

"And these were the boots you took?"

"That's right. They're a bit on the small side, but they kept the water out."

"Did you see whose boots they were?"

Ed shook his head. "No, like I said they was all on the shelf."

"And nobody kicked up a fuss?"

"No, I expected them to, but they was quiet as priests who've lost their crosses in the brothel."

Murdoch frowned, not liking Ed's simile. "Do you mean to say that the owner of the boots couldn't afford to admit it?"

"Well, I didn't think that then, but now you're saying they was taken off a stiff it makes sense the cove wouldn't moan."

"And you're sure you don't know who that was?"

"There was a lot of men milling about, the ones going into the bath and the ones getting out. He probably nabbed somebody else's. Tramps are always doing a swap when they can get something better. It goes with the territory."

244

"There you go, he's told you the truth," said Olivia. "Are you going to live up to your end of the bargain?"

"Let you go, you mean. Not likely. It would mean my job. The other officers know what you've been up to."

"Frig. I thought you might be a man of your word."

Olivia looked as if she might haul off and slug him so Murdoch smiled.

"Let's say I'm not releasing you just yet. But if you co-operate I will promise that not only will there be no charges, I might be able to get you a small honorarium for public service."

"What's that?" asked Tim.

"Money, lad."

Olivia stared at Murdoch. "What the hell do you want us to do, put on a show for the inspector?" She sucked in her cheeks. "I do a good imitation of Mary Queen of Scots, come back from the grave. Is that what you had in mind?"

Murdoch laughed. "No. I don't think history is quite up his alley. This is what I have in mind, listen up." He explained his plan and both Olivia and Ed expressed their admiration.

"We'll turn you into a plunger yet," said Olivia, "and I know just the place to go."

There was a tinge of sadistic pleasure in her expression that made Murdoch uneasy.

Chapter Twenty-Seven

OVER THEIR PROTESTS, MURDOCH left Ed and Tim in the cell and set out with Olivia. As they hurried along Wilton Street toward River Street, the widow's veil rippled behind her, like an ominous black sail on a pirate ship.

The second-hand clothes shop Olivia took him to was run by a "sheeny man." *Shop* was giving the place too dignified a name, as it was a derelict stable in a laneway off Sumach. Empty lots flanked it on either side and the house to which it had once belonged was boarded up. There was no sign and the door was closed, but Olivia didn't hesitate. She opened the door just wide enough for them to enter and Murdoch followed her inside. The place was dark and reeked of old manure and old clothes. There was only one oil lamp and in its dim light, Murdoch could just make out the old trousers, shirts, socks that were piled on rickety tables or hung on hooks on the walls. There were so many, Murdoch wondered if half the poorer population of the city had sold their clothes. He hoped nobody he'd ever nabbed came in while he was here. They'd think he'd got the shoot and gloat.

At the rear a man, wrapped in a shawl, was sitting on a high stool. He was hunched over an open brazier and barely made any acknowledgement of their presence. The rest of the shop was empty.

Murdoch recognized him. He'd often seen him trudging the streets with his cart, ringing his bell and calling out for bones, bottles, and rags. He was small, thin, and wiry, probably younger than he first appeared with his long, dark hair and a full, ragged beard.

"Afternoon, Mr. Gold," said Olivia and she threw back her veil, gazed around, and like a swimmer embarking on a refreshing dip, she dived into the chaos, Murdoch following helplessly behind her. Within minutes, she pulled out a pair of worn corduroy trousers from one heap. "These should fit."

Gold said in his hoarse, accented voice. "Everything's been fumigated, missus. No need worry."

Murdoch eyed the trousers doubtfully. "They look as if they belonged to a teamster."

Olivia snorted a friendly contempt. "You ain't lived on charity before, have you? You takes what you can get and make 'em fit. If they're too long, roll 'em up. Tighten them with your belt." She shoved aside some greasy-looking trousers to make room on the table for her find, then moved on to a rack of jackets and suits. A quick sort and she held up a brown-and-white check jacket that must have been owned by a player in a summer vaudeville show. The beer stains down the front were visible even from two feet away. "Here's a coat'll go nice with that brown."

Murdoch was about to protest but thought better of it. He wasn't outfitting himself to make a court appearance.

"How much?" she asked Gold.

"Take trousers and jacket both, yours for one dollar."

"One dollar! Don't make me laugh. I could buy new ones for that."

"Feel coat cloth, missus. What's wrong with you? That's best worsted, only been worn once."

Perhaps he meant that the previous owner had never taken it off, thought Murdoch.

"It's not worth thirty cents," said Olivia and she flung the jacket away in disgust. She scrutinized Murdoch. "Let's see. Perhaps you don't need a jacket. You could get away with wearing that old sealskin coat, it's shabby enough."

Murdoch winced. That coat had stood him in good stead for a long time.

248   "We should change the fedora," added Olivia.

"I've got excellent stock of hats. Very low prices," Gold interjected. "I can't make a living to sell at these prices but for you . . ."

He got down from his stool and squeezed around one of the tables. There was hardly room to move in the small space. He lifted a black felt hat from a lopsided shelf and blew the dust off it. "Here, missus. This one English made. Best quality fur felt."

Olivia took the hat and inspected it. The trim around the crown had long gone and the inside sweatband was dark from use. Murdoch removed his fedora and tried on the new one. It was tight.

"That'll do," Olivia said.

Murdoch adjusted the hat slightly. It had an unpleasant sticky feel to it.

"What have you got in the way of flannel shirts?" Olivia asked Mr. Gold.

"Flannel shirts? Who ever sells me flannel shirts? I've got good linen from gentlemen. Hardly worn. Look here." He poked at a pile of clothes on a nearby table.

Olivia did a rapid and experienced sort of the shirts that were heaped together but none of them satisfied her. Then she picked up a heavy woollen jersey, the kind typically worn in outdoor athletics. Mr. Gold might have been telling the truth about fumigation but he certainly hadn't bothered to clean the goods. This sweater was caked in dried mud, as if its previous owner had come directly off the soccer field.

Olivia beamed. "We'll take this one."

She added it to the pile she was building and continued her exploration, Murdoch trailing behind her

249

feeling peculiarly childlike. Mr. Gold shuffled round the tables, sometimes swooping in to show her a very fine cravat, or a pair of *kashimir* socks. All the time the two of them wrangled with each other about the price, or the quality. Olivia was utterly unmoved by Gold's moans.

"Twenty cents for a pair of threadbare combinations like this! I'll give you a dime and that's being generous."

She took three pairs of socks and at Murdoch's questioning, she whispered, "One pair for your feet, one for your hands, one pair for Ed. You don't mind, do you? They're only two cents each."

Finally, they were done and all that remained was to find a pair of boots. There were three shelves at the back of the shop displaying dozens of boots, all of which retained the shape of their previous owner's feet so that Murdoch felt as if he were looking at the disembodied remains of a defeated army.

Gold glanced at Murdoch's shoes, then picked a pair of scuffed brown boots from the shelf. "These just came in today. Very fine, very fine. See leather lining, keep you warm all winter. For you, forty cents."

Olivia inverted the boots, which were bent up at the toe and worn at the heels.

"Fifteen cents and not a penny more."

"You're ruining me, missus. Twenty or nothing."

"Sold!"

"Shouldn't I make sure they fit first?" asked Murdoch.

She shook her head. "Beggars can't be choosers. You'll have to get used to them."

She went back to the hook where she'd found the check jacket. "If you throw in this, I'll give you a dollar thirty for the lot."

Gold frowned. "Missus, I have wife, five little children. How can I face their sweet hungry faces if I come home with only one dollar and thirty cents? When they say, Poppa, how much you earn today since six o'clock this morning? How I tell them that it was only one dollar and thirty cents? And my wife, she has such pain in her teeth. I must take her to dentist but on one dollar and thirty cents, I cannot do it."

"I thought you told me you had four children?"

"Four, five, what's difference? They all have to eat."

Olivia held up her hand. "One dollar and forty-one cents, for your children's sake."

"Fifty-one cents for my wife's teeth."

"All right. But that's the limit."

Perhaps, Murdoch thought, teeth were her weak spot.

The sale made, Gold gathered the goods to parcel them up.

Murdoch gave the money to Olivia, who in turn handed it over. Murdoch hoped he'd be reimbursed by the inspector, who was apt to fuss about expenses he hadn't authorized in advance.

251

Gold handed him the brown paper parcel. "Good luck to you, mister, whatever you doing. I hope it's legal."

Murdoch followed Olivia out of the shop into the laneway where the air felt blessedly fresh.

"We have to hurry," she said. "If you're going to get into the workhouse, you've got to be there by five o'clock. If there are too many casuals they'll turn you away."

"I'll change at the police station," said Murdoch. "You and Ed can go on ahead so nobody sees us together. I'll arrange for the police matron to look after Tim."

"He can come with me, I won't do a bunk."

"Olivia, I'm not going to put temptation in your way. Tim stays."

"Mr. Murdoch, when you die and they cut you open, they're going to find you don't have a real heart of flesh and blood, they'll find something all black and shrivelled up."

Chapter Twenty-Eight

THERE WAS A FULL-LENGTH MIRROR in the hall outside of the duty room where constables were expected to make sure their uniforms were in order. Murdoch surveyed himself. Crabtree stood behind him.

"I'd arrest a man looking like this, George."

Everything about him appeared seedy; the baggy trousers, the loud check of the stained coat, the rough, high-necked muddy jersey that had a hole in the front, and the shabby black hat drooping low on his forehead.

"You're most convincing, sir, except for your skin colour and your eyes. I'm afraid you look too healthy."

"Not much I can do about it at this late date. I should have consulted Olivia and Parker. At least I didn't trim my moustache yesterday, which I was going to do." He rubbed at his chest. "Damn, I swear this jersey is as scratchy as a hair shirt." He grinned wryly. "Good practice for Lent, I suppose."

He took his belt in another notch. He'd tied string around the trousers below the knees and he looked like a navvy.

"You can have these when I've done, George. They'll fit perfectly. "

"My wife wouldn't let me in the door, sir."

"The worst thing is these bloody boots. My toes feel as if they are in a vice. I can understand why our plunger friend seized the first opportunity to exchange his own boots for some that looked better. The feet set the tone for everything else."

"You believe his story, do you, sir?"

Murdoch nodded. "I'm inclined to. I only hope he's not as good a liar as he is a plunger. If we can find the man he stole the boots from, we might have our murderer."

"I hope the fellow hasn't moved on, sir."

"He'd better not have or all my misery will have been in vain."

Murdoch knew that no tramp would talk freely to him as a police detective and he hoped that going to the workhouse in disguise would work. They might open up if they thought he was one of them.

He looked at the clock on the wall. "I've got to get going. I'll slip out the back way so nobody sees me. I told Parker to go on ahead and get himself a place. Olivia is going to apply for outdoor relief at the local depot and see if she can pick anything up from the other paupers." He scratched again. "Information, I mean, I'm already getting plenty of the other kind."

"If you don't reappear in two days, shall I come in search of you, Sir?"

"You'd better, George. I can't imagine the casual ward at the House of Industry is on a par with the Avonmore."

"You never know. One of the councillors was complaining in the *News* the other day that the casuals are getting better treatment than some decent folk."

"Well, I'm about to find out."

Once he was outside, Murdoch was glad he'd taken Olivia's advice and bought a second pair of socks to wear as mitts. There was a fierce cold wind blowing, but he deliberately didn't protect his face. Twenty minutes wasn't going to turn his skin the colour of tanned leather, but it would have to do. He'd walked no more than ten minutes when he began to hobble. The socks were well darned and that combined with the stiff unyielding boot quickly rubbed a blister on his heel. It was getting close to five when he reached the corner of Bay Street and Elm, sharp stabs of pain shooting up from his foot. A large constable was walking his beat along Dundas Street and Murdoch quickly turned his head away, pretending to wipe his nose with his sleeve. He recognized the policeman from the police games last summer. He'd almost won the fat man's race. Fortunately, he didn't recognize him, but Murdoch was aware that the officer had given him a good once over.

The casuals who were applying for a night's lodging at the House of Industry were expected to go to the rear of the building and when he arrived there, Murdoch groaned. About forty men and a few women were already lined up on each side of the big double doors. Ed Parker was fairly near the front. Crabtree had found him a pair of crutches and he was drooping over them.

Murdoch joined the end of the line. There was a tramp in front of him, with a grizzled beard and shaggy hair sticking out at wild angles from under his plaid cap. His weatherbeaten face was deeply lined, but he was big-boned and seemed strong so it was hard to say what his age was. He nodded in a friendly manner to Murdoch.

"New, are you?"

Murdoch shrugged, not sure which answer, yes or no, would take him further.

"You ain't bin a wayfarer long, I knows that," said the man.

"Just got the bird two months ago," replied Murdoch.

"Wife and nippers to feed, I bet."

"You've hit the nail on the head."

The man scrutinized Murdoch for a few moments, his grey eyes disconcertingly shrewd. "What did you do before you was sent packing?"

"I was a lumberjack up in Huntsville. Good one, if I do say so myself. Then I went and hurt my back. The

256

bloody bosses said it was my own fault and they wouldn't wait for me to get better. Out I go, arse over turkey. So I came down to the Queen city, see if I could get work."

"Family still up there, are they?"

"That's right."

"You ain't going to be much help to 'em in the workhouse."

"I know that, but I'm not gonna be much help if I starve to death either, am I?"

A shambling youth in front of them suddenly giggled and at first Murdoch thought it was in response to his mild witticism, but then he recognized the loose smile and vacant eyes of a simpleton. If his brother Bertie had lived, he would have been like this man, although, God forbid, Murdoch wouldn't have let him beg for a bed in the workhouse. The lad saw his glance and ducked his head quickly.

"Don't mind him," said the tramp. "He'd laugh if a bird shit on his head, wouldn't you, Alfred?" The simpleton giggled again in delight, but Murdoch was glad the tramp's voice had been kind not contemptuous. "We need folks like him in this gloomy world, where men haul off and kill each other over an eggshell."

"Or a pair of boots." Murdoch thought he'd throw in a little bait.

The other man grimaced. "When you've been a tramp longer, you'll know *that* is a very good reason

257

for killing somebody. Good boots is worth their weight in gold." He looked down at Murdoch's feet. "Yours ain't so good, brother, if you don't mind me saying so."

"They're bloody vile. I might as well be wearing horse shoes."

Alfred was giggling up a storm as they talked and he was drawing attention to them, which was something Murdoch didn't want. He stuck out his hand to the older tramp.

"My name's Williams." The tramp had a dirty old sack, tied at the neck with string, slung over his shoulder and he lowered it to the ground. He was wearing filthy woollen mittens, cut off at the fingers.

"Jack Trevelyan at your service, but everybody calls me Traveller. Like name like nature." They shook hands. The tramp's grip was strong and Murdoch lowered the estimate of his age a few years.

"Alf, shake hands with our new friend Williams," Traveller said to the simpleton, who promptly grabbed Murdoch's hand and pumped it vigorously, smiling happily.

"Good morning, good morning to you."

Finally, he let go and began to stare into space, muttering to himself words that Murdoch couldn't understand.

"Wouldn't have any baccy on you, would you?" Traveller asked.

258

Murdoch started to reach in his pocket, then he realized he'd left his pipe and pouch back at the station in his own clothes.

"No, I don't. Sorry."

"No need to be sorry, they won't let us smoke anyway, but I was gonna warn you that if you did have a pinch you should hide it. They're not above searching your pockets and if they find baccy or booze, out you go. Same with money. If you've got more than a few coins, you'd better stow it in your boot. They'll take it from you otherwise. You have to be skint to stay the night."

"I don't have a cent on me."

Murdoch hoped his nefarious plan would be excused by the seriousness of his investigation. Heaven forbid he be a burden on the taxpayers.

He glanced at the lineup in front of them. Many of the men were carrying sacks with billy cans tied to them.

"What've you got in your sack?" he asked Traveller. "Your good clothes?"

The tramp laughed, showing a sparse crop of stained teeth. "I don have any clothes but these uns on me back. It's mostly old newspapers I'm carrying. You never know when they'll come in handy. That and me tin which I use for me tea and sugar. I've got me pipe in there and me baccy pouch, but they're wrapped in the papers so I'm hoping they won't find it."

"Do they always search?"

"'Course they do, but they leave the job to the old-timers who live here and have to work off their keep. Most of them, thank the Lord, are usually too feeble to know what they're doing. What they're really on the

259

MAUREEN JENNINGS

lookout for is the demon drink. You're crossed off the list
for the rest of the season if you try to smuggle in liquor.
'Course that ain't so hard if you know how."

Two men joined the line behind them. One was
young and rough-looking and Murdoch could see he'd
been in a fight recently. There was a goose egg over his
eye and a raw scrape on his jaw. His companion was
older and his face had the purplish colour and puffy
look of a drunkard and he smelled like it too. He'd heard
this last remark.

"It's bleeding hard to get through the night. No baccy,
no grog, no food. We're supposed to go to sleep, but
how can you when you're sharing a ward with forty men
whose bellies are rumbling like a goddam army band
and whose nerves are screaming for a bit of comfort?"

"Don't we get any supper?" Murdoch asked in dismay.
This was another thing he hadn't taken into consideration
and he hadn't had anything to eat since this morning.

"God forbid any of us tobies should be treated like
human beings," growled the other tough. "It's tea and
turn out here. It'd cost all the fat coves too much dash
if us had a bit of food in our bellies before bed. Sean
here is right. You ain't going to get much sleep, what
with the bronchitis, the consumption, the drunks craving
their tots. You'll see." He touched his knuckles to his
forehead the way sailors do. "Name's Bettles. My partner's Sean Kearney."

"Williams." Murdoch was prepared to shake hands,

260

but the other man made no move to do so. Instead he jabbed his finger at Traveller. "You, I know."

Traveller returned the salute but his expression was mocking. "Old pals, aren't we, Ned? How'd you get that mouse? Did you win?"

Bettles scowled. "None of your business."

"He ran into a door," said his pal. "Ned won."

Bettles rubbed his hands together. He had no gloves. "Ain't they open yet? It's frigging perishing."

It was much colder now that the last vestige of daylight was gone and neither of the newcomers had overcoats.

"We wouldn't be standing out here if they was open, would we," said Traveller.

"You might be. You gaggers all look ignorant enough."

Murdoch stiffened at this gratuitous bit of nastiness, but Jack grinned in such a way that the display of his yellowing canines gave the impression he'd use them if he had to.

"Ah brother, we are but mirrors," Traveller said.

Before Bettles could respond, there was a shifting and ripple of movement down the lineup and Murdoch saw that one of the doors had opened. A tall man in a long black mackintosh and black leather cap stepped through. He held up his hands for attention, which he got immediately.

"For those of you who are new here, I'm Gowan and I'm your tramp major. That means you listen to me if you know what's good for you. Now, I'm telling you right now we don't brook no insubordination here so don't think you can break the rules and get away with it. You won't. Rules are to be obeyed. For your own good, mind you. We've got everybody's welfare at heart here. And no bellyaching about the bed or the food. You're bloody lucky you're being given a free place for the night. Bloody lucky. I don't get anything for free. I work. Is that clear? Do we all know where we stand?"

Some of the men nodded but most didn't respond. Murdoch saw anger cross Bettles's face. Traveller didn't show any expressions but he muttered, "I know for sure I'm bloody well standing outside the bloody workhouse, mate. That is very clear to me. I'm not confused about that at all."

Alf giggled and Murdoch grinned at him, but the others were too intent on watching Gowan.

"Hands up if you were here last night."

A dozen or so men held up their hands, including Traveller, Kearney, and Bettles. Good, thought Murdoch, that limited the number of men he had to watch.

"You repeaters, you know what to do then," said Gowan. "You get to go into the bathhouse first. Chances are you'll be less filthy than those who are here for the first time although some of you will get lousy in twenty-four hours if I know anything about it." He stepped back. "Come on then. Report to Hastings at door A. The rest of you lot go in door B and give your name to the man there. Tell him where

262

you've come from and where you're going to after here."

"Heaven, I hope," whispered Traveller. "They'll be sure not to run into Mr. Gowan there."

The men started to move in the direction of the gate, but Gowan raised his arms and bellowed again. "Hold on, where's your manners?" He put his hand to his eyes as if he were searching for something. "Any ladies here?" He guffawed. "No, of course not. You women then, come on through. Door on the right."

Three women, all elderly, shuffled through the gate, their heads bent, their bodies shrunk into their shawls.

Gowan let them through, then stepped aside from the gate. "Let's move, you toffs." There was a surge forward and Murdoch was forced to move with them, not sure what to do next. It wouldn't do him much good to be with the newcomers. He was saved by Traveller, who caught him by the sleeve.

"Get in with the repeat group. The bath's a lot cleaner if you're in first."

"I'm not registered."

"Leave it to me."

Behind the iron gates was the lumberyard where Murdoch knew the casuals were expected to chop and cut wood during the day to earn their keep. The so-called labour test had been in existence for two years now and the city councillors considered it a great success. The elderly and infirm were excused, but the others had to work or leave.

On the far side of the yard were two arches and in front of each one was an elderly man in a black mackintosh and beakless cap like Gowan's. They held ledgers in front of them. The smaller group of tramps moved to the archway on the left, which had a large A over the lintel. Parker was hopping on his crutches and he'd exchanged a quick glance with Murdoch as he was pushed past him by the throng of men. At the entrance, they stopped abruptly and formed a ragged line. Bettles and Kearney had shoved to the front, but Traveller had got a firm grip on Murdoch's arm and they were close behind.

"Hurry up, goddamn it," said Bettles as the elderly clerk fumbled with the pages in the ledger. He was checked off, Kearney followed, and behind him came Alfred, who for all his simplemindedness knew enough to muscle his way to the front of the line. Next was Traveller.

"Jack Trevelyan," he said and the clerk began to search for the name.

Traveller leaned over and pointed with his finger. "There I am. And there's the fellow behind me. Thompson, Joseph." He turned around to Murdoch. "Right, mate?"

"Right."

The clerk gazed at Murdoch with bleary eyes. "I don't remember –"

264   "Come on, Hastings," called one of the remaining men. "We're freezing out here. Check him off, for God's sake."

The clerk did so and with Traveller leading the way, Murdoch went through archway A.

Chapter Twenty-Nine

TRAVELLER HAD MURDOCH by the sleeve, which was just as well because the men were shoved and pushed as they hurried toward the stairs at the far end of a whitewashed corridor. The new casuals were slower getting through their arch because their names had to be written down, but two or three of them came through their door at the farther end and some of the men in Murdoch's group yelled at them to keep back. They scrambled down a short flight of steps, turned at a sharp angle, and went through yet another door that another palsied elderly man held open for them. He was bleating feebly, "Gentlemen, slow down, please slow down," but nobody paid him any heed.

Murdoch was thrust through into a long, dimly lit room. The air was suffocatingly humid, which felt good after the cold, but there was a strong smell of carbolic that made his eyes sting. At the far end of the room were two huge boilers and facing them a row of bathtubs, partitioned by wooden walls. The tubs were already filled with steaming water. To the right was a set of shelves and next to them stacks of wooden boxes. He was pushed toward the shelves where another nabber in a holland apron was calling out, "Put your clothes in a box. Don't forget your chit. All clothes in the box. Boots on the shelves." The men started to strip off their clothes.

Traveller grabbed two boxes and gave one to Murdoch. Looped around the handle was a strip of leather with a wooden numbered chit. Traveller unfastened it. "Don't lose this. Hang it around your neck. You won't get your clothes back until the morning. They fumigate them." He grinned. "We're cleaner than most good citizens, if you ask me."

Murdoch took off the fedora and his sealskin overcoat and dropped them into the box. There was a long bench underneath the shelves where several men were sitting and removing their boots. Murdoch could see how easy it would be to switch his for somebody else's. Most of the boots were shabby and in bad condition, which confirmed his suspicion that the original owner of the good boots Parker had stolen would have raised a ruckus unless it was in his interest not to do so. All of the tramps, including Traveller, had strips of cloth wound around their toes and as they unwrapped them, Murdoch recoiled at the stench. Their clothes might be fumigated but they weren't washed.

Caught up in the surrounding sense of urgency, Murdoch peeled off his mud-caked jersey and trousers and struggled out of his union suit. Traveller was on one side of him, Alf on the other. Ed seemed to have been shoved to the end of the row and was hopping awkwardly as he tried to get his trousers off without putting his sprained ankle to the ground.

Alf, giggling nonstop, was already naked. His body was soft and hairless but his torso was dotted with bedbug bites. Traveller was wearing a truss and he hung it up on a peg, then tapped Murdoch on the arm. "Come on, take that tub at the end. It's warmer by the boiler."

He padded off across the floor, which was some kind of hard granite tile, and headed for the line of bathtubs, half of which were already occupied. Traveller's body was pallid except for his weathered neck and lower arms. Murdoch was shocked to see a crisscross of stripes across his back. Jack Trevelyan had been flogged at some point in his life. Murdoch hurried after him to the adjoining tub. The water was very hot and he jerked his foot back when it touched the surface. Then he gritted his teeth and climbed in, slowly lowering his rear end into the bath. There was just enough water to cover his hips and he saw his legs turn red. The carbolic in the water caused his blistered heels to sting painfully.

267

"You 'ave ten minutes. 'Ere is soap," said a voice at this ear. Another nabber. He had a French accent and his hair and moustache were thick and dark, worn long the way favoured by the Frenchies at the logging camp. He gave Murdoch a small piece of soap and shuffled off to the next tub. He limped badly and Murdoch could see his left foot was twisted inward.

Murdoch rubbed the soap between his palms. It was poor quality, gave as much lather as a stone, and smelled strongly of tar, but he washed as best he could, then sank down into the hot water. At home, he usually bathed once a week on Saturdays, in a small zinc tub in the kitchen. The workhouse bathtub was longer and he could stretch out his legs. It seemed that he had been in the water hardly more than two minutes when he heard a shrill whistle and the Frenchman called, "*Finis. Finis.* Out, if you please. Next group in."

Another small ghostly man appeared around the partition with towels over his arm. He handed one to Murdoch and moved away.

"Come on, mate, get a move on," a wiry little man, very hairy with bandy legs was already standing by the tub and Murdoch was obliged to get out. He wrapped himself in the thin, rough towel and headed back to the bench. From there he had a view of all of the tubs. The first group of occupants was getting out and was quickly replaced. Murdoch saw Ed Parker get into his tub, grimacing with the effort. He'd followed on the most elderly of the tramps, who had smelled gamey from a few paces and Murdoch didn't envy him.

Traveller was drying himself off and he pointed to a stack of nightshirts. "Get one of those."

Frenchie stopped him. "No dress yet, monsieur. The doctor must examine you."

Murdoch looked over at Traveller in dismay. The big man shrugged.

"They'll be most likely checking for small pox. There was a case at one of the country workhouses last week."

The door to the corridor opened and in came a slight, grey-haired man who wore spectacles and stooped slightly. It was Dr. Uzziel Ogden. Murdoch turned to the bench as if he were looking for his boots and got his astonishment under control. He didn't think the doctor would betray him, but he couldn't be certain.

Suddenly Frenchie gave a shout and pointed to the second tub. The one that Parker was in.

"Monsieur Doctor, come quick."

Ogden rushed over and Murdoch saw that Ed was lying with his head under the water.

"Get him out, he's drowned," called the doctor. Frenchie and Ogden grabbed Parker's arms and hauled him into a sitting position. His eyes were closed and his chest wasn't moving.

"He's not breathing. Help us, here," said Ogden and willing hands took Parker by the legs and Parker was hauled out of the tub and laid on the wet floor. It was all Murdoch could do to hold back but he had to.

269

MAUREEN JENNINGS

Ogden knelt down beside the prone man, turned his head to one side and began to lift Parker's arms up and down over his head in a pumping action. He did this several times, then with a splutter Ed opened his mouth and water poured out.

Ogden thumped him hard on the chest, causing him to cough violently. After a few moments, he sat up.

"What on earth happened?" asked the doctor.

"I, er, I don't know, sir. I must have slipped and banged my head."

"My God, man, you could have drowned." The doctor spoke as angrily as if Parker had brought this on himself. Which of course he had. "We'd better not take any chances. Let's get him to the infirmary. Can you walk?"

"I believe so, sir. I mean, I have sprained my ankle but that's got nothing to do with drowning."

"Frenchie, help him."

"I'd be grateful if you'd come too, sir," said Parker. "I am feeling a bit dizzy, if truth be told."

Ogden tutted but didn't refuse. "Put a shirt on him," he said to the nabber. "And get his crutches." Once dressed, Ed hopped slowly out of the bathhouse, supported by the two men.

Murdoch exhaled deeply in relief. "Hey, I'm getting cold, can't we get out of here?"

"I don't know, the doctor . . ." said the elderly attendant who'd let them in.

270

There was a loud knocking on the other door and somebody shouted, "Hurry up." The nabber jumped. "Get your nightshirts then."

Murdoch slipped his over his head. It was a heavy linen and fell to his feet, but it didn't smell too clean, as if the laundry was two tramps ago.

"Put on your boots and come this way," said the nabber, and he opened the door Parker and the doctor had taken. The casuals followed him down a short, cold corridor, to yet another door, which the attendant unlocked. Murdoch felt as if he were in a jail. This door opened into a long, high-ceilinged room filled with narrow beds, each spaced about four feet from the other. Between each bed was a commode bucket. The floor was covered with a worn oilcloth. Two large clocks hung at each end of the whitewashed room. The narrow, high windows were curtainless. Like the bathhouse, the dormitory was pungent with sulphur and carbolic.

Traveller beckoned to Murdoch and led the way to the centre of the long aisle where a large woodstove blocked the way. Alf trailed behind them and Bettles and Ward were close at his heels.

"It gets cold in here during the night," said Traveller. "Better to have a bed near the stove."

He pulled back the thin grey blanket on one of the beds and got under the cover. There were no sheets or cases for the pillows. The other men were also starting

271

to get into bed, even the young farm labourer. Murdoch sat on the bed next to the tramp's. "My God, Traveller, it's only six o'clock."

"They'll wake us up at six in the morning and like the man told you, you probably won't get much sleep. There ain't anything else to do anyway except get some kip. Goodnight to you."

He pulled up the blanket so that it completely covered his face.

The next batch of men was arriving now and they began to choose their beds. Alf had taken the one beside Murdoch, but he was sitting up, propped against the wall, watching, greeting some of the newcomers with his facile smile. Ned Bettles and his pal Kearney had taken the beds across the narrow aisle from Murdoch and they were lying on top of their blankets.

"Oi, Williams, did you bring any baccy in with you?"

The old nabber who had let them in heard that. "I will remind you men that no smoking or drinking is allowed."

"We know that, old man, no need to shake your fetters. But I need to make my water."

"You must use the commodes provided for that purpose," fussed the man.

Bettles swung his legs off the bed and lifted the lid of the pail beside the bed.

"Hey. Somebody forgot to empty it," he scowled.

The nabber scuttled over to inspect. Murdoch could see that the pail was indeed almost full.

"Nothing we can do about that now. You'll have to use somebody else's if you have to."

He turned to Murdoch, who had stretched out his legs. "You are not allowed to put your boots on the beds."

Murdoch knew the poor old man was only doing his job, but he was irritatingly fussy.

"What other rules am I supposed to know?"

"No spitting is allowed and you must use the commode provided."

"So I understand."

The old man didn't react to his sarcasm, but he said earnestly, "Lights will be extinguished at nine o'clock. After that time, there is to be no talking. Silence must be kept."

He hurried off to scold a young newcomer who had got onto one of the beds with his boots on.

Murdoch removed his own and stowed them underneath his bed. The nightshirt was itchy and he felt peculiar to be going to bed at this time of night. Some of the men were talking to each other, but they were the new casuals. The regular tramps didn't talk, not even Bettles and his companion. They got in the beds and like Traveller immediately got underneath the blankets.

Murdoch leaned back and looked up at the dark windows. His stomach rumbled and he realized he was 273 very hungry. It was going to be a long night.

Chapter Thirty

THERE WAS NOWHERE ELSE to sit except on the narrow, hard bed and the ward wasn't that warm so after a little while, Murdoch followed Traveller's example and got under the blanket. Candles were burning in the wall sconces but they were inferior wax and threw off little light. He shifted, trying to make himself comfortable. He would have liked his pipe; he would have liked one of Katie's hot stews, but most of all he wished he had something to read. There was nothing to do except go to sleep and it was only a quarter past six.

"You're looking like you've lost your best friend." Traveller had opened his eyes and was grinning at Murdoch. "Finding the life a little quiet, are you?"

"Like the grave. I'm tempted to rouse all the men and start up some sea shanties. That'd liven things up."

"You'd get thrown out in no time. The bosses don't like rowdy behaviour. You might get away with singing a few hymns, but you'll have a hard time finding many in this bunch who know the words. Besides, hymns aren't popular with this lot of unrepentant sinners. They've had them stuffed down their gobs too many times and had to act grateful . . . Just a minute, this'll cheer you up." He brought his hand from underneath the blanket and keeping whatever it was hidden in his fist, he handed something to Murdoch. "Be careful. There's always somebody ready to do a Judas for an extra bowl of soup." He pressed a small vial into Murdoch's palm, then rolled onto his back and closed his eyes. "Save some for me," he muttered.

Murdoch glanced around him. As far as he could tell in the poor light, nobody was watching him. He waited a few minutes, surreptitiously unscrewed the top of the vial, then slid down the bed and pulled the blanket over his head. Carefully, he took a couple of sips from the bottle and almost choked as a burning liquid hit his throat. He struggled to suppress his coughing and waited while the fire in his empty belly raged. Still under cover of the blankets, he replaced the top of the bottle. *Save some for me*, indeed. One sip would last him a week.

He felt a tap on his shoulder and pulled the blanket down to nose level. Traveller was leaning across the gap between the beds.

"You all right?"

"What the hell was that?"

The tramp chuckled. "It's homemade. I got it from a toby in the country. He calls it witch's milk. Powerful, ain't it?"

The burning in his gut was subsiding a little now and Murdoch was feeling a bit light-headed.

"If you've had enough, give it back to me. Don't let it be seen," said Traveller.

Murdoch handed over the little bottle. "How did you smuggle it in here?"

"Easy. My truss comes in handy."

Murdoch felt a spasm of uneasiness at the memory of how warm the vial had been. Traveller disappeared underneath his blanket and Murdoch heard a smothered cough. A few minutes later, the tramp's head reappeared, his face even redder than before.

"That'll make you forget your troubles in no time."

Murdoch burst out laughing. "It'll make you forget more than your troubles if you drink too much of it. What is it?"

"It's a secret formula, but I think my chum makes it from potatoes."

Alf giggled from the next bed. He hadn't been asleep after all. "Can I have some?"

"No, you cannot," said Traveller. "We drank it all." He pushed down the blanket and sat up. "I'm wide awake now. That's the sinister side of that drink. It don't put you to sleep right away."

The simpleton bounced on his bed like a child. "Will

276

you tell us a story, Mr. Traveller? Mr. Williams hasn't heard your yarns before."

Murdoch seized the opportunity the boy was giving him. "Great idea, I'd like that, as I'm awake now myself."

"What story do you want, Alf?" Traveller's voice was indulgent. Even in the dim light of the candle, Murdoch could see the tramp's eyes were glistening. He must have taken a really good slug of the witch's milk.

"Tell him how you got your stripes. That's a good one."

Murdoch laughed. "I have to admit I was curious about them myself. They look kind of severe."

"Thirty-five lashes. Fifteen the first time, twenty the second, and I got them while I was detained at Her Majesty's pleasure. Now I suppose you want to know what I was doing in the penitentiary?"

"If you want to tell me."

"Why wouldn't I? I ain't ashamed. Not everybody who goes to jail is a criminal, you know."

Not wanting to stop him, Murdoch nodded sympathetically.

Traveller settled himself more comfortably and laced his fingers across his chest. "I was born and bred in Newfoundland, but I left when I was fourteen. No future there that I could see. My family was most wiped out by the influenza so there was nobody to weep for me. I signed up on a whaler. Got to see a lot of the world. I was a hot head, drank too much even for a sailor, but I was doing well on the ship. You can make

277

a lot of money on just one voyage if you're lucky. But then, like now, there's always some cove who wants to pull down a big healthy lad and in back then, it was the first mate, a weasel fart-catcher of a bastard who took a scunner to me from the moment I put my foot on the deck. Like I said, I was always a hot head and I took exception to the sneers and the duties I'd pull, which were always the coldest and the messiest. According to him, they was never done right so I was always up on some charge or other and me pay docked. He was always ready to hand me a stotter to the head if he thought I looked at him the wrong way. One night, he went too far and shoved me headfirst into a bucket of fish guts. I took exception and turned around and slugged him."

"Hooray," exclaimed Alf in delight and he boxed the air with his fists.

Traveller continued to stare up at the ceiling. "So the cove, he fell down, cracked his ugly head on the mast. He's a drivelling idiot for the rest of his life. I was charged and sent down, but the captain gave me a good testimonial so I only got three years and a bit of triangulation. Fifteen stripes. I wouldn't have got that except I wouldn't eat humble pie. Why should I? I was defending myself."

278   He paused and Murdoch saw that even after so many years, he was still bitter about his treatment.

"Well, like I said, I've bin given thirty-five all told. Those first ones for standing up for myself, the other twenty for the same reason. Near the end of my sentence, I took on a guard who could have been the kith and kin of the first mate. He wanted to stick my head in the piss bucket. I refused and another three years was added on to my sentence for that little tap."

Alf laughed in delight. "Some little tap. I know your little taps, Traveller."

The tramp frowned. "Be quiet, Alf. Our friend here will get the impression I'm a violent man, which I ain't."

Trevelyan was presenting himself as a wronged man and Murdoch wondered how true that was.

"Like I said, Mr. Williams, I was a hot head in those days, but I'm as meek as a lamb now. Fighting ain't worth the trouble it brings."

"But you'd do it again, surely? You couldn't stand for that kind of treatment."

"That's the truth, I couldn't, but I have a cooler head now and I'm more canny about seeing trouble coming. The tobies all know I won't put up with shite and they keep their distance."

"They're ascared of him," chirped Alf.

"Anything else you want to know, son?" Traveller asked Murdoch.

"How'd you end up a casual?"

"Same way you have, I don't wonder. I'd lost my appetite for the sea when I came out of the peg, but I couldn't get a job that was steady. I never was much good about gaffers, but when I came out the aversion

279

was even stronger and I couldn't abide any man who always had to prove he was boss. If they paid fair and treated me decent, I'd work for them and willingly, but that kind of cove was hard to find. To most of them I was as low as an un-baptized savage. They acted surprised sometimes that I could even understand English. Given that I also like to keep on the move, that I get stir crazy now if I stay in one place too long, you have what you see here, a wayfarer, as they like to call us."

"Hooray," said Alf again. He'd spoken too loud and Bettles, who was in the bed opposite, growled out a curse. The dormitory was quieter now, most of the men seemed to be resigned to going to sleep.

"It must be a hard life," Murdoch said softly.

"Not if you know the ropes, it ain't so bad." Traveller winked at him. "You ain't said much about yourself though."

"Not much to tell." Murdoch braced himself for the questions he expected to come at him, but the tramp suddenly yawned.

"Why don't we save it till the morning? I'm in need of my kip, now while I can. Alf, you lie down and close your eyes, do you hear me?"

"Yes, Mr. Traveller." The boy immediately slid under his blanket. "Good night, Mr. Williams."

"Good night, Alf. Good night, Traveller."

The tramp rolled over onto his side and grunted a response. Murdoch lay back. He was feeling ravenous.

He sighed and rolled over onto his stomach to flatten the emptiness. The sour smell from his pillow was nauseating, but there wasn't anything he could do about it.

Murdoch didn't know what time it was because the room was too dark to see the clock, but he felt that he hadn't slept long. He hadn't been able to fall asleep after Traveller's story and was still awake when the old nabber had come in to blowout the candles at nine o'clock. After that, he'd tossed and turned for what seemed like more than an hour. Silence must be observed, the attendant had said, but the dormitory was noisy. Men snoring, talking in their sleep, getting up to make copious water in the bucket. One man had the deep racking cough of the consumptive that he knew all too well from hearing Arthur Kitchen's for the past four years. Somebody at the end of the row had a nightmare and had started crying out. Two or three men closer to him shouted curses at the fellow, whoever he was. Alf giggled nervously even in his sleep.

Traveller was right about the room getting cold. The stove was not stoked up and drafts poured through the gaps around the window frames. One blanket was not enough and Murdoch wished he had his own warm quilt. Added to all that, the straw mattress was prickly and hard. Was this all worth it? he wondered. So far he hadn't come across any new evidence. Ed's departure

281

for the infirmary had saved Murdoch's bacon, but it also meant Ed hadn't identified his own boots. The description Mrs. Bright had given of a tramp walking across the Gardens could fit anyone of a dozen men here, as could that of the man Mr. Swanzey had encountered in the greenhouse. He tried to cheer himself up with the hope that his suspect was here, one of the handful of men who were repeaters.

Murdoch sensed rather than heard somebody beside the bed. He opened his eyes, saw a silhouette of a man bending toward him. He had something in his raised hand. With one swift movement, Murdoch rolled onto the floor, dropping into a crouch, and straining to see in the dark. The figure backed away and he heard a familiar giggle.

"Alf, what the hell are you doing?"

Murdoch tried to keep his voice low but the youth had startled him. Anger followed.

"You said you was hungry," whispered Alf. "So I was going to surprise you and put a piece of bread under your pillow." He showed a crust to Murdoch. "I smuggled it in my boot, but I wrapped it up good in some newspaper."

Murdoch got to his feet. "That was kind of you, but I'll wait until morning. Why don't you go back to bed."

"Yes, why don't we?" growled a voice from the bed across from them. Murdoch heard the scratch of a match and a light flared, illuminating Bettles's face.

282

There was a sconce directly behind his bed and he reached up and lit the candle.

"What the hell's going on?" Kearney stirred in the adjacent bed and also sat up.

"Little Alf was having a tryst with his sweetheart."

"He was giving me a piece of bread," said Murdoch.

"My, touchy, aren't we?" Bettles turned to Kearney. "What do you think, Sean? Have we uncovered a couple of nancy boys?"

Kearney swung his legs over the side of his bed. Bettles did the same. The simpleton knew exactly what was in store for him. He dropped to the floor and scuttled underneath his bed, whimpering like a frightened dog.

Somehow, Bettles had managed to smuggle one of the bathhouse towels into the dormitory. He'd covered his pillow with it and now he pulled the towel away and began to twist it into a rope.

"Perhaps these two need a bit of a lesson, Sean."

Kearney had a towel as well and he picked it up and started to twist it. "I'd say that's a good and necessary thing to do."

Both men stepped across the aisle, blocking any chance Murdoch might have to get away from the wall. He was trapped between Traveller's bed and his own, both of which had heavy metal frames bolted to the floor. He had nothing to defend himself with except the thin pillow and he grabbed this and held it in front of himself.

283

Bettles grinned. "Fat lot of good that's going to do you, Mr. Nancy Boy. This is the casual ward, or did you forget? I'll split that thing in two with one swing."

The moment hung in the balance, Murdoch on his feet, ready for the attack, the two men opposite him, just as ready to move in on him. Nobody had raised his voice and the rest of the ward appeared to be fast asleep.

As far as Murdoch knew, that included Traveller, but suddenly, with as quick and easy a movement as Kearney had made, he sat up and pushed away the blanket.

"Put it down, Bettles, that'd be despoiling of public property and we can't have that, can we?" His bare feet dangled over the edge of his bed. He was no longer a young man, but at that moment, nobody would have doubted his ability to make good his command. In his hand, a blade gleamed dully in the light of the candle. It was a razor.

Bettles grimaced. "I ain't got no truck with you, Traveller. This fellow's a Miss Molly."

"No he ain't."

"Alfie here was a going to climb in bed with him."

"No he weren't. The lad's as simple as a puppy dog. Now, I suggest we all calm down and get some kip. Before you know it, we'll be called."

Traveller got off the bed with such speed that both Bettles and Kearney jumped back.

"Suit yourself," said Bettles. "He's in the bed next to *you*, not me."

284

If Traveller hadn't been blocking the way, Murdoch would have swung a punch at the man and hang the consequences, but neither Bettles nor Kearney were within reach. They slowly eased back to their own beds, allowing the towels to untwist.

"Maybe we'd better leave the candle lit," said Traveller. "Just so we know there won't be anybody wandering around where they shouldn't. And I mean anybody."

Alf giggled and stuck his head out from under the bed.

"You can come out now," said Traveller. "Get into your own bed and don't stir till sun-up even if the whole ward is starving. Do you understand me?"

"Yes, Mr. Traveller."

Alf scrambled into bed and Traveller sat back down.

"Thank you," said Murdoch.

Murdoch looked over at Bettles and Kearney, who were stretched out on their beds, as ready and alert as wolves. Had they guessed he was a police officer and used Alf as an excuse to trounce him?

"Don't worry about them two," said Traveller. "I've had all the sleep I want. You can get some more kip and I'll make sure our friends don't move."

"No, I'll do it. I'm wide awake myself. What have we got, another two hours until the call? I'll stay up."

It was true what he said. He was hardly going to fall asleep when the man in the next bed possessed a vicious-looking open razor that he clearly would have

285

no hesitation in using and two husky thugs across from him wanted to see blood.

Traveller shrugged. "Suit yourself. Wake me if you need to. Don't even let those two take a piss." He lay down and pulled his blanket up around his shoulders. "Don't let that fool boy bring me his mucky sandwich either."

Chapter Thirty-One

THOMAS HICKS COULD SEE HIS WIFE, *Emily, sitting across from him at the table. He felt terribly ill and knew he'd vomited down his nightshirt. He couldn't catch his breath no matter how hard he tried and his head was throbbing so violently he was afraid his skin would split apart at the temples. He tried to cry out for help, but Emily didn't seem to notice. She was drinking her tea in that dainty precise way he remembered so well. He knew that his bladder and bowels had voided and he was ashamed even in front of her. He wanted to move, to stand up and get away from the pain in his chest, but he couldn't.*

She put down her cup and saucer and folded her hands neatly in her lap.

"Have you come for me at last, dearest?" he managed to ask her.

"Yes, Tom, I have, " she said and her smile was so sweet, his eyes filled with tears and he wept.

———

"Sleep that knits up the ravelled sleeve of care." Murdoch had studied *Macbeth* in the fifth standard. Brother Julian, who was stupefyingly dull, had taught the class and he and his pupils had never progressed beyond the thorny hedge of the unfamiliar language. Brother Julian seemed to find Shakespeare as foreign and uninteresting as they did. However, just once, the play had come alive when quite out of the blue, the Brother said that Shakespeare had understood, even in that long ago time, how disease of the soul can affect sleep. "Macbeth hath murdered sleep," proclaimed the Brother, his voice unusually resonant. "His guilty conscience prevents him from sleeping."

Murdoch had suffered from insomnia as long as he could remember, and Brother Julian's remark had thrown him into a dark period as he tried to discover if his own soul was indeed sick and, if so, how he could heal it. Fortunately for him, there was a priest, Father Malone, who was attached to the school, had listened to the young boy's painful confessions, reassured him, and absolved him. But the insomnia never went away and many a night Murdoch found himself lying awake, waiting for dawn to come when he could fall asleep.

288 He thumped at the scrawny pillow as he tried to get more comfortable. Staying awake this time was a choice, which made matters a little easier, but he still felt the familiar twist of utter loneliness in his guts. He was

sharing a room with about sixty other men, but he felt alone, the perpetual outsider. What would they do if they knew he was spying on them? Did he have copper written all over him? He hoped not. He thought his own cover story was plausible and they'd seemed to accept it. He could just make out the shape of Bettles and Kearney across the aisle. They were both lying still and their sleep seemed genuine. Traveller was on his back, snoring softly, his breathing deep. Murdoch owed him a debt now for his intervention. From the beginning, he had been most friendly. Was he like that with every newcomer or was he currying favour? Did *he* suspect the truth?

Murdoch could hear Alf, in the next bed, snuffling and whimpering periodically in his sleep like the puppy Traveller had called him. Murdoch let his thoughts drift. He wondered if anybody was awake at home. Katie might be tending to the twins. Perhaps Amy had got up again and was helping her. She was so good with the babies. Murdoch grinned to himself. She wasn't like any teacher he'd known. The nuns at his school were strict, but in the early years he was a studious and obedient boy and he'd liked school and done well. It was later, when his Aunt Weldon had sent him to study with the Christian Brothers, that school descended into unremitting misery. Murdoch chafed at the strict and unjust rules, the capricious dishing out of punishments, but above all, he loathed what he perceived as the superstitious ignorance of the Brothers. Most of his teachers seemed poorly educated, hardly one step ahead of their pupils. He began to challenge them, to speak back, and almost every day he was caned for some infraction, supposed rudeness, or simply because that day the Brother felt like beating his pupils. The worst, the man who became his hated enemy was Brother Edmund, a big-boned, hard-faced man who before he'd found his calling had worked for a horse breeder somewhere in Alberta. This Brother boasted that there wasn't a horse or a boy he couldn't break. Murdoch had desperately wanted to prove him wrong, but the contest was impossibly unequal. By the end of his second year, Murdoch knew he had only three choices. He could leave the school without an education of any kind, endure a brutality usually reserved for hardened criminals, or stop questioning everything, learn whatever he could and go silent. He chose the last option and Brother Edmund crowed.

Murdoch's jaw had clenched at the memory. Unlike Traveller, his body no longer carried the scars of the floggings the Christian brother had administered with such undisguised delight, but his soul did. He'd heard a few years ago that Brother Edmund had died from diphtheria and Murdoch's first reaction was one of regret that he'd never gone back to the school, found the man and given him the thrashing he deserved.

Amy Slade's pupils would never carry that kind of memory, quite the opposite.

He hadn't told her what he was up to, but Charlie would have explained why he wasn't at home. She'd be eager to hear his tales when he returned, he knew that. He was lucky to have her and Seymour, and he'd come to rely on their company the way he had on the Kitchens. As long as he'd been living with the Kitchens, he'd had some feeling of family and he dearly hoped Arthur would recover. Murdoch would like to have his own family, he knew that. He and Liza had talked about having children, had even picked out names.

Murdoch sighed. The possibility of finding a wife seemed remote now that Enid had left him. Maybe he should go back to professor Otranto's dance studio. There were some very attractive young women there, but he didn't feel comfortable dancing with them, treading on toes, his hands sweating on the silk of their dresses. He was out of practice and he'd be sure to make a bollocks of the waltzes.

If he were at home in his own room, he would have got out of bed at this point, pushed back the rug, and done a few reverse turns. If he did that now, they'd probably send for the doctor and he'd get committed.

Thank goodness Dr. Ogden had been drawn away by Parker. Clever Ed. All that trickery paying off.

Somebody at the far end of the ward got up to use the commode. He seemed to be ill and groaned and broke wind alternately until he voided. Murdoch hoped he wouldn't forget to empty that bucket.

291

The nightshirt was itchy. He scratched his chest remembering the bedbug bites on the men going into the bath. Somewhere in the city, people were sleeping in soft feather beds with linen sheets that were washed regularly. They were warm and fed. Of all the men in this room, how many deserved this wretched fate? Less than one-third in his estimation. The others, through the misfortune of injury or ill health, were sentenced like convicts to a wandering life with no home or family and little prospect of getting out of the mire. The more time a man spent in the casual wards, the less chance he stood of getting back to a respectable job. Employers were suspicious of the wayfarers and as he'd already seen, they were the first to be suspected of a crime if one occurred in their vicinity.

Was it one of these men who had attacked Charles Howard so viciously? In his mind, both Bettles and Kearney were capable of it. Bettles had shrugged off his bruised face and the minister didn't seem to have marks on his knuckles, but he could have struck out with his elbow, an object in his hand, anything really. Which of them had been wearing Howard's boots before Parker took them?

Murdoch sighed and pulled the threadbare cover up to his chin. He'd better start acting more like a detective and less like a tramp if he was going to find out.

292

———

Josie groaned and tried to sit up, but the room swam nauseatingly in front of her eyes and she dropped back to the pillow. She reached over to touch her mother, who was lying beside her.

"Ma, can you get me some water, I'm desperate thirsty."
She thought she'd said this, but she wasn't sure. Her head ached and she felt as if the air was so heavy it sat on her chest making it hard to breathe.

"Ma," she said again and she turned her head. A cold, clammy fog from the lake had crept into the room and she was finding it hard to see anything clearly. She so wanted to go back to sleep, but she knew she shouldn't. Through the deepening mist, she tried to see her mother's face.

"Ma, get up. It must be late."

Esther stirred and Josie saw her struggle to get out of the bed. She knew she was trying to get to Wilf.

She always puts him first, she thought irritably. Can't she see I'm dying?

Chapter Thirty-Two

THE DOOR OPENED and the old nabber, Hastings, came in carrying a handbell, which he began to shake vigorously.

"Wake up, men. Wake up. It's six o'clock. Wake up."

The men stirred in a movement that rolled down the ward like a feather bed being shaken by an energetic servant. Some of the men sat up quickly, others groaned and rolled over, but nobody stayed asleep. Traveller sat up and got out of bed at once.

"Nothing else happened, I presume?" he asked Murdoch.

"We were quiet as the grave. I'd better pinch myself to know I'm alive."

Traveller chuckled. "Well my stomach and my bladder are telling me I'm still quick. Do you have to use the bucket?"

"I do indeed."

"Use it now then. The last one has to empty it."

Murdoch took his advice.

He hardly finished when he felt a tug on his sleeve. Alf was standing behind him.

"Can I come in with you?" he asked and nodded nervously in the direction of Bettles and Kearney.

"Of course."

"Line up in front of the door," the nabber called.

"Come on," said Traveller. "It's best to be at the front of the line for the dining room."

Murdoch and Alf followed him, shoving through the other men, and got into the first group already waiting at the door.

"You five men at the back, you bring down the buckets," called the nabber before leading the way down to the long hall where they'd left their clothes. Murdoch thought they must have looked a proper sight, sixty men of all ages and sizes, shuffling along in their nightshirts and boots. It was cold in the corridor and he was glad of the warmth of the bodies pressing around him. Alf hung on to Murdoch's shirt as if he were a child with his father. They halted at the door past the bathhouse.

The nabber hopped on a small stool by the door and rang his bell.

"Find your clothes and get dressed quickly. Put your nightshirts in the bin provided. Don't forget to hand over your tabs. When you're ready, wait in front of the doors at the far end."

295

"Are we in the army?" Murdoch asked Traveller.

"More like jail," he replied.

As they stepped over the threshold, an overpowering rotten egg smell hit Murdoch's nose.

"Phew, what's that?"

"It's the burning sulphur they use to fumigate our clothes. Stinks, doesn't it?"

Hunger and cold made all of them move speedily and within ten minutes they had lined up facing the opposite doors. Murdoch hadn't enjoyed getting into his dirty clothes but at least he was warmer. All the men were dressed for the outdoors, clothes piled on top of clothes when they had them. Murdoch was struck by the hats the men were wearing: battered fedoras, plaid caps, fur forage hats, anything to keep their heads warm.

The nabber shoved his way through the crowd and jumped onto yet another stool.

"For those of you who haven't been here before, I will tell you that you will be served two slices of bread and one bowl of skilly. One mug of tea. Don't moan and complain because you won't get any more than that. It's not our fault. That's all the council allows us."

"I could eat that four times over," Murdoch whispered to Traveller.

"Not here you won't unless somebody's sick and can't eat, and who gets his food is a matter of luck."

Hastings opened the door, leading the way back upstairs.

Because of Traveller, their little trio was among the first to spill into the room. The dining room was long and narrow with several wooden tables and benches in rows down the centre. Traveller took them directly to a long serving table where four men, old and withered, were standing ready to serve them. Two of them dished out the oatmeal, the third man had a bin of slices of unbuttered bread, and the fourth was filling mugs from an urn with a liquid so pale it was hard to believe it was tea.

Murdoch collected his bowl of skilly, his two slices of bread, and a mug of tea. Following Traveller, he went to one of the tables and slid into the bench, Alf close beside him.

His stomach was growling painfully and he spooned up some of the oatmeal as fast as he could. It was watery, lukewarm, and tasteless.

"Put some salt in it, it'll taste better," said Traveller. There were metal shakers spotted along the table and Traveller smothered his oatmeal. Nobody spoke while they consumed the unappetizing meal. Murdoch was ravenous, but even so, it was hard to enjoy dry bread that was on the verge of being stale. He followed Traveller's advice with the bread too and dipped it in his mug of tea. Both Alf and Traveller finished before he did and he saw them scouting the table to see if anybody was dawdling over the oatmeal and who might be persuaded to give it up. There wasn't anybody, even though Murdoch could see several of the out-of-work

297

labourers were pulling faces and muttering to each other.

Bettles and Kearney had taken seats at the end of their table and Murdoch glanced over at them casually and without pausing in his gulping down the porridge, Bettles managed to flick him the thumb.

Traveller, who didn't seem to miss anything, jerked his head in a warning.

"Don't let him get to you."

"He's riding me."

"'Course he is but you're the winner if you keep your temper. Besides, t'ain't nothing to do with you, son. That son of a bitch was just hoping to best me, is the truth. You're the bait."

"Why do you say that?"

Traveller didn't answer immediately, wiping the inside of the mug with his last piece of bread.

"Traveller's the king," giggled Alf. "They's always going for the king."

Trevelyan grinned. "You ain't been going around the circuit like we have, Mr. Williams. Us regular tramps become like a court, you might say. We knows each other and we knows our place. I ain't the oldest, Jesse over there is the oldest, but I'm the strongest and I know the ropes. Sooner or later one of the bucks wants to challenge my position. It's happened to me since I was a nipper. I was born big and stayed big. And there's always some cull wants to best me so he can be king." His keen eyes met Murdoch's. "They're too stupid to realize that they're going to be king of a court filled with courtiers who wear rags and are society's castouts."

"Let them have it, then."

"If it were a matter of stepping aside so they could have first go for the pig's food they serve us, I'd do it willingly, but it ain't that simple. Some of these fellows like Bettles won't be satisfied till they see blood. It's what you might call primitive. Us men are the same as the wild creatures. We've got to prove who's got the biggest cock, excuse my language. So as long as I've got the strength, I've got to fight them."

"And when you don't have the strength?"

"Then there'll be a new king, won't there?"

Murdoch couldn't tell how old Traveller was. Certainly close to middle age. He was big and looked strong, but more than that he had a formidable presence.

Jesse, the old tramp who was sitting next to Traveller, apparently lost in his own world, suddenly said, "Here, Jack. I can't stand this tea. Do you want the last of it yourself?"

He shoved his mug toward Traveller.

"Thank you kindly. Even this cat's piss is better than none at all, though I'd give my right fingers for a good hot, strong cup of char with heaps of sugar."

He gulped down the tea, wiped his mouth with his sleeve.

Murdoch would liked to have gone on talking to him, but Hastings appeared again with his bell.

299

MAUREEN JENNINGS

"Listen up, all of you. This meal is being served to you courtesy of the taxpayers of this city. In return you are expected to work. You will follow me to the lumberyard, where you cut and split wood. Those who are physically capable of this work must do it or you will forfeit your dinner. If you are incapable you will be excused and if you can prove that you have prospects of getting work if you leave this morning, you must say so. I will remind you, however, that we are experienced here in the ways of tramps so don't think you can pull the wool over our eyes. Who here is going for a position this morning?"

Of all sixty men, a half dozen raised their hands.

"You can leave then, but report to the manager in the lumberyard first. Don't try any gammon, we'll know."

Murdoch nudged Traveller. "Why aren't more of the men trying to find proper work?"

"'Cos there ain't any to be found. It's easier to stay here and chop wood than trudge around the city and get turned down every time you try for something. At least you're guaranteed a bowl of soup for dinner."

The nabber saw them talking and he scowled. "Quiet, you two. I haven't finished. Is there anybody here who ain't going to pay for their keep?"

Four men raised their hands.

"You've got to move on then."

"That's what I was planning to do," growled one grizzled tramp. He must have gone through the bathhouse, but his clothes were so wretched and dirty, his skin so weatherbeaten, he seemed filthy. The other three men were similar and Murdoch gathered they were at the end of their permitted three days and preferred to take their chances on getting dinner and leave the workhouse. He hoped none of them was the one he was looking for and he tried to memorize what they looked like.

"Are you going to work?" he asked Traveller.

"I am, I've got one more day here."

"What about your hernia? Will it give you trouble?"

Jack winked. "I never know when that damn thing is going to act up. Sometimes I can't do anything, sometimes I can. Today, I'm all right."

The nabber rang his bell again. He must enjoy doing that, thought Murdoch.

"The rest of you follow me. Orderly and quiet now."

The men at the table began to move out from the benches.

"Hang back," Traveller muttered. "It's better to be with the last group in the lumberyard. They might not have enough piles for everybody."

They followed the nabber out of the dining room and back down the stairs. He pushed open a heavy door.

"Don't think you can get away with shirking because you can't. Remember, you can still be turned out." 301

As he walked out to the lumberyard, Murdoch entertained himself with the fantasy of stuffing the old codger's head into his own bell.

Chapter Thirty-Three

A MAN IN A BLACK OVERCOAT and fedora was waiting for them in the yard. He was short and stout, with grey side whiskers and a walrus moustache. A gold pince-nez, with a gold chain, was perched on his stubby nose. Everything about him said *minister*, especially his nervous smile as he watched the tramps coming through the door. Murdoch saw Parker, hopping on his crutches, come out from the infirmary side. He didn't look any the worse for wear, rather the opposite, to Murdoch's jaundiced eye. Ed looked rested, far better than he himself felt. There were three nabbers, also waiting, one of them the boss, Gowan, from the day before.

The tramp major blew on his mittened hands against the cold. "All right then. The sooner you start working, the sooner you'll get warm. Over here is the Reverend Elmore Harris, who in case you should want to look him up, is the pastor of Walmer Road Baptist Church. He's the manager for today and he's here to help me sort out the wheat from the chaff or, to translate for you heathens, the liars from the truth-tellers."

One of the attendants handed him a list, which he stared at.

"The following men will step forward, Barnes, Carson, Keats, and Stepney. I understand you're claiming to be unfit to work. Let me see you with my own eyes."

The old man who'd given Traveller his tea stepped forward. The others were also elderly and one had the racking cough of the consumptive, currently aggravated by the cold air.

Gowan inspected them as if they were cattle he was buying. "What do you think, pastor?"

"I'd say they are definitely excused. I think the fellow on the end should go over to the infirmary and see if he can get some cough medicine."

"That's Stepney. Go on then and count yourself lucky. The other three of you can carry the wood when it's split and stack it in the carts over there. That's not too hard. Now who has refused to work? Step forward where I can see you and state your name."

The four men who had put up their hands in the dining room did as he said and Gowan made an obvious point of writing down their names.

"Off you go, then. I know who you are so don't expect to come back here and freeload off decent citizens. And if you bother anybody for money, you will be charged with vagrancy and thrown in jail."

Traveller snorted at that and muttered to Murdoch, "Sometimes jail is better than being in here. You get more to eat."

Gowan tossed his record book to the nearby nabber.

"Now then, some of you know what to do, some of you don't, so I'll explain. All of those logs over there, kindly donated by Elias Rogers, have got to be sawed into four pieces. Those blocks then have to be chopped and split. That's not too complicated for any of you, is it?"

The nabbers began tagging various men and directing them to the trestles. All of the logs had been previously cut to length, and in spite of the circumstances and the cold, and the perpetual itching of his jersey, Murdoch felt a surge of pleasure at the sweet raw wood smell. He inhaled as if it were a perfume, aware of the quizzical glance from Traveller.

A nabber touched his arm. "You can chop."

Traveller, Alf, Bettles, and Kearney had also been designated as choppers and they stood together waiting until the first block of wood was sawn off. Murdoch seized his chance and strolled over to Parker, who had been given the job of counting the number of blocks. He was perched on a spare trestle, a pad and pencil in his hand.

304

"Feeling better, are you?" Murdoch asked.

"Thank you, sir. I am that."

Murdoch moved a little closer and turned so that he was standing beside Parker and appeared to be casually looking over the tramps getting to work. "Do you see your boots?"

Ed focused on his pad. "It's hard to tell. They weren't special, just old black boots. There are four coves I've seen who could be wearing them."

"Point them out."

"The simpleton who was by you in the queue for one, and the man in the yellow muffler."

"There's two with yellow mufflers, which is it?"

"The younger one with the bruise on his mug. Also, the cove in the plaid cap who was beside you."

"Who else?"

Before Ed could answer, Gowan called over to them.

"Oi, you. Williams. What do you think you're doing? This isn't a church club. Get busy or I'll put you on notice as a shirker."

"Quick, who else?"

"Maybe the old guy who just got sent off to the infirmary."

"Did you get a look at the ones who left?"

Ed shook his head. "No, sorry."

"I'll come back," Murdoch muttered to Ed. "Keep looking."

He went back to where Traveller and the others were starting to stack their blocks ready for chopping.

"How's the lad doing?" Traveller asked Murdoch.

305

"He seems all right."

"Did you know him from before then?"

"No, I was just concerned. He could have drowned."

Traveller grinned. "Mebbe. But everybody knows if you can get a night in the infirmary you get some grub and a better breakfast." He jerked his head in the direction of the manager. "Gowan's watching you. He's a mean son of a bitch. You'd better get busy."

Murdoch removed his hat and his sealskin coat and placed them on the ground out of the way. The sun was sparkling on the patches of snow and the sky was a brilliant blue. The price for this brightness was icy temperatures and his breath was like smoke in front of him, the cold air penetrating through even his thick jersey.

The choppers were picking up axes that were lined up against the fence. Murdoch went to get his. He tested the blades on a couple. None were very sharp, but one of them was balanced well enough so he chose it and returned to his spot.

One of the men had finished sawing his log. He had the wide shoulders and smooth movements of a logger and his logs were appearing fast.

"Where was your crib?" Murdoch asked him as he picked up two of the blocks.

"Huntsville. Know it?"

"Sure do. I was a chopper there myself about twelve years ago."

Traveller heard him.

"I thought you said you was just now from a camp and that you'd hurt your back."

"That's right. It wasn't Huntsville, though."

He stood one of the blocks on top of the other and took a swing at it, feeling the satisfaction of seeing the wood divide cleanly into two pieces.

"Your back seems fine now," said Traveller.

"Bit sore, but it'll do." And he stacked another piece of wood. Alf was next to him making wild and futile stabs at chopping his block of wood. Murdoch stopped what he was doing.

"Here, Alf. Let me show you. Best to put one piece of wood on top of the other. It's easier on your back that way. Now hold your axe nice and loose, don't clutch it like that. It's important to aim for the crack in the wood. See that one there. Stand with your legs apart and bend at the knees as you come down. Here, like this."

He showed him and split the wood cleanly. Alf laughed as if he had shown him a magician's trick.

Bettles and Kearney had been leisurely collecting their blocks and Bettles called over to them.

"You're in a good humour this morning, Alf. You must have slept well. Lots of lovely dreams, I suspect, from the noises you were making."

Alf nodded uneasily. Murdoch was standing close to Traveller and he saw the tension in the tramp's body. 307

"You must have had good dreams yourself, Bettles," said Traveller. "For a while there I thought I was in a pigsty what with the stink and the snorting going on. Then I realized it was all coming from your bed. I hope you changed your blanket this morning."

Alf made the mistake of giggling, little beads of saliva bubbling out of his mouth. Suddenly, Bettles stepped forward and grabbed his crotch. "Don't laugh at me, Alf. I don't like it."

Alf shrieked as Bettles squeezed his testicles. Gowan turned around.

"What the hell's going on?"

Bettles stepped back while poor Alf clutched himself, tears in his eyes.

"What's going on?" Gowan repeated glaring at them.

Traveller put his arm around Alf's shoulder. "The poor lad bumped into a trestle. He'll be all right."

The trestles weren't close by, but Gowan didn't question the explanation. "Watch where you're going, you knocky lad."

Alf was still convulsed with pain and Traveller started to walk him up and down. Murdoch struggled to contain his own anger. He didn't dare get drawn into anything. All he could do was vow to himself that he'd see that Bettles got paid back.

Gowan stabbed his finger at Bettles. "You, get chopping or I'll throw you out. There's plenty of blocks coming now. You too, Traveller. The boy can sit out for a few minutes, but you ain't his nurse so you can leave him."

Traveller returned to the trestle and picked up his axe. He didn't say anything, just stacked his blocks and started to chop. Both Bettles and Kearney were tensed and ready for retaliation, but as none was forthcoming, they had no choice but to pick up their axes and start to work. Murdoch cautiously resumed his chopping as well. Jesse was collecting the split pieces of wood and carrying them over to carts near the wall. For the next little while, everybody was busy, the yard filled with the thunk, thunk of the axes. Murdoch was starting to sweat despite the cold.

What happened next was so fast, he didn't see it. He had bent down to stack his next block of wood. He glimpsed Traveller raising his axe to swing at his own piece, but somehow the axe flew out of his hand. Bettles was standing about eight feet away and the axe caught him on the side of the head. He dropped to the ground, blood gushing from his split scalp. Kearney yelled and ran over to him, as did Murdoch. Bettles groaned and tried to sit up.

"Don't move," said Murdoch. He went to get out his handkerchief, forgetting he didn't have one. "Damn it."

The pastor and the tramp major came over to see what had happened.

"Do you have a handkerchief?" Murdoch asked them and Reverend Harris quickly handed him one of fine white linen. Murdoch wiped away some of the blood from Bettles's head.

309

"Hold this tight against your head and sit up slowly," he said to Bettles.

"What the hell happened?" asked Gowan.

"My axe must 'ave slipped," said Traveller. "The wood is wet. I trust I haven't caused this man a serious injury,"

The manager swirled around and glared at him. "What the hell were you doing? You could've brained the man."

"I told you my axe slipped. Ain't that right, Kearney? You saw what happened. It was an accident."

The Irishman could only nod. Bettles looked murderous. The blood was spilling through his fingers and down his hand into his sleeve.

"He should get to a doctor," Murdoch said to Gowan.

All the men had stopped their work and were standing gawking.

"You, Kearney, help him to the infirmary. The rest of you, the opera's over, get back to work."

Bettles managed to get to his feet but shook off Kearney's hand.

"I can manage," he said. He looked over at Traveller but didn't speak. He didn't have to. His message was obvious. With the pastor hovering on one side and Kearney on the other, he left the yard, drops of blood marking their path. Even Alf was quiet.

Traveller turned back to the piece of wood he'd been chopping. "He'll be all right. Scalp wounds always bleed a lot."

310

He grinned at Murdoch, who restacked his log. He made sure he wasn't standing where there could be another accidental slip.

About half an hour later, Kearney and the minister returned.

"How's Bettles?" asked Murdoch.

"He's on the mend. The bleeding has stopped," answered Harris.

"Thank the Lord," said Traveller in a loud voice. "I am spared having the death of a man on my conscience."

He was palpably insincere.

Kearney moved as far away from Traveller as possible and work continued for two hours without pause, although even the young loggers slowed down. Murdoch saw Harris say something to Gowan, who at first shook his head then with obvious reluctance got down from his stool and left the yard. Murdoch wiped his forehead. He was among the younger men there and certainly one of the fittest and he was finding the relentless work tiring as he'd had no real food since yesterday. The miserable bit of bread and skilly didn't count.

Gowan reappeared, followed by the two elderly nabbers, both carrying buckets. Hastings rang his bell for attention and the tramp major bellowed, "Listen up, you men. You're lucky today. Our manager, Reverend Harris, has a tender heart. He has asked me to give you a ten-minute respite. Not that some of you need it from what I can see, but he's the boss. You can get a cup of water from the bucket here, but no more than ten minutes." He took out a large steel watch from his vest pocket. "I'm timing starting now."

With so much sawdust flying around, all of the men were thirsty, but they had been well trained and they lined up in two docile lines, each dipping in the bucket, gulping down the water, then passing the iron cup to the next man. Murdoch deliberately hung back so he could get next to Parker. He went first and he gulped the metallic-tasting water and handed over the cup, with a slight nod. Ed drank, then hopped away, Murdoch walking beside him.

"Well?"

"I managed to get a better look at Traveller's boots. I think they're mine."

"Are you sure?"

Ed screwed up his face. "Not sure exactly, but they could be."

"Damn it, Ed. You said that about Alf's boots, and Bettles."

"Well they could be too. I told you old boots look alike. But both those coves are my size."

312 Murdoch didn't think Alf could be a murderer, but from what he'd witnessed so far, he wouldn't eliminate Bettles and probably not Traveller.

Gowan rang his bell. "Back to work, you men. We don't want you to catch cold now, do we?"

Murdoch walked back to his spot, hefted his axe, and swung down at the block of wood. A searing pain shot up from his lower back and he yelped. He tried to straighten up, but his body refused to co-operate and all he could do was stand bent forward. He took a few steps, hoping the pain would ease but it was excruciating. No matter how hard he tried, he couldn't stand upright. He dropped the axe and hobbled over to Gowan.

"I'll have to stop, my back has seized up."

Gowan guffawed. "Of course it has. Well you can stop Mr. Williams but if you do, you'll have to leave. No tasty hot soup for you."

"I think he really has hurt himself," said Harris timidly. "He probably got chilled. He's been working hard, I've noticed. Surely we can make an exception."

"Begging your pardon, sir, but you don't know these men like I do. They're better actors than a music-hall troupe."

It was all Murdoch could do not to grab the man by the throat and throttle him. The only thing that pre-vented him was the fact that he was bent over in an agonizing and undignified way.

"Thank you for your kind words, Mr. Harris. You can stuff your hot soup up a place where it will surely burn, Mr. Gowan. I'm leaving."

Parker, who was sitting nearby, grinned, but Murdoch sensed the fellow was rather enjoying his discomfiture. He crept back to where he'd left his hat and coat, feeling as if he had suddenly aged twenty years. Traveller stopped chopping.

"Sorry you hurt yourself, Mr. Williams. That old injury, I suppose."

Murdoch nodded. Traveller picked up his coat for him and helped him to put it on. Alf patted his back solicitously and smiled at him.

"Are you coming back here tonight?" Murdoch asked Traveller.

"Mebbe. Or we might go over to the House of Providence. They have better food even if you do have to go to mass in the morning. What about you? What will you do?"

"I'm not sure of anything except I won't be here another night."

"Goodbye, then. Perhaps our paths will cross again."

As far as Murdoch was concerned, they were going to cross very soon.

He shook hands with both of them and hobbled as best he could out of the yard, Gowan watching him to see if he could catch him malingering.

Chapter Thirty-Four

THE PREVIOUS NIGHT, SARAH DIGNAM had retired to her room as soon after supper as she could without exciting a barrage of questions from Elias about her health. As he believed all illnesses to be caused by poor bowel function, he was apt to ask her embarrassingly personal questions no matter who was present. Fortunately, his attention had been diverted by May Flowers, who had refused to leave her good friend until she was reassured she was exhausted and thinking only of bed. May had remained until almost eleven o'clock, and Sarah heard her high-pitched laughter as she cheered Elias up. He was laughing too and she wondered if he would ever give up his lifelong dedication to bachelorhood and succumb to the full bosomy charms of her friend.

Sarah felt a stab of loneliness at the thought, so intense she closed her eyes. Her love was dead and any possibility of finding fulfillment in a matrimonial embrace was gone. She touched the back of her hand to her cheek. She was hot. Her head was aching and her throat felt dry and sore. She was coming down with something, she was certain. She had slept so badly that she stayed in bed late even though Walters had fussed outside the door. Thank goodness Elias was a late riser and he hadn't come with some new physic.

Sarah reached for the bible under her pillow and turned to the Song of Solomon. She didn't really need to read it. The verses were so familiar to her by now, she could recite them by heart.

"I found him whom my soul loveth: I held him, and would not let him go until I had brought him into my mother's house, and into the chamber of her that conceived me."

She was in the room where she had been born, perhaps conceived, although she was not comfortable imagining her tiny mother having connections with the large burly man she knew as her father. Elias had taken their father's room after he died, and she naturally had requested to have the pleasant front room that had been her mother's bedchamber. She had replaced little over the years, changing the wallpaper only once. However, the green and burgundy flock she chose was so similar to the previous covering, she hardly remembered the old one. The mahogany bed was the same as her mother had used, but Sarah had brought in her own dresser and wardrobe. Her room was a comfort to her. Elias had never stepped foot in it since their father died and he had come to wake her with the news.

"By night on my bed, I sought him whom my soul loveth: I sought him but I found him not . . . I held him and would not let him go . . ."

She had never held Charles or been held by him. Not so long ago, when she was leaving the church, she had turned her ankle on the steps and he had caught hold of her arm. She had pressed her hand into his as she regained her balance. Even through the leather of her glove, she could feel the strong sinews of his hand and it was all she could do not to press his palm against her cheek.

She touched the plain gold cross that was hanging around her neck.

"A bundle of myrrh is my well beloved unto me; he shall lie all night betwixt my breasts."

Tentatively, she placed her hands on her breasts, soft and pendulous under the silk of her nightgown.

"His left hand is under my head and his right hand doth embrace me."

No man had caressed her in the way that she knew men caressed women.

When she was a child, she'd heard the cook chatting with one of the maids. The girl had a follower, whom Sarah had seen coming to call for her on Sunday mornings. The maid had said to the cook, "He stroked my diddies." And she'd squealed with excitement when she

317

said it. Sarah had later asked her nanny what the word meant and she had been alarmed at the upset her innocent question had caused. The maid had been dismissed immediately and even the kind old cook had been severely reprimanded. "Little pitchers have big ears," said Nanny and afterwards as long as they had servants, Sarah felt the constraint between them.

"This thy stature is like to a palm tree and thy breasts to clusters of grapes."

She moved her hand down to her stomach, which in spite of her small frame, felt too full and flabby without her corset.

"Thy belly is like an heap of wheat set about with lilies."

Chapter seven had been May's responsibility and she had done a very poor job. None of the passion of the verses made sense as symbolic of Christ and the church. Charles had said to think of the holy state of matrimony and the sanctified love between a man and his wife. Sarah had wondered about Charles and if he had thought of the joints of his wife's thighs as jewels, *"the work of a cunning workman."* She had pushed that thought away at once, of course. She didn't like Louisa. Thank goodness she didn't come to the prayer circle, flaunting her position. Sarah noticed how she always made a point of placing her hand on Charles's arm, as if to claim her possession. When she spoke in company, she frequently said, "Charles and I," reminding everybody present that they were bound together.

318

True love needed no such ostentatious display, as Sarah well knew.

Charles had asked her to present chapter eight, "and especially let us look at verse six," were his exact words. "Let us especially look at verse six."

"Set me as a seal upon thine heart, as a seal upon thine arm: for love is strong as death; jealousy is cruel as the grave: the coals thereof are coals of fire which hath a most vehement flame."

Sarah got out of bed and went over to the mirror. Her fine hair was hanging loosely about her face, she had been too tired to braid it last night. She was quite grey now, not blonde, and in the dull morning light, she looked old and haggard. *"You have such fine eyes, Miss Dignam, if I may say so."* No, that is not exactly what he'd said, he said her blue dyed caperine brought out the colour of her eyes but he might as well have said she had fine eyes. He, himself, had startlingly beautiful blue eyes. She'd asked May if she thought so too, but her friend had only looked at her curiously. "They're not that unusual," she said, but then May never acknowledged any of Sarah's enthusiasms, ever.

She closed her eyes, trying by an effort of will to remember Charles how he had been, not the way he was when she had last seen him, with a bloody socket where his eye had been. How many times had she imagined pressing gentle kisses on those eyes, taking the black lashes as delicate as moth wings into her mouth.

319

Abruptly, she opened her eyes and met her own image in the mirror. She reached into the drawer, took out the piece of bloodstained paper, and held it against her cheek. His hands had touched it and therefore she was touching him.

"The watchmen that went about the city found me, they smote me, they wounded me: the keepers of the walls took away my veil from me."

She had to tell the truth no matter what the cost. She owed it to Charles and the love he had declared to her.

Walking eased the spasm somewhat, but Murdoch still couldn't stand up straight by the time he reached the police station. Fortunately, Seymour was on duty and Murdoch didn't have to go through a long explanation about why he was dressed the way he was.

"What the heck happened to you?" Seymour asked.

"I was overzealous. I forgot I wasn't twenty years old any more."

"Was it worth it?"

"I'm not sure yet, but we might have some evidence on the case. I want you to send Crabtree and Dewhurst over to the House of Industry right away. There are four men there I want brought in for questioning. The names are Bettles, Kearney, Trevelyan, also known as Traveller, and a simpleton named Alf. Keep Bettles and Kearney

320

in a separate cell from the other two. Also make sure Ed Parker comes back to the station. I haven't finished with him." Murdoch scratched at his chest. "Oh God, I had a bath last night but I'd dearly love to sit in a hot tub for a couple of hours. I must get out of these clothes. Do they smell as bad to you as they do from here?"

Seymour nodded. "'Fraid so. Rotten egg kind of smell."

"That's the sulphur they use for fumigating." Murdoch started to go toward the rear door then stopped. "Charlie, could you send out for a couple of meat pies before I keel over from hunger?"

"Of course."

"And if you don't mind, I'm going to burn these clothes. They will probably stink, but I can't bear them for a minute longer." Standing still hadn't helped his back and he groaned as he went to open the door. "Where is Crabtree, by the way? Any new developments on the case?"

"Not that I know of, but I had to send him out on another case. We've had one of those bloody tragedies with carbon monoxide gas fumes. Typical story, people use the worst coke because that's all they can afford and the landlord doesn't get the chimneys cleaned properly. An entire family, including one poor cripple lad, died upstairs and an elderly man in a room down-stairs. Two other occupants are very ill, one might not

321

live. Crabtree and Dewhurst are at the house now."

Murdoch stared at him "Where is it?"

"Sherbourne Street, south of Gerrard."

"Do you know the names of the people?"

Seymour checked the notepad on his desk. "The elderly cove downstairs was a Thomas Hicks and the family upstairs was Pugwell, no sorry, Tugwell. There was Mrs. Tugwell, her young crippled son, and her grown daughter."

"My God, Charlie, when did this all happen?"

"Sometime in the night. Why, do you know them?"

"I was just there yesterday. The Tugwells were on Howard's visiting list, a family whose application he rejected."

Seymour whistled through his teeth. "Are we looking at a coincidence here or are the incidents connected?"

"I don't know, but I'd better get up there right away. How were they discovered?"

"One of the local ministers dropped in early this morning and found them all dead. He got one of the neighbour's boys to run for the beat constable. Fortunately, it was Burley's watch and he's a good lad with a clear head in an emergency. He figured out what had happened, and opened all the windows. He had to smash some of them apparently. He just got the other two women out in time or they'd be dead too."

"Damation, Charlie. What the hell is going on?"

"Look, you'd better get over there. I'll send Fyfer and

322

Wylie to pick up the tramps. We'll hold them here until you get back."

Murdoch went to head out the door.

"Will, you should change your clothes first."

"Damn. You're going to have to help me, Charlie."

Chapter Thirty-Five

MURDOCH HAD RETRIEVED his wheel from the station and he found that although bicycling was easier than walking, getting on and off the bike was a problem. He had difficulty straightening up when he parked his bicycle near the house on Sherbourne Street. There was the usual crowd of onlookers gathered outside by now, not nearly as well dressed as the one that had gathered outside the church, but the morbid curiosity was the same. A police ambulance waited in front and Burley was keeping guard at the door. He greeted Murdoch with a salute.

"Good morning, sir."

"The bodies are still here, I presume?"

"Yes, sir, and the physician has just arrived."

"The air has cleared now?"

"Yes, sir."

They both glanced back at the house. The front windows on both floors were smashed.

"I hear you acted very promptly, constable. Well done."

Burley flushed with pleasure. "Thank you, sir. I'm keeping my fingers crossed that the two ladies will live. They was both unconscious but they revived a bit in the air."

"Have you had time to inspect the fireplaces?"

"No, sir, but Constable Crabtree and Constable Higgins are in there now."

Murdoch took a deep breath, not because he feared the carbon monoxide might be still lingering in the house but because he didn't relish what he knew he was going to see.

He went inside. The door to Hicks's room was open. His body was in his chair close by the hearth. A book was at his feet where it had fallen. His eyes were open and his face was covered with the typical red blotches caused by monoxide poisoning. There was a sour smell of vomit in the room and Murdoch could see Hicks's dressing gown was stained down the front. Constable Crabtree was at the fireplace, holding a lantern so he could examine the chimney.

"Find anything, George?" Murdoch asked. As best he could he bent down to look. Crabtree glanced at him startled.

"I did it chopping wood. I'll explain later," said Murdoch. "Aim your light, will you?"

The constable did so. "Looks like a brick came loose and caused a blockage." Murdoch reached up and

325

released a small shower of debris. "The whole bloody thing needs repairing. I wish we could prosecute the miserly landlords who prey off poor people like Hicks. They take their money and do nothing. It's disgusting."

He eased himself away.

Crabtree poked in the coal scuttle, which was by the hearth. "He was burning the cheapest variety of coke. The fumes must have backed up. He probably didn't know what was happening. The same with the people upstairs, who were all in bed asleep. As I understand it, there were three of them in the family and we did find the bodies of two females in one bed and that of a young man in a cot by the window." He paused. "The sad thing was, it looked like he'd tried to get out of bed, probably feeling ill, but he couldn't do anything. Apparently, he suffered from the palsy." Crabtree consulted his notebook. "The two women who live in the room next to Mr. Hicks are sisters, Miss Emma and Larissa Leask. There's a connecting door that's been plastered over but not very well. The only reason they survived at all is that they always sleep with their window open, but Miss Emma is elderly and she is critically ill at the moment. Next to the Tugwells on the second floor are a man and his wife, Mr. and Mrs. Simon McGillivary. They are in the hospital but expected to recover, although Mrs. McGillivary is with child and the doctors are most concerned about the baby's future welfare. On the third floor there are three tenants. A German man,

Mr. Werner Einboden, and his wife, Gudren, on one side of the stairwell and a bachelor by the name of Philip Taylor on the other. He works a night shift at the newspaper office and he wasn't at home. The Einbodens both have severe headaches, but other than that they are all right."

"Where are they now?"

"Across the street with one of the neighbours, a Mrs. Cole."

"Does the blocked chimey look like an accident to you, George?"

"It's impossible to say, sir. He may have killed himself. Suicides will do this sort of thing to make it look like an accident so the family doesn't lose out on insurance. You talked to him, sir. Did you think he was unbalanced?"

"He was a lonely man full of sorrow, but I wouldn't say unbalanced and I'm sure he'd know his act could cause the death of other people."

"Not everybody realizes how monoxide travels, sir."

"Mr. Hicks was very well read. He used to be an engineer, he told me."

"It's hard to imagine somebody blocked that chimney deliberately. But I suppose we have to keep that under consideration, don't we, sir?"

"He never went out. He'd hardly sit there while some cove went and stopped up his chimney. Besides, what earthly reason would anybody have for murdering a frail old man like this?"

327

Crabtree didn't answer. They'd both seen enough of human depravity to know almost anything was possible.

Murdoch went over to the dead man and, with difficulty, bent to pick up the book that had fallen from Hicks's lap. It was the Book of Common Prayer.

"I was going to bring you a book to read, but I didn't get around to it. I only wish you'd had a chance to read some more rollicking tales, Mr. Hicks."

"Shall I go and round up a jury, sir?"

"Yes, indeed, George. I'll go upstairs and talk to the physician. Who is it, by the way?"

"Dr. Ogden again."

"Good."

Murdoch waited until the constable had left, then he gently closed the staring eyes of the dead man. He made the sign of the cross.

"May God have mercy on your soul."

Stiffly, he climbed the stairs to the second floor and went into the Tugwells' room. Dr. Ogden had just finished her examination of the bodies and she turned to greet him.

"Good afternoon, Detective Murdoch. Oh dear, you have lumbago, I see."

"Yes, ma'am. I was chopping wood."

"Do you have a female at home?"

"Er, no, ma'am, I'm not married."

"I don't mean that. I mean is there somebody at home who could use an iron on you?"

"Er, I'm not quite sure what you are asking me, doctor?"

She smiled slightly. "The best treatment that I know of is to have somebody apply a hot iron to your lower back muscles. It should be done over thick brown paper, but one or two treatments like that will cure you in no time."

It was on the tip of Murdoch's tongue to say, "Yes, Sister," but he caught himself.

She turned her attention back to the bed where Esther Tugwell and her daughter were lying side by side. Except for the pallor of their skin, they could have been asleep. Dr. Ogden had removed the tattered quilt to do her examination, but otherwise the situation was clearly as it had been when they went to bed. There was no sign of disturbance or struggle. Murdoch could see the same red blotches on both of their faces that had been on Hicks, but neither of the women had vomited. The son was a different matter. He had obviously tried to get out of bed and he was entangled with his blanket, half on the floor.

"Rigor mortis is well established but carbonic monoxide poisoning tends to delay the onset so it is more difficult to determine with accuracy when death occurred. But I'd say they all died at approximately the same time, which would be no earlier than ten o'clock last night but could have been as late as one or two in the morning."

329

"Is there any doubt that the monoxide was the cause of death?" Murdoch asked.

She snapped the clips shut on her medical bag. "None at all. There are no signs of trauma to the bodies, except for the lad bruising his face when he fell to the floor. I intend to do the postmortem examination this afternoon. You can attend if you wish or I will have the results sent to you immediately."

The other constable had been standing by the window, looking a little queasy.

"Higgins, did you examine the chimney in this room?" Murdoch asked.

"Yes, sir. It was clear."

"Poor innocent souls," said the doctor.

"I understand the fumes originated down below with a blocked chimey."

"It looks that way, ma'am."

She tugged her gloves on. "No matter how much you might warn them, people are so careless. He was probably using coke."

"Yes, he was. A poor quality."

"That wretched fuel should be outlawed."

"It's cheaper, ma'am."

"I'm aware of that, detective. As far as I am concerned the poor are often their own worst enemies." With that she headed for the door but paused in front of Higgins. "Constable, you should go outside at once.

330

The gas can linger for a long time. Mr. Murdoch, don't
forget my suggestion concerning your back and above
all, keep your bowels open."

"Yes, ma'am."

Chapter Thirty-Six

MRS. COLE, THE NEIGHBOUR who had offered refuge to
the German couple, was a young woman, plump and
pretty, who was obviously newly married and set up in
her own house for the first time. The furnishings were
sparse and cheap but brand new and the air was thick
with the smell of beeswax polish. She served the three
of them underbaked cake and weak coffee but with such
kindness and hospitality, Murdoch thought Mr. Cole
was a lucky man.

The Einbodens, who were seated on Mrs. Cole's best
couch, seemed desperately poor, spoke little English,
and were extremely nervous. It took a while for
Murdoch to make himself understood and in turn to
understand their replies. What he finally came away
with was that Hicks may have had a visitor late that
night, but as he was in the habit of reading out loud
they couldn't possibly swear to that. Nobody had visited

the Tugwells and Josie had come home with her usual noise about nine o'clock. The Misses Leasks were spiteful old women who didn't like foreigners and they had nothing to do with them. The same with Mr. and Mrs. McGillivary. They never saw Mr. Taylor. Only for Thomas Hicks did they shed a tear. Metaphorically. They were both too afraid of Murdoch to show any emotion other than a cringing subservience.

After an hour, he took his leave. Burley was standing guard at the rooming house, but the ambulance had left and the blustery wind had scattered the curious like, pieces of newspaper. The constable had nothing to report and Murdoch headed for the station. Sitting down for so long had stiffened up his back and even riding his wheel was painful.

Seymour greeted him as soon as he walked into the station. His usual dour face was beaming.

"Very good news, Will. We brought in the tramps and I think we've nabbed our man. See here." He held up a man's silver watch. "It fits the description exactly of Reverend Howard's piece."

Murdoch took it from him and flipped open the lid. Inside was engraved the date, *October 30, 1892*, and the initials, *C.H.*

"Excellent. Who had it?"

333

"Jack Trevelyan. It was hidden in the lining of his coat. Constable Fyfer gave them all a thorough search that I doubt they'd experienced since the midwife pulled them into the world. He's a good officer, that one."

"Indeed. What did Traveller have to say for himself?"

"Says he found the watch in the Horticultural Gardens on Tuesday. Says he hid it because he was spending the night in the workhouse and you can't trust anybody in that place."

"What about the other three?"

"The simpleton is enjoying himself, as far as I can see. Won't stop giggling. He didn't have anything hidden. Bettles and his mate are as tough a pair of natty lads as I've come across. They both had knives tucked in their boots and almost ten dollars between them hidden in their coats. So much for being paupers. They're richer than I am."

"Let me talk to Traveller. Will you have him brought to my office."

"Do you want him cuffed?"

"We'd better. But, Charlie, can you bring in some food. He hasn't had anything to eat since yesterday."

The sergeant chuckled. "You're in luck, Will. Katie sent me off this morning with a pork pie that would feed an army. I've had my fill. He can have the rest of it."

The mere mention of Katie's pork pie made Murdoch's stomach growl.

334

"If there's enough for two, I wouldn't mind some later."

He walked slowly to his cubicle of an office and eased himself into the chair behind the desk. Within a few

minutes, he heard footsteps in the hall and Constable
Fyfer appeared in the threshold.

"He's here, sir."

If Murdoch hadn't heard them he would have smelled
them coming. The odour of sulphur permeated the
cubicle. "Bring him in."

Fyfer pulled aside the reed curtain and stepped back
so that Traveller could enter. Murdoch had expected
the tramp to be surprised when he saw him, but he
merely grunted and sat down promptly on the chair.

Murdoch nodded at Fyfer, who withdrew to the hall.

"Good afternoon, Mr. Trevelyan," said Murdoch.

"Good afternoon to you. How's your back?"

"Sore."

"You should have known better than to put your
block on the ground like that."

"I know. I was also chilled . . . you don't seem surprised to see me."

"Not the least. I suspected you was a nark from the
beginning, that's why I kept you close to me. I weren't
totally sure until we was in the ward. You gave yourself
away there."

"In what way?"

"Well it was how you handled those toe rags, Bettles
and Kearney. You knew what you were doing, for one
thing. And I thought to myself, This cove ain't no wayfarer." Traveller chortled. "We tobies tend to fight a bit
more dirty, if you know what I mean. Like they was

335

about to. But it was good what you did with Alf last night. I would have taken care of him, but what you did was manly."

Murdoch couldn't help but grin. Here was Traveller, up to his neck in hot water, dishing out compliments like he was a schoolteacher.

"And you got me out of trouble so I'm grateful to you for that," said Murdoch.

Traveller shrugged. "I'd have done it for anybody. I told you, those scum was after me." He raised his hands. "Would you consider taking these off. I ain't so stupid as to cause trouble in a police station."

Murdoch called out to the constable. "Fyfer, will you uncuff Mr. Trevelyan? And will you tell Sergeant Seymour we're ready?"

The constable came in and unlocked the handcuffs and Traveller rubbed at his wrists. "They was put on too tight."

Fyfer looked as if he would like to stand by and get in on the proceedings, but Murdoch nodded at him to leave.

Traveller gazed around the cubicle, taking in the shabby furniture. "I would have thought a detective would have a fancier place than this."

"Money's tight everywhere."

"Ha. Ain't that the truth."

Murdoch reached in his drawer and took out his pipe and a packet of tobacco. "Have you got your pipe?"

"No, it's taken a walk. And me baccy."

"You can use mine." Murdoch pushed a box of matches and the tobacco packet across the desk. "It's a good Bull Durham."

Traveller filled the pipe, lit up, and drew in deeply, letting go with a sigh of appreciation. "I suppose you're wanting to ask me about the watch I found. I hear it used to belong to some poor fellow who got himself murdered."

"Who told you that?"

"The constable who found it in my coat."

Damn, thought Murdoch. Fyfer should have kept that to himself.

"Where *did* you find it?"

"Like I told him. In the Gardens."

"Where exactly?"

Traveller blew out some smoke. "Near the entrance to the greenhouse. I was in there keeping warm a couple of days ago and when I was leaving, to get to my hotel, which was about to open, I saw the watch lying on a bench."

"There might have been a reward offered, why didn't you turn it in to the police?"

Traveller grinned at him. "'Cos you lot would immediately suspect me of stealing it and I'd be bothered with a lot of questions like now and it is very unlikely I'd get a reward. I don't have a watch to keep track of my appointments so I thought finder's keepers."

"What day was this exactly?"

"Can't say exactly. Wayfarers tend to lose all track of time. Wasn't yesterday, could have been the day before, but I won't swear to it."

I bet you won't, thought Murdoch. Vagueness is a good defence until you find out where the trouble is.

"Did you see anybody while you were in the greenhouse? Did you talk to anybody?"

"Yes, I did as a matter of fact. A gawdelpus. A good fellow he was. He gave me two nickels."

"Did you ask him for money?"

"Not me. You and me both know that's against the law."

"What time was it when you encountered this charitable gentleman?"

"I can't tell you that. Like I said, we tobies don't have a good sense of time. We had a little chat or, more precisely, the gentleman talked to me about my sins. They always like to practise Sunday's sermon on folks like me, do the gawdelpuses. Then he walked off and I stayed thinking about my Saviour for the next little while, then I left too. When I found the watch it was reading ten minutes to five."

"So you must have met up with him about, what, half an hour earlier?"

"It's possible, but I wouldn't swear to it."

Murdoch sighed. He was up against a professional here.

"How long were you in the greenhouse altogether?"

"It's hard to say. I had a little kip on a bench so maybe a couple of hours. I left just before five o'clock to get to the spike. You know how it's better to be there early." Traveller took another deep draw on the pipe. "I'm curious, by the way, as to what you were doing there? It can't be because you're a pauper, even, begging your pardon, with a crib like this."

"Frankly, I was looking for you. Maybe not you specifically but a tramp I thought might be able to answer some questions concerning Reverend Howard."

"Do you suspect a wayfarer killed the gentleman?"

"Yes, I do."

"It's always easier, isn't it, to pin the crime on one of us? Saves you a lot of work."

"That's not the reason."

Murdoch pulled the box out from underneath his desk and put Howard's boots on the desk.

"Have you seen these before?"

"No, can't say I have, but they look uncommon good boots. Not yours, are they?"

"They originally belonged to the murdered man. They were taken from his body by somebody who wore them in the workhouse, where they were stolen a second time. I obtained them from the second thief."

"Must be good boots."

339

Murdoch drummed his fingers on the desk. He wasn't getting very far with the wily old fox. "Tell me, Traveller, have you ever been in Guelph?"

There was a flash of wariness in the man's eyes. He paused to draw on the pipe again. "Yes, I've been there. Just last week as a matter of fact. It's more comfortable than the House of Industry, I promise you that. Wish I could have stayed."

Murdoch tapped at the boots. "Do you swear to me you didn't take these from the pastor's body?"

Traveller's face was briefly hidden in a cloud of smoke. "I'm getting the impression it don't matter much what I say. You've got me tagged as the murderer and I can protest till I'm blue in the face but you ain't going to change your mind."

He put down the pipe and held out his hands to Murdoch.

"You'd better put the cuffs on right now and make your arrest. It'll look good for you."

There was a knock on the wall outside and Seymour pushed through the reed curtain. He was carrying a plate on which sat a thick wedge of pork pie.

Murdoch held up his hand. "Never mind, Sergeant Seymour, Mr. Trevelyan isn't hungry after all. In fact, he's going back to the cell. Put the handcuffs on him."

Seymour deposited the plate on top of the filing cabinet by the door and Murdoch saw Traveller cast one quick glance at the aromatic pie.

Murdoch watched while the sergeant led the docile tramp away.

Chapter Thirty-Seven

SEYMOUR RETURNED a few minutes later.

"Are you going to charge him, Will?"

"Not at the moment. Contrary to what he thinks, I'm not partial to making tramps scapegoats. He's bloody evasive for sure but that might be habitual and nothing to do with the murder. But I do know this, George, our Mr. Traveller will only tell me when it suits him. I want you to get him to remove his boots and bring them here. He'll have to go in his socks." Murdoch pointed at the piece of pie on the cabinet. "Is there more of that?"

"Like I said, Katie made enough for an army. There's at least two more servings left in the dish."

"Good."

Murdoch grabbed the plate and stuffed the pie into his mouth, swallowing it down in two gulps. Seymour grinned at him.

"Shall I give Katie your compliments?"

341

"Cardboard would have tasted good, but don't tell her that." He wiped his mouth with his handkerchief. "All right, let's bring in Alf. You don't need to cuff him."

Seymour left, taking the plate with him, and Murdoch managed to drop the boots into the box again and put the watch underneath his notebook.

He could hear Alf giggling as they approached the cubicle. Seymour brought him in and indicated he should sit in the chair.

"Hello, Alf," said Murdoch.

The boy stared at him in bewilderment. "Are you under arrest too?"

"No, lad. I'm actually a police detective. I was only pretending to be a tramp because I'm trying to find a very bad man."

"Is he a tramp?"

"He might be."

"Mr. Traveller isn't a bad man, but Mr. Bettles is."

"How long have you known Mr. Traveller?"

"A long, long time."

"A few months? A year or more? How long exactly?"

Alf laughed. "Weeks and weeks. He looks after me." Murdoch could see the lad was shivering with fear and he smiled at him.

342   "I just want to ask you a couple of questions, Alf, then the sergeant is going to take you outside and get you some hot pies with gravy. You don't have to be afraid. Nobody will hurt you."

Murdoch hoped he could make good this promise, but he also knew there was much truth in Traveller's accusation. Tramps and simpletons were easy marks and Inspector Brackenreid, for one, wasn't a patient man especially when a person of the better class had been killed.

He took the watch out of the drawer. "Have you ever seen this before, Alf?"

The boy nodded eager to please. "Yes, sir. I saw it just this morning. Did somebody pinch it?"

"Where did you see it?"

"The pastor in the woodyard was wearing it. Don't you remember? He looked at it a lot, I noticed."

Murdoch sighed. He vaguely recalled Reverend Harris consulting a silver watch.

He leaned over and lifted out the boots from the box. "What about these? Have you ever seen anybody wearing these? You can look at them if you want to."

Alf examined the boots, turned them over, bent back the soles, and sniffed at them. "Good boots," he said, a note of pride in his voice. Alf knew boots.

"I want you to think back. Not last night, but the night before that, did you notice if any of the tramps were wearing them?"

Alf thought about the question sombrely. "Them's good boots. You'd better take care of them. When you get into the bath they could get nicked, good boots like that."

343

Murdoch dragged over the other box with his foot and took out the pair of boots he'd found in the greenhouse.

"Have you seen these boots, Alf?"

The boy laughed out loud. "'Course I have. They're mine."

Murdoch did a quick check of the boy's feet. He was wearing shabby black boots very like the ones on the desk. "You've got your boots on, Alf. Did you have two pairs?"

Puzzled, Alf looked down, then grinned. "No, only ever had but one. They could be mine though."

Murdoch reached over and patted the boy's arm. "Thanks, Alf. Do you have a family you could go and stay with?"

"No, sir. They throwed me out. 'Alf,' they says to me, 'you eat more than the horse does so we're throwing you out.'"

"Where did you live?"

Again Alf assumed his thoughtful expression. "I don't rightly remember, sir. In the country it was though." He giggled. "'You eat more than the horse,' they says to me."

Murdoch reached in his pocket and took out a fifty-cent piece. "Here, my lad. One of the constables is going to take you to get something to eat and you can have whatever you want."

"Cake and custard. Can I have cake and custard?"

344

"Of course. As much as you can get for fifty cents."

Alf grabbed Murdoch's hand and planted a wet kiss on it. "Thank you, Mr. Williams. I'll save some for you for tonight."

There was no point in explaining to him that he wouldn't be coming back to the workhouse, so Murdoch just nodded. He called for Fyfer to collect him and as they were leaving, Alf asked, "Is Mr. Traveller coming for cake too?"

"Not at the moment. He's helping us to find the bad man."

"That's Mr. Bettles. He was going to hurt me. You and Mr. Traveller saved me."

Alf looked as if he was going to rush over and give Murdoch another kiss, but Fyfer tugged his arm and led him away.

Murdoch went through the same routine of hiding the watch and the boots. He hadn't really expected Alf would be of much help, but he'd had to try it.

There were footsteps in the corridor and the now familiar smell of sulphur wafted over as Higgins pushed Bettles through the reed curtain into the cubicle and shoved him into the chair.

"The man thinks he's a barrister. He keeps moaning that we're not telling him what he's being charged with." 345

Bettles looked like a casualty from the battlefield. The doctor had trimmed away his hair where the axehead had cut him and wrapped his head in a bandage, now bloodstained. The bruise under his eyes was turning yellow at the edges.

"As I live and breathe, it's Mr. Williams. That is unless you have a twin who's a down-and-outer, which I'm inclined to doubt. How's the mayor going to react when he discovers one of his officers is eating at the taxpayers' expense?"

To Murdoch's gratification, he seemed genuinely surprised. Higgins, who didn't know about Murdoch's undercover sojourn into the workhouse, looked puzzled. Murdoch nodded at him to leave and faced Bettles.

"I didn't get much sleep, the food was both lousy and inadequate, and I've hurt my back. I'm telling you right now, I'm not in a good skin this morning and I don't have patience for somebody trying to throw out horse plop. I am investigating a serious crime and you, Mr. Bettles, are a suspect. Do I make myself clear?"

Bettles rubbed his knuckles against his forehead like a sailor. "Ay, ay, sir. What you say is clear enough, but I don't have a frigging notion what this serious crime is that I'm supposed to be party to."

Murdoch stared at him for a moment. Bettles had light blue eyes, cold and lifeless as the scales of a dead fish. He could read nothing there, except wariness. He put the pair of boots and the watch on his desk.

"Do you recognize any of these objects?"

"Am I allowed to touch?"

346

Murdoch nodded and Bettles took his time examining each boot.

"These here look like any dozen tramps might have on their feet, but these ones are good boots. What do you mean 'recognize'? They ain't mine, if that's what you're getting at."

"Do you know whose they were?"

"Sure do. Our friend Traveller was wearing them on Tuesday when we went into the workhouse." Bettles scowled at Murdoch. "Don't tell me the old cove is accusing me of stealing his frigging boots? Is this the serious crime you're talking about?"

"You know bloody well it isn't. We're talking about a murder here, Mr. Bettles. These boots belonged to the murdered man. They were stolen from his body. Would you be prepared to go into a court of law and swear that you saw Mr. Trevelyan wearing them on Tuesday night?"

Bettles leaned back, a smirk of satisfaction on his face. "That depends. Memory can be so unreliable, can't it? We tramps tend to stick together. I wouldn't want to get him in trouble if it weren't true. You said I was a suspect. Is that just because I'm a wayfarer or have you got something else to pin on me?"

"Where did you spend Tuesday afternoon, Mr. Bettles?" 347

"Ah that's easy. I was nice and cozy in the pauper's common room at the House of Providence. The nuns took pity on me because I had a touch of bronchitis and they let me sit by the fire all afternoon. You can ask them."

"I intend to."

"I should have stayed there, but my three days was up and I was sick and tired of the idolatry." He squinted over at Murdoch. "I'm a Methodist born and raised."

"But you'll accept their charity."

"I'll accept the wampum of a savage if he gives me grub."

Murdoch found himself drumming on the table again. He knew Bettles was too wily to offer an alibi that couldn't be proved. Too bad. Murdoch had been looking forward to incarcerating him.

"By the way, you'll find out when you ask the Sisters that Kearney was with me. I thought I'd save you the trouble of questioning him."

"That's considerate of you."

Bettles shrugged. "Who went to the Grand Silence, then? Who was it you think Traveller did for?"

"I didn't say Jack Trevelyan did for anybody. But I'm investigating the murder of a man named Charles Howard. He was a pastor."

"What happened? Did his sins catch up with him?"

348   "Why do you say that?"

"Well it wouldn't be a thief that killed him, would it?"

"How can you be so sure?"

"Them church coves don't usually have much dosh.

No, correction. They don't usually *carry* much dosh with them in their pockets and such so as folks will think they're Christly but as we all know most of them are a bunch of hypocrites." For the first time, Bettles's eyes had life in them. "I know you despise us men who have come down in the world and need to beg for our supper, but let me tell you, Mister Detective, you get to know the ways of the world when you're looking up from the bottom."

"Name names."

Bettles laughed. "I have a funny kind of brain, mister. Memories come and go like birds on a branch. Sometimes they land and sometimes they don't." He touched his forefinger to the side of his nose. "Just let me know if there's anybody you particularly want to hear about and if I know, I'll tell you."

Murdoch wanted to reach over the desk and knock the smirk off his face and he might have if he wasn't virtually crippled. But he also knew that Bettles was hardened against intimidation or threats of any kind. All the currency the man had was the insinuation, probably real enough, that he had secret information.

"The thing with detective work, Mr. Bettles, is that you never know how long an investigation is going to last. I'm going to have to keep you here until we've made more progress."

"That don't worry me. It's warm enough and I know by law you're going to have to feed me. It'll be a nice

349

change from chopping logs." He stood up. "We're done then?"

Murdoch raised his voice and called to the constable who was outside in the corridor.

"Take Mr. Bettles back to the cell."

"Do you want to talk to the other fellow?" Higgins asked.

"Not now. Get Crabtree to take his statement concerning his whereabouts on Tuesday afternoon."

The constable took hold of Bettles's arm and led him out. Murdoch got to his feet and a stabbing pain ran up his back. He managed to straighten up slowly. "Did his sins catch up with him?" Bettles had asked. The trouble was the question was a valid one.

Chapter Thirty-Eight

LOUISA HOWARD WAS PALE AND HAGGARD, her eyes red-rimmed from lack of sleep and too much weeping. The drawing room where she received Murdoch was oppressive in the fading afternoon light. All of the mirrors had been soaped and the pictures turned around to face the wall. Black crepe ribbons festooned the fireplace and the window frames.

When he showed her the watch, she clasped it and kissed it. "Does this mean you have apprehended his murderer?"

"Not quite. It was in the possession of a tramp in police custody, but he swears he found it in the greenhouse of the Horticultural Gardens. This may or may not be true. We also have Mr. Howard's boots. I showed them to your maid, Doris, and she is certain they were your husband's. They were almost certainly worn by a tramp, but again we have as yet no definite proof which

man this was or if he was indeed the person who murdered your husband."

Louisa was twisting a black silk handkerchief round
and round over her fingers.

"But you say you do have a man in custody?"

"Yes, ma'am, I do."

She frowned at him. "But not yet charged?"

"No."

"I fail to understand why not."

"Mrs. Howard, I promise you we are doing everything we can. But I cannot arrest a man unless I am
certain he is guilty."

"He had Charles's watch and his boots."

"We know he had the watch, but we don't know if
he had worn the boots."

Louisa compressed her lips into a tight thin line. "Mr.
Murdoch, our Lord Jesus taught us to love our enemies,
but I tell you in all honesty, as each day dawns and I
see my fatherless children and I feel my fatherless child
stir in my womb, I am less and less able to obey those
teachings." She tugged on each end of the handkerchief.
"I want to see Charles's killer hanged. I will have no
peace until I know this has happened." Her eyes filled
with tears and she wiped them harshly away. "I cannot
weep any more."

Murdoch hesitated, searching for words that wouldn't
hurt her anew. "Mrs. Howard, I understand how you
feel and I would never persist in my inquiry if it weren't

352

necessary, but there are some more questions I need to ask you."

"What questions, surely you know enough?"

Her voice was harsh, but Murdoch also thought he detected fear. She had gone curiously still, watching him. Oddly enough her expression reminded him of the one he'd seen on Traveller's face. She was seeking to avoid the place where the trap was set. "Did his sins catch up with him?" Bettles had asked.

"On Tuesday, when I was here with Dr. Ogden, Mr. Drummond came to call on you. You refused to admit him. Why was that, Mrs. Howard?"

She glanced at him in surprise. This was not what she thought he was going to ask. "Mr. Drummond is no friend of mine. He was strongly opposed to Charles's appointment as pastor of this church. I could not bear the thought he might be coming here to gloat. He can have whomever he wants now."

"I understand Mr. Swanzey was the candidate Mr. Drummond supported."

"Yes, he was. Fortunately, Matthew is a man of humility and piety. He was quite reconciled to the choice and was most generous in his support for Charles. Unlike Mr. Drummond, who made it plain for all to see that he despised my husband. That is why I did not admit him and have no desire to do so even now."

"It must be difficult for you that his house is so close to yours."

353

"It is. I believe he stands in his shop doorway all day long, watching us. Why, I don't know, but it is most unpleasant."

On his way to the house as he walked along Gerrard, Murdoch had seen Drummond doing just that.

Her anger toward the elder had enlivened Louisa and she jumped to her feet and walked over to the fireplace, stretching out her hands to the blaze.

"Is that all you wished to know, Mr. Murdoch? I must confess I am feeling very tired."

Murdoch paused, trying to find the tactful way to ask his next question.

"There is something else, ma'am, and forgive me for the delicacy of the topic . . ."

He could see her back tense but she didn't turn around.

"I repeat, sir, I really am most fatigued. I don't think there is any more I can say to you."

"This concerns Miss Dignam."

Again Murdoch had the distinct impression this was not the question she expected. She glanced over her shoulder in surprise.

"I realize she has had a dreadful shock," continued Murdoch, "and she is most upset, but I wondered if she had a special relationship with your husband."

354   This question did bring Louisa about to face him. "Special? What on earth do you mean, special?"

"Miss Dignam is a spinster and perhaps has been a lonely woman. Sometimes in those circumstances, women develop fanciful notions about men such as their doctors or their ministers."

He hated himself for putting it that way. He could almost hear Amy Slade's voice castigating him.

Louisa Howard actually laughed. "Sarah Dignam fancied herself in love with my husband, is that what you're getting at?"

Murdoch nodded. "So you were aware of it?"

"Of course I was. Half of the parish knew. She was making quite a fool of herself. Always coming with little gifts, waiting around after prayer meetings, coming early. Staring at him with eyes that would put a puppy to shame. Poor Charles, she was driving him to distraction."

Neither Mrs. Howard's voice nor her expression were in the least kind. Murdoch wondered why she had so little sympathy.

"Surely you don't suspect Miss Dignam, do you?"

"I'm just gathering information, ma'am."

"She is a pathetic old soul, but I've never considered her to be deranged. And why would she kill the man she adored?"

She didn't wait for an answer, which was just as well. Because Murdoch would have had to say that Miss Dignam might have considered herself to be spurned. And hell hath no fury like a woman scorned. That path was quicksand and not one he could in conscience explore with the widow herself. He'd have to speak to Miss Flowers.

His back was seizing up on him and he eased forward in the chair, trying not to wince.

"I won't keep you much longer, Mrs. Howard, but there is one other matter I should tell you about."

"Yes?" Damn, there it was again. Wary as a wild cat.

"When I was here before I asked you if your husband had any enemies. You told me about the work he did as a volunteer for the city's charitable institution and we both thought it worthwhile questioning some of the people applying for charity who he would have visited."

"Yes? It is of no matter now."

"It may be more than we think. I did make inquiries specifically of the ones he had been forced to reject. This morning I discovered that one such family has died in what is probably a tragic accident."

"Why are you telling me this? Surely it has nothing to do with my husband's death? Poor people die all the time. He could not have been responsible."

"I did not mean in the least to imply that he was. The cause of death was carbon monoxide poisoning. The chimney was blocked in the downstairs room and the fumes came up into their room. The downstairs lodger died as well and two other people were made quite ill."

"I am sorry to hear it, but perhaps you can under-stand that my capability for sympathy is somewhat limited at the moment."

"Of course, ma'am. But I wonder if your husband ever mentioned this family to you. The name is Tugwell,

Esther and her daughter, Josie, and son, Wilfred."

Louisa's shock was palpable. "Tugwell? No, I never heard the name before."

You're a bloody poor actress, Murdoch said to himself.

"You say it was an accident?"

"It would appear to be so. As I said, the source of the carbon monoxide was the downstairs chimney. The fumes filled the house. The Tugwells got the worst of it as they were directly above."

For some reason he couldn't fathom, that seemed to relieve her.

"Mr. Murdoch, I realize you are only doing your duty but all this talk of death is most upsetting. I really must ask you to leave." She leaned over and tugged hard on the bell pull. "You have your culprit and I beg you not to bother me again until you have made that arrest. Then I shall be happy to receive you."

Doris came into the room.

"Please show Mr. Murdoch out, Doris. And I will receive no more visitors today."

"Mr. Swanzey is here, madam. I was just about to let you know."

Louisa looked flustered. "Yes, of course. Show him in. Goodbye, Mr. Murdoch. Forgive me if I sounded rude, it's just . . ."

"I quite understand, ma'am. I will keep you informed of my progress."

357

Doris opened the door and Swanzey came in. He hesitated in the doorway, but Louisa held out her hand to him.

"Matthew, dear friend. I'm so glad to see you."

Murdoch saw Swanzey flinch, but then he hurried across to her.

Murdoch left. He felt like a hound that had suddenly hit the scent of the fox. He didn't know where the creature was hiding, but he was sure he was on its trail.

Chapter Thirty-Nine

WHEN MURDOCH RETURNED to the station, Olivia Bagley and Ed Parker were both sitting on the bench in the main hall waiting for him. Olivia was wearing an appalling array of rags as to be almost unrecognizable. She didn't have her false teeth in and when she saw him she smiled a gummy grin.

Murdoch beckoned to them. "Come with me."

They followed him back to his cubicle. He'd forgotten to get an extra chair, so Olivia generously offered the one seat to Ed and she stood beside him. Murdoch went behind his desk.

"We've done what you wanted," said Olivia. "I'd like to get my boy now."

"As soon as I hear your report, you can both go," said Murdoch. He took out his notebook and fountain pen. "Ed, let's start with you. Oh, by the way, I'd like to thank you for your prompt action in the bathhouse.

I would have been discovered for sure if you hadn't diverted Dr. Ogden."

Ed looked at him oddly. "Why do you say that?"

"Because he knows who I am –" He saw the expression on Ed's face. "Hold on, are you saying you didn't throw a fit in the bathtub as a distraction?"

"Well, er, as a matter of fact, no. If you get into the infirmary, you at least get some supper and it's quieter."

"Parker, you were supposed to be helping me in there."

He shifted in embarrassment. "Sorry, Mr. Murdoch, I didn't think. As soon as they said a doctor was coming in, I knew I could get myself transferred . . . but I did let you know which of the coves might have my old boots on."

Murdoch had collected boots from all four of his nabs and lined them against the wall.

"Have a look at those. Can you identify any pair as yours?"

"I'll have to try them on."

"All right. Mrs. Bagley, help him, will you?"

Olivia came around and undid Ed's laces, easing off the tight boots. Both of them made ostentatious noises as she removed the boot from his injured foot, she of sympathy, he of pain. Murdoch waited until Ed had tried on all three of the other pairs, his expression heavily concentrating, as befitted a man conducting a test of such importance. He tried on each boot a couple of times, even got to his feet and hopped around the tiny space of Murdoch's office.

Finally, Murdoch put a stop to it. "Well?"

"It's very hard to say, sir. I'd only had the boots a couple of months myself, but of all of them, I'd pick these ones."

"It's them for certain," chipped in Olivia. "Who'd got them?"

Murdoch saw no reason not to tell them. "Jack Trevelyan was wearing them."

Ed and Olivia exchanged glances. "Does that mean he was the one who did for the pastor?" asked Ed.

Before he could answer, there was quick rap on the wall outside his cubicle and Gardiner thrust his head through the reed curtain.

"There's a message for you, Mr. Murdoch. Dr. Ogden called. She wants you to telephone her right back. She says it's urgent."

Murdoch got out of his chair as quickly as he could while the two plungers eyed him curiously.

"I'll be right back, don't touch anything," said Murdoch.

"Couldn't stand us a cup of tea, could you, seeing as how we're helping you with your inquiries? We're fair parched, aren't we, Ed?"

Ed nodded vigorously. "Do you mind, sergeant?" Murdoch asked Gardiner. It was clear the sergeant wasn't happy with the request.

"If you think it's necessary, I'll have Callahan make a pot for them," he said.

Murdoch made his way to the telephone table in the front hall. He picked up the receiver and the constable connected him, then went off on Gardiner's orders to mash the tea. Murdoch was glad to have the privacy. Callahan was a nosy chap and Murdoch was sure he stored up bits of dropped information to use later, like a chipmunk gathering nuts. Gardiner, still in a sulk, went back to his desk.

The telephone rang for such a long time Murdoch was on the point of hanging up when Dr. Ogden answered, sounding slightly breathless as if she'd run to the telephone. He picked up the mouthpiece.

"Dr. Ogden, William Murdoch here. I understand you wanted to speak to me."

"Yes. Good. I've just completed the post-mortem examination on Mr. Hicks and I thought you should know immediately that I found prussic acid in his stomach. As soon as I cut him open I could smell it. Very distinctive odour of bitter almonds."

"Good heavens."

"Prussic acid is a favourite poison of suicidal persons, but I don't remember even seeing a bottle when I first examined him. Did you find one or a suicide note?"

"No, neither." Murdoch hooked his foot around the spare stool by the desk, pulled it over, and sat down, suppressing his groan. "Could it have been an accident?"

362

"That is most unlikely. You can hardly mistake a bottle labelled 'poison' for a glass of water. There wasn't a large amount in the stomach but sufficient to bring about unconsciousness almost immediately. That's why it's so often chosen by self-murderers, it acts quickly before they have a chance to change their minds. But it's most peculiar you haven't found the bottle. You'll have to search thoroughly."

"I intend to, ma'am."

"It is not completely out of the question that Hicks took the poison somewhere else in the room, say, then walked back to his chair where he collapsed. I'm wondering if he didn't block the chimney himself, hoping his death would seem like an accident, not even thinking he would cause the deaths of innocent people. You'll have to see if he left a will or has an insurance policy on his life."

"Yes, I'll do that. I must say when I met him, he didn't strike me as a man who was in a precarious state of mind."

"Ah yes, but these people are cunning. I've known instances when the closest family members had no notion at all of what was going on in the suicide's mind. Did you say anything that may have upset him?"

Murdoch considered her question. "Not that I am aware of, although he did talk about his deceased wife whom he was sorely missing."

363

"There you go, then. Does he have children?"

"He said not. Was there any other wounding to the body?"

"None."

"Could another person have forcibly administered the poison, for instance?"

"I saw no such signs."

"Have you examined the other bodies yet?"

"No. I will report back to you when I've done so."

She disconnected and Murdoch hung the receiver on its hook. Goddamn it. So much for his sensitive nostrils sniffing the air. It seemed that the Tugwell connection to Howard's murder was a coincidence after all. And he supposed that Louisa Howard's odd reaction to the news of the tragedy had to do with her hearing that in some way her husband would be held responsible. Poor old Hicks. He got slowly to his feet and walked over to Gardiner.

"Will you send a couple of the constables over to the house on Sherbourne Street. Have them take Mr. Hicks's room apart. We're looking for a bottle of prussic acid and maybe even a suicide letter and any papers at all concerning his affairs, a will, insurance policies, that sort of thing. I'll come as soon as I've finished here."

"I'll have Fyfer and Higgins go over at once." Gardiner hesitated. "Will, I have to tell you, I am a Christian man, but I'm itching to get my hands on that tramp. When are you going to make the arrest?"

"I don't know. We don't have enough solid proof yet."

"Leave me alone with him and I'll beat the confession out of him."

Murdoch nodded. "I'll take care of it, Henry."

"The pastor deserves justice. He was a true servant of our Lord."

"Yes, I'm sure he was. Tell Fyfer I'll join him as soon as I can."

He made his way back to his cubicle. Olivia had taken over his chair and she was in the process of gulping down her mug of tea. Murdoch saw how greedily she was drinking and he felt guilty.

She moved back to Ed as soon as Murdoch came in.

"Everything all right, then? Not terminal, are you?"

"What?"

She grinned hideously. "You just had an urgent call from a doctor and you come back looking like thunder. I just wondered if she was telling you bad news."

"Never you mind. Let's get on with this."

Murdoch sat in his chair and was rewarded by the stab of pain. He winced.

Olivia noticed. "Eddie said you hurt your back. You should put a mustard poultice on it. And take a purge."

"Thank you, Mrs. Bagley. Now do you have any news for me?"

She smiled slyly. "As a matter of fact, I do. I went to each depot in turn and started up a good chin with the others in the queue. Lot of walking it was but I will say, it's the first time I've felt stuffed for weeks. And if you ever want to know, the soup they serve at St. Peter's Church is the best."

365

"Thank you, I'll keep that in mind."

His tone made her a bit huffy. "Just trying to be helpful. Well, anyway, the third time round, I went to the depot just up here on Oak Street. And let me tell you, Mr. Murdoch, I got the sixpence. There was a young woman in front of me, a bit disreputable if you ask me but I did like you said I was to do and engaged her in conversation. 'I was lucky with my Visitor,' says I. 'He coughed up a ticket right away.' 'That so,' says she, 'well you were dead jammy, weren't you.' 'Did yours give you a hard time,' I asks. 'Ha,' says she. 'I just got a new one. The first was tight as pigskin as usual, but this one was willing to give me a ticket all right under certain conditions.' 'What conditions?' asks I. 'You *know* what,' she says, 'I get my docket as long as I – him.' And she used a word I won't sully your ears with repeating but in common parlance it means have intimate connections."

"With the Visitor?"

"Precisely. 'But isn't he a clergyman?' I asks because most of the Visitors are. She laughs like I'd said something very funny. 'Where've you bin all your life, in a manger? Reverends are the worst. And I'm not the first this one has bin after.' 'That isn't right,' says I, which it isn't. 'You *have* been brought up in a manger,' says she. 'It happens all the time. You'd better watch yourself. He'll be after you next. He's not fussy.' I would have gone on talking to her, but we were about to get our soup then and that's all she could see."

Murdoch stared at her. "Did she tell you the man's name?"

"No, the chin went pretty much as I've told it to you."

Olivia looked at him, clearly expecting to be congratulated. Murdoch managed to beam at her.

"Well done indeed, but there's no possibility she was making it up, is there?"

"None. Why'd she tell me something like that if it weren't the truth?"

Ed interrupted. "Some people like to stir up trouble, Livvy. They're in the dirt and they feel they might as well fling some of it around."

"This weren't like that. She let her hair down because she thought we were sisters. As if I've ever. Plunging's one thing, selling yourself for a bit of coal and a loaf of bread is another."

"Have you ever had anything to do with any of the Visitors?" Murdoch asked.

"No." Olivia lifted her shoulders in pride. "We've managed to fend for ourselves, haven't we, Ed?"

"But you were in the workhouse on Tuesday."

"That was an emergency. We didn't get much dosh that day, the weather was too bad, so Ed decided he'd be better off taking a turn in the spike. I begged him not to and I was right. Look at all the trouble it's landed us in."

Parker was about to protest and rekindle what was obviously an ongoing argument. Murdoch tapped his

367

pen on the notebook. "All right, never mind that now. Mrs. Bagley, what did this woman look like?"

"It's hard to say, she had a shawl over her head."

"You've got to do better than that. You said a young woman. About how old? How tall? Was she dark or fair?"

"I just told you, she had a shawl over her head, I didn't see."

Murdoch knew perfectly well that this was Olivia's way of getting her own back. Under protest, she had done what he asked her to, but she wasn't going to make his life easier. For all her protestations, she did see the woman in the queue as one of her own kind. Murdoch wasn't and never would be. He laid his pen beside the notebook and leaned over the desk.

"Mrs. Bagley, your son is probably missing you and you have indicated you miss him. I need to talk to the girl who was telling you this story. I'd like to get a description of her so I can find her. Until your memory gets sharper, Tim is going to have to stay where he is."

Normally, Murdoch wouldn't have behaved like a bully but he was tired, hungry, and his back hurt. He'd hardly finished what he was saying when he realized he'd made a mistake. He saw an expression cross Olivia's face and he knew he now embodied all the tyrannical wardens, police officers, doctors, all those who had power to determine whether she ate or not, whether she had money to live or not, and above all who had

368

rule over her life. She stared back at him with anger in her eyes.

"I'm sure Tim is getting some good grub where he is so I doubt he's missing his ma that much so I ain't much worried about him. But you can't get blood out of a stone, Mr. Detective, no matter how much you stomp on it. I don't remember anything at all about this woman. Nothing."

In his own frustration, Murdoch flashed back at her. "Very well. I'm having you taken to the Mercer. Perhaps a little time in solitary confinement will jog your memory. I will talk with you tomorrow."

Ed gaped at him in dismay. "Begging your pardon, sir, but that don't seem fair to me. Livvy is doing her best."

"Is she?" Murdoch knew his voice was too loud. "Let's put it this way, Mr. Parker. A man, who for all intents and purposes was a thoroughly decent human being, has been brutally murdered. He leaves behind him two young children and his wife is carrying their third child. Last night, a kind old man died. He may have taken his own life, I don't know for certain, but because of him, three other people lost their lives, one a crippled boy. Another woman is deathly ill and may not live. I met this old man and all he wanted to do was read books. He met Charles Howard, who was also the Visitor for the family that lived upstairs, and is now dead. I was starting to believe that was purely a coincidence, but I

369

don't like coincidences. Now you're telling me about a woman who claims that one of the esteemed volunteers for the city might be what I would deem a rapist."

There was a silence as they looked at him; Olivia's eyes were dark.

Murdoch made himself calm down. "Perhaps you can understand why I am not feeling much patience with poor memories. I intend to clear up this bloody case if it's the last thing I do."

He leaned his elbows on the desk and rested his head in his hands. To add to his misery, he was developing a throbbing headache. "The woman you met in the queue may be able to help us. I beg you to help me find her."

She sucked in her cheeks, a gesture that added twenty years to her face. "If I cannot remember, there's nothing I can do, is there?"

Murdoch sighed. "So be it." He rubbed at his temples. "Mrs. Bagley, I apologize for trying to threaten you. I should not have done that. I'll have Tim released and you can go home. But you have to report back here in the morning. If you try to scarper, I'll put out a bill for you and you will go to the Mercer for sure whether your son misses you or not. Perhaps something will come to you in a dream."

She shrugged. "I doubt that." She helped Ed to his feet and handed him the crutches. She waved her finger at Murdoch. "If you want to cure your lumbago, you should go home. Take a purgative or some such."

She didn't say "rat poison," but he knew that's what she was thinking.

Chapter Forty

MURDOCH WAS BEGINNING to feel as if he could fall asleep on the spot. He longed to be at home, in bed, with his stomach full of Katie's hot pork chops and potatoes. However, even fatigue couldn't wipe out the pain of his lumbago and there was no comfortable position, sitting hardly better than standing, and walking agony. The only kind of movement that didn't hurt was bicycling and he was glad to get on his wheel and head for Hicks's lodging house, where the two constables were searching. Before he left the station, he instructed Gardiner to give Traveller a good dinner and a pipe of tobacco but not to release him as yet.

"What about the other two toe-rags?"

"If Burley comes back and the Sisters have confirmed their alibi, we'll have to let them go, but don't feed them. And make sure they tell you where they're going next."

He was pedalling slowly along Wilton when he noticed somebody huddled in the doorway of the grocery shop at the corner. Murdoch stopped.

"Alf, what are you doing here?"

The boy looked completely miserable, his nose reddened from the cold.

"Hello, Mr. Williams. I've done my three days at the workhouse and my brother threw me out so I don't have nowhere to go."

Murdoch cursed under his breath. Gardiner must have turfed Alf out of the jail when Murdoch released him.

"And you have no money for a doss house, I presume?"

"No, sir. Mr. Traveller was going to look after me but I don't know where he is."

Murdoch took out his notebook and began to scribble a note. "Alf, I want you to take this note to the House of Providence. Do you know where that is?"

"No, sir."

"All right, I'll tell you in a minute. When you get there you must ask for Sister Mary Mathilda. Say it to me."

Alf repeated slowly, "Sister Mathilda."

"Give her this note. She'll give you something to eat and she'll find you a bed for the night."

Before Murdoch could stop him, the simpleton jumped up and grabbed his hand and planted a hearty kiss on it.

Murdoch pushed him away gently. "That's enough, Alf. Now put the note in your pocket . . . that's it. Off you go. Straight down Parliament Street to Queen Street. Then you turn left. Show me your left, Alf. Good. Just before St. Paul's Church is the street that leads to the House of Providence. You can see it. I'm going to come to the House in the next few days and I will expect a good report."

Alf giggled in real joy. "Can Mr. Traveller come too?"

"Not at the moment. And Alf, Sister Mary Mathilda is a lady, a nun, and you mustn't grab her hand or kiss her without asking. That's not polite."

"No, sir. I won't."

"Get going then. Fast as you can."

Obediently, Alf trotted off and Murdoch watched him to make sure he'd got it right. At the corner, he turned and gave a big exuberant wave as if he was far away and bidding farewell to a longlost friend. Murdoch felt a pang of sorrow. His brother, Bertie, used to stand on the pier and send off the fishing boats with just that exuberance. Most of the fishermen tolerated him, but their father was always irritated. *He looks like a fool. Don't let him act like that.* The chastisement came down heavily on everybody in the family, especially their mother.

374   Murdoch waved back.

He continued on his way along Wilton to Sherbourne.

Fyfer greeted him at the door to Hicks's room. "We found this in his cupboard, sir. It's his will, written three years ago. There's fifty dollars as well." He handed an envelope to Murdoch. "We've turned his room inside out, sir, and there isn't a trace of a bottle of prussic acid nor a suicide note."

Higgins was shaking out the last of the books in the bookcase.

"Be gentle with those books, constable," said Murdoch. Higgins looked bewildered but began to move a little slower. Murdoch opened the envelope. Inside was a single piece of paper headed.

The last will and testament of Thomas Elijah Hicks. Dated this 20th day of June 1893.

Being of sound mind, I Thomas Hicks do hereby write my last will and testament. I bequeath all of my worldly goods, to wit my books and bookcases to the Toronto Public Library to dispose of as they see fit. My personal effects I donate to St. Stephen's Anglican Church to dispense among those who have need.

My body I bequeath to the Toronto Medical School so that our new young doctors may learn.

I request my burial be simple and that I be buried next to my beloved wife, Emily, who resides in the Mount Pleasant Cemetery. I have left enclosed sufficient money to cover those expenses. My solicitor has a copy of this will. His office is 31 King Street West. Mr. Eric Deacon.

The will was signed and witnessed by two people who gave their occupation as clerk.

The money was a mix of crumpled notes from various banks and of various denominations. In spite of his poverty, Hicks had saved enough money for the burial he wanted.

"Higgins, I want you to take this paper and go to Mr. Deacon. See if this was the last will that Mr. Hicks had drawn up. Find out if he had taken out any insurance policies."

The constable left.

"Let me just show you something, sir," said Fyfer, and he led the way over to the window. The curtains had been opened when Dr. Ogden did her examination, but Murdoch hadn't paid a lot of attention.

"This is an old house and the frame is cracked. Somebody has gone to a lot of trouble to seal the window."

He indicated the newspaper that was stuffed into the gaps around the frame.

Murdoch looked puzzled. "He's keeping out the drafts. I've done that myself."

Fyfer smiled, happy at his own astuteness. "Look at the date on the newspaper. It's yesterday's *Globe*. This was just done. I take that as too much of a coincidence. Man blocks any air, then that same night dies from carbon monoxide poison. It would be easy to dislodge a brick in the chimney and create a block. We all know the danger of burning cheap coke without proper venting. I'd say it's a clear indication of self-murder."

Murdoch sighed. "But why do both? Why take prussic acid and also set up carbon monoxide poisoning?"

"There'll be an insurance policy, mark my words, sir. They'll pay for an accident, not for suicide."

"But why haven't we found the bottle of prussic acid?"

"It must be here somewhere, sir. It wouldn't just walk away."

"But it could be carried. What if somebody else gave him the poison?"

"Offed him for his insurance money, you mean?"

"Fyfer, you've got insurance on the brain."

"Sorry, sir. I just took out an indemnity policy myself, maybe that's why. My parents will do well if I'm run over by a streetcar."

"Leaving aside the possibility of an unknown person being the beneficiary of the as-yet-unfound insurance policy, somebody could have poisoned him with the prussic acid, maybe even at his own request, then set it up to seem like a tragic accident with the blocked chimney."

"But why go to all that trouble, unless they stand to gain something? . . . Yes, sir, I know what you're going to say but what if the murderer was a friend? What if Mr. Hicks says to that friend, Hey, I'm tired of living without my old lady, will you poison me, because I'm ascared to do it myself, but then make it look like an accident so none of my friends will be upset and think

377

the less of me? Was he a papist, do you know, sir?"

"No, I believe he was a Presbyterian. At least he was reading the Psalms, but I suppose he could have been any denomination."

Fyfer was looking a little smug and Murdoch held up his hand. "All right. That theory doesn't hold water. If Hicks wanted to kill himself, he could have easily set up the carbon monoxide poisoning and made it look like an accident. It's the prussic acid that's thrown a wrench in the works. That doesn't make sense. According to Dr. Ogden, the poison acts quickly. Hicks was an old man and she believes he would have gone unconscious almost immediately. "

Murdoch was sitting at the table, which was easier on his back. There was a teapot on the table but no cups. Over by the sink, Hicks's few mugs were on their hooks. Murdoch reached over and removed the lid from the teapot. There was some tea left in the bottom. He took a good sniff.

"Damn, I should have checked this before. Have a smell, Fyfer, there's prussic acid in there all right." The constable confirmed his suspicion. "We'll get this to Dr. Ogden right away. So you have to be right about there being a second person. The mug is washed and hung up. Hicks couldn't have done that."

"Whoever it was, friend or foe, wasn't thinking too clearly, were they, sir? They should have emptied out the teapot. Either that or made it blatant and left the bottle in the cupboard or something. They must have taken it with them."

"As you say, Hicks's guest wasn't thinking clearly. He, or she, must have been distressed at what they were doing."

"They probably thought nobody'd suspect. Criminals don't realize what doctors can find these days when they cut you open. So what do you think, sir? Was it a friend or a foe?"

"It's hard to believe the man was deliberately murdered. If ever a man seemed harmless, Thomas Hicks did."

"So's an anthill until you kick it," said the constable somewhat ambiguously. "Shall I get started on questioning the neighbours, sir? See if anybody noticed anybody coming in."

"Dr. Ogden thought he died about midnight so I assume the second person came about ten o'clock. The German woman who lived upstairs said she heard voices. That's probably who it was. Get some help, Frank. I want every resident on the street interviewed. The usual. Did Hicks quarrel with anybody? What sort of man was he and so on." Murdoch stood up and pressed his hand into the small of his back. "Lock the door, will you, and leave the key at the station. I'm sure his landlord will be wanting to rent out the rooms immediately and I'm not going to let him. I'm going home for a short spell, but if anything of a dramatic nature comes up, come and get me."

"Yes, sir. By the way, I know a good treatment for lumbago."

"Don't tell me, take a purge?"

"That's right, sir. Works wonders. Remember that attack I had last winter when I was shovelling out snow in front of the station? I was bent double, but I took a few Ayers pills and they got me right as rain in no time at all."

"I'll keep it in mind."

Chapter Forty-One

BICYCLING SEEMED TO EASE the spasm in his back and Murdoch was able to dismount and bring his wheel into the house without too much difficulty. He stowed the bicycle in its usual place under the stairs and was about to go up to his room when he noticed a black astrakhan coat and a silk hat hanging on the hall stand. At the same time, he heard the now familiar sound of a foghorn emanating from Amy's room. This was followed by a convincing rendition of a loon calling. Then a burst of man's laughter. She was home early from school. And she had a visitor. The loon sound became a lovely liquid finch song. More laughter and applause. Murdoch stood listening a few moments longer when suddenly the door opened and Amy came out into the hall. Right behind her was a man he had never seen before, a tall, well-dressed fellow whose face was a glow with pleasure. Murdoch felt himself turn scarlet with embarrassment and would have liked to get up the stairs in a hurry but he couldn't. Amy saw him, and to his eyes, she likewise seemed disconcerted.

"Good afternoon, Will. I didn't expect you home so early."

"Nor I you."

"It's a half holiday today."

"Oh yes, I forgot. You did mention that."

The man was still standing behind Amy, eyeing Murdoch with frank curiosity. He leaned toward her and said cozily in her ear, "This must be the famous Mr. Murdoch, the police detective you told me about?"

She stepped away from him. "Yes, that's right. Allow me to introduce you. Will, this is Mr. Roger Bryant - William Murdoch, my fellow lodger." She smiled. "And my saviour."

"What an enviable position to be in your life, dear Amy," murmured Bryant.

"What I meant was that Will took me into these lodgings when I had nowhere to live." She sounded slightly irritated and Murdoch could feel some tension easing inside his chest. Mr. Roger Bryant might be acting like a masher, but Amy was having none of it. Who the hell was he to be on such familiar terms with her? Murdoch stepped forward to shake hands, but no will power in the world could force his back muscles to release sufficiently for him to stand completely straight.

"Will, what have you done to your back?"

"Touch of lumbago, nothing serious."

"Ah, how unfortunate for you," said Bryant as he shook hands. He was a couple of inches taller than Murdoch, perhaps a little older. He had attractive blue eyes, thick wavy brown hair, and a luxuriant moustache, waxed to fine points on either end. His breath smelled faintly of wine.

Amy turned and removed the hat and coat from the stand and handed them to him.

"My dear, one would almost think you are trying to get me out of here in a hurry," said Bryant.

"You said you had an appointment."

"So I did but it does not have nearly the same appeal as your wonderful lodging house does. Thanks, as you say, to your landlord here."

Murdoch and Amy spoke at virtually the same time.

"Oh, I'm not the –"

"He's not the landlord."

That made them laugh and Mr. Bryant frown. He took Amy's hand and bowed over it. Murdoch was certain he would have kissed her fingers, but she pulled away before he could do so.

"Please think about what I said, Amy. I will await your reply."

He took a gold-topped ebony cane from the stand and with a brusque nod at Murdoch he left.

Amy closed the door emphatically behind him. "Roger's an old acquaintance of mine," she said to Murdoch, who

383

was leaning against the stair wall. Amy bent down and picked something up from the floor. "Oh dear, this is your letter, Will. It slipped off the table. It's from Great Britain. You've been waiting for it, haven't you?"

Murdoch took the letter from her. It seemed distressingly thin.

Amy turned away. "I have to practise some more of my songs for tomorrow. Take care of your lumbago. I'll see you at suppertime. "

She headed back to her room.

Murdoch felt as if there was acid in his stomach. She had every right to have visitors, to know men who acted like suitors. She had every right, of course she did. And why wouldn't she be attracted to a man who was handsome and obviously rich. His coat alone would have cost Murdoch two weeks' wages and the gold-topped cane another month's.

Traveller would probably have said, We're just the same as the creatures of the wild. The one with the biggest cock always wins the female.

Appalled he was thinking this way, clutching Enid's letter, Murdoch made his way up the stairs.

On the other hand, Amy hadn't seemed exactly won over by Mr. Bryant in spite of the jollity he'd heard coming from her room.

384

The dream was one that recurred over and over, only small details changed but the import was always the same, he was trying desperately to rescue his mother or Susanna or Bertie and couldn't. This night's dream was particularly vivid.

He seemed to be in the school dormitory in his hard, narrow bed. It was very dark and although his eyes were open, he couldn't see and he strained desperately to make out the vague shapes around him. He was also finding it impossible to sit up, as if he had no power in his body. He sensed rather than saw that over in the corner of the big room, his mother and sister were both sitting on a bed that resembled one of the flat-topped rocks that jutted out from the beach on the south arm of the cove. They were surrounded by some kind of dangerous sea animals, half seal, half rat, which they were trying to fend off. He had to get to them if only he could move. Bertie was crying, but he didn't know where he was.

Murdoch woke up. He could hear babies wailing and it took him a few moments to come out of his dream and realize it was the twins downstairs. He'd been struggling so hard, he'd almost moved himself off his bed but he was lying on his back and when he tried to sit up, he couldn't move without a shooting pain up his spine. Slowly, there that's it, roll to one side, now push. Argh. He was sitting straight up at least, his feet dangling over the side of the bed.

From downstairs, the wails lessened. One of the twins at least had stopped crying. Katie was probably feeding him. In a moment the other quieted down. Murdoch could make out a murmur of voices, then the

385

sound of the door opening and closing. Amy was leaving for school. With an effort and another moan, he stood up and shuffled to the washstand. She hadn't come into the kitchen for supper last night, and Katie told him she'd said she had a headache and was going to eat in her room. Seymour had gone out for one of his regular meetings and even Katie, who loved to sit with him and chat, had pleaded exhaustion and gone to bed so he had eaten alone. He was pretty tired himself, but when he managed to get upstairs and into bed, sleep had eluded him as it so often did. He'd read Enid's brief letter through again. She'd begun by saying, "I might not have occasion to write for a long time . . ." and the words were seared in his mind. Her father was about the same as he had been, the weather was damp, she'd had a cold. Then in her last paragraph, she said that "an old family friend" had come to visit, the man, now a widower who "got along just wonderfully with Alwyn." That was a particularly sharp stab, considering how long it had taken Murdoch to win the boy's affections. All these "old acquaintances" were getting under his skin. Enid's letter was friendly enough, but the tone was as cool as a cucumber, as if he, Murdoch, were the old acquaintance, not a man who had been her lover. Only at the end of the letter had she said anything truly personal. "Think of me sometimes, Will." He glanced over at the lovely ormolu clock on the mantelpiece that she had given him just before she left. "At least I can be sure you will be reminded of me from time to time."

Damn. He felt both guilty and irritated at her timidity. He had cared for her deeply and even now the memory of the lovemaking they'd experienced stirred him. She was the first woman he'd ever had intimate connection with. He'd loved Liza passionately but both of them had believed in the sanctity of marriage and the love was not consummated.

"The grave's a fine and private place, But none, I think, do there embrace."

Liza had encouraged him to read poetry, although it wasn't quite to his taste. Like Mr. Hicks, he preferred rollicking adventure stories. But one day, he'd come across Marvell's poem when he was browsing through some of the poetry collections at the library and he'd rushed home to read it to her. Oh God, when was that? June probably, he remembered it was a lovely sunny evening and Liza was wearing a light summer dress. She listened seriously to the poem and laughed. "You can praise my bosom as long as you like, Will," but then she kissed away his scowl with a frustrating passion. "We'll be married soon." But they weren't married soon, or ever would be.

"None I think do there embrace."

He poured water from the pitcher into the bowl on the washstand. He'd expected the water to be cold, but it was lukewarm and he smiled. Dear Katie must have crept into his room with a jug of hot water, expecting

387

he would be waking soon. He was later than usual, but he was finding it hard to move fast. He couldn't be bothered to sharpen his razor and paid the price by nicking himself on the chin. Blood coloured the water immediately and he dabbed at the wound with the towel. Another damn.

He hadn't read Marvell's poem to Enid. She was not playing the coy mistress with him. The opposite. She had made it clear she wanted to be his wife. It was he who was holding back.

Serves you right then, he said to himself. Why should she wait for you? Now she's probably being courted by the old family friend who has conveniently lost his wife, that, thank goodness, Alwyn, who as we all know is very particular, actually likes.

He sponged himself down as best he could and dried off. The room was cold, the fire in the hearth long burned out, and he tried to hurry. He got into his under-shirt all right, but his trousers were a problem and he had to shuffle from one foot to the other before he could get them on. He'd been so intent on that struggle, he hadn't heard the knocking on the front door, but as he was wrestling with his socks, there were footsteps on the stairs and a light tap on his door. Katie said softly, "Mr. Murdoch, there's somebody here to see you."

He opened the door. "Is it Constable Crabtree?"

Katie turned a little pink at seeing him half-clothed. "No, Mr. Murdoch. It's a lady. She is most apologetic about coming here at this hour, but she says it's urgent. Here's her card."

Murdoch took the calling card and read, *Miss Sarah Dignam.*

"Good Lord! Show her into the parlour, will you, Katie? Tell her I'll be right down."

"Shall I make tea?"

"Yes, indeed and toast too if you don't mind. With lots of butter."

He returned to his room and pulled on his shirt. The celluloid collar of the shirt was stiff and as he fumbled with the button, some of the blood from his chin transferred to the edge of the collar. Damn and blast to that. Hurriedly, he knotted his tie and put on his jacket, which fortunately hid the blood spot. Bending over to tie up his shoelaces was almost impossible and required contortions he didn't know he could ever repeat. He felt as if he were taking so long, he half expected Miss Dignam, who had taken such an unorthodox step as to call on him at his lodgings, to be coming upstairs to greet him. Fortunately, she was contained enough to be still waiting in the front parlour. Katie had brought in the tea and a rack of toast, but Miss Dignam was sitting motionless in the chair. Like Mrs. Howard, she looked as if she hadn't slept and she too seemed to have aged. However, in spite of her pallor and the deep lines etched around her eyes and mouth, she retained the vestiges of a sweet prettiness, now fragile and desiccated as a

389

pressed flower. The short blue cape she was wearing accentuated her blue eyes.

"Miss Dignam, I'm so sorry to keep you waiting."

"No please, it is I who should apologize for coming at such an early hour and to your own lodgings. I first went to the police station, but the sergeant said you had not arrived and I managed to get out of him where you lived so I came here directly."

The strangeness of the visit couldn't totally distract Murdoch from the hunger pangs in his stomach and he indicated the tea trolley.

"May I offer you some tea and toast."

"No, thank you." She must have noticed his yearning glance at the teapot because she said, "Please, have your breakfast. I have waited this long, a few more minutes won't make that much difference. "

Murdoch poured himself a cup of tea, added milk and sugar lumps, and took a piece of the toast. Miss Dignam sat staring into the fire, which was just getting going in the hearth. She looked so grey and sombre that he paused for a moment. Good God, had she come to confess to the murder of Charles Howard? He put down the toast, uneaten.

"I'm ready now, ma'am. Why is it you wanted to see me?"

"Mr. Murdoch, I have done nothing but pray to our Lord for guidance ever since this tragedy happened. I am aware that what I did was against the law and I am quite prepared to take my punishment." She reached into her jet-beaded reticule and he thought she was looking for a handkerchief but in fact she removed an envelope, which she handed to him. "I have not told you the complete truth on two counts, Mr. Murdoch. I hope you will understand and forgive me when I explain why. There is something in the envelope that you should see."

Murdoch opened the flap. Inside was a piece of paper that had smudges of brownish red on the edges that he recognized as blood stains. He unfolded the letter.

To the board of directors.

It is with a heavy heart that I write this letter. I wish I was not privy to the information I have just now received which I must impart to you

The letter stopped with a sharp upward zig of the *u*. "Where did you get this, Miss Dignam?"

"I took it from Mr. Howard's desk when I found him."

"Why did you do that, ma'am?"

She didn't answer, only clasping her hands more tightly together. Murdoch was aware that in the adjoining kitchen, Katie had started to sing to the twins. Miss Dignam raised her head and listened for a moment and an expression of intense loneliness crossed her face. Hearing the lullabies sometimes affected Murdoch the same way.

"Ma'am? You didn't answer my question. Why did you take the letter?"

His voice was by no means sharp, but she shrank back into the chair. "When you first came to talk to me, Mr. Murdoch, I had the impression that you are a kind man and I must trust that impression now because what I am about to tell you could easily invite your ridicule and contempt and frankly, I would find that hard to bear." Finally, she met his eyes. "You see, Mr. Murdoch, what I have to tell you is that Charles Howard and I loved each other."

All he could think of was Louisa Howard's angry words: *Poor Charles, she was driving him to distraction.*

Miss Dignam didn't seem insane. She was speaking calmly, not weeping, and the only sign of emotion was a slight flush on her thin cheeks and a brightness to her eyes. "Let me explain," she continued. "When Charles was chosen as our new pastor, he was not the unanimous choice. Our previous pastor was a conservative man who died as he had lived, without much reverberation. Some of us had been hoping for a minister who might bring new vigour to the church and Charles was such a man. He was well travelled and urbane and had actually experienced the battle of Khartoum, as a civilian, you understand, not a soldier. He had many stories to share with us and he brought exactly the breath of life we needed." She paused. "My throat is a little dry, Mr. Murdoch, perhaps I will have a cup of tea after all."

392

He poured the tea and waited while she sipped at it. He didn't know where all this was leading, but he knew he must be patient. And there was something about this little wan woman that tugged at his heart.

She replaced her cup on the trolley. "It fairly soon became apparent to me that Charles was developing special feelings for me. His wife is a good woman but, I regret to say, rather shallow and far too caught up in the prestige of her position as a pastor's wife. I say that only to you, of course. May Flowers shares my view, but that is all we have shared. I do not gossip, Mr. Murdoch. I never told Miss Flowers what was happening between Charles and me. I did not know how we were going to resolve our dilemma, but I trusted he would find a way and on Monday, by certain signals that he sent me, I knew he was going to openly declare his love."

"What were these signals, Miss Dignam?"

Unexpectedly, there was a flash of fire in her eyes and her voice was stronger. "I know what you're thinking, Mr. Murdoch. How could a woman such as I, no longer in her youth, be an object of attraction to a man in his prime? A man who is already married? I myself doubted it many times, but finally I was convinced. The signs? A woman knows these things. They were in his special smiles to me, the way he would touch my hand when we parted, the expression on his face when he thanked me for my little gifts but especially the way he was in our prayer meetings." She smiled slightly,

393

remembering. "There are some things that transcend differences of age or station. Ours was a meeting of minds, an excitement created by the awareness of mutual understanding that was shared by no other woman."

Staring at him with eyes that would put a puppy to shame.

"You asked me earlier why I had taken the letter from Charles's desk . . . I did so because I thought it might have something to do with us and our dilemma."

"You thought he might be writing a letter to his wife?"

"I glimpsed the first few words and that is what I assumed. Perhaps I have not made myself clear, Mr. Murdoch. Charles had asked me to comment on the text for that Monday."

She paused again and Murdoch could see how hard she was struggling for control. "You see, this was his way of signalling to me his intention."

"I'm afraid I don't understand, Miss Dignam."

There was a flicker of impatience across her face. "No, of course not, how could you understand? The text in question that Charles asked me to study was from the Song of Songs, chapter eight, verse six; 'Set me as a seal upon thine arm: for love is strong as death; jealousy is cruel as the grave. . .' You see, Mr. Murdoch, Charles was about to discuss how we could realize our love publicly and somebody has made sure that wouldn't happen."

Chapter Forty-Two

MURDOCH REMAINED WITH MISS DIGNAM for another half an hour, during which time, seemingly relieved at having unburdened herself of the secret, she wept ceaselessly. However, when he pressed her to say more about what she had insinuated, she became shifty. "He was the soul of discretion, but I cannot say with complete certainty that his wife was oblivious."

Half the parish knew. She was making quite a fool of herself.

Finally, Murdoch escorted her home where he left her to the untender mercies of her friend Miss Flowers, who appeared to be staying at the house. He didn't know what to make of her statement, whether to believe her. On the surface, it wasn't likely, but then he hadn't known Reverend Howard. Perhaps the intellectual compatibility she was convinced they shared had been seductive. On the other hand, what if she had expected

Howard to declare his love? According to Mrs. Howard, he was going to declare the exact opposite. Had that driven Miss Dignam into a kind of madness? She didn't strike him as cunning, but what if her madness took the form of a sort of amnesia? What if she had killed Howard and now didn't remember? Fyfer had said she was covered in blood when he saw her. Her explanation for that was plausible, but what if there was a more sinister reason? The attack had been vicious and it was hard to see Miss Dignam capable of it. Murdoch ran his fingers through his hair. While he was on the subject of sinister, could he believe the newly widowed Mrs. Howard? Her murdering her own husband also seemed most unlikely, but as Miss Dignam had quoted to him, "jealousy is cold as the grave." And many a time he'd heard the Christian Brothers warning their young charges about trifling with a woman's affections. "Hell hath no fury like a woman scorned." Murdoch, shy and awkward around the few young women he did meet, had been rather afraid of that possibility and vowed to deal honourably with any woman he might encounter as an adult. He winced at that thought, still not at all sure he was behaving honourably toward Enid Jones. On the other hand, jealousy was a powerful emotion, as he knew all too well, that could take over a man or a woman, and he was beginning to wonder if the green-eyed monster wasn't somehow at the centre of this murder.

He parked his wheel in the stable that adjoined the station, enjoying for a moment the warmth and smell of the old white horse, Captain, who was standing, already partly harnessed in case he was needed to pull the police ambulance. There had been complaints from the drivers that the horse was getting too old and slow for his job, and Murdoch knew it wouldn't be long before he was dispatched to the knackers. He gave him a quick pat on his wide rump, glad he was ignorant of his fate and left him to munch on his hay.

When he entered the hall, Murdoch found a sleepy and sullen-looking pair of queer plungers waiting for him. Damn, he'd forgotten he'd told them to come first thing and he was much later than usual.

"Good morning, folks. I'll be right with you," he called out a cheery greeting and went to hang up his coat and hat on the peg by the door.

Charlie Seymour was at his desk and he came right over. "Bettles and Kearney are confirmed to be at the House of Providence on Tuesday. The admitting Sister says they were there on Monday night and didn't leave until close to five on Tuesday. The nuns didn't want them to stay any longer. She says they are malcontents."

"How certain is she of the time when they left?"

"Very certain, apparently. She had to get a porter to escort them out just before the new applicants were admitted at five o'clock."

397

"Howard was dead by three-thirty that afternoon so unfortunately that means those two bits of scum are in the clear."

"Shall I let them go then?"

"Wait until I've got Olivia and Parker in the duty room. No point in them being seen as narks. Bettles is the type who will take any excuse to throw his weight around. How's Traveller doing?"

"He's been pretty quiet except for singing sea shanties at six o'clock this morning. He says he thought we needed livening up."

Murdoch grinned. Traveller had taken his advice.

"I'm going to talk to these two first, then you can bring him in." Murdoch eased himself up.

"How's your lumbago?" asked Charlie.

"About the same."

"Did you speak to Amy or Katie? They'll probably have some suggestions for what to do."

"I'm sure they will, everybody does, but no, I didn't see either of them at supper so I haven't had the benefit of their feminine wisdom."

Seymour gave him a searching sort of look. This wasn't the place to go into it, but Murdoch was burning to know what Charlie knew about a certain Mr. Roger Bryant, rich man.

Murdoch beckoned to Olivia and Ed to follow him and they went down the hall to the duty room. There was more room in here than in his cubicle and as it

398

was between shifts for the constables, they wouldn't
be disturbed.

"Sit down, please. Ed, how's your ankle?"

"Better, thank you, sir. Somebody gave me a nickel
this morning."

"Ed!" exclaimed Olivia warningly.

"I weren't doing nothing wrong. I was just standing
there waiting to cross the road and I took my hat off
to wipe my brow and before I knew it a kindly lady
had dropped me a coin."

Murdoch chuckled. "Before you know it, kindly
ladies will have paid your rent. You'll be able to milk
that injury for a long time."

"Frankly, sir, I can't earn near as much just acting like
a cripple as I can plunging. I think folks like the excitement of plunging."

Murdoch took the big blackened kettle off the hob
and poured more hot water into the teapot. The constables waited a long time before they emptied out the
pot and it was already half full with tea leaves.

"Do you want some tea?" he asked.

Ed was about to say yes but Olivia got there first.
"No, thank you. We've already had our breakfast."

She was very cool this morning and Murdoch knew
he was still in her bad books.

He poured three mugs of tea anyway. "Mrs. Bagley,
I'm sorry I was rude to you yesterday. It was un-
called for."

399

She stared at him in surprise. "Well . . . apology accepted. You're just doing your job, I expect."

"You've been very helpful, both of you. I was frustrated with my own lack of progress."

Both Ed and Olivia reached out and took a mug of tea. Wordlessly, Murdoch offered them milk and sugar. He filled up his own mug and for a moment, there was silence in the room, broken only by the clink of the spoons. Ed smacked his lips.

"Now that's what I call a good cuppa. It'd take the blacking off the stove."

Olivia gulped down the tea in a way that told Murdoch she had lied about having breakfast.

"I did think some more about what you said, yesterday," she said. "I can't promise you that I remember a lot more than I already told you, but some things did come back."

Murdoch smiled appreciatively and nodded at her to continue.

"The woman was young. Younger than me by five years at least, about my height and she had a plaid shawl over her head. And a brown or black skirt. She was lathy, but then all the paupers get that way, don't they?"

Murdoch sighed. He knew Olivia was telling him the truth, but it wasn't much to go on. There were likely several young, thin girls of medium height in the pauper queue and most of them would be wearing plaid shawls and dark skirts.

400

"Would you recognize her again?"

Olivia frowned. "Hmm. I might if I was close up."

"Would you go back to the House with me and see if we can find her? They open the gates for the soup at noon, don't they?"

Olivia shrugged. "I'll go on one condition. You'll have to put your old clothes on again. They'll all know you for a frog and I don't want to be seen as some kind of nark."

Murdoch groaned. "You don't know what you're asking. I haven't stopped scratching."

They both grinned at him. "You'll get hardened to it," said Ed.

"Where are your duds, then?" Olivia asked.

"I asked the sergeant to burn them."

"That's a waste. There was still some use in those clothes."

"Tell you what," said Ed. "I can't stand in no queue with this ankle. We're about the same size, why don't we do a swap? You take my hat and coat at least."

Murdoch didn't want to be impolite, but Ed was a good six inches shorter than he was and the coat and hat in question were decidedly on the seedy side. But he had no choice.

"Thanks, Ed."

"You'll look good as a detective, Eddie," said Olivia.

Murdoch checked the clock above the fireplace. "It's almost eleven o'clock. How far away is your boarding house?"

"We're out on Queen Street in the country."

"Too far to go there and back." Murdoch reached for his notebook. "There's a butcher shop just down from here on Parliament." He scribbled a note, tore out the page, and handed it to Olivia. "The owner's name is Mr. Davies. Give him this and he'll make sure you have one of his best sausage rolls." The look he caught in her eyes confirmed his first suspicion. They hadn't had the money to buy breakfast. "Come back by half past eleven and we'll go to the depot."

"Can I have another splash of char before we go?" Olivia shoved her mug across the table and Murdoch poured her some tea that was by now soot black.

When they'd finished, he walked with them to the front doors and they left both livened by the prospect of further adventures and sausage rolls. Murdoch was about to return to his own cubicle when the telephone rang. Callahan answered and waved at Murdoch to indicate the call was for him. He picked up the receiver.

It was Dr. Ogden. "Detective Murdoch, I have just finished my post-mortem examination of the Tugwell women. I thought you'd like to know the results right away. The older woman was in poor condition with signs of early consumption. Her daughter had gonorrhea."

402

"I see. And that would mean that any of her most recent er, customers, would have contracted it?"

"Undoubtedly. "

"And Mr. Howard showed no signs of the disease?"

"Of course not. Did you expect him to?"

"Not necessarily. I'm just making sure I have all the facts."

Her voice on the other end of the telephone sounded cold. "Charles Howard was a respectable man of God. You forget I knew him. I cannot for the life of me imagine he would consort with a prostitute."

Once again, her tone of voice grated on his nerves. "It's surprising how many men conceal dark secrets, doctor."

"You don't need to remind me of that, Mr. Murdoch. I have seen too many of their innocent victims, their wives, in my consulting rooms."

"Quite so." Murdoch signalled to Callahan to pull over the stool for him. "Dr. Ogden, I wonder if I could get your opinion on another matter concerning Charles Howard."

"I can only spare you five minutes. I must get to my surgery."

Murdoch eased himself onto the stool and turned away so that the constable couldn't hear him. As succinctly as possible he related Miss Dignam's story.

The doctor actually guffawed. "Good Lord, the woman is delusional. She'll get herself committed to the lunatic asylum if she goes on like that."

"So you don't think it's likely that Reverend Howard was in love with her?"

403

"Utterly out of the question. Charles was always amiable to the women of the congregation. Who knows, perhaps he was a little excessive, but the fact is, he adored his wife. You haven't seen Louisa Howard at her best, Mr. Murdoch, but to say that he would choose Sarah Dignam over her is absurd. What man would willingly reach for a withered winter apple when he could have a ripe plum?"

Her tone was scornful and Murdoch felt a brief pang of guilt on behalf of the male half of the population. "Is there anything else, detective? I really must hurry."

"No, thank you, ma'am. I won't keep you any longer."

They hung up and Murdoch handed the telephone back to Callahan.

He walked over to the desk.

"Charlie, tell me something honestly. If given the choice between a shrivelled-up apple and a lush plum, which would you take?"

Seymour looked at him in bewilderment. "Is this a trick question?"

"No, well sort of. Which would you choose?"

"Neither. Plums give me the stomachache and an old apple isn't worth it. I'd go for a pear. I like pears."

"Thanks, Charlie. I'm going back to my office for a while. There's been a new development in the Howard case. Come down as soon as the patrol sergeant relieves you and I'll fill you in."

404

Murdoch returned to his cubicle and sat down at his desk. He knew what his answer would be to the doctor's question and he pitied the woman who had given her heart so completely to a man who, it would seem, was doing no more than his job called for.

Chapter Forty-Three

MURDOCH TOOK OUT his magnifying glass and began to examine the letter Miss Dignam had brought him. The writing was scrawled as if in haste and there were two or three blots on the copy. Unless Reverend Howard was habitually in a hurry, the letter seemed to indicate urgency. Murdoch knew that many people made fair copies of their letters once they'd composed them. He'd done that himself with important letters. Was there another copy of this letter that was complete? According to Doris, she hadn't mailed anything that morning and Sarah Dignam had said this was on Howard's desk. The only copy then and obviously interrupted. Murdoch studied the letters again. There was a dot after the last word, not a full stop, this was higher up. Murdoch took out a piece of paper from his desk drawer and started to write.

My name is William Murdoch.

Then he paused as if to think about his next word and his pen remained in the air. He wrote the words again but this time pretended to hear something outside. Sure enough, he found he had rested his pen on the paper, leaving a small dot. Thin evidence maybe but likely indicating Howard had been interrupted rather than stopped on his own volition. What was the information, *just now received*, that caused him such distress and that he dearly wished he didn't know. *A heavy heart.* Suggested sorrow, disappointment. *I dearly wish I was not privy to the information* implied a confidence bestowed. *I must impart to you* was quite formal and suggested he was addressing some kind of authority. Did it concern the applications for charity? Had he been told somebody was cheating? That was not unlikely, but the language was too severe surely for what was such a common human failing. What people had said about Howard didn't seem to reflect a dour man of no compassion, quite the opposite. Given what Olivia had just told him, Murdoch had a strong suspicion he knew what Howard had learned.

Murdoch tried to put himself in the pastor's skin. His wife said that their luncheon together had been completely normal. He had not seemed distressed or preoccupied and as far as she knew he had no appointments. Assuming that was the case and Howard was not a master of deception, something had occurred to upset him after he arrived at his office. There was no

407

post delivery so it couldn't have been a letter. His book open on the chair suggested he had been interrupted but, at that point, peacefully. What if somebody came to see him who confided in him some news that distressed him in the extreme? Howard had then begun his letter, which he never finished. He had been killed as he sat at his desk writing it. There were two possibilities. First, he had a visitor who gave him distressing news but who then left. Howard started to write his letter and was interrupted a second time by somebody he either knew or certainly didn't fear. That person stabbed him, reasons unknown. Perhaps connected to the letter, perhaps not. The second possibility was that the first visitor and his killer were one and the same. They either left and came back or were still in the room when Howard started to write his letter. What if the pastor had threatened to betray the secret revealed to him and his assailant silenced him forever. On the other hand, the disturbing information of course was not necessarily the reason for the murder. The two events could be coincidental and Howard could have been killed by a tramp, probably Traveller, as everybody wanted to believe.

Murdoch was about to get up and put the letter in the filing cabinet when he heard rapid footsteps coming down the hall toward his cubicle. He didn't need the bellow of Brackenreid's "Murdoch!" to guess who was coming to see him. He braced himself. The inspector never visited Murdoch's tiny office unless he was so irate he couldn't wait to send for Murdoch to come upstairs.

Brackenreid thrust aside the reed strips that served as a door to the cubicle. Murdoch took one look at his flushed face and knew the inspector was suffering from the painful aftermath of overindulgence, a situation that was becoming more and more frequent of late. A rant was about to be delivered.

"Murdoch, you were supposed to report to me first thing this morning regarding the Howard case. Why haven't I heard from you?"

"The case isn't closed yet, sir."

"I understand you've arrested a tramp who had Howard's watch in his possession. What more do you want?"

"I haven't arrested him as yet. I'm keeping him here for further questioning. He swears he found the watch and at the moment I don't believe we have sufficient evidence to charge him. There are some puzzling aspects of the case that I would like to be sure of before I do so."

"Puzzling aspects? Puzzling aspects? It's you who are the puzzle, Murdoch. A tramp was seen going into the church on Tuesday afternoon –"

"Beg pardon, sir. He was seen crossing the Gardens, not entering the church."

"Nonsense. It's obvious that's where he was heading. He went in, found Howard in his office, and demanded

409

money. The pastor refused him and in a fit of fury he stabbed him and kicked him to death. He then stole the poor man's watch and boots. He has been found with the watch in his possession. What the hell is puzzling about that, Murdoch?"

Murdoch bit his lip. It was certainly plausible, countered only by his own misgivings and a feeling he had about Jack Trevelyan. Really, he should show Brackenreid the letter.

"Sir, give me another day and I promise I will hand you a full report."

"Give me an arrest, Murdoch, that's what I want and we can both rest easy."

Suddenly, Brackenreid's attention was caught by the poster on the wall announcing last summer's police games. Murdoch had put it up there because he placed second in the fiercely competitive bicycle race. Whether it was the memory of his detective's success over their rival stations or whether the inspector's ire had been sufficiently vented, Murdoch didn't know, but Brackenreid actually softened.

"You have until tomorrow morning, Murdoch."

Then he looked up as if he was about to salute the portrait of Her Majesty Queen Victoria and left, the reed strips swaying and clacking in his wake.

Murdoch took a deep breath. He had a lot to do. Walking was out of the question and in spite of a sleety rain that stung his face, he retrieved his bicycle and pedalled over to Carlton Street.

Drummond was standing at his doorway looking out onto the deserted street.

"Don't tell me you ate all that oatmeal already?" he greeted Murdoch.

"No, I'm here for a different reason." Murdoch leaned his wheel against the curb and came over to the shopkeeper.

"I'd like to have a serious word, Mr. Drummond. Can we go inside?"

Drummond looked as if he might refuse but changed his mind and reluctantly stepped back and led the way into the shop, which was even more barren than before.

"What do you want?" he asked, his voice belligerent.

Murdoch felt like answering that he'd like to give him a good shaking, but he kept his voice as polite as he could manage.

"When I was here last time, I realized you have a very good view of the church from your store."

"What of it? It's free, ain't it?"

"I get the feeling you spend a lot of time observing the comings and goings along the street."

"What if I do? Is that against the law?"

Murdoch bit his lip. A quick slap across the man's head wasn't going to help matters and Drummond was much older than he was, after all. "I believe that Reverend

411

Howard had a visitor shortly before he was murdered, and I wonder if you, yourself, saw anybody enter the side door that afternoon about one-thirty or so?"

"What if I did?"

"It's not against the law, Mr. Drummond, but shall we say the law would be served if you do have information you haven't yet given me."

"She wouldna have been the murderer, you can be sure of that."

"Who is the 'she' you are referring to?"

Drummond knew he'd slipped and he actually appeared nervous. He rocked back and forth on his heels for a moment, then swirled around, started to fiddle with the few potatoes, moving them around in the bin. He didn't say anything for several moments and Murdoch began to wonder if he should charge the old pizzle with obstructing the course of justice and take him to the station. Drummond must have read his mind because he said, "I did happen to glance out on the street just as a woman was going by. I saw her enter the church."

Murdoch took out his notebook. "What time was this and what did she look like?"

"It was quarter past one. The church bell had just chimed. As for what she looked like, I didn't pay much heed. She weren't that posh. Maybe a black or dark brown coat."

"Did you notice this woman come out?"

"I did. She was in there about half an hour. She

walked back the same way she'd come and turned down on Sherbourne Street."

"And you didn't see anybody after that?"

"Not a soul. The tramp would have entered the church from the front. I didn't know anything had happened until I heard all the commotion. The constable set off the alarm bell and you can hear that blasted thing for miles."

"Why didn't you come forward as a witness at the inquest, Mr. Drummond?"

"It slipped my mind. It wasn't important."

"That was for me to decide."

Drummond grimaced. "Women were always calling on him. Oh the ladies loved our pastor, they did. As if a handsome set of whiskers has anything to do with the Lord. This one was all dressed up in her Sunday best. Her hat was a joke with purple feathers five feet high at least."

Murdoch frowned. "Was she a young woman?"

"Not her. Mutton dressed as lamb, she was, with her fancy fur collar and that ridiculous hat."

"She was wearing a fur collar?"

"That's right. It looked like a dead squirrel had fallen on her shoulders."

"And you're sure she'd turned down onto Sherbourne Street?"

"That's what I said, didn't I?" He raised his grizzled eyebrows in a ferocious leer. "Mebbe our good pastor

413

had given her one of his uplifting chats because she was walking much faster on the way back." He shoved one of the potatoes against the bin wall as if it were a bowling ball.

"You didn't like Reverend Howard, did you?"

Drummond's glance slid away and he shrugged. "I could deny it, but there's dozens who'd tell you otherwise. Besides, I don't hold with slyness and namby-pamby characters masquerading as good Christian souls."

"Is that how you saw Howard? A phony?"

"I told you already we didn't agree on the direction our church should take. To my mind, he came in under false pretences, then as soon as he was here, he started to show his true colours." Drummond touched his forefinger to the side of his nose and lowered his voice to a conspiratorial tone. "He had certain leanings, if you know what I mean. You mark my words he would have had us all worshipping graven images like the papists do."

Murdoch closed his notebook with a snap. "Thank you, Mr. Drummond. I will be calling on you again, seeing that you deliberately withheld important information."

"You kenna prove it was deliberate. People forget, you know."

Murdoch headed out of the door to his bicycle, Drummond trotting after him.

"Who was she? I didn't know it was important. What are you going to do? Detective, answer me!"

Chapter Forty-Four

MURDOCH WAS STILL FUMING when he arrived at the lodging house on Sherbourne Street. Constable second class Whiteside scrambled to his feet, literally caught napping as Murdoch entered.

"Good morning, sir."

"I want to check something in the upstairs room, constable. You can stay where you are."

The poor lad looked disappointed and Murdoch sympathized. It must be excruciatingly boring to spend your shift sitting outside a door in an empty house.

The Tugwells' room was unlocked and he went inside. The window sash was still up and the room was cold and damp. He went straight to the wardrobe in the corner of the room. There wasn't much inside. A pair of boy's trousers, a shabby brown coat, and two dark-coloured dresses, a jacket of tatty navy wool that he had seen Josie wearing. On the upper rack were two hats, one was the gaudy red plush that Josie was wearing when he first met her, the other a black felt with long purple feathers, which she had worn to the inquest. Murdoch guessed this hat might be considered the family's Sunday best. Josie wears it to an inquest, Esther to call on the pastor. On the second rack of the wardrobe, curled like a little moribund animal, was a fur neckpiece.

Murdoch looked around the cramped room where the entire Tugwell family had lived. Wooden crates served as cupboards for their few possessions and the bedcovers were bleached sacking. Already the place was gathering dust, but he had the feeling that normally Esther kept it as clean as she could. There was a washstand by the window and two chipped mugs had been set to drain dry on one of the crates. He went to the fireplace. The coal shuttle was almost empty. On the mantelpiece in pride of place was a photograph, a family portrait taken when the family had known better days. Mr. Tugwell sat on a chair, a child on his knee whose face was slightly blurred as if he hadn't been able to sit still long enough for the photographer to snap the picture. Behind was a pretty, young Josie and Esther, fuller of face, smiling at a hopeful future. Murdoch determined he'd try to find some relatives at least who would honour these few possessions and dispose of them rather than letting the rag-and-bone man come and pick them over.

He said a prayer for the poor souls who had died here, then hurried downstairs to the constable.

"Unlock the door, if you please. Come in with me and bring that candle."

The hall where the constable had been sitting was gloomy and he'd lit the wall sconce.

Once inside, Murdoch went directly over to the hearth. "Constable, I'm having a hard time bending down. Will you take a careful look at the floor right about here? Is there anything you see? Use the candle, it's dark in here."

Whiteside crouched down close to the floor and wiped his fingers on the threadbare carpet.

"Just bits of plaster, sir." He glanced up at the ceiling. "Looks as if they came from up there."

Murdoch strained to look up. All of the ceiling was cracked and chipped but here, just to the right of the chimney, there was a fairly large piece of plaster broken off. The lathes of the floor in the room above were visible. No wonder the carbonic monoxide gas had infiltrated the Tugwell room.

That had been the point.

When he walked into the station, Seymour beckoned to him. "Our tramp friend is insisting he talk to you. He refused to say a word to me, but I'm thinking he's ready to make a confession."

"I don't know about that, Charlie. I've made a discovery. You know we kept saying, Who would want to kill old man Hicks? Well I'm sure now he was just

417

unfortunate. The intended victims were the Tugwells. The murderer was diabolical. He knew that by creating carbon monoxide in Hicks's chimney, the gas would drift up to the next floor. He must have given Hicks prussic acid to make him unconscious so he could block the chimney and stuff the windows. Then he used a broom handle to aggravate a missing patch of plaster in the ceiling and left the rest to fate."

"My God, but same question, why kill them?"

"I believe Mrs. Tugwell went to visit Howard shortly before he died. I think she may have told him something incriminating about somebody, God knows who, or exactly what, at this point but I'm starting to guess. The *what* part anyway. Josie Tugwell was on the game. Perhaps her mother told the pastor about Josie's customers." He took Howard's letter out of his pocket. "Miss Dignam took this from the pastor's desk, but for her own convoluted reasons that I'll tell you about later, she didn't admit to it until this morning when she brought it to me. It's not addressed to anybody and it's not finished, but listen to this: 'It is with heavy heart that I write this letter. I wish I was not privy to the information I have just now received which I must impart to you.' What does that sound like to you, Charlie?"

418   "If, as you say, Esther Tugwell came to confide in him, she wasn't talking about some piece of gutter slime who dipped his wick when he could, but somebody respectable, somebody known."

"Exactly. And I'm wondering if that same pillar of society came to the office while Howard was writing his letter. There could have been a big confrontation and the selfsame respectable cove killed him."

Seymour whistled through his teeth. "My goodness. This is a new turn of events. So you don't suspect our man, Trevelyan, at the moment?"

"I'm ruling out nothing. Let's see what he has to say, shall we? I'll pay him a visit." He headed for the cells at the rear of the station. "Keep an ear out will you, Charlie? If I yell, come quick."

Murdoch slipped aside the peep-hole cover in the cell door. Traveller was lying on his back on the hard, narrow bed, his eyes closed. Murdoch unlocked the door and went in. The tramp was alert instantly and he rolled over and propped himself on his elbow.

"Mr. Murdoch, ye're a busy man. I asked to talk to you an hour ago."

"Forgive me for not coming running, I was investigating the case."

"And what did you find then? The mayor committed the crime? Or maybe it was Reverend Power wanting to get rid of the non-believer?"

Murdoch was in no mood for jokes and he felt irritated. "What did you want to talk to me about, Mr. Trevelyan?"

"Oh, it's Mr. Trevelyan, is it? I thought we'd progressed to Christian names at least. I was going to call

419

you Willie and you can certainly call me Jack if you like. Or even Traveller, which I prefer."

He was grinning in a good-humoured way and Murdoch shrugged. There were two beds in the cell and he perched on the opposite one.

"Do you have some baccy?" Trevelyan asked him. "I'd fain give my soul to the devil for a pipe of good black Durham."

"Here." Murdoch fished out his own pipe and tobacco pouch and handed it to him. He waited until the tramp had lit up and taken a deep, grateful pull. The tiny cell was filled with pungent smoke.

"There's some people coming to see me in about half an hour, Traveller, so I'd be glad if you'd get a move on."

Traveller eyed him shrewdly and beamed his gap-toothed smile. "I'm getting more and more the sense that you ain't got me on your hanging list. Am I right?"

"I'm not sure you ever were, but I do know you're holding out on me. You're not telling me what really happened in the church on Tuesday."

"What makes you think I was in the church? I recall telling you I was catching a kip in the greenhouse."

"Let's just say you left something behind." In answer to Traveller's raised eyebrow, he added. "A smell. There was a powerful smell of sulphur in the church. Fumigation every night and the clothes stink. I know mine were terrible."

420

Traveller laughed. "Folks think we tramps smell like that because we ain't washed, but that ain't it. I've had a bath three days in a row and been fumigated three days in a row." He sniffed at his sleeve. "They reek. If hell smells this bad I'm going to live a very good life and make sure I don't end up there."

"Start with telling the truth then. That should give you some marks in God's balance book."

Traveller drew in some smoke and blew it out slowly. "All right. I was in the church that afternoon. It was a cold day and I've sometimes slipped in there for a little kip before finding my bed for the night. It was empty at that hour and I goes upstairs to the balcony and stretch out on one of the pews. I've dropped off nice when the next thing is I'm wide awake because I can hear coves shouting downstairs. They must have been loud because they was in the back where the offices are." He puffed on the pipe again and Murdoch shifted impatiently. "Just rein in a bit, Willie, I'll say it in my own good time. It's not often I have such rapt attention from a frog. I know what you were going to ask me, but no, I couldn't make out what they were saying. All I can tell you is that one in particular is real mad about something. He's shouting more than the other. It don't go on too long, hardly enough to say how do you do, how are you, and how's your mother's health. Then they shuts up and a few ticks later, I hear a door slam shut so I gathers one of them had left by the back way.

421

MAUREEN JENNINGS

All nice and quiet now and I tucks myself back into my
wooden bed. I ain't interested in other folks' barneys. I
drops off properly this time, but wouldn't you know I'm
woke again cos I hear somebody come pitter-patting
down the aisle. I takes a peek and I sees this lady. She
kneels down in front of that rail they've got in the front
of the church. Oh no, Jack, don't tell me we're in for a
prayer meeting, I says to myself. I know how it'll be if
I get found." He sniffed. "I'm leery of the type of Christian
ladies who fancy themselves good Samaritans but who
want you to keep your place and that ain't asleep in the
balcony of the church. Anyways, she doesn't stay long
on her knees but trots off through the door at the back
of the church. I'm a sitting there wondering if this ain't
a good time to leave when the next thing I know, the
woman is shrieking her head off. She don't come back
into the church, but I can hear her outside, crying like
she's seen the devil himself. I thinks it might be wise to
do some investigating myself so I slips down the stair-
case that leads to the back of the church where the
offices are. Well, I can smell the blood right away and I
know something bad has happened and I'd better not
linger. The door to one of the offices is open and I can
see a man lying on his back. He has a knife sticking out
422   of the side of his neck and his face is all smashed in on
one side." Traveller paused to take a particularly long
pull on the pipe. He blew out slowly. "Needless to say,
the poor cove is no longer one of the living –"

"How long do you think he had been dead?"

"Well I didn't touch him, but I got the sense it wasn't long. The wounds were still oozing." The tramp glanced over at Murdoch. "Would you say I am being of assistance to the police in this case and that will balance out any little sins I might have committed?"

"Yes, yes. Get on with it, for God's sake."

"Well, you know now how important a good pair of boots is to a tramp. I see the poor dead fellow is wearing a pair that are a sight better than mine. He obviously don't need them any more, so I get them off fast as I can and then let myself out by the side door. There weren't anybody around, thank goodness, so I go straight over to the Gardens so I could change the boots."

"Did you also take the man's watch?"

Traveller shook his head. "I didn't see no watch. I told you the gospel truth when I said I found that one in the entrance to the greenhouse." Again he took a pull of the pipe. "I'm thinking it might have been laid there as a trap. The chain weren't broke for one thing. I should have known better but there you go, we're all human, aren't we? It was a handsome piece and I couldn't resist it."

Traveller had a good point about the watch, Murdoch thought.

"Did you see a biscuit tin in the church?"

423

"A tin? Oh, you're right. I forgot. It was laying right beside the body. I seen it under the lady's arm when she was a praying. She must have dropped it when she came on him dead like that. I did pick it up. No sense in wasting good food. I ate the cake and left the tin under a bush in the greenhouse if she's looking for it."

"Was it a man who was arguing with the pastor?"

"Of course it was. There wouldn't be shouting like that if one of them was a lady, would there?"

"Would you recognize the voice if you were to hear it again?"

"Nope. Like I said, I couldn't even make out words, just that they was having a big barney. That much was clear."

Murdoch tapped his fingers on the bed. "You tell a good story, Traveller, but then you've had lots of practice. How do I know it's true? It could just have easily been you who went into the pastor's office, asking for money. He was distracted by something and wouldn't talk to you. You became enraged and struck him with the letter opener, then kicked him in the side of the head. This version fits the facts just as well."

Traveller laughed out loud, genuinely amused. "Look, Willie, if I had lost my temper and done in every man who ever turned me down, I'd have been hung more times than fifty cats have lives." He gazed at Murdoch through the haze of smoke between them. "Speaking of overhearing, I heard you and your inspector having a barney earlier. He's hell bent on sending me to the gallows. I'm charged and convicted with him. I thought about it and decided I'd better tell you the truth so as to give you a chance to find the real culprit."

It was Murdoch's turn to laugh. "And here I thought you had repented of your sins and wanted to help me."

Traveller waved his pipe. "That too."

Chapter Forty-Five

Olivia and Ed were waiting for him in the front hall.

"You'd better hurry up, we don't have much time," said Olivia. "There's sure to be a long queue already."

"I'm ready. I just have to change coat and hat with Ed."

"What's he going to do now?"

"He can stay in my office."

"That's a laugh. Ed in a frog's job. Let's hope he won't have any plungers to deal with."

"Don't worry, all he's going to do is sit there and shut up."

Clearly Olivia was a mite jealous of Ed's change in status, even if it was pretend. As for him, he was beaming and when Murdoch slipped on the dirty-looking hat and the long, heavily stained coat, he could see why. Even with the sealskin coat, Ed was definitely getting the better end of the exchange.

Leaving him safely ensconced behind the desk with

a copy of the chief constable's annual report to keep him occupied, Murdoch and Olivia set out for the depot. She had softened toward him again and chatted away as they walked up Parliament as fast as he could manage.

"Ed and I are thinking of getting hitched this summer."

"I thought you didn't believe in marriage?"

"Who told you that? It'll be good for business and Tim needs a father as he's getting older."

She seemed oblivious to the fact that her business as she called it was on the other side of the law. Murdoch had promised them a pardon if they helped him and he hoped he'd be able to honour that promise.

"We'll invite you," she added.

The depot was at the corner of Parliament and Oak Streets on the front steps of the Methodist church. The queue of applicants was already about twenty strong and Olivia and Murdoch slipped in at the end. A trestle table was set up in front of the church doors and two well-dressed ladies were standing behind it with aprons over their fur coats and soup ladles at the ready in their hands.

"Where's your pail?" Olivia hissed in Murdoch's ear.

"I didn't think to bring one."

She smirked at him triumphantly. "No good at this, are you? Good thing I have mine."

He glanced around and saw that all the other people in the queue were carrying enamel or tin pails of various sizes and shapes. The majority of the applicants were women. Behind him an old lady, wizened and toothless, muttered to herself and avoided his glance. She was carrying a blackened iron pot. In front of him was a coloured girl, about ten years old, who had a scarf tied over her summer bonnet for headgear. There were only two other men in the entire group, one middle-aged and bone thin, who shifted restlessly from side to side as he waited, the other younger and fierce-looking. He stood slightly apart from the others, ashamed of being in such company.

"Do you see the girl?" Murdoch asked Olivia.

She shook her head. "Not yet."

The church doors opened and two men came out carrying a large, steaming soup pot between them, which they hoisted onto the trestle table. The queue stirred and shuffled forward. The women who were serving were friendly and brisk.

"Give your dockets to Mrs. Heller as you come up," called out one of them. "Hurry up now, get it while it's hot. Hold up your pail, there's a good girl."

This was addressed to the ten-year-old. She received her dollop of soup, covered it with a tin lid, picked up two slices of bread from the bin, and hurried away. Her pail wasn't that large and Murdoch wondered how many people it was supposed to feed.

From where he stood, the soup smelled good and the eagerness with which the applicants in the queue stared at the pot confirmed they felt the same.

Suddenly, Olivia nudged him with her elbow. "There she is, over there."

A young woman with a plaid shawl over her head was walking slowly up the road. She had a pail in her hands, which were ungloved.

"What do you want me to do?" Olivia whispered.

"Nothing at the moment. Just get your soup. And let her get hers, then we'll talk to her."

He could see the woman scanning the group and he ducked his head. He didn't want anything to frighten her away and he could feel his heart beating faster in anticipation. She might hold the key to the murder.

She joined the end of the line just as Olivia and Murdoch were moved forward. He was so obviously in pain the two women serving at the trestle table smiled on him with sympathy.

"He forgot his pail," said Olivia as she held out hers for her serving. The older of the two women, a sweet-faced matronly woman, reached down and brought out an enamel bowl from a box beside her.

"You can use this, but you'll have to eat your soup here."

Mrs. Heller intervened, "Do you have your docket?"

Murdoch groaned to himself. He'd forgotten all about that. "No, I don't."

She frowned at him, her good humour vanishing, a woman who was wise to the ways of paupers. "You did receive one, I hope?"

"Well, I, er –"

"'Course he did," Olivia jumped in. "He's on Reverend Howard's list, if you want to check."

429

"We don't go by lists," said the woman. "You have to present us with a docket." She reached into a cloth bag on the table and pulled out a white slip of paper. "It looks like this." She'd raised her voice as if he had suddenly become hard of hearing.

Olivia turned to Murdoch and snapped, "You'd forget your head if it was loose." She swivelled back to the church woman. "I'll vouch for him, missus. He hurt his back chopping wood and I think it affected his brain."

Some brave soul from the rear of the queue shouted out, "What's the hold up?"

The older matron hesitated, then nodded at her companion. Ungraciously, Mrs. Heller seized the bowl and spooned half a ladle of soup into it. Olivia's pail was filled next and they picked up their bread and moved away quickly from the line, making their way over to one of the benches by the curb. Most of the people in the queue left immediately after they'd received their helping but some, like them, sat on the bench to eat the soup while it was indeed hot. Murdoch had no utensil with which to eat the thick glutinous liquid so he followed the example of a man next to him and brought the bowl to his lips and half drank, half chewed it down. Although the colour was an unappetizing grey, and the consistency was that of wallpaper glue, it was surprisingly tasty and he had no trouble eating it. Olivia took out a spoon from her pocket and used that.

The bread was dry and Murdoch used it to sop up

430

the last bit of soup. He wiped his mouth on his sleeve.

"Oi, that's Ed's good coat," said Olivia. "I'm going to buy him a new one."

The young woman in the shawl was now at the front of the line and she received her helping, got her two slices, and started to walk away.

"Go and talk to her, quick," said Murdoch. "Tell her who I am and that I must talk to her about what she said to you. I won't prosecute." He squeezed Olivia's arm. "Please give me a good reference, I'm depending on you."

"Take care of my pail." She got up and hurried over to the girl. They were out of earshot, but Murdoch could follow what was being said. First the surprised greeting, then the sudden alarmed glance in his direction (he smiled), then the vigorous shaking of the head, then more talking, Olivia's hands gesticulating (another smile from him), finally a reluctant agreement. Olivia took the girl's arm and led her to the bench. She was even younger than she had seemed from a distance, but poverty had worn away most of the prettiness she might have had. She had the pasty skin typical of somebody who doesn't eat decent food. Her dark brown eyes were hard and wary.

"Mr. Murdoch, this is Ida. She's agreed to help but only if you promise she won't get into trouble."

Murdoch stood up and touched his hat. "Hello, Ida. It's not you I'm after. I want to follow up on something you told Mrs. Bagley."

"I told who?"

431

"Me," said Olivia.

"Are you the frog's shill?"

"No, I'm not. He's making me do it."

Murdoch was irritated by this remark and his voice was sharp. "Let's say we struck a bargain. Both sides benefit."

Olivia sucked in her cheeks. "We've all got to make a living in this sorry world, haven't we?"

"Yes, we do, and that includes me," Murdoch snapped back at her.

Ida had watched this exchange with interest and for some reason it seemed to bring her more over to Murdoch's side.

"I'm getting perishing here while you two barney. Can we get on with it so I can go home?"

Murdoch forced himself to calm down. "You mentioned a certain man to Mrs. Bagley here. You said he was a Visitor with the city. Do you know his name?"

"Can't say as I do."

Murdoch reached into his inner pocket and took out his money clip. He had five one-dollar bills. He pulled out two of them.

"Will this further our conversation?"

"Two won't, but three might. I'm not that chatty."

432   "All right, three dollars and no more."

Ida took the money from him and stuffed it inside her jacket. Then she laughed, a loud, coarse laugh that was nevertheless genuine.

"You should have heard first and paid after because truth is I really don't know the cove's name. They don't introduce themselves. They'll ask for yours, mind. They ask all sorts of questions of *you*. They poke around your room to make sure you really are starving and freezing and not just malingering. Mostly they want to see if you are hickey and even if you've downed some vile brew to help you forget your godforsaken life, they don't give a pauper's dilberry. You're shit out of luck if you're caught. Then like God Almighty himself, they decide if you are going to get a docket for a few bits of coal that won't last more than three days and food that isn't enough to feed a dog anyway and for this you have to bob and bow and look ever so grateful or you're off their list."

This flood of bitterness washed over Murdoch. "Are they all like that, all the Visitors?"

"Yeah, they all are. Some just have more cream on the top than others, but underneath they're the same sour milk."

She plopped herself down on the bench and removed the lid from the pail. "I'm going to have my pig's swill now. Talk away."

"The man who propositioned, er –"

"I know what that means. The man who wanted to have some touch up in exchange for a couple of dockets."

"What did he look like?"

Ida raised her pail to her lips and, like Murdoch had, half ate, half drank the soup. "Can't tell you that either, he was muffled up. Didn't want his mug to show."

"Was he tall, short? Fat? Thin?"

She sighed. "Let's put it this way, mister. I wasn't paying much attention. They're all the same to me because from where I'm working I usually can't see their faces anyway."

Olivia snorted in disapproval.

"There's bin so many, I can't tell one from the other," continued Ida. "I make it a point, really. Why should I remember them? They don't want to know me,"

Murdoch couldn't help himself. "But you're hardly twenty, surely?"

She snickered. "You're out by two years, mister."

"I'd have said close to thirty myself," chipped in Olivia.

"Nobody asked you, did they?"

Both women looked as if they would like to continue in this vein, but Murdoch quickly brought Ida back to the matter at hand. "Had this man been to see you before?"

"No. I do know that much. This one was new. But he was a gawdelpus, I can tell you that."

"How do you know?"

"He had to say his prayers first. 'God forgive me for what I am about to do and forgive this daughter of Eve.' Horse plop like that. I ain't looking for forgiveness. Then he prayed even worse afterward about what a wicked man he was. He got himself all worked up, made me nervous. But it's all bollocks as far as I'm concerned. If it bothers your conscience so bad, don't

434

do it. Or go somewhere private and flog the bishop."
She wiped the bread around the rim of the pail to mop
up the last vestiges of the soup. "Do you know what
kind of soup this is?"

Murdoch shook his head.

"Nor me. S's good though."

Murdoch hadn't finished half of his second slice
and he offered it to the woman. She nodded thanks and
stuffed it into her mouth, licking her dirty fingers. Olivia
made it clear what she thought of such disgusting manners.

Then Ida snapped her fingers. "You know what, that
old Tom did give me a name. Some of them like you
to say their name, then they can pretend they aren't
really paying for it. I get it all the time. 'Oh Ida, tell
Johnny he's got a lovely big cock.'"

Olivia looked shocked and glanced at Murdoch in
dismay. Ida grinned more. "This one wanted me to
scold him. That was fine with me. 'Oh, you are a very
bad man. You shouldn't be doing this, Mr. Howard.'"

Murdoch flinched. "That was his name? Howard?"

She shrugged. "That's what he said. Christian name,
Charles. I made a joke of it, 'Oh Prince Charlie how
'ard you are.' But he didn't like that at all. I thought he
might even haul off with a stotter." She stared at
Murdoch. "Why've you got that face on? Don't tell me
he's your best friend?"

435

Chapter Forty-Six

MURDOCH TRIED TO COMPREHEND what the girl had just said.

Ida poked him. "Oi. You know for a copper you give too much away on your ugly mug."

Olivia was also gaping. "She ain't talking about the pastor that was done in, is she?"

"What pastor that was done in?" Ida asked, her hard eyes flashing with excitement.

Murdoch didn't answer. "Ida, when did this Visitor last come to see you?"

"Monday afternoon. That's their regular hours. But come on, what's the gabble on a dead pastor?"

"I'm investigating the murder of a Reverend Charles Howard. He was killed on Tuesday afternoon."

Ida upended the pail to make sure it was truly empty. "Too bad for him."

"And too bad for you too. No more bargains to be made," said Olivia.

"Oh I don't know about that. I'm planning to meet the cove this very afternoon, as a matter of fact."

"Dead men don't meet up with anybody, the last I heard."

Ida laughed, her hearty coarse laugh. "Most of the men I deal with *are* dead. That's why they come to me. It's my job to bring 'em back to life."

Murdoch jumped in. "What do you mean, you're planning to meet this man today?"

"Just what I said. He came by on Wednesday and said to meet him in the Gardens after I'd done at the depot."

Olivia turned to Murdoch. "So it isn't the pastor. She's talking about somebody else?"

"It would appear that way. Either he gave out Howard's name or it's an amazing coincidence."

"Too bloody amazing to be believed, if you ask me."

Ida frowned. "What are you two gabbling on about? Are you saying the dead gawdelpus was named Charlie Howard?"

"That's right," Murdoch answered.

She snickered. "Cheeky tom then. Must have read about it in the papers. It happens. The best one I ever heard was a cove telling me he was the prime minister . . . come to think of it, maybe he was."

437

"Watch your tongue, Ida Harper," said Olivia suppressing a laugh.

Ida seemed to be enjoying her role as teacher of the game. "They'll say anything to keep you off the track just in case you fancy putting a bit of a squeeze on the wife. One fellow said he was dying and he was a virgin and his doctor had recommended female connections before he passed on. Said it might prolong his life." She laughed. "Must have, because he's still in the land of the living six years later. Big nob with city council. This Howard cove tried to excuse his little sin by telling me he hadn't had conjugal relations for weeks because his wife had one under her apron."

"Didn't you tell me the pastor's wife was expecting?" Olivia exclaimed to Murdoch.

"Yes, she is. And he wouldn't have learned that from the newspaper. "

Ida tapped Murdoch's arm. "Is that all because I have to get going?"

"You swear it's one and the same man who came to see you on Monday? You said you couldn't tell one Tom from another."

"Not to look at, but I know voices. He sounded like he had a cold, but that was probably a lot of gammon too. Of course it was the same one. And he wants the same thing. He must have been happy with our exchange of favours." She wiped her mouth with a filthy handkerchief she took from her pocket. "I'm off. He won't wait."

Murdoch grabbed her by the arm. "You're not going anywhere. I need to talk to this fellow." He took out his money clip and removed the last two dollars. "Here. Take this and I want you to swap shawls with Mrs. Bagley."

"This is my good wool," protested Olivia.

"So's mine," said Ida. But the truth was her shabby plaid was far inferior to Olivia's hand-knitted shawl, as they both knew.

"Please, ladies. We don't have much time."

Reluctantly, Olivia removed her shawl and handed it to the other woman.

"Ida, what is your last name and where do you live? No, you won't get into trouble, but I'll have to come back to talk to you."

"I'd like that," said the girl with a lecherous smile that elicited another snort of disapproval from Olivia. "It's Harper. Ida Harper and I live at 310 Sherbourne, the first room at the back." She wrapped the shawl over her head. "Do I get to keep this?"

"No."

"Yes."

Olivia and Murdoch spoke simultaneously, and he had the feeling he had just said goodbye to half a week's wages.

"Where exactly were you to meet this man?"

439

"In the Horticultural Gardens. There's a greenhouse on the south side, the one with the water wheel and the pond. It's nice and private with all the shrubs."

"He's taking a risk, ain't he?" said Olivia. "People go through there."

"Not so much at this time of the year. He said it was convenient for him."

"In what way, convenient?"

"He lives close by. He can boil the kettle, pop out for a bit of dock, and be back in time to mash the tea. But if you want my opinion, he's the kind that gets excited if there's summat of a risk involved."

Murdoch got to his feet. "Ida, thank you for your help." He took Olivia by the arm. "Come on. We have to hurry."

She allowed herself to be led away. "I still don't know why I had to give that tart my good shawl."

"Because I want you to pretend to be her."

She stopped in her tracks. "Pretend to be a tart? Never. Besides, it sounds dangerous. You seem to suspect this cove of doing for Mr. Howard."

"I don't know that for sure. I just want to talk to him. You'll be quite safe, I promise you."

"You and your promises. You couldn't defend a fox from a rabbit in your condition."

She was right about that, and the last thing Murdoch wanted was to see her hurt. "All I want you to do is be there so he at least comes into the greenhouse and I can identify him."

She studied his face. "Did your ma want you to be a copper?"

440

"I don't know what you mean."

"If she did, she'd be beaming on you right now the way I've seen the mothers of some of the bloody priests. They go to every mass and think they're Mary Herself."

Murdoch didn't know if he completely understood the comparison and Olivia's comment opened up all sorts of possibilities for future reflection but not right now.

"Lumbago or no lumbago, Olivia. I won't put you in danger."

She gave his cheek a quick pat. "Don't worry. I'm good at taking care of myself."

It didn't take them long to reach the Horticultural Gardens. The grounds and the outside of the pavilion looked as deserted as ever.

"We'd better not be seen together," said Murdoch. "I'll go in first."

"What if he's already there?"

"So much the better. Then I won't have to involve you."

Olivia frowned. "Hold on. You're not thinking straight. You could go and arrest some innocent geezer who's just in there sniffing the flowers. You need to catch this cove in the act. Don't say no. You wouldn't be able to prove a thing unless he actually says or does something."

"Olivia, I can't –"

She interrupted him. "I told you, I can take care of myself. Besides it's worth my while to get in good with the frogs, especially you with your conscience."

441

Murdoch was about to protest again, but she stopped him. "Get a move on, for Christ's sake. I'll wait here. If he is inside, you'll have to walk on by, but at least you'll get a gander at him."

She was right.

"Give me five minutes. If I'm not out by then it means he isn't there and I'll have found a hiding place. The greenhouse where they're supposed to meet is to the left through the connecting door. Near the end of the path, right next to the water wheel, you'll see a tool shed. I'm going to try to hide in there."

She nodded and pulled the shawl closer around her face. "Poo, this thing stinks."

Murdoch left her there, pushed open the door into the greenhouse, and headed for the connecting door to the left. When he went through, he was disappointed to see the place was quite deserted, no muffled man on the prowl. He'd been jolted when Ida said this rendez-vous was convenient for her Visitor. There were two men who fitted into that category, Swanzey and Drummond, and both would know the more intimate facts of Howard's family life. He grimaced. So much for intuition. Until now, he wouldn't have suspected either one capable of misusing his position as Visitor the way this one was. And certainly not of killing Howard. But one of them had.

442

Chapter Forty-Seven

MURDOCH WALKED DOWN the ramp and along the path to the bend where the pond and water wheel were. His back was worse. He felt sympathy for women condemed to wear tight corsets. His entire lower back felt as if it was being held fast by whalebone. Running was impossible however much he willed himself to override the pain.

Ida's Visitor had chosen well. This section of the greenhouse was completely secluded, the windows obscured by the lush shrubs and the entrance quite hidden by the bend in the path. A bench was at the corner. He smelled again the soft perfume of the hyacinths.

The entrance to the little hut was through a gate with a notice, WORKMEN ONLY, and a short path led to the door. Murdoch thanked God it wasn't locked and stepped inside. The one small window must have been broken because it was partially boarded over and the interior was dark. Murdoch opened his eyes wide, willing himself to see through the gloom. After his eyes adjusted, he could see now that he was in a tool shed, with gardening implements, spades and forks, stacked around the walls. The hut was in disrepair and there were gaps in the wood slats. He could hear the splashing as each paddle of the waterwheel hit the stream rushing from the wall. By pressing his face to a space between the window boards, he could see the path but only a few feet to his left. It was too late to find another place now, but he might have attempted it if Olivia hadn't suddenly appeared. She walked by, paused, and turned to face the way she had come. Murdoch tensed. Just as suddenly a man appeared a few feet behind her. He was fairly tall, bundled up in a long black coat. A muffler was wrapped around his neck and face and his black fedora was pulled down low.

Who was it?

Murdoch saw rather than heard Olivia greet the man. The noise of the wheel drowned out her words, but some sort of exchange went on. She was keeping the shawl wrapped around her face all this time, but she shook her head. Murdoch could see the man recoil and suddenly, he reached and yanked the shawl away from her. Olivia backed away. Murdoch knew she was talking fast to assuage him, but he looked around. He shouted and this time Murdoch could hear him.

"Who the hell are you? Where's the other whore?"

Olivia continued to back down the path, but the man followed. Suddenly, he grabbed her by the arms and started to shake her violently. To Murdoch's horror, Olivia went completely limp and collapsed in the man's grip. He struggled to pull her to her feet, but he couldn't. Murdoch had to move and he shoved open the door, yelling, "Let go of her, I'm the police."

The man turned, saw Murdoch, and dropped Olivia to the ground. The only way out was down the path and he went to make a run for it. Olivia, however, was blocking his way and as he jumped over her apparently lifeless body, she reached up and grabbed him by the ankle. With perfect timing, she sat upright and shoved him away from her as if she were tossing a caber. He lost his balance and fell sideways against the low wall of the pond, toppling over into the water. Arms flailing, he tried desperately to stand up but the pond bed was too slippery and he couldn't find his footing. Olivia had scrambled to her feet and Murdoch hobbled by her, stepped over the wall himself, and tried to reach her assailant. However, he too slipped off a rock and fell to his knees. The other man tried to get to his feet, but he slipped again and fell backwards. This time he landed directly in the path of the waterwheel, which was continuing its relentless turning. The edge of one of the paddles caught him on the top of the head, stunning him. Then the next paddle struck him.

And then the next.

445

Desperately, Murdoch reached for him and managed to grab his trouser leg, but he couldn't move him. He called out to Olivia and she leaned over the wall and seized the man's other leg. Together they managed to drag him away from the wheel. He was inert and the water was scarlet. He had lost his hat, the scarf was still tightly wrapped around his face, but above the scarf was only a ghastly mess of blood and bone.

Murdoch managed to get the body partly out of the water onto the wall, and panting from the effort, and the pain in his back, he climbed onto the path and bent double until he could get his breath. Olivia had stepped away.

"Are you all right?" he gasped at her. She was white.

"He would have killed me if he could. I saw it in his eyes. He must have known the game was up and he panicked."

"Are you hurt?"

"Naw. That's an old trick I used. He grabbed me and I let my entire weight collapse. Took him by surprise."

Murdoch straightened up. "Olivia. We'll have to get some help. Do you think you can run to the station?"

She nodded. "Don't know about run, me legs have turned to jelly, but I'll do my best. He's quite done for, ain't he?"

446

"Yes. Tell the sergeant what has happened and say we need an ambulance. "

For a moment she didn't move but stared into the red pond. "Who is he?"

Murdoch reached over and pulled the sodden scarf away from the man's face. What was left of his jaw was thin and clean-shaven, the open mouth loose now.

"His name's Matthew Swanzey."

Epilogue

"HE WAS A GOOD MAN, as quiet as a mouse. Never a moment's trouble. He never complained about his meals like some of them do. I just can't believe what you're telling me."

Swanzey's landlady had been repeating variations on these words for the past ten minutes. Murdoch and Crabtree had gone to the dead man's lodgings and had yet to get past Mrs. Kew's disbelief and distress at what she'd heard from them.

"He was always so considerate. Why just last week I came down with a touch of phlebitis and he brought in my tea to me instead of me waiting on him. Then he sat and read aloud from the Psalms."

The memory brought on more tears, and Murdoch edged toward the door.

"Mrs. Kew, I'm going to need to see Reverend Swanzey's room. Constable Crabtree will stay here with you. I wonder if I couldn't trouble you for a cup of tea? We could all do with one, I'm sure."

Having something to do calmed the poor woman and Murdoch was able to go upstairs to the front room that had been Swanzey's. He stood in the threshold for a moment. He had rather expected the room to be neat and austere and it was. Mrs. Kew's taste ran to lace and red plush with a plethora of ceramic ornaments, but Swanzey's was as plain as a monk's. The room was quite spacious and the furnishings barely filled it. There was a narrow bed with a white coverlet beneath the window; a wardrobe; a bookcase, half empty; a washstand; and, in the centre of the room, a small round table with two wooden chairs. There were no pictures on the walls, the floor was uncarpeted. Murdoch could see an envelope propped up against the large bible on the table and when he went over to investigate it, he was startled to see that the envelope was addressed to him.

Murdoch was stripped to the waist, lying on his stomach on the kitchen table with brown paper across his lower back. Amy Slade was beside him, testing the iron for heat.

"Are you sure this will work?" Murdoch asked her.

"It's a proven remedy for lumbago. You'll feel much better afterwards."

She brought the iron down to his back and started to iron as if he were a shirt or a sheet. Murdoch found it

449

was not a disagreeable sensation, quite pleasant, in fact, although lying on his stomach was uncomfortable.

"Go on. I am quite able to iron and listen at the same time."

"Swanzey started out by saying that if I was reading the letter it meant he was either dead or in prison. In either case he wanted to explain what he called 'the regrettable occurrence,' which is about the most ludicrous expression I've ever heard to describe a brutal murder of an innocent man. Regrettable occurrence, indeed. As I suspected finally, the pastor had discovered Swanzey was misusing his position to get sexual favours from the female paupers on his list. When he was confronted, Swanzey said, and I quote, 'The devil threw a cloak of darkness over me.' Apparently, he couldn't bear the notion that he might not continue to be God's voice and servant, something he said he had yearned to be all of his life."

Amy pressed on the iron. "I can almost feel sorry for the fellow. He sounds like a tormented soul."

Murdoch tried to turn his head to look at her. "This tormented soul, as you call him, killed five people."

"I'm sorry, Will. I don't condone in the least what he did, but it seems as if he was mentally imbalanced."

450 "You're more charitable than I am. I think he was a miserable worm of a man, obsessed with himself and what he saw as his spiritual struggles. He took no responsibility for murdering Charles Howard, blaming

it all conveniently on the devil. The only reference to his preying on powerless women was what he called 'the vices of my blood,' which were again the result of the devil putting temptation in his way. He said the Tugwells were Lucifer's agents and that it was God who arranged things so that Swanzey was present when Louisa Howard received the blackmail letter. That gave him a chance to cover his arse, excuse the expression, and silence them."

"What was this letter? You haven't told me."

"I spoke to Mrs. Howard last evening and she acknowledged she'd received a letter from one of the Tugwells accusing her husband of improper conduct. I think that as soon as they knew the pastor was dead, one or the other of them cooked up a little blackmail scheme. As Olivia would tell me, it's an old trick. The dead man can't protest his innocence. She had wanted to show the letter to me, but Swanzey persuaded her to destroy it. He must have been afraid the Tugwells would betray him if pressed too hard, because of course, it was him, not Howard, who was the guilty party. So he immediately took steps to make sure they didn't. He visited trusting, lonely old Thomas Hicks, put prussic acid in his tea, and as soon as he was unconscious, he blocked the chimney. He probably brought him the cheap coke as a gift. Fortunately for us, he made a mistake and left with the bottle of prussic acid; otherwise it would have been written off as the kind of tragic

451

accident that is always happening to poor people. I wonder if that was God manipulating him or the devil? Carbon monoxide gas is indiscriminate, but Swanzey didn't care if he killed a household of people as long as he silenced Esther and Josie. Ida Harper, another woman he coerced, said she never saw his face, but Josie must have."

Murdoch felt his face going red at the anticipation that Amy would ask him how Ida could have had connections without seeing Swanzey's face, but she didn't.

"Poor Mrs. Howard, to get a letter like that."

"She was relieved when I explained it to her. She said that she'd always found Matthew Swanzey to be rather repulsive, but I don't know if that's an opinion rewritten after the fact. As far as I can tell, he was a respected member of the church. Speaking of the church, according to Mr. Swanzey, the devil also seemed to have blinded the members of the congregation and the church Synod who chose Howard as their pastor and not him. Swanzey was convinced that he was truly God's beloved servant and these things were sent to test his faith. The Almighty just wasn't revealing his hand yet, but it was a matter of time before Matthew would be taken up and exulted as the supremely eloquent witness to the Good News gospel. Another quote from the letter, 'The voice of the Lord is in my ear and I will heed his commands to the extent of my ability.' What a colossal conceit. Strip away all that religious folderol and you've got a man seething with jealousy. Howard won the coveted appointment, he was handsome and charming. Women loved him. Swanzey could only get acquiescence from starving women. No wonder, he even took the dead man's identity when he found himself succumbing, once again, to the vices of his blood, as he called it."

Amy tapped him lightly on the back of the head. "Lie still. You're tightening your muscles and you'll make things worse."

But Murdoch couldn't stop. "I presume it was at God's bidding that he murdered those four innocent people, including a crippled child. But he was completely silent on that little matter."

He closed his eyes. "I should have been on to the man earlier. There was an overcoat hanging in Swanzey's office. He must have come in, then been called to Howard's office where the pastor was in the midst of writing a letter that would destroy Swanzey's career. If I'd followed up on that bloody coat, I might have got him before he killed Hicks and the Tugwells."

Amy paused. "You don't know that, Will. He was cunning. He might have come up with a perfectly good explanation for the coat. What killed those people, alas, was that one of the Tugwells saw an opportunity to get some money. And the ultimate responsibility for their plight lies with society and our tolerating such poverty." Amy came around to the head of the table and peered at him. "I know you don't agree with me, but I'm not going to argue the matter right now. I need to get the other iron, this one is getting cold. Are you all right so far?"

"Quite, thank you. I've never felt like a shirt before, but now I know what that must be like."

She laughed. "We'll probably have to do this a few more times, so you'd better get used to it."

She turned over the brown paper and applied the fresh iron to it. They were quiet for a few moments while she worked.

"He did say something at the end of the letter that has stayed with me. 'If I am in the bosom of our Lord when you read this, I shall know what His judgment is and that is the only judgment that matters to me.' Let's hope he got a nasty shock. On the other hand, God has infinite mercy so who knows? But that's a topic for another day."

Amy returned the iron to its stand on the stove. "I think that's it for now."

"Can I sit up?"

"Yes, slowly though."

He eased himself into a sitting position on the table. His lumbago did feel much easier.

454 Amy smiled at him. The warmth of the iron had brought a flush to her face and her eyes were shining. She hadn't pinned up her hair and it was loose around

her face. Murdoch was suddenly acutely aware that he was sitting in front of her in nothing but his undervest and trousers.

"Is there anything else I can do for you, sir?" Her voice was teasing.

"You could marry me." His words popped out before he could stop them.

She started to laugh but stopped when she saw his expression.

"Will . . . I . . ."

"I mean it. Miss Slade, I, William Murdoch, would like you to be my wife. If I could kneel down I would, but I'm afraid I might not get up again." He caught her hand and held it between his. "Please, dear Amy, do say yes."

She pulled her hand away. "Oh, dear, I, er, no, I couldn't."

"I'm sorry, I –"

"No, please don't look like that. It's not you at all. But marriage . . . Will, surely you know how I feel about marriage?"

"No."

"I suppose you could say, I'm against it."

"I see."

"No, you obviously don't. Marriage isn't entered into on an equal basis. Women give up their identity, men don't. How would you feel if by marrying a woman you

455

had to surrender your name, give up your job that you love, and be expected to wait on her hand and foot? And in addition you had to swear to obey her? What outdated nonsense that is."

Amy was looking even more flushed at this point.

Murdoch reached for his shirt, "Thank you for the lecture. I'm sorry if I touched on a sore point, that was not my intention."

"Will, I've hurt your feelings and I didn't mean to. I'm so honoured that you asked me."

"Even if it is an invitation to humiliation and servitude?"

"No, you don't understand. Marriage as an institution I can't abide, but marriage meaning a physical and spiritual connection between a man and a woman, I don't disapprove of." She ducked her head, suddenly shy. "Dear, honourable Will, so many times I've walked away from you rather than risk making a complete fool of myself because I so wanted to –" She stopped.

Murdoch stared at her, not initially comprehending, but Amy touched his arm.

"If you would consider me as your wife in that sense, I joyfully accept."

"Are you saying what I think you're saying?"

456   "Let's put it this way. I won't iron your shirts, but I will iron your back willingly and with love as long as you want me to."

Her use of the word *love* almost made him want to weep. He tried to stand, but he couldn't straighten up and he was forced to look at her with his head bent.

"Can you crouch down a little and seal that with a kiss?"

She obliged.

Author's Note and Acknowledgements

For the convenience of my plot, I have moved Chalmers Church from its real location, which is long gone. There was a Presbyterian church at the corner of Carlton and Jarvis, which is now a Lutheran church.

The House of Industry, also known as the city poor house, was at the location I have given it on Elm Street. Only the facade remains today, but it is easy to stand before it and feel the impact it might have had on the destitute and desperate people of the time who had to line up for their daily soup.

And speaking of soup, the unidentified soup that Murdoch swallows at the food depot was typical of the period. I came across a recipe while visiting the Judge's Lodging Museum in Presteigne, Wales. I made it, and it is exactly as described.

The poor house procedures I have used in the story were as depicted.

The current Dundas Street East was then named Wilton Street.

I have tried to be as accurate as I can be with all the historical details and regret any errors, however small.

———

As always, I am grateful to many people for their help in the making of this book.

Elaine, the librarian at the Pelham Library, was not only a gracious host but took time to inform me about the structures of the Presbyterian Church.

Jim, woodsman extraordinaire and regular member of the dog-field gang, set me straight about the subtleties of wood-chopping and axe-throwing.

Linda Wicks, the archivist at the Sisters of St. Joseph library, brought me fascinating registers and patiently waited for me to finish reading through them.

I especially owe thanks to the folks at McClelland & Stewart, especially Bruce, Cass, and Dinah, who have supported me so enthusiastically and produced covers I love.

My agent, Jane Chelius, is the best.